Praise for

TALL, DARK AND DEADLY

"O'Clare writes edgy suspense with tough-as-nails characters who endure more than most can imagine and they
come out stronger on the other side."
—*Romantic Times BOOKreviews*

"The best book I've read this year!"
—*New York Times* bestselling author Lora Leigh

"A gripping novel filled with suspense and danger."
—*A Romance Review*

**ST. MARTIN'S PAPERBACKS TITLES
BY LORIE O'CLARE**

Tall, Dark and Deadly

Long, Lean and Lethal

LONG, LEAN AND *Lethal*

LORIE O'CLARE

St. Martin's Paperbacks

LONG, LEAN AND LETHAL

For information address St. Martin's Press, 175 Fifth Avenue, New York, NY 10010.

ISBN: 978-0-312-94343-1

Printed in the United States of America

St. Martin's Paperbacks edition / October 2009

St. Martin's Paperbacks are published by St. Martin's Press, 175 Fifth Avenue, New York, NY 10010.

10 9 8 7 6 5 4 3 2 1

ACKNOWLEDGMENTS

There are many reasons, other than those listed in *Long, Lean and Lethal*, as to why those who helped me research this book need to remain anonymous.

The swinging lifestyle is frowned upon by many, but there are many who approve of it. They are professionals, homemakers, retired, and students. They come from all walks of life. To you and me they appear "normal," hard-working, and live by high standards and morals. From what I learned, they are good people. They do have morals and values that are commendable. They are just different ideals on life from those who don't swing.

For those of you who are active in this lifestyle, and who candidly answered my questions—thank you! You opened up your homes to me, shared your experiences with me, and yes, some of you had some hilarious stories to tell. You know who you are! And as promised, I have kept your identities anonymous. Thank you again, from the bottom of my heart. You have helped bring the characters in this book to life. On behalf of Noah Kayne and Rain Huxtable, thank you again. We're eternally in your debt!

ONE

Special Agent Noah Kayne with the FBI stood in the middle of his motel room, squinting against the bright light coming in through the open door.

"I've got a car on the way for you," Police Chief Aaron Noble told him. Although probably close to fifty, the chief looked like he was in good shape. He also looked like he wished he were anywhere but here. "As soon as it's here you can follow me to the station."

"I've already briefed myself on the case." The file proved interesting reading on the plane and while he waited for a ride to come get him, since they didn't have a rental car for him at the airport. "Three murders so far."

"So far? Is that how Bureau people are trained to think?" Chief Noble scrubbed his forehead with thick, long fingers. "Homicide connected the first two deaths several months ago. Exact same murder weapon."

Noah didn't expect anything different out of the chief. He'd yet to be sent in to aid an investigation and not found at least someone with the local law bitter that he was there. But he also knew, according to what he'd read in the brief, that there would be another murder, probably soon, if he didn't get a handle on the situation and put some shock tactics out. It was a tricky business: scare the perp too much and he'd never catch him, but let the murderer think he still controlled the situation and more people would die.

"More than just the same murder weapon." Noah glanced over at the case book that was sent to him prior to his flying out here to Lincoln, Nebraska. It sat on the table on the other side of the king-size bed that filled most of the space in the otherwise mediocre motel room that would be home to him until he cracked this case. "According to your officer's reports, the two women were shot from the side, while sitting in their cars. Our perp intended for each of them to die quickly and with no pain. It's almost execution-style, but from what I read here, these are crimes of passion. Someone hated these people enough to pull the trigger at close range, possibly during conversation, without hesitating."

"I agree that we have one murderer." The chief glanced over his shoulder at the open door and then walked over to it, glancing outside. "The females died instantly. There was hardly any blood in their cars, which meant the heart quit beating quickly."

When the chief moved, Noah walked around the bed and then over to the table. He slumped into the chair, although the last thing he felt like doing was sitting.

"Your records here show your male victim also died instantly with the same shot to his left temple. He wasn't in a car, though."

"Parking lot. He died right next to his car. The engine was cold, and we arrived within less than an hour after death. My guess was that he was heading home after work. Again though, no sign of struggle." Chief Noble closed the motel room door and joined Noah at the table. "Your car should be here in a few minutes, so go ahead and give me your take. You've read the bible." He nodded to the thick file folder in front of Noah. "The third death occurred a month ago. They've all gotten cold. Tell me what your Bureau can do to help me."

So much for picking the chief's brain. Noah knew the attack all too well, though. If solving crimes were just that, life would be a hell of a lot simpler. But there were always politics and egos. Neither impressed Noah one fucking bit.

"*The Bureau,*" he started dryly, emphasizing the first two words, "is going to help you find your killer," and ignored the chief when he straightened, his expression jumping to the defensive. "Or more specifically, I am. You've got no witnesses, nothing at any of the crime scenes that connects any of these deaths together. But what you do have are similarities: same weapon, all shot in the left temple, quick and neat."

"Those similarities aren't going to get you shit. I may not be a Bureau man, but I'm not an idiot, either."

"Well, the main focus right now is motive. Once motive is established, the rest falls into place. All three people murdered were part of a swingers' group. They were all married, with terms to their marriages most wouldn't approve of."

The chief shoved his fists into his slacks pockets. "This is your baby, Kayne. All that matters is that we find the perpetrator, preferably before anyone else dies. And they say you're the best."

"I do what I do. I'm not interested in your flattery." Noah ignored the chief's condescending glare. "Honestly, I wouldn't be here if these murders didn't match similarities in other parts of the country. Your officer already working on this case let them get cold. If I can connect your three deaths to several that occurred in Dallas, as well as Kansas City, I'll get a better idea of what I'm working with."

"All I know about those murders is what I saw in the papers and on the news. They call him the Swinging Killer." If Chief Noble found any humor in that, he didn't give indication. His expression was stone cold, serious. "How are you going to determine if they're connected?"

"I'm going to walk alongside your killer, get to know him, what makes him tick. You aren't going to hear from me, or see me, until it's time to take him down. I go undercover and stay there until the job is done."

"I see," the chief said, and pushed his chair back. Most local law enforcement liked being kept abreast of what

Noah was doing when he was in their town. Chief Noble's reaction didn't surprise him.

Noah watched the chief walk over to the curtains and then mess with them until he found the long, narrow wand that opened them. Light flooded into the room when he pulled them back and also gave him and Noah a view of the large parking lot outside. He empathized with Chief Noble's frustration. Noah hated admitting he needed help. It was a fault, a character defect, but he'd been told more than once he had many.

Laurel had been very good at listing all of them toward the end.

"You know as well as I do that not even the Bureau is going to let you run loose on the street without checking in and confirming what you've got, and what you know." Chief Noble gave him a hard "don't fuck with me" kind of look.

Noah swore the chief's expression could be patented and labeled as the initial response any chief of police gave him when he explained his tactics.

"I'll go over your evidence and interview your officers," Noah began, reciting standard procedure. "And I'm sure you've got my supervisor's phone number if you've got any problems. But trust me, Chief; this is how it's got to be done. You've got three perfect murders on your hands. No clues. No motive—yet. And they aren't going to stop. I'm going to become your killer's best friend."

The chief nodded once. "There's your car and your new partner."

"Partner?" Noah caught the chief's smug look but refused to take the bait. "I work alone. Always have. It's in writing."

"Call your supervisor, and yes, I do have her number," Chief Noble said smugly. "I know your track record, Kayne, which is why I requested you. You aren't married, are you?"

"No," Noah said sharply, refusing to think about the matching rings that still sat in his top dresser drawer at his apartment in D.C. He focused instead on Brenda committing him to an arrangement that fell outside the accepted parameters without discussing it with him first. "And I'll call Brenda right now."

Brenda Thornton, who might possibly be the closest he had to family in this bitter world, knew him sometimes better than he knew himself, which pissed him off to no end. They'd discussed these murders, all happening in three different cities, and all with parallels that were uncanny. It was decided an agent would go to each town, move in, and get acquainted with the discreetly quiet group of swingers in each community.

"Feel free to call your supervisor." Chief Noble walked over to the door and opened it. When he turned and looked at Noah, the brightness outside created shadows on the chief's face that made his smug expression seem almost demonic. "And good thing you aren't married. Bigamy is a crime in this state, and you're about to meet your wife."

Noah reached for his phone, but his hand was suddenly too damp to pull it free from his waist. "What did you just say?"

"Your wife," Chief Noble reiterated. "You're going undercover and we're investigating murders among married couples in a swinging community. Only makes sense that you would need a wife."

Brenda never said shit about a fucking wife. "Like I said, I work alone."

"Not on my case you won't," the chief growled, nodding to someone outside. "Rain, there you are. It's about time you got here."

"It took longer at the car rental place than I thought it would." A lady with a soft, sultry edge to her voice, like she'd just woken up, spoke just outside the room. "I don't do minivans and it took a while to change the paperwork."

"You're entering into the world of middle-class suburbia. And what's wrong with a minivan? My wife loves hers." Chief Noble stepped forward and reached for the person just out of Noah's view. "Come inside first and meet your new partner," the chief coaxed.

"We've discussed this already," she snarled under her breath, and walked into the motel room. "I'll get cozy with your killer, but I'm doing it alone. And why did you want me to meet you here? This isn't suburbia, unless you think we're dealing with cheating spouses and you want to set me up as one."

Noah took advantage of the moment when she adjusted her eyes to the dimly lit room. Most tall women tended to slouch a bit, as if being tall embarrassed them. Since he stood over six feet, it was something he'd always noticed, and it bugged him.

But Rain, who probably was a good five ten, held on to every inch with pride. She didn't have an athletic or voluptuous build. Instead, curves faded into hard, flat planes that stretched until they softened and filled out into perfectly rounded hips, the kind a guy would grab on to when taking her from behind. Her faded jeans were snug, helping to round out her curves, and her plain blue sleeveless shirt hugged her slender waist, ending just before her jeans began and giving him a peek at those hard abs.

She wasn't buffed out, although she looked like she could hold her own. Her shoulders were smooth and round. Straight, thick dark hair was gathered in a clasp at her nape, showing off her long, perfectly curved neck that he stared at for a moment, focusing on that soft curve just above her collarbone. He bet she would feel like silk.

Her breasts weren't small but were not too big, either. Although he noticed the outline of a bra under her shirt, as he watched, her nipples hardened. Rain sensed his scrutinizing gaze. He'd bet damned good money she was aware of him appraising every inch of her. And his attention affected her. It affected him, too.

But when he shot his gaze to her face, her expression was hard and her focus was on the chief.

"It makes no sense whatsoever to bring the FBI in on

this case. An outsider isn't going to help." Rain didn't lower her voice, focused on Chief Noble, and ignored Noah. "This is my case, Chief, and you know it. You think I'm not capable of bringing down our guy alone?"

"He's got the expertise. You've got the knowledge of this town and the community. Both of your skills are superb. These are very elite, exclusive, and private swinger groups. They don't allow just anyone into their inner circle. The best way to get to know the suspects, and hopefully our murderer, is to enter their ring as a married couple." Noble sounded like he'd rehearsed his speech for this exact moment.

"Find someone else." Rain turned to leave, still not having given Noah as much as a second glance. "I'm not entering into a swingers' group as a married woman, or a single woman for that matter. I don't understand why I can't interview them and gather what I need to make an arrest as a cop. But if you think I can't handle my own investigation without help, I'm out of here." She tried walking out the door.

Chief Noble must have been on a fairly good basis with his officer. She didn't look shocked when he took her arm, escorting her back into the motel room. "The minute our killer becomes aware that the FBI is in town on this case, they will change his or her MO. I don't have to tell you that, Rain."

"Then send FBI home," she sneered. "I can handle this."

"Noah Kayne, meet Rain Huxtable, your wife." The chief rocked up on his heels like he was witnessing two kids on their first date. For the first time since he'd arrived at the motel room to meet Noah, the chief looked very pleased with himself, like he had pissed off two for the price of one.

Noah didn't flinch at the chief's introduction, although he would rip Brenda a new one first chance he had to speak with her. Rain turned her head slowly, and then raised one eyebrow, giving him a quick once-over.

Noah didn't consider himself a Greek god. More times

than he counted, he'd been told he had that bad-boy look. Whatever that meant.

It still stung a little when she said, "Right, whatever," and returned her attention to Chief Noble without as much as a blink of an eye. "Why didn't you tell me that you had some guy here before I got here?"

"This is *Special Agent* Noah Kayne," the chief offered, stressing Noah's title.

This time when Rain looked at him, her gaze traveled over him slower than before. He quite honestly couldn't say that he'd ever seen such soft baby blues look so incredibly defiant.

"Why didn't you tell me that you had some special-agent guy here?" She made his title sound like curse words.

"Head down to the station," the chief continued, turning toward the door. "I want a breakdown by five on how you plan on nailing our Swinging Killer."

Rain followed the chief out the motel room door, leaving Noah to grab his key card and bring up the rear.

"We're already in the process of interviewing," Rain told the chief. "I've got reports that I've put on your desk that have statements from friends of our victims who were interviewed when they came into the station. I've read the reports. There are some good leads in there. You don't think I can break this case on my own?"

Chief Noble reached his squad car and looked over the hood, squinting against the bright afternoon sun. "Your partner might have ideas. Brainstorm together and let me know what you come up with."

It seemed he ducked into his car quickly and took off just as fast.

Maybe the chief ran from his detective because she might have too abrasive a personality and he wasn't in the mood to deal with it. If Noah were a compassionate man, which he wasn't, he might feel sorry for the detective when she stood there for a moment, watching the squad car leave the parking lot. He didn't care that the tall, sexy detective felt betrayed. Hell, he'd been given the shaft, too.

"Where's my rental?" he asked, keeping it civil. For now, they were stuck together and there was work to be done.

She had one hell of a fine-looking ass. "It's the green Taurus. But it's not your rental; it's my rental."

She kept walking, offering a view that won over searching the parking lot for his car. When he finally did glance up, Rain held keys in her hand and paused at the driver's-side door of what he guessed was a brand-new Taurus.

Noah stopped next to her and held his hand out for the keys.

Rain looked at his hand and her disdain didn't leave her face when she lifted long, thick lashes and graced him with her baby blues. "I'm driving. Get in on the other side."

"I always drive."

"Not with me you don't."

Noah knew a test when he saw one. Rain probably challenged anyone who crossed her path. If he'd known he was going to have the sexy Amazon cop tossed in his lap he would have researched her. But sometimes there was something to be said about first contact and initial reactions.

"Detective, you can give me the keys or I'll take them from you. But if we're going to be partners you might as well get accustomed to shotgun."

She rolled her eyes, looking disgusted, and turned to slide the key into the keyhole.

Noah wrapped his fingers around her arm and Rain spun around, a long strand of dark hair flying free from its confines and drifting over her face. Her eyes turned a stormy, turbulent shade of blue and her parted lips were a soft red, full and moist.

"Just try and manhandle me, Bureau man, and I swear to God you'll regret it," she hissed, willingly showing off her quick temper. Her sudden quick breath and the fiery flush that spread over her cheeks proved one thing: sparring with him got her off.

There wasn't a damn thing wrong with good Klingon sex.

They were going to be partners, paired together without either of them knowing beforehand. There needed to be stipulations, understanding of each other's nature, in order for them to appear the part they were about to play. Getting to know Rain Huxtable was paramount, prior to anything else they would learn together. He didn't mind pushing her a bit to learn her true colors.

Noah tugged her toward him. Rain resisted, turning her back to the car and then leaning against it when he let go of her arm. It wasn't hard to remove the keys from her hand, especially with the element of surprise in his corner. She might be taller than most women, and fine-tuned to perfection, but he was stronger than she was. He covered her hand with his, parted her fingers, and slipped the rental keys into his palm.

"You can slide in through this side, or walk around the car," he whispered, keeping his reaction to physically touching her well under wraps. "But you're riding shotgun. That isn't open to discussion. When we get to the station, you can take the lead."

Rain tried shoving her way around him. Noah pushed his body against hers, holding her where she was, pinned between him and the car. Most women leaned their heads back, exposing their necks to him. And he knew his size intimidated many. But Rain barely adjusted her head to glare at him.

"Are you getting your rocks off, Bureau man?" she snarled, moistening her lips as her tongue darted over them.

"Trust me, cop woman; you'll know when I do." He liked her height, he decided. Her creamy skin was soft as silk, but it covered a warrior's heart. And the way her dark hair and baby blues contrasted against her complexion made for a distracting, if not professional model quality, picture. She looked like the type of woman a man would keep as a trophy, but so far she acted like a woman who would rather see a man bleed than submit to him. "But until we get to that point, let's get a few things straight."

"Don't hold your breath. Macho men don't turn me on," she purred, relaxing her body and dropping her hands to her sides. Rain didn't take her gaze from his, though. "And all we need to understand about each other is that if you do as you're told, and don't ever touch me, we'll get along just fine. Unless of course you don't mind a leash and collar. Now that might get me wet."

She couldn't be serious. Studying her facial expression, her captivating eyes, had him guessing she was messing with him. It also showed him he was grossly out of practice in figuring out if a woman was flirting with him or picking on him. He'd been 100 percent loyal to Laurel for over three years. Obviously her sense of loyalty was defined very differently from his.

Noah grabbed Rain's arms, this time moving her away from the door and turning her around. He almost gave her a quick slap on the ass, just to see her reaction. But there was a serious and dangerous criminal to catch, and although Noah somehow doubted Rain would scream sexual harassment, he also didn't want her thinking that all that mattered to him was getting down her pants.

"Get in the car, Rain," he instructed, admitting being impressed by her distracting good looks but knowing as well the last thing he wanted to do was fuck her. Any type of relationship, physical or otherwise, would take more out of him than he had to offer. One-night stands were it for him, and would be from here on out. "Let's see if you navigate as well as you spar."

Noah unlocked the car and then slid behind the wheel, impressed that he barely needed to adjust the seat. He watched Rain walk around the front of the car, her expression tight as she reached the passenger side and then climbed in next to him.

The car smelled brand-new and he noticed less than a hundred miles on it. Other than the round sticker on the dash that said "Thank you for not smoking," there wasn't any other indication that it was a rental. Noah let the engine run for a moment while he worked the sticker until he successfully removed it from the dash.

"Don't tell me you smoke," she said, shooting him a side-glance.

"The less this looks like a rental, the better." He'd give the outside a once-over to check for any stickers a rental agency might have affixed to it later. "Have you done a lot of undercover work?"

Her smile was smug and colder than the glare she shot at him. "Damn shame you haven't had time to research me." She pointed toward the exit, not answering his question. "Head on out and go north. The station isn't far from here."

He felt her gaze travel up and down his body and was very aware of the distance between them. But more than that, a sizzling sexual current hung heavily in the air. Rain might be playing tough and coming across as put out big-time by being forced to spend time with him, but he got under her skin as much as she did him. They would either fight or fuck, and he wasn't sure either would make her a good partner.

TWO

Rain leaned back in her office chair and scratched her scalp. She'd been strapped to FBI man all day long. Granted, he was reasonable enough to acknowledge that her game plan for proceeding looked good. And there was some solace in knowing he had no clue they were to be teamed together, either. But that didn't make the idea of working with him, or having him around her like a fucking shadow, any more appealing.

"Cherish these moments alone, girl," she mumbled, staring at the ceiling and stretching while she yanked the clasp that held her hair at her nape until her hair fell free over her shoulders. She continued raking her fingernails through her hair and enjoying a quiet moment to pout.

Her skin tingled as if he were still watching her. Noah's unnerving dark eyes seemed to be able to read her thoughts, delve into her soul, and learn the answers to his questions before she spoke. He was too intense, too much in her space. She didn't like it.

Worse yet, she wasn't sure she'd ever seen a man as dangerously good-looking as Noah. With his broad, pronounced cheekbones and long, straight nose and dark wavy hair that wasn't quite black but a rich chocolaty brown bordering his regal-looking face, he reminded her of one of those heroes from a dark shape-shifter-type movie that her father used to love watching. Noah would have been the nemesis, the unknown who appeared, aided in saving the day, but definitely wasn't who he professed to be.

"Lord," she muttered, not sure if more coffee would help or if she should simply call it quits for the day. Rain lifted her head, staring at her doorway and the hallway outside her office. Noah would also be the type appearing without a sound out of nowhere and watching her without her noticing it. No one stood in her doorway, though. "Definitely need to call it quits for the day," she grumbled, cradling her head with her hands and letting it fall back so she could stare at the ceiling some more.

Noah had taken off to make some phone calls. She didn't ask what calls or when he'd be back. If she had, he would think she cared, or that she might be interested in him. And she didn't care. She wasn't interested. Rain just wanted to cherish the alone time.

God, she didn't want a partner. Chief Noble knew she didn't want a partner. There was no way she could risk herself working that closely with someone else again.

Two years ago she had lost her father and it might as well have been yesterday. The pain from him dying just wouldn't go away. Then last year Bowen, her partner for four years, was killed during a bust. He took a bullet meant for her. Anyone she truly loved, or dared opening up to where she could call them friend, died, or disappeared from her life. The pain was too intense. And as much as being alone really sucked, it was better than having her heart sliced open again. The pain was too intense.

"Crap!" Rain leaned forward, grabbed her hair clasp off her desk, and snapped and unsnapped it in her fingers. She couldn't do shit to change the past. "All you have to focus on is keeping anyone else from dying."

Rain glanced at the wall clock and then picked up her yellow legal pad. Staring at the notes she'd scribbled throughout the day, she considered what she'd tell the chief when he showed up. It was almost five, and if Chief Noble was good at anything, it was his word. He would be punctual; he always was. More than likely he would saunter in, anxious to learn if she'd killed FBI man or if they'd come up with a kick-ass game plan.

Rain and Noah hadn't so much created a strategic method of attack yet as they'd shared info, learned what each other knew already about the case. Glancing at her notes, she had learned a few things today she hadn't already known. But Noah didn't know all the details surrounding the murders here in Lincoln, either. There were two murders in Kansas City, four in Dallas, and three here. The similarities were uncanny, making it appear pretty damned clear they were all committed by the same person, or possibly group of people. Maybe there were swinger haters out there intent on doing damage to the promiscuous lifestyle.

If Chief Noble expected her to show her gratitude for bringing in the FBI, he would have one hell of a long wait. It wasn't going to happen. She was good. Damned good, the best he had. And it hurt like hell that he'd contacted the Bureau without discussing it with her first. She could solve this case without Noah's help. Without anyone's help. Rain would have convinced Chief Noble of that if he'd given her the chance.

She didn't deny Noah had skills—he was FBI. That

didn't mean she couldn't take this on by herself. She didn't need Noah. Even if going undercover as a married couple might be a good idea since they were investigating murders committed inside a clique of married couples who didn't open up easily to those outside their circle, it wasn't the only way to crack the case.

Worse yet, there was something about Noah that went beyond him being FBI. The way he looked in his blue jeans, how his broad, muscular-looking chest filled out the short-sleeved T-shirt he wore, the entire package, distracted her too much. That was the problem, and why she relished a moment to herself, if only to get her head back on straight and focus on something other than his large, muscular Renaissance man–type sex appeal.

She leaned forward and reached for her phone, then punched the main number down on the first floor. "Betty," she said, noticing for the first time that she sounded tired. "Will you let me know when the chief comes in?"

"He's already here," Betty Boop, as a lot of the guys called her, squeaked cheerfully through the phone. Her short crop of black hair and large dark eyes earned her the nickname. "And who is the tall, dark, and brooding sexy hunk that is with him?" she asked, lowering her voice conspiratorially.

"I have no idea," Rain said dryly.

Betty snorted and then mumbled something before hanging up. Rain didn't care if Betty didn't believe her. Betty knew most of what was going on in the station from her perch at the service counter. More than likely, she knew more about Noah than Rain did.

As Rain adjusted her chair to move closer to her computer, her stomach growled. And her clothes itched. She absently clicked her way around a few sites until she came upon the profile for Special Agent Noah Kayne. The chief didn't bother telling her until he sent her to get the damned rental that she would have a partner on this case. After she got Mr. FBI dumped in her lap before noon, lunch had been the last thing on her mind. Now a hot meal and even hotter shower sounded better than anything else she could think of. Other than getting even with the chief for neglecting to mention that her new partner would be an obnoxious, stuck-on-himself Bureau man, whose dangerous gaze and relaxed, confident movements reminded her too much of a hungry predator. Rain wouldn't allow herself to be his next meal.

Moving the mouse again, she glanced at the clock and realized it was after five. Betty had mentioned that the chief was with Noah. There wasn't anyone else in the station who came close to tall, dark, and brooding. If he and the chief were plotting without her, she'd chew their asses.

"Maybe I should just go home and assume FBI doesn't need a partner after all," she growled, standing and heading around her desk.

She stopped when the door opened and Noah entered, meeting her gaze immediately and looking as if he knew exactly what her thoughts were. Not many men looked at a woman like they were sincerely interested in what was going on in her mind. Hell, most men didn't seem to notice that a woman had a mind. But Noah, with his thick dark hair that waved around his face and made him look about as non-FBI as a guy could look, gave her all of his attention like she was the only thing on his mind. And he searched her face as if knowing her thoughts mattered more to him than anything else.

In spite of how her body reacted to those possessive eyes, she forced herself to look away first and focus on the chief, who was right behind Noah. Then, the insane afterthought hit her and she remembered that her hair was disheveled. Rain grabbed her hair clasp.

"You said five," she snapped, glaring at Chief Noble while pulling her hair against the back of her neck and then securing her hair clasp.

"And since you were too busy to join us, we were forced to come to you," Noah said with a soft baritone, and then walked right up to her, cupping her cheek against the palm of his hand, brushing his fingertips down to her jawbone, and then moving around her.

She froze, completely taken aback that he would physically touch her in the office. Not that she would let him touch her no matter where they were, but here, in front of the chief?

Noah's touch was so relaxed, his movements so comfortable and confident. They were strangers. He shouldn't touch her like that. But then he shouldn't look at her like that, either. It was as if they'd known each other forever and his hands were on her every day. And her body reacted to him like she already knew how good he was.

Hell. He probably sucked in the sack.

"The meeting was supposed to be here," she growled under her breath.

Noah ignored her comment and moved behind her and then made himself very comfortable in the large office chair she'd been reclining in. The chief rested his rear on the edge of the desk and crossed his thick arms over his barrel chest.

"I was headed here when Noah found me," the chief said dismissively. His usual scowl was in place, and she doubted he even noticed the exchange between her and Noah. "Sounds like you've got him up-to-date nicely on everything so far."

"If I'd had some notice that he was going to be assigned to me—," she began.

"The FBI believes we're possibly dealing with hate crimes," the chief said, interrupting her. "Noah was filling me in on their suspicions so far. Although the group here in Lincoln isn't as evolved as the ones in Kansas City and Dallas, they are growing, and becoming more open about who they are. And I like what you two have got going so far. This just might work," the chief added, finally looking at her with his watery gray eyes.

"What hate crimes? We didn't discuss this." She shifted her attention from Chief Noble to Noah.

"You're finding out now." Noah's expression turned

blank as he met her gaze, as if they were complete strangers and hadn't spent the last few hours shut in the detectives' brainstorming room. "I only found out when I touched base with my supervisor. We've got a new lead."

Rain dropped her focus to the floor, chewing her lower lip. This was her case. She'd been working on it since the first murder a couple of months ago. Maybe there weren't a lot of clues. Maybe it was one of the tougher cases Lincoln had seen. But it wasn't too tough a case for her to crack. Noah offered this new lead as if it were a prize to bring to the table. But damn it, Rain would have discovered the connection soon enough.

She wouldn't admit Noah came up with good arguments and was incredibly easy to brainstorm with. None of that was the point. She was good enough to handle this case alone. She'd earned it. Since entering the force, Rain had worked her way up the ladder, never arguing over any case given her, and proving to everyone she wasn't riding on her last name for favors. In spite of how incredible her father had been, Rain had shown the entire force she was equally incredible, and by her own right.

"When Noah touched base with his supervisor just now, she sent him information on several Web sites that might be fronts for generating income that is then being sent to bank accounts around the country. We might have money laundering involved in these murders, too."

Rain looked at Noah. Excitement sizzled inside her. A new fact to add to the whole picture, new information. She wanted every detail. "How do you know we aren't dealing with two completely unrelated crimes? How are these Web sites linked to our murders?" she asked, playing devil's advocate.

"Between the murders and the bank transfers? I'm not sure." Noah never took his gaze from hers. "Whoever is running the operation knows what the hell they're doing. The bank accounts were created by people who don't exist. All transfers are done electronically. The sites aren't generating that many hits, yet somehow they're generating enough money to then transfer to the bank accounts here in town and around the country. So far, I haven't been able to trace the IP address to a physical address."

"Write down the Web sites for me." Rain pointed to pen and paper on the desk. "If the Web sites are fronts, they will be keeping a close eye on where their hits come from and will get nervous if they discover law enforcement is checking them out. I'll take a look once I get home. I have some connections here in town." Rain walked to the other side of the desk and then turned to face both men. "A few gurus when it comes to Internet information. Locating the owner of an IP address, or finding out who holds the domain and then subpoenaing them to give us the owner's address, shouldn't be a problem."

"The IP tends to move around, which is odd in itself, but always is here in Lincoln." Noah's gaze dropped from her eyes to somewhere lower than her face. "My hunch is that we've got a connection."

"You two will focus on everything happening here in Lincoln," the chief announced. "You're going undercover and getting cozy with every couple who had anything to do with the victims. Focus on the money laundering and these Web sites as well and if there's a connection, it will pop up sooner or later."

"We've already got profiles on each couple where one of the spouses was murdered," Noah said, tapping Rain's file that held most of her information she'd gathered since working on this case before he arrived. "We'll visit the clubs these people belonged to, learn where they shopped, find their friends."

Rain picked up her file, balancing it in her hand while sifting through the reports inside. "Each couple appears pretty unique to me. We've got Roberta Swanson, married eighteen years, full-time employee working IT where her husband also worked. They had three kids, only one of them still at home, three dogs, two cats, and a saltwater fish tank. They didn't belong to a church but were active bowlers."

"Lynn Handel was murdered next," Rain continued. "She was murdered five weeks after Roberta died. Both women were shot while in their cars. Roberta was leaving her house. She was shot in her driveway. But Lynn was returning home when she received the fatal shot, again in her driveway. Both women were killed exactly the same— one bullet to the left temple, died immediately, other than shattered glass there was very little cleanup. And no witnesses or anything that forensics could find to help wrap up either case."

"So we know both women were married and both were shot in their cars." Noah crossed his arms over his chest, watching her, his focus moving from the file in her hand to her face.

Rain didn't dwell on Noah's distracting good looks. Nodding once, she returned her attention to her file, licking her too-dry lips and willing her heart to beat a bit slower as she continued. "According to Lynn Handel's widower, they were a month shy of their tenth wedding anniversary. They had one son, who was eight. The Handels didn't belong to a church and weren't bowlers. Lynn worked as a teller at a bank and according to her co-workers, other than the usual complaints about her husband, nothing seemed amiss in her life. No financial or personal tragedies. No enemies."

"When did you put together the connection that both of these couples were swingers?" Noah asked.

Keeping matters on business made talking to Noah a lot easier. Nonetheless, Rain studied Chief Noble's focused expression as she reiterated what she already knew.

"Two weeks after Lynn died, George Lapthorne was shot to death in the parking lot outside of the building where he worked. There was no confirmation that he was heading home, since he was the last to leave the office, but his wife reported in her statement that he usually got home from work around seven. The time of death was six thirty.

"George was on his second marriage and had just celebrated his seventh wedding anniversary. The Lapthornes went all out with a huge barbecue, which about twenty people attended to celebrate. The Handels and the Swansons were on the list of those invited. This was when I discovered we had more than just casual friendship as a connection between these families with murdered victims. Lincoln isn't so small that everyone here knows everyone. It's a pretty good-sized city. Yet that barbecue invitation list the Lapthorne family showed me also contained names of other victims' families."

Rain looked at Noah and his large hand that covered her mouse. He moved it, clearing the screen saver, and then focused on the monitor. When he looked away from her computer screen, the glint in his eyes stirred more than resentment inside her.

The computer was still open to his file. Noah let his attention drift down the screen, probably scanning the information on him, but then shifted his attention to her. The slight smirk on his face was probably nothing Chief Noble would think twice about.

She clearly saw Noah believed he'd just proven her curiosity about him was piqued. Otherwise, she wouldn't have been researching him when he wasn't in the room. As she watched, that glint started smoldering.

Rain looked away, pressing her lips together and scowling. It wasn't her fault if his ego decided her interest went beyond professional. She sure as hell didn't need to confirm it. Just because he was sexy as hell, more aggressive than any man she'd ever met, and caressing her with eyes that offered a silent invitation didn't mean he turned her on. Noah was in her way. Good looks and charm could rot in hell.

"Last I remember hearing, we're a town of about two hundred and forty thousand," Chief Noble offered, turning his attention to Noah. "This is the first time in our recorded history we've had murders connected like this."

"We've got a list of murders getting colder and colder every day," Noah said, his expression tight and unreadable.

He didn't appear to be insulting her, but it still rubbed hard when he brought up that there weren't any substantial clues brought in yet.

"Each murder was cleaner than anything I've run across in my years as a cop," she said, feeling a need to defend her credentials. "There were no fingerprints. None of these murders were sexual. We've had nothing to trace back to the killer."

"Those are the hardest to crack," Noah said, his baritone softening, as if soothing her.

Rain didn't want consolations. She wanted clues.

"I've got the boys sweeping a house right now. An hour or so and we should be able to get you two moved in." Chief Noble slapped his leg. "I have all the faith in the world with the two of you digging into this mess, you'll find what we need to slap a warrant on someone."

So much for heading home for that hot bath. Like she would be able to soak if she were in a house she didn't know with a man she shouldn't get to know.

Her phone chirped and she moved to it quickly when she saw the dispatch button blinking. "Huxtable here," she said, her throat suddenly dry.

"I've got a disturbance with weapons, possible code black." Betty, the dispatcher, had a natural high pitch to her voice, making her sound younger on the phone than she actually was. As innocent as she sounded, speaking the morbid words, Betty Boop was a shrewd woman and an excellent dispatcher. "The caller reported a female, Caucasian, gun wound to the head. Medics and coroner are en route."

"Ten four," Rain said, while an unpleasant sensation rippled through her. Female shot in the head—their perp had struck again.

She scowled at Noah when he ran his finger across his neck and shook his head. "No, ma'am," he whispered, his baritone bordering on dangerous.

Rain looked away from him, closing her eyes as she

pinched the bridge of her nose. Like she needed him reminding her what was and wasn't allowed once they went undercover.

"Betty, dispatch the call to Gomez. Instruct her to call me immediately once she's on scene." Rain hated having to give up the call.

"I'd like to speak with Rain alone for a minute," Chief Noble said, nodding to Noah when he stood and held her gaze for a moment before walking out of the office. "What do you think of him?" the chief asked, closing the door behind Noah.

"Does it matter?" Rain leaned against the desk, staring at the phone, wishing she were hurrying out the door to the crime scene.

"I need my best man to get down and dirty with these people, and I don't have to tell you that you're the best I got."

Rain blew out a breath of resignation and shot Chief Noble a quick glance. She was the best he had, and part of proving that to him was accepting this case and working with FBI, even though it hurt. God, what she wouldn't have done to crack this one on her own. "What are your orders, boss?"

"Check out a computer from the supply room and then gather up any personal items you want." Chief Noble patted her shoulder before heading for the door. "By the time you two are ready to move in, your new home should be ready for you. Give it an hour or so. Once you're up and online, log in to the station here so that you can stay briefed on any new leads pulled in at our end."

"Chief?" she asked, searching his face when he raised an eyebrow, looking at her inquiringly. "Was it your idea to bring FBI in?"

"No. It wasn't. Rain, I know you could have handled this case alone. But we quite possibly have a murderer, or murderers, working up and down the Midwest. We have to cooperate."

She nodded once, wishing she felt more solace in knowing her chief knew she could have brought this one down alone.

"You're bringing a lot to the table," the chief continued. "Don't think the FBI won't appreciate that."

She was sure Noah would greatly appreciate all of her work. He'd probably take credit for it, too, once this was all wrapped up. That thought left a bitter taste in her mouth. There was something wrong with being attracted to a man who she believed might screw her, and not in a good way.

"I've got a list of people compiled who knew all the victims. I planned on interviewing each one of them." At least Chief Noble would know all the work she'd done on this case so far. "There are a few clubs each of the victims belonged to that I plan on checking out."

"Take FBI with you. The two of you will probably make a good team."

"When did you find out we'd be working together?" she demanded, searching the chief's face, but his expression remained the same.

He looked tired, stressed, and only shook his head slightly before sighing. "I just found out yesterday. Would it have made a difference in your reception of him if you'd known ahead of time?"

"Maybe," she said, crossing her arms, and knowing in her heart she probably would have shunned Noah Kayne just the same whether she'd known about working with him ahead of time or not.

One look at Chief Noble suggested he believed the same. "You'll make a good team," he reiterated.

Rain grunted, thinking twice and still wanting to say something very crude but holding back. The chief headed out the door, leaving it ajar, and Noah stepped back inside. She'd never stood outside the office and eavesdropped so she wasn't sure how secure the walls or door was. Either way, she hadn't said anything she regretted.

Noah gave her an appraising look. "No offense, princess, but I'm not thrilled about this, either."

Rain stiffened. He wouldn't know how painful his words were to her. "Don't ever call me princess. I'm not yours, or anyone else's, princess." Only her dad called her that, and he was gone now.

"Whatever you say, boss," Noah drawled.

"There's some progress," she grunted, and moved around the other side of the desk to grab her purse.

She noticed how he moved easily, silently, in spite of his size. Obviously very comfortable with himself, Noah appeared like a deadly predator. If she didn't get a grip on how her body reacted to every movement he made, it would be a hell of a time being around him 24/7.

"It was a joke." Noah stood at the door, his hand on the doorknob, and watched while she gathered her things.

"Just great. He thinks he's a comedian." She let him open the door for her and headed into the hallway. Once again she would have to let him drive. He still had the keys.

Rain didn't offer directions this time when they left the station, and Noah didn't ask. He made it to the motel easily enough and left her in the car, with it running, while he gathered his things. Then tossing a duffel bag in the backseat, with the computer they'd taken from the station in the trunk, she played navigator as they headed to her house so she could pack.

"Do you live alone?" Noah asked when he pulled into her driveway and parked the rental.

"Yes." She got out on her side, knowing he would follow her inside without invitation.

He was right behind her when she unlocked her front door and then punched her code into the pad on the wall to silence the security system her father had installed for her right after she bought the house. Noah closed the door behind him. Her dead-bolt lock snapped into place as he locked them inside.

Rain waved her hand in the direction of her kitchen.

"Drinks are in the kitchen if you want," she offered, then trotted up her stairs.

As many times as she'd come home late at night and traipsed through her home without turning on lights, tonight her legs were wobbly on the stairs, forcing her to slow down. Her skin prickled as she hurried to her room. It wasn't a sense of unease, more of trepidation, of fighting the sensation that solving this case might be as intense as dealing with a man so aggressive that his willfulness almost matched hers.

Although, damn, maybe she should fuck him and get it out of both of their systems so they could focus on this case. Rain did a full circle in her bedroom, her mind stuck on images of what it would be like to have sex with Noah, before she walked back out of her room and down the hall to the bathroom.

She grabbed a suitcase and overnight bag out of her linen closet and then stood for a moment, outside the bathroom door and at the top of the stairs, and listened to the movement downstairs.

It didn't surprise her with Noah's confidence level that he would have no problem making himself at home in her house. She listened as cabinets opened and closed quietly. It sounded as if he searched her entire kitchen. Part of her ached to hurry down there and keep a close eye on him so that he wouldn't invade too much of her space, but at least with him in her kitchen he was kept busy and wouldn't saunter upstairs and make it even harder for her to think than it already was.

She would not let her imagination travel to the possibilities of what might happen if he did come upstairs. Hurrying down her hallway, Rain hit the light switch with her elbow and then tossed both suitcases on her bed. A quick shower, pack some clothes and toiletries, grab food, and she'd be good.

Rain had pulled a change of clothes out when her cell phone rang. Unhooking it from her waist, she glanced at the number and then answered quickly.

"Hello," she said, knowing if the chief was calling her this soon after speaking with her, it wasn't good news.

"Rain," he said, sounding tired. "How are you doing?"

"I'm fine," she said, guessing she probably sounded as worn-out as the chief, yet for different reasons. They hadn't even started digging into this case and already she was emotionally exhausted trying to keep her thoughts from undressing and mounting Noah.

"I thought you would want to know that our latest victim died from a gunshot wound to the temple. She was in her car." Chief Noble sighed. "Victim is identified as Lorrie Hinders. She and her husband own a nursery here in town."

Rain hissed through her teeth and then kicked off her shoes and headed for her bathroom. "Any prints? Witnesses?"

"Nothing."

"Damn it."

"Call me as soon as you've got your computer hooked up at the house. If the reports aren't loaded by then, I'll e-mail everything on our latest victim," he said solemnly. "And Rain?"

"Yes?" She closed herself in her bathroom and flipped on the light.

"I need you to work with Noah. I know you don't like it. When I was over at your new home earlier today I noticed the living-room furniture is a bit worn-out. That couch was hell. Make him sleep on it if it will make you feel better."

She almost laughed out loud. "Sounds like a damned good plan."

"I know you can crack this."

"I know I can, too," she told him honestly, again feeling that anxious excitement creep over her skin. She promised to call when she and Noah were set up at the house and then hung up.

Rain stripped quickly and turned the water to hot. Between aching to leap headfirst into this case and figure out who was killing these people and why, then thinking about living with Noah, it was all she could do to remember how to wash herself.

Somehow, thirty minutes later or so, she lugged her packed luggage down the stairs. Noah hurried to the bottom of the stairs, reaching for the suitcases before she reached him.

"Who was on the phone before you showered?" he asked, his expression all business.

Rain released her bags to him and he took them to the front door. A couple paper sacks, filled with food from her kitchen, were already there. The impulse to ride his ass for assuming he could pack up her food hit her hard, but it was a good idea. They would need to eat.

Her stomach growled, not that she needed the reminder that she was half-starved. Heading for the kitchen to see if he'd left anything she could munch on, she started to call out over her shoulder. Noah was right behind her.

"The chief," she told him. "When we get the computer hooked up, he'll have the latest intel for us."

"Our victim?" Noah asked.

"Same as the others."

His expression hardened and she sensed the same anxiousness that crept through her bite at him.

"Then we better head out, unless there's anything else you want to take."

"Food," she said, deciding not to elaborate, and instead opened her refrigerator. He'd pretty much cleaned her out, not that there had been all that much food in there to start with. There was never time to grocery shop, and cooking wasn't exactly her favorite pastime. Closing the refrigerator, she edged past Noah and headed to the bags by the door.

She looked at everything piled by her front door. "Looks like you've got it all covered."

"I hope you didn't mind. It will save us a trip to the store, at least for tonight. You didn't have a lot of groceries."

"I've got enough for me, or I did until you packed me

up." Squatting in front of the bags, she sifted through the few canned goods and snack foods she kept on hand until she found an apple and a candy bar. It wasn't exactly what she had in mind for supper, but it would do.

Straightening, she was all too aware of how close Noah stood to her. An image of him wrapping his arms around her entered her mind, and her premonition proved correct.

Noah wasn't gentle. He didn't wrap his arms around her and pull her against him passionately. Not that she wanted him to. He grabbed her arm and flipped her around and then gripped her jaw. Her insides swelled so quickly that a tightening in her womb made it damned hard to breathe, let alone think.

Noah held her face and stared into her eyes with a look that went beyond dangerous. "In less than an hour, Rain, the world will see us as a married couple. We're going to need to act the part."

"They won't see us when we're alone," she whispered, hating how easily he made her react to his touch.

"Are you saying you can turn emotions on and off?"

"There's no emotion. That would require liking you," she hissed, searching for anger to help cool the heat that so quickly simmered and took over her insides. "This was supposed to be my case."

"You're hot as hell for me right now," he whispered.

"And you're a pompous ass." She tried turning away. She needed to fight with him, get really angry. Otherwise she would melt against that steel chest of his and submit to demands she feared she wanted as much as he did.

But Noah tightened his grip, his kiss punishing and demanding. He wanted her to submit, to admit that there was an attraction. And because he wanted that, more than anything she would not give it to him. She growled fiercely, striking out with her hands until he let go of her.

The disappointment in his eyes mixed with an almost victorious, if not determined, look on his face. "At least I know now that you won't kiss just any good-looking man."

"Go to hell," she grumbled, yanking at her shirt to straighten it and then turning and heading toward her kitchen.

Not that there was any reason to go there. Her pussy was soaked and her insides throbbed with frustrated tension and a craving she knew would get worse the longer they were together. If she made it through the night without fucking him it would be a goddamn miracle.

Noah was hot as hell, which was obviously something he knew already. He was attracted to her. Again, no new news there. Rain licked her lips, still tasting him. As quick a kiss as it was, she still tingled from it. From the brief taste of him to the way he grabbed her, demanding control and command, just like he did in every walk of his life.

Rain knew how to control, too. And she knew how to command a situation. But above and beyond all of that, she knew letting her guard down for one second, allowing Noah inside, even if just to appease the need he'd created inside her, would bring pain. It always did. As good as Noah might think he was, he wasn't good enough to prevent the hurt and regret that would inevitably follow.

Been there, done that, Rain thought to herself while placing her palm against her hard, cool counter. No more pain, only gain. She needed to focus 100 percent on this case, and the only way to do that was to keep Noah at arm's length, publicly and privately. There were plenty of married couples who never touched each other. No one said she and Noah needed to go undercover as a happily married couple.

She hated the emptiness that filled her, slowly replacing the throbbing aroused state she'd experienced moments before. Nonetheless, she embraced it. Then heading for her refrigerator to grab one of her water bottles and pocket a few cans of Diet Dr Pepper, she scowled when the light from her refrigerator glowed in the dark kitchen, and she stared at her cleaned-out fridge.

"He's good," she whispered. Then closing her refrigerator and making quick work of opening and closing cabinets, she made note of everything he took. Her mental inventory calculated the value of the missing goods at somewhere around one hundred dollars. "The FBI can pick up my grocery bill," she muttered to herself, although she felt no satisfaction in tabulating the debt now owed her.

Noah came toward her up the walk with the car running in the driveway. "Lock your house up," he instructed, his serious expression showing he'd also put himself back into a mind-set of being all business. The seductive glaze in his eyes was gone. "Was there anything else you wanted to take?"

"No. You appear to be very thorough." Her suitcases and bags of groceries were packed in the car.

"I always am," he informed her, and then headed to the rental car before she could think of a snide remark.

THREE

"Talk about half the pieces of a fucking puzzle missing," Noah grumbled, and pushed his chair away from the kitchen table.

Standing and stretching, he scratched his bare chest and glanced at the clock on the microwave. Rain had left over thirty minutes ago to buy more groceries. He didn't argue that more food in their new home would be nice, and even added a few items to her list. Noah guessed Rain already felt the same frustration that ate at him, part of it being from this case that had absolutely no fucking leads and the other part being a bit more personal.

Rain might have told him to fuck off. And Noah sure as hell wouldn't rape her. But it didn't take an experienced detective to sense the tension sizzling between them. If he were smart he'd call it a night and crash before she got home just to avoid the discussion of sleeping arrangements. And so he could get the bed.

Walking barefoot to the refrigerator, Noah pulled out a bottled water and wished it were a beer. He stared at the charts that he'd printed and the stack of reports and list of addresses of friends and locations of businesses each of the deceased had frequented. Then moving so he stood over the table, he looked at the information they had so far on the murder that had occurred earlier this evening.

He looked up when he heard the garage door open and headed over to the door off the kitchen that led to the garage. Rain parked the rental and cut the engine. The trunk popped open at the same time that the garage door automatically closed. Noah flipped on the interior garage light, not liking that it didn't come on automatically. Maybe doing some minor home repairs would help all of the information in his head fall into place, because at the moment they didn't have one single fucking lead.

Noah frowned when Rain grinned broadly at him as she climbed out of the car. "I'm not unloading groceries. I've already done my half of the chore. I'm so good I can bring home the bacon and get our first big break at the same time."

"Oh yeah?" He headed toward the trunk and then pulled out several bags, glancing at their contents before adjusting them in his arms. "I have no doubts you're very good. But what is this first big break?"

Something had her wound tight. Her pretty blue eyes glowed and her expression was free of the hard angles he'd seen earlier when she was pissed. He liked her smile, and how her dark hair made her skin look creamy. At the moment, though, as she shifted from one foot to the other, hardly able to contain the vibrant energy twisting around inside her, Noah wondered if she might start jumping, or flapping her hands with excitement.

Instead she followed him into the kitchen, holding true to her promise not to help haul in groceries. "I went to the grocery store that is less than a mile from here. I could show you on a map how it's also within a mile of where three of our deceased lived. While I was discussing grades of meat with the incredibly talkative butcher, a small line formed behind me. Most of your eight-to-fivers do their shopping at this time."

Rain was bursting at the seams to tell him something. Noah put the sacks of groceries on the counter and turned to the garage to grab the remaining bags.

"So you found the gossip center for married women?" He pinched her cheek as he walked by, which confirmed her level of excitement when she didn't slap his hand away. "Married life obviously suits you well."

"It suits me very well when one of the women standing next to me, and the butcher, get into a conversation about Sheila Lapthorne, the widow of one of our victims." Rain followed him and stood in the doorway to the garage while he lifted the two remaining bags out of the trunk and then closed it. "They were commenting on how it doesn't surprise either one of them that she's still part of the club even after her husband's death. You could tell they were speaking in a kind of code, trying to be discreet. But apparently the woman buying meat and the butcher are also both members of this club."

"What is the club?" He stepped into the kitchen and Rain closed the garage door behind him.

"I'm not sure if it has a name. And yes, I did ask." She reached into the sack next to him and started pulling out several wrapped packages of meat, then walked around him to the refrigerator. "I said that we were new in town and if there was some type of club for married couples I'd love to hear about it."

Noah glanced over at her while she arranged meat in the freezer. Investigation work got her off. She didn't blink an eye at him when she accepted more meat that he handed to her, and he decided he wouldn't comment that she had bought enough from the butcher to feed a small army.

"When I said that, the lady next to me got quiet. But the butcher—you'd think I just asked him out for a drink. His reaction wasn't what I expected."

"Is the butcher flirting with my wife?"

Rain rolled her eyes at him. "Whatever," she said, although the temper she had displayed earlier was gone. Adrenaline pumped through her and she blew off his comment with a wave of her hand. "It wasn't so much what he said but how he looked at me."

"What did he say?" Noah already knew how the butcher would have looked at "his wife." Rain glowed at the moment, and if she looked anything at the store like the way she did now, Noah wouldn't be surprised if she had bought all this meat at an incredible discount.

"He said it would depend on what type of married couple we were." She bunched up one of the empty bags and searched for a trash can. Then, not seeing one, she shoved it in the corner of the counter and went at the next bag, this time pulling out a bag of apples and a couple loaves of bread. "So I asked him what kind of married couples participated in their club. The woman next to me cleared her throat and when I looked at her she was noticeably blushing. But the butcher changed the subject, and although I was next in line, he asked what she needed. So I waited until he got her meat wrapped for her, and then asked again about the club."

Noah found the six-pack of beer he had asked her to buy and pulled two bottles out. After putting the remaining bottles in the refrigerator, he opened them both and handed one to Rain.

"Let me guess, it's a swingers' club."

Rain took the bottle and feigned her surprise. "How did you know?"

"I'm an investigator. You just gave me all of the clues. A club that doesn't have a name, and when people discuss it they use a code of sorts. Then you said that when you asked about it the woman next to you blushed." He tipped the bottle to his lips and savored how cold the beer was as it went down smoothly. "What did your butcher say?"

Rain took a quick gulp of her beer and then put the bottle on the counter. "He told me that there are some married folk here in Lincoln who get together at each other's homes. He said it was an alternative-lifestyle type of club and that it wasn't for everyone."

"And you said?"

Rain grinned at him and burped. "I asked if it was wife swapping."

Noah fought the urge not to grin at her triumphant look. He doubted she knew how fucking sexy she looked right now, burp and all. She looked sincerely happy. More than likely when the adrenaline quit pumping through her veins she would remember how much she resented him being here and pushing in on her scene and "her case."

"I think 'wife swapping' is an antiquated term these days," he said, and turned to survey the grocery situation. They now had trash bags but no trash can, so he opened the box of bags and pulled one free of the roll. Once he opened the bag, Rain helped gather the empty grocery sacks until the kitchen was in order again.

"Actually, I think the terms used to describe polyamorous lifestyles vary from region to region," she offered quietly while stuffing the last of the grocery bags into the trash bag. "But I acted like it was something I was into, and the butcher was very anxious to share information on his club."

"I'm sure." Noah doubted any man would turn down the opportunity to make the move on Rain. Hell, he'd already tried several times, and had yet to get a rise out of her like what he saw in her now. Taking another swallow of his beer, he remembered the same glow on Laurel's face when she tried convincing him she didn't love him any less even though she wanted to have sex with the friend Noah had chosen to be his best man. The beer didn't go down as smoothly this time, but Rain didn't seem to notice when Noah put the bottle down on the counter a little harder than needed.

"Most swingers are very comfortable with their lifestyle and although they'll remain discreet about it, if asked and the surroundings are conducive to sharing information they will willingly discuss something that they believe is a wonderful pastime," she added, opening the cabinet under the kitchen sink and stuffing the trash bag half-full of trash under it, then closing the cabinet. "Most aren't ashamed of it, but don't talk about it openly because others judge them down."

"You sound like you approve of it." He swore she gave him the same look Laurel did when he accused her of wanting his permission to be unfaithful. Like he was the insane one.

"All I care about is we just got a big break into a case where an hour ago there were no leads whatsoever," she informed him, her glow quickly fading. "I suppose you're all for swinging?"

His personal life didn't have shit to do with this case. Especially a personal life that was very much over. "I don't disapprove of what these people are doing," he said, meaning it. It wasn't for him and never would be. Vows were taken for a reason. If a couple wanted to rewrite those vows, like Laurel even suggested doing, then they might as well label it something other than marriage. None of that had anything to do with solving this case, though. He wasn't here to preach to a damn soul; he was here to nail a murderer. "If all parties are consenting, and no one is getting murdered," he added, unable to keep the growl out of his voice.

Rain picked up her bottle of beer and then opened a cabinet and pulled out a box of crackers that she'd just put away. "The butcher told me they are a very laid-back group, with no preconceived notions about anyone. He said if we would like to learn more I should bring you into the store tomorrow so that you could discuss it with him. All he asked was that we not talk to him about it while customers were around."

"Of course." Noah looked at the box of crackers in her hand. "You buy all that meat and plan on eating crackers for supper?"

"If you think I'm fixing you supper after busting my

ass buying all of those groceries," she snipped, once again showing him the feisty, hotheaded Amazon princess he'd spent the day with. "Not to mention, I just got our first lead," she added triumphantly, her long dark hair flowing like silk over her shoulder and parting around her full, round breast.

"You forget, princess, I've been in your kitchen already. There was dust on your stove. I'm not going to chance that meat you bought being ruined during preparation when for all I know you might not even know how to boil water." He moved around her, swiping her hair behind her shoulder, where it was confined at her nape by a pretty hair clasp. He loved the feel of it in his hand before letting it go, and watching it flow down her back. "Just don't want you ruining your appetite while waiting for your dinner," he whispered over her shoulder, and noticed her visibly shiver. "I wonder if there's a grill here," he added, feeling blood drain to his cock, leaving him somewhat light-headed as he grew hard. The cool air helped a bit when he opened the freezer and surveyed all the neat white packages.

"I told you not to call me princess." Rain turned her back to him and looked at the work spread out on the table that he'd done while she was gone.

Other than placing their suitcases in the one bedroom of the two in the house that was furnished, he didn't take time to inspect the place other than for security purposes earlier. Satisfied all windows and doors were locked securely, he got busy lining out what they knew so far on the case. Leaving Rain to browse over his charts, he searched the garage for a grill and then headed out the back door to find a deck that desperately needed weeds cut back from it.

There wasn't any desire to comment on her not liking his nickname for her. There were worse names he could call her, and she did have that tall, willowy, regal look about her he doubted she could change if she tried. Besides, she wasn't the only one who was excited about moving forward with this case. Noah didn't want to argue with her. He wasn't in the mood. When she wasn't biting his head off and was willing to talk shop, Rain wasn't so bad to be around. And she sure as hell wasn't bad to look at.

"Score!" he mumbled when he pulled the cover off of a propane grill. After inspecting the tank and making sure all the valves were working properly and set right, he started the thing up and then grinned. "We feast tonight." Memories came to mind of grilling for Laurel while she sat outside with him, doing her nails or simply complaining about her job with the navy as a civilian doing IT work.

Leaving the grill and the sordid memories, Noah slid the glass door open, deciding greasing it might make it open and close easier, and paused as he studied Rain.

She leaned over the table, writing something on one of his charts. "I'm almost positive that I remember her calling him Butch," she said, although she didn't straighten when she spoke out loud. "Either way, until we get confirmation, 'Butch' is short for 'butcher' and it can help label him."

Noah came up behind her, focusing on her ass perfectly positioned for him and the way her shirt snuck up her waist, revealing her creamy skin and slender back. Her hair flowed down her back, like a river of black ink, shiny and enticing. His fingers itched as he stared at the smooth-looking strands, confined at her nape and then ending just where her shirt ended, adding to the view of her flesh exposed above her jeans. Noah got hard as a fucking rock just thinking about what it would be like to take her like this.

Grabbing her hips, he leaned into her when she jumped.

"Holy crap! Don't do that," she hissed, straightening quickly and jumping to the side of him.

Her hair bounced at her nape and fought the constraint of the hair clasp that held it. Now wasn't the right time to pull it out of her hair, although when he saw her briefly earlier today with it down he ached for the opportunity to watch all those thick dark wavy strands fan over her bare shoulders. Instead, he reached up and pushed her hair to the side while sliding his other hand around and pressing it against her belly.

"How do you like your meat?" he whispered into the curve of her neck.

Rain noticeably shivered but growled at the same time. "It's going to be dismembered if you don't watch yourself," she threatened.

Noah chuckled, hearing her gasp. Instead of fighting to make him let her go, she went still. Daring to push her just a bit further, he stretched his fingers over her stomach, until the tips of his fingers grazed the bottom of her breasts. It took more effort than he expected to keep the sudden rush of desire from exploding inside him.

"You would hurt the man who offers to feed you?" he growled, his voice hoarse. He pressed his mouth over the silky smooth curve in her neck and tasted her, then scraped his teeth over her flesh.

"God damn it," she cried out, and then almost knocked the table over when she fought to jump out of his arms.

Noah grabbed her arm and steadied the table at the same time. "Steady, girl. You can handle it."

"That's not the point," she wailed, and pulled free of him as she backed up another few steps and then ran her hands over her hair, causing several strands to fall free and curve around her flushed face.

"What's the point? You don't like meat?" He straightened the stack of papers that was next to his chart and noticed her handwriting alongside one of the columns.

"Yes, I like meat, medium rare. Go put yourself to use and cook it," she said, her voice breathy, although the edge of irritation was as obvious as her aroused state.

Her nipples were hard as stone and poked against her shirt. He guessed she wore one of those silky-type bras that offered some support but did little when it came to hiding her nipples harden. And damn, they were distracting as hell at the moment.

Noah forced his attention to her face, willing himself to back off. It was hard finding arguments to substantiate doing so, though. What he had with Laurel was over, and it amazed him when he'd acknowledged how quickly he'd fallen out of love with her when she'd continually pressed him to agree to her fucking other men, believing if she allowed him to watch, or even partake, that would convince him to agree to the terms. After a monogamous three-year relationship with her, believing she was the one to the point where he'd bought the rings and popped the question, he never imagined anything she would say or do would make him quit loving her. He'd been wrong.

Which today made him a free agent. Add to that the fact that he and Rain were supposed to be a married couple and his body insisted his mind accept the fact that coming on to Rain was okay to do.

Rain didn't look at him but instead focused on the table while combing her hair with her fingers and adjusting her clasp behind her neck.

"Rain," he said, and watched as her gaze shot to his. "Come here."

"No," she answered quickly. "Why?"

"It's okay. Come here."

"I'm fine where I am." Her baby blues sparked with that passion he was starting to see ran incredibly hot in her when she was challenged.

"Come here," he said again, keeping his voice calm, nonthreatening.

Rain needed a challenge to feel stimulated. It showed off her intelligence, her craving to take on more than what life offered the normal soul. And when that stimulation kicked in, Noah saw the desire, the craving to touch and be touched. And he saw how she fought to keep her urges to respond to him hidden, as if somehow letting him see he made her hot would be showing a weakness in her.

"Why?" Her eyes turned a deeper, darker shade, like rare, pure sapphires.

"Please." He didn't move but held his ground, waiting, watching her ponder his request.

Until finally she responded, slowly, first one step, and then another. Rain held her head high, almost looking him in the eye without having to tilt her head back too far at all.

"Happy now?" she snapped, and pressed her lips together as if giving in to his request to move closer to him irritated the hell out of her.

"Almost." He moved his hand behind her neck.

Rain didn't flinch, didn't move a muscle, and continued glaring at him. Try as she would to look put out by his actions, he didn't miss her quickness of breath, the way her tongue darted out quickly to moisten her lips before she pressed them closed again. And then how she held her breath, waiting, watching, as he moved his fingers over her hair and took her hair clasp in his hand. It unsnapped easily and her dark hair flowed freely, swaying over her shoulders and falling in waves against her flushed cheeks.

"Tell me, Rain," he began, his voice a hoarse whisper. It was so damned hard not to tell her how beautiful she was. "Would it be better if we fucked now and got it out of our systems? Or should we continue to fight it and try simply to focus on this case?"

"I don't know," she answered, her voice cracking, and then she swallowed and looked down at her hair clasp in his hand.

Her hair fell in thick waves around her face, adding to her sultry sex appeal.

"Let me know when you do." Noah placed her hair clasp on the table and then left her standing there as he headed outside.

A hot shower helped get some of the kinks out after sleeping on the couch. Noah was headed for the kitchen and coffee when his cell phone buzzed that following morning.

He grabbed it on the second ring and then searched for the can of coffee Rain had bought the night before.

"How's it going, Kayne?" Brenda's voice cracked, her usual hoarse tone first thing in the morning from too much coffee and cigarettes. "Married life treating you well?"

He pulled the coffee can out of the freezer, where he finally found it, and then started searching for a can opener. "Pull a stunt like this on me again and I swear to God I'll quit."

Struggling with the electric can opener and the large can, he ignored Brenda's easy laughter and instead breathed in the fresh smell of coffee as the lid peeled away.

"It was short notice when this case came in," she explained, all business. "I've got Foreman in Kansas City and Roper in Dallas, each with a small team. You were my first choice to send to Lincoln. I hear it's a thriving metropolis in the Midwest," she added, as if making an effort to show her distaste for small towns would smooth over his frustration with being given the assignment without being told he would be "married" to a local cop.

"I haven't gotten out to see the sights yet," he grumbled, digging the scoop out of the can and then searching until he spotted a coffeemaker next to the stove. Thankfully the Lincoln Police Department understood what necessities had to be included in a kitchen for undercover work.

"I hear you had another homicide there last night," Brenda continued, obviously already dosed on her caffeine and ready to debrief him.

"I've worked up a comparison chart on all of our victims," he offered. "Didn't find one damn similarity in the lot of them, but we might have something worth following up on today."

"What's that?"

"Rain had already learned a connection existed between several of the spouses who were killed. They knew each other. She obtained an invitation list to a party that more than one of the couples were invited to. But last night, Rain met the butcher at a grocery store near this house we're staying in." He finished setting up the coffeemaker and then left it to percolate while heading toward the back door. When he stepped out on the back deck, it looked worse in the daylight than it had last night. "Apparently he willingly talked to her and she confirmed he knew at least one of the couples whose spouse was murdered."

"Sounds like this could get interesting."

"We've got confirmation, we think, that these couples might have all had another connection," he told her, walking along the edge of the deck and testing the durability of the wood. It appeared sturdy, just neglected. "We're going to go visit this butcher today together. Rain already gave him the impression we might be interested in joining a group he mentioned to her that is for couples who share similar interests."

"They're all swingers?" Brenda offered, although none of this was news. They already knew those being murdered were all swingers.

"Sounds like it," he added, knowing if she took this to a personal level, he had other things to do than spend the morning listening to his supervisor try to play counselor. "Sheila Lapthorne, the widow of George Lapthorne, is apparently attending swinging events that the butcher is part of. We're going to look in on more of the details today."

Brenda didn't say anything for a moment, and Noah stiffened, ready for any reference she might make to this case and his personal life, or what had been his personal life. Noah didn't label many people in his world as personal friends. Brenda had been his supervisor for five years now. During the hardest moments with Laurel he'd shared some of the ugliness with Brenda, and he prayed now she wouldn't make him regret confiding in her.

"You know I need to ask how you're handling all of this," she said quietly.

"You wouldn't if you didn't know anything," he growled, making it clear he didn't want to discuss any connection this particular case had with his personal life.

"A good supervisor has to know everything about her agents. You know that as well as anyone," Brenda said quickly, sounding defensive, as if suggesting he wouldn't open up to her hurt her feelings. She was made of tougher stuff than that. "You're going to enter into a lifestyle you recently denounced to the point you broke off your engagement."

"I'll keep you posted once we learn anything," Noah informed her, speaking before she could continue. "As with any case, you've got me one hundred percent. If you thought otherwise, you would have given this case to someone else."

"You were the first man who came to mind," she said slowly.

He didn't want to hear why, and feared it wasn't because of his impeccable track record. But the last thing he wanted was to pursue the direction of this conversation.

"I'm going to get coffee." He'd given his update; there wasn't anything else to talk about.

"So have you fucked her yet?"

"Who says I'm trying to?"

Brenda's easy laugh didn't surprise him. "I take it that's a no. You must be slipping. I remember back in the day you were a damned slut."

"Maybe I was once," he conceded, unwilling to defend his reputation from his younger days without caffeine in his system. "When it was one case after another, a diversion helped from time to time."

"And you don't need a diversion now?"

"Is that why you assigned me to this case?" He regretted asking as soon as the words were out. He really didn't want to hear the answer.

"I needed my best investigator. That's why I assigned you to this case. But if the cop you're now working with is bringing forward unpleasant memories," Brenda said slowly, "I might be able to get you partnered with a better investigator."

"Rain is a good cop, Brenda. And given the fact that neither one of us wanted a partner, Rain is giving it her all to perform the best that she can. No cop likes being hitched to FBI; you know that."

He turned to check on his coffee and saw Rain leaning in the doorway to the kitchen, arms crossed, dressed in loose-fitting running pants and a small tank top that showed off her perfectly shaped breasts. Her cocked eyebrow and pursed lips showed she overheard him mention her and sing her praises.

"Detective Huxtable should be honored to be on this case. You make sure she follows your leads and if in any way she starts hindering your progress, you let me know. We can put another agent in undercover with you," Brenda offered. "I agreed at the time that a local cop would be best at your side since she knows the town, and since she was already familiar with the case. I need you to crack this one, but if she's not working out as a partner . . ."

"I never said she wasn't." Noah grabbed the pot of coffee, turning his back on Rain, and filled his cup.

"I've done extensive research on all of these murders in all three cities. One of the strong factors is that these people are a very discreet group of people. We can't get on the inside unless we send in a couple. And a happily married couple, who are carefree and appear, how shall I say it, very sexually active with each other?"

"I get where you're going with this," Noah interrupted.

Rain had moved in next to him with coffee cup in hand. "How far will it go for me when I tell your supervisor that she's not my boss?" she asked, obviously having overheard Brenda's voice through the phone.

"What did she say?" Brenda wheezed at the other end of the line.

"I'll touch base with you later today." Noah left Rain to get her coffee and moved to the kitchen table. "We're hitting the streets today and I'm hoping to tie together some of these names. Once we do, hopefully we'll be able to figure out a motive."

"That is, once we follow up on my lead," she said louder than she needed to.

"What did she say?" Brenda snapped. "If that little cop thinks she can mouth off at me—"

"Enough!" Noah barked, returning to the coffeepot and taking Rain's cup from her hand. He poured her coffee and handed it to her. "Brenda, I'll call you later this afternoon. We need to follow up on the lead Rain rounded up last night with the butcher I mentioned to you." He turned and glared at Rain and mouthed, *Satisfied?*

"I'll be in and out of meetings all day. Leave voice mail if you don't reach me."

"I always do," he said, and then hung up after she said good-bye. Tossing his phone on the counter, he turned and leaned against it and sipped at his coffee while watching Rain.

She took a long drink of her coffee and then blessed him with an incredibly innocent look. "Was that your supervisor?" she asked.

Noah drank more coffee even though it was hot and burned all the way down. "I need caffeine and a hot shower and then we'll head out."

He walked past Rain and headed down the hallway. She was right on his heels. "You know, I'm a damned good cop. Maybe there weren't any strong leads on this case before you came to town, but I am the one who rounded up our first break into this mess."

"I know." He walked into the bathroom and checked the towel, decided it was fresh enough, and then turned to face her determined expression. "Don't worry about Brenda. I'm sure she's on to something else now and not even worried about you, or me."

"I could have been FBI if I wanted to. I didn't," Rain continued, glaring at him like he'd been the one to chastise her. "I wanted to work in my community, help those around me."

"Sounds like a good reason to be a cop."

She kept going as if he hadn't spoken. "There might be bad cops out there, but there's bad FBI, too. And just because I'm a cop doesn't mean I can't do undercover work, or create a profile." She sipped her coffee, watching him over the rim with bright blue eyes. "And you think I don't know how we need to act around these couples in order to break into their little clique?" she demanded.

"I'm sure you do."

"But I'll tell you right now," she snapped, barely letting him speak. Rain pointed her finger at him. "No one tells me I have to fuck someone. No one, do you understand?"

She wasn't going to shut up. Noah pulled off his shirt and tossed it to the floor. When Rain continued ranting about being insulted since she was just a lowly police officer, Noah figured there would be one way to make her quiet. He pulled down his jeans and boxers and tossed them with his shirt.

"Crap, Noah!" Rain fell backward into the hallway. Rain's baby blues got wider than round orbs glowing in the dark.

Noah chuckled. "I'm not sure if that's a compliment or an insult."

"Go to hell," she yelled, and stormed down the hall-way.

Noah shut the door and then turned on the water in the tub, adjusted it, and pulled the tab for the shower. Her surprised and shocked expression was priceless. He climbed into the shower and wondered what thoughts ran through her head now that she'd seen him naked.

FOUR

Rain got out on the passenger side of the rental and straightened the mid-thigh-length dress she'd chosen to wear today. Noah came around the car in his relaxed-looking blue jeans and snug-fitting T-shirt. Corded muscle rippled underneath the cotton, showing off Noah's well-developed body. Rain blinked to get the image of him standing naked in front of her and then saw the buns of steel she'd caught a glimpse of when he'd turned around earlier in the bathroom.

Goddamn. He was a perfect fucking package.

"This place looks a hell of a lot different during the day," she mused, glancing at the handful of cars in the parking lot. "It was packed here last night."

"Let's go see if we can find our butcher." Noah held out his hand.

Their undercover work started now. If she hesitated in taking his hand, anyone watching might think they weren't the happy couple. And both of them agreed on the way here that presenting themselves as comfortably married and good friends would make it easier for other couples to open up to them.

Rain slid her hand into his and strong fingers wrapped around hers as Noah led her to the store. The ring she'd put on her finger before leaving the house pinched her flesh. Noah had a matching band on his left hand. They were now officially the happily married couple.

"We're going to make him think we're established swingers," Noah said quietly, matching her pace and walking close enough to her that their arms brushed against each other. "Follow my lead when we say we're from D.C. I know the area well, so if by chance anyone else does, too, they won't be able to pull anything over on us."

"I'll just say you never let me leave the house," she quipped, and then glared at him when he smiled broadly. "Because I work at home. I'm an artist."

"Can you paint?" He looked surprised.

"Actually, yes, I can." And setting up a canvas often helped relax her mind and enabled her to figure out the obvious. When it came to tough cases, her father used to always tell her that letting the creative juices flow helped clear up clues that were often right under her nose.

Rain's excitement grew when they neared the back of

the store and she spotted the stocky butcher, standing behind the counter and weighing meat for an older lady. He glanced up at Rain and smiled but then returned his attention to the customer.

"Is that him?" Noah asked.

"Yes." She knew she was tall for a lady, but she still needed to glance up slightly to stare into Noah's eyes. She liked that about him.

But when Noah looked down at her, the intense glow in his eyes caused her insides to quicken. A warmth spread over her and she couldn't look away.

"He wants to fuck you, you know that, don't you?" Noah whispered, searching her face while waiting for her answer.

Rain got the impression that how she answered would tell him something about her. "Why do you say that?"

"Do you mean to tell me that you don't know when a man wants to fuck you?"

Rain smiled and glanced over at the butcher. She and Noah stood to the side and out of the way, but the butcher gave her his attention when she looked at him. The older woman must also think the meat department in the grocery store a place to deliver new gossip, because she went on about a neighbor's trials and tribulations while putting in a new swimming pool.

Rain turned into Noah, moving closer to respond when a mother with toddlers pushed a grocery cart past them. "Some men are more obvious about what they want than others," she whispered, her mouth close to his ear.

Noah let go of her hand and slid his arm around her, keeping her pinned against him while turning his head so that his mouth was inches from hers. His eyes looked more brown than green today, and his dark hair was slightly tousled. But it was all that hard-packed muscle pressing against her and making her nipples feel pinched as they hardened that distracted her the most.

"It's called discretion," he whispered, shifting his

attention and glancing around them before looking at her again. "I'm sure you noticed his wedding ring. If your butcher is a swinger, he's got permission from his wife to fuck other ladies, if they and his wife consent."

"I know what a swinger is," she retorted, snapping at him even though her whisper was barely audible.

"Do you approve of their lifestyle?"

She didn't want to admit that possibly her knowledge was lacking and that any information he had on the lifestyle would be helpful. Good cops didn't pretend to know something they didn't, however. It ate at her pride, but she straightened, which resulted in him pressing her closer to him, and looked him square in the eye.

"I've never partaken in any swinger activity," she said quietly. "If that is what you're asking."

"Would you?" Again he searched her face.

"I assume you're asking if I would while working this case." Her stomach twisted, as she suddenly wondered how far they would have to go to solve this case. More than likely, she wouldn't have to fuck Noah, just make appearances believable while under the scrutinizing public eye.

"If it helps us with this case, would you watch me fuck someone while you fuck someone?"

His rough whisper scraped over her flesh and his words presented a very erotic image that made her heart beat faster. She hated that he probably felt the sudden thumping in her chest.

"Would you fuck someone to help catch a murderer?"

"If the situation merited it, yes."

Rain nodded and became acutely aware of his thumb moving up and down along the curve of her spine. "Have you ever fucked someone simply to gain information?"

"No." He didn't hesitate answering.

"But you would."

"You're avoiding answering my question."

"We're supposed to be a team on this case, right?" she whispered, daring to shift her weight and brush her body against his. "Therefore, it seems to me that knowing what my husband enjoys, and is willing to do, is the best way to answer your question. You just said a swinging couple is a couple who mutually agree to the terms when it comes to their sexual activities. Obviously I wouldn't do anything my husband wouldn't do."

The conversation affected Noah, too. His eyes glazed over and a small, very satisfied-looking grin appeared on his face. He looked ready to say something else, but then his attention shifted, and his grip on her relaxed.

Rain turned as the butcher approached them, her flesh sizzling when Noah's hand slid up her back and his fingers wrapped protectively around the back of her neck. If she didn't already know they were here to give appearances that they were swingers, Rain would swear Noah's body language screamed "mine."

"Rain, it's good to see you again," the butcher said in a smooth, deep baritone. "And this must be your husband." He held out his hand to Noah. "Ned Flynn. But everyone calls me Butch."

"Butch, it's good to meet you." Noah's baritone deepened to match Butch's as he took his hand off Rain and shook hands with the butcher. The men sized each other up as they shook hands.

Butch was a thick man, maybe around five ten or thereabouts. Rain would put him at about the same height as her. His brown hair was cut short, not quite a crew cut but close. She decided he wasn't unattractive, although he wasn't someone she would single out. It was his personality, the friendly glow in his eyes, and his eagerness to seek a person out and start a conversation that probably made him good at what he did, and his part of the store the local gossip hangout.

"I tell you what," he said, letting go of Noah's hand but then gesturing for them to follow. "I've got a fifteen-minute break. Come on outside with me. We'll visit for a few. That is, unless you have shopping to do."

"We're good," Noah said amiably, once again taking

Rain's hand in his and then falling into stride alongside Butch. "Looks like you've got a good community here."

"The best." Butch smiled at Rain when they walked through the automatic opening doors and stepped outside into the morning sunlight. "Where are you two from? I didn't get a chance to visit much with your wife last night."

"D.C. I set up computers and networking for businesses." Noah laughed like he just told a good joke and let go of Rain's hand to hold his up in the air. "But I don't do personal computers or make house calls."

Butch's crow's-feet lengthened when he grinned broadly. He looked at her and chuckled. "I don't know. House calls can be fun from time to time."

Rain winked at him and he cleared his throat. If there was a crime in this man's past, he was very confident that he'd covered his tracks. Butch spoke easily and didn't hesitate in answering questions, like he was an open book.

"That they can," Noah agreed. "Rain didn't say what kind of swingers you are. We aren't really a BDSM couple. Rain isn't submissive. She would just as soon tie you up as be handcuffed to a bed."

"I saw that in her right away. Not much of a submissive at all." This time Butch grinned at her with admiration, as if he'd just sung her praises.

"Back home, there were a few clubs we attended when time allowed. My wife was excited that possibly there was something here where we could make new friends."

"We're not organized to the point where we have a meeting hall or a Web site or anything like that," Butch offered, and then waved at a lady who parked not too far away from where they stood next to the stall where grocery carts were returned. Butch leaned against the truck parked there. "Some folks meet and then we never see them again. Others, like me and the wife and a handful of other couples, are old-timers." He winked at Rain. "But not too old, I promise."

"Good thing," she said, and then let Noah wrap his

arm around her shoulder and pull her against him. "As long as your group isn't overwhelmed with drama. We're in this for fun. Obviously we don't want to become friends with people who aren't honest and sincere."

Butch's expression sobered. "My dear, we're all overwhelmed with drama. I'm afraid it's human nature. But we do try to keep it out of our parties. Obviously when some of us have known each other for so many years, we tend to get involved, and care about each other's personal lives. But no one will expect you to share anything you don't want to share."

Rain noticed Butch didn't take the bait and open up about the crimes that had wreaked havoc in his friends' lives recently. It could be the result of Butch being discreet. Since he believed her and Noah to be a new couple in town, possibly he didn't want to scare them away by announcing people in his group were recently murdered.

"We'd like to come to your next gathering, if we're welcome." Noah also grew serious. "Sounds like the best thing to do is meet everyone and let them meet us."

"You're right, and in luck. We're doing potluck Friday night over at the Gamboas'." Butch glanced down at his watch. "I need to get back in there before those kids make a mess of my counter. Give me your phone number and I'll have the wife call you tonight with all of the details."

Rain watched Noah search his pockets and then make a show of not having a pen or paper. Excusing herself quietly, she hurried away from the two men and went to her and Noah's rental, which was several stalls down. She noticed the woman Butch waved at get out of her car and watch with interest while Rain reached into the car for the notebook in the front seat. Tearing a piece of paper out of it, she then tore that piece of paper in half, pulled the ballpoint free from the cover of the notebook, and wrote down their names and, after hesitating for a moment, jotted down her cell-phone number. She didn't know Noah's number.

She glanced at what she'd written—"Rain and Noah"—with her number scribbled underneath. Looking outside the car, she saw Butch and Noah speaking with the woman who had given her the once-over and waved to Butch before parking. The lady definitely qualified as pretty and Rain wondered if she was part of Butch's "club" as well. Rain shook her head, reminding herself that just because people were attractive didn't make them swingers. In fact, it would be her luck that most at the potluck Friday night would be plain looking, if not ugly. On impulse, she looked back at the piece of paper, pressed it against the notebook cover, and started to write Hudson as their last name. It was her undercover last name, and now it would be Noah's, too.

Anyone might do a search on them after attending the party, and with murders going on in this exclusive circle of friends someone would be smart to do so of any newcomers. She hated that Noah might give her shit for assuming his last name, but the facts couldn't be ignored. Noah was FBI and it would be harder to trace him than it would be her. She pressed the pen to the paper and wrote "Kayne" after Noah's name. Rain and Noah Kayne. Staring at it twisted her stomach in knots. Noah had insisted last night it be their undercover name. Submitting to him in any way bugged the crap out of her. He was right about this though and she was woman enough to admit it.

When she hurried back to the group, apologizing since she knew Butch needed to get back to work and using the excuse that she couldn't find a pen for taking her so long, she handed the piece of paper to Noah for him to give to Butch.

It was an easy move, and one that neither Butch nor the lady who now stood next to him batted an eye at, but it allowed Noah to see how Rain presented them as a couple.

"Very good." Butch accepted the paper and then pulled his wallet out of his back pocket and slid the paper inside. "I've got to go earn a dollar. We'll talk to you tonight."

Noah said good-bye to the lady and then turned and placed his hand on Rain's back. He didn't say anything until he'd opened the passenger door for her, closed it after she slid into the car, then walked around and joined her on the driver's side.

"What did you think?" he asked as he started the engine, secured his seat belt, and then looked over his shoulder, glancing her way as he backed out of the stall.

"I think if he's done anything wrong he doesn't feel a lot of remorse."

"I doubt he's guilty." Noah headed toward the parking-lot exit. "But do you think he knows anything?"

"I know that he knows at least one of the deceased's widows. Last night he discussed with that woman that Sheila Lapthorne was still going to the parties." Rain reached over her shoulder and pulled her seat belt around and snapped it. She reminded herself that she didn't need to impress Noah with her responses. This wasn't a quiz. But it was important to go over the details of any conversation with a partner, especially when the conversation wasn't recorded. "So we know that he's aware of the murders. He didn't give any indication that there's anything going wrong, though, possibly because he doesn't want to scare away newcomers."

"Which gives us insight into his nature. Butch can play like life is sweet when actually it stinks like shit."

"Exactly." She continued brainstorming when Noah pulled up alongside an ATM that stood by itself in the parking lot.

Her thoughts were distracted when he unhooked his seat belt and then stretched his long body behind the steering wheel so that he could pull his wallet from his back pocket. Corded muscle strained against his jeans and she focused on his muscular legs, remembering again what he looked like naked. Her mouth went dry when Noah pulled a card out of his wallet.

"We're going to do some shopping. I think it would be

a good idea to set you up an art studio. If we decide that we need to record, or get to a point where we want to bring a group of people together and learn more details about what they know, it would be best to do it at our house. So it's time to make the place look homey."

"And who is flipping for this bill?" She looked at the credit card in his hand.

"Compliments of the FBI, princess, we're going to turn our home into a love nest."

"Call me princess again and the only thing you'll need to buy is a doghouse," she growled, hating that he used the pet name her father had used for her. "And it better be large enough for you to sleep in."

"You can go from sweetheart to bitch in less than a second," he growled.

She didn't care if he sounded offended. "I'm no one's princess," she muttered, and wished her dad were still alive so she could talk to him about this case. Some of her best memories were of sitting on the porch with him after supper and mulling over the facts of whatever case she was working on at that time.

Noah didn't comment but worked the ATM and then slid his card and a thick pile of cash into his wallet. Instead of heading out, he looked at her with a brooding stare and studied her for a minute.

"Someone burn you bad?" he finally asked.

His question shocked her and she stared out the front windshield, once again seeing her dad appear before her. Her father might have been stricter than most, but he'd also been her best friend. She wondered what he would have thought of Noah. Dad didn't approve of any of the men who had ever come sniffing around her. Granted, most who did weren't that impressive to Rain, either. It hadn't bothered her much when he'd encouraged her to send each and every one of them packing.

"No," she answered, not seeing any reason to add that she'd never stayed in a relationship long enough to get burned. "Why would you ask?" Then bested by curiosity, she added, "Did someone burn you?"

Rain looked at Noah in time to see the dark, almost ominous shadow spread over his expression. "Seared to the core," he offered easily. "And I asked because you're very evasive."

"Maybe it's because I need to remain grounded so we can focus on a very important case." She tried reading him, curious whether he'd been joking about being burned terribly.

"Should I take that to mean my incredible good looks and charming personality are distracting you?" The dark, dangerous look she'd noticed a moment ago disappeared quickly when he offered her a roguish grin.

She couldn't help smiling at him, having a feeling that Noah probably had left more than one lady stranded high and dry. "Try and tell me you aren't aware of how you affect women," she sneered, rolling her eyes as she looked ahead of them. "I can't imagine you've ever had a problem getting any woman to do exactly what you want her to do."

"You have no clue," he growled, a harshness in his tone snapping her attention back to him. Noah hit the accelerator, taking them around the ATM machine and to the exit. He didn't elaborate, and as curious as this dark side of his was that reared its ugly head and disappeared before she could analyze it, Rain knew it wasn't any of her business.

Adjusting herself in her seat, she decided to play navigator. "Take a right when you get out of here. I know the perfect hobby store that should have everything we need." They would work better together if they kept their conversations on the case, and not on each other. There wasn't time, or the desire, Rain reminded herself, to get attached to this man. Her life was her work. A good man might relieve sexual tension from time to time, but whenever Rain allowed herself to get too close to anyone all it did was fuck up her life.

This case was too damned important to allow anything

to mess it up. And that meant keeping a safe distance from her partner, even while being in his arms. Rain kept her attention on the road, refusing to look over at Noah. She couldn't help wondering what was in his past, though, that caused his expression to darken at times.

Over the next few hours they did more shopping than Rain had done all year. And she admitted, although her feet were killing her when they returned "home," it was a blast buying so many things.

Noah left her, hauling off his score of yard work tools, and Rain found herself alone in the house to arrange and decorate. They were in a two-bedroom ranch-style home, with both bedrooms and the bathroom lining each side of the hallway. Rain entered the small, empty bedroom with the easel and canvases, along with bags of paints and other supplies. She lost a good hour organizing and arranging while mulling over their conversation earlier with the butcher, pondering what to expect out of Friday night, and going over faxes that came through while they were gone. When her phone rang, it dawned on her that all of this time Noah hadn't come back inside.

"Hello," she said, after glancing at the number and not recognizing it.

"Is this Rain Kayne?" a woman asked.

Rain snapped to attention. "Yes. Hi, who is this?" she asked in as cheerful a tone as she could muster.

"This is Brandy Flynn. I believe you and your husband chatted with my husband, Butch, at the store earlier today."

"Yes. We did. Hello." Rain walked into the kitchen and pulled a Diet Dr Pepper out of the refrigerator and then looked out the back door.

"Butch mentioned a potluck we're going to Friday over at the Gamboas'. I spoke with Jan and she's excited to meet you two," Brandy said cheerfully.

Rain barely caught what Brandy said as she focused on Noah's bare back. Sweat glistened off all of that muscle as he pushed the mower over the grass. The back deck was wet and looked a lot better than it had the last time she looked at it. Noah was doing a bang-up job of making the yard look cozy and inviting. Not to mention, even though he was probably filthy and stunk, he looked more than inviting as well. Invitation, hell. Rain imagined walking outside and demanding he stop mowing and fuck her in the semi-private backyard.

She blinked and focused on her conversation. "Noah and I are thrilled to possibly make some new friends that are into what we're into," she offered, impressed she didn't stutter while pinching the bridge of her nose and closing her eyes to focus on the conversation.

"Swinging," Brandy offered, and then laughed easily. "Forgive me. We're a laid-back group and pretty open when around each other. My husband says you are both gorgeous people. I'm sure we'll all love you both!" Again her laughter sang through the phone.

Rain wasn't sure whether she should say something flattering about Brandy's husband or not. "We're both more into personalities instead of physical appearance," she said, and then wondered if she could pry anything out of Brandy. "It matters a lot to Noah and me that we have common interests with our friends. Can you tell me about the people who will be there? Are all of them married couples?"

"Yes. Most of us are married. And it is kind of a prerequisite for all of us. We prefer associating with couples over singles. Let's just say that way everyone has something to offer," she said, again laughing. "But there are a couple of single people, if you're into that."

"Are there single men, or women?"

"Well, Sheila," she started, and then paused.

Rain hoped Brandy might mean Sheila Lapthorne and decided to press. "Yes?" she encouraged.

"Oh, she is a wonderful lady. She recently lost her husband. We're all trying to be very supportive."

"How terrible," Rain said, glancing again out the back door but then looking away when Noah caught her looking. "What happened?"

"Well . . . ," Brandy began.

This time Rain didn't say a word. She would wait out the silence to hear what Brandy would say about George Lapthorne's murder.

"It was a terrible accident, really, hunting accident."

"Hunting accident?" Rain popped open the can of soda and then headed into the master bedroom where the computer was set up. She plopped down in front of it and opened a notebook, then grabbed a pen.

"It was very unfortunate that it happened. George should have known better." Brandy sounded firm, but then her tone softened. "Of course it isn't something that any of us discuss at the parties."

"Oh no. Of course not." Rain wrote "Hunting accident" on the blank page and then wrote "George" next to it. Above it, she wrote "Brandy Flynn." "I just wanted to get a feel for everyone going there. I'm afraid I don't know much about hunting. What is everyone else like?"

"We're all very good friends and committed to each other. If you fit in, I'm sure you'll become part of our tight community," Brandy said matter-of-factly.

"Who all will be there Friday night?"

"The Gamboas of course—Ted and Jan. We'll be there. Then there are Susie and Steve Porter. Steve is sort of our leader. You'll also meet Richard Swanson, and I'm pretty sure Elaine and Oscar Phillips will be there. They've been accepted into the group now. And then, of course, Patty and Joanna," Brandy said and finally took a breath.

Rain quickly wrote down the names as Brandy rattled them off. She underlined Richard Swanson's name. Then searching through the copies of the police reports, she found the information on Roberta Swanson. Her husband's name was Richard. Rain licked her lips, anxious to milk as much information out of Brandy as possible without making it sound like all she cared about was the names of those who matched the murderer's victims.

"Who is Richard's wife?" she asked, pointing at his name after writing it down on her notepad.

"Richard is a widower," Brandy said, and then cleared her throat.

"So there are a fair amount of single people in the group?"

"Richard's been with us forever. No one is going to ask him to leave." Brandy laughed, but there was a forced sound to it. Suddenly she sounded a bit nervous. "Anyway, it is a potluck party. But we won't ask you to bring anything since it's your first time with us. The address is Twenty-three twenty-three Pine and the party starts at eight. I can give you directions if you tell me where you live," she offered.

"We insist on bringing something." Rain again shuffled through paperwork until she found the address for the home they were staying in. "Noah's a good cook. What is everyone else bringing?"

"You aren't bringing anything," Brandy said firmly, but then her tone lightened. "I insist. You're coming as our guests. Now, tell me your address. I'll give you directions. Butch said you were new in town."

"We are. And Noah always insists on driving. I'll never learn my way around at this rate."

Brandy's laughter was once again melodic, relaxed. There was something she was very nervous about discussing, which made Rain itch to press further into the topic of the murders.

"What do you do while he works?"

"He hasn't started his job yet. We're still getting settled in." Rain scribbled on the side of the notebook paper that Noah needed a start date. They would have to keep their stories straight. "But our address is Thirteen-ten West Elm Street."

Rain listened while Brandy gave directions, and repeated them back to her so it sounded like she wrote them down. And she didn't bother to comment when Brandy told her to take a right when it should be a left. Rain knew exactly where the house was for their Friday night potluck.

"If you need help with anything around town, give me

a call," Brandy said when she'd finished with her directions. "Otherwise, we'll see you Friday night."

"Sounds good. Bye for now." Rain hung up the phone and leaned back in her chair, staring at her notes. "She knows something," she guessed, musing out loud. Then as an afterthought, she scribbled "right instead of left" in the margin. In case Butch overheard the directions being given, Rain and Noah would need a reason why they found the place with Brandy's directions.

Rain's stomach fluttered as nervous excitement rushed through her. The back door opened and closed and Rain watched the hallway and listened while Noah opened and closed the refrigerator and then his heavy footsteps creaked against the floor as he walked through the house.

The sun no longer reflected against the sheen of sweat clinging to all that bare muscle. Noah filled the doorway, no shirt, faded jeans, and with a beer in his hand. Rain took in the picture, a view dangerous and dripping with sex appeal, and then looked away quickly. But even as she tried focusing on the notebook page with her notes scribbled on it, the image of him standing in front of her naked appeared in her mind. Her heart pounded against her ribs while it grew noticeably warmer in the room.

"What have you been doing?" His question sounded normal enough, but his deep baritone, rushing over her skin like an invitation, added to the view he offered her, seductive and incredibly enticing.

"I just got off of the phone with Brandy."

"Brandy?"

Rain glanced at him. He didn't move from where he stood. "Brandy Flynn is Butch's wife."

"Oh." One eyebrow shot up and then Noah moved into the room, the smell of his deodorant and freshly cut grass oddly creating an appealing, almost erotic aroma. "You took notes? You get something off of her?"

Rain sighed and opened and closed her pen quickly, making it click while staring at what she'd written down.

Noah put his hand on the back of her chair and his knuckles scraped against her shoulder blade.

"Just an impression, I'd say," she began, and then leaned forward and pointed at her notes while explaining the phone call while he watched over her shoulder. "I don't know her," she concluded. "But it was how her vocal inflection changed, the way she laughed and then evaded and even lied about certain things. She knows something."

"She might know a lot," Noah offered easily. "And you seldom know a perp when you interview him. It's signs like you just described that help determine if guilt exists or not. We use those signs to know where to push with an interrogation."

"But this wasn't an interrogation," she reminded him. "Brandy viewed it as a phone call to get acquainted with new people in town and invite them to a party. I couldn't push too hard."

"You'll get your chance." He moved his hand and squeezed her shoulder, then stroked her hair. "The fact that we have people with knowledge of the murders proves we're moving in the right direction."

"Moving at a snail's pace."

"Solving a murder takes time. And we've got four murders, more if these deaths are connected to the ones in Kansas City and Dallas."

"You don't think I know that?" She dropped her pen and moved out of the chair and away from his gentle caresses.

"I know that you know that." Noah drank from his beer, watching her over the bottle while his Adam's apple moved in his neck with each swallow. He put the bottle on the desk by the computer before it was empty. "We've got a full day before that party and the opportunity to learn more about these people and find out what they know."

"Our killer could be among those people," she blurted, aware of the possibility that their murderer might be closer than they thought.

"Could be." Noah moved closer to her, although it also

meant he moved toward the door, which might have been all he intended to do. "What do we do now?"

She ached to touch him. He didn't seem to have a problem continually caressing her, stroking her skin or petting her hair. Rain knew that if she reached out and even so much as pressed her fingertips into that solid, muscular body all her resolve would fade away. All it would take was the slightest movement and she could answer his question without uttering a word.

Rain lifted her gaze to his face, realizing she'd been focusing on his rippling chest muscles, and saw his serious yet relaxed expression. His question was sincere, with no suggestive undertones. Noah's mind was on the case, which was where her thoughts needed to stay.

"We've got some names here. I can search online, see if we have any priors, learn where each of them live, where they work. I can find out if any of them recently purchased a gun. The best thing to do is lay down all of the facts first." She looked toward the computer, encouraging her mind to continue on its brainstorming path. "The fax came through with a list of names who are friends or acquaintances of each victim. Everyone on that list is a suspect until we eliminate them. We need to find out where each one of them was at the time of each murder, what their relationship was to each victim."

"I need a shower and then I'll help you." Noah reached for her, as usual touching her without hesitation as if it were the most natural thing for him to do. "Unless of course you want to come scrub my back and then we can research them together."

She made a face and hoped it looked like the idea didn't appeal to her. "Go take your shower," she grumbled, although her voice was huskier than she wanted it to be.

Noah cleared the distance between them so quickly she barely noticed him move until he stepped into her space. Grabbing the hair at the side of her head, he tugged hard enough for her to feel the pinch against her scalp. Then, as he seemed so good at doing, Noah pressed his lips over hers, kissing her thoroughly before letting her up for air.

"Next time then," he whispered, his mouth close enough that it would take nothing to kiss her again. "Maybe I'll get you dirty later and then wash your back."

After Noah left the room, Rain grumbled her frustration, still feeling where he touched her even after the shower started. It was impossible not to imagine him naked, seeing the water slowly soak the dark hair on his chest, and picture sudsy streams flowing down all that corded muscle.

"Damn him," she growled, reaching for her pen but then tossing it on the notepad while frustration ate at her furiously.

She almost jumped when her phone rang again. Staring at the number for a moment, Rain contemplated sending the call to voice mail. Maybe talking to someone who had nothing to do at all with anything in her life right now would help.

"Hello." Rain moved to her bed, plopped onto the edge of it, and pulled her legs to sit cross-legged.

"Rain, how are you doing, sweetheart?" Jimmy Malcom, her on-again, off-again lover, who conveniently lived thirty miles away in a smaller town, sounded as jovial as always.

"I'm fine, Jimmy," she said, knowing he didn't want to hear the details of her life.

"Great!" he said, the grin obvious in his voice. "It's time for us to play catch-up. It's been a while."

"It has been a while," she agreed, staring at her toenails while focusing on Jimmy's deep voice. For a while, Rain had contemplated making Jimmy a more serious boyfriend. Her father never knew about him, and wouldn't have approved if he did. But the physical distance between them made Jimmy a safe lover. When she was with him she could play his devoted girlfriend, and when she returned to Lincoln she could clear her head from the romance and focus entirely on her work.

"Remember when we went out to the lake last summer?" he asked, chuckling as he pulled forward the memory.

"How could I forget?" Rain smiled, remembering when they had rented a paddleboat and then tried making out in it. The thing capsized, soaking both of them. It proved a fair amount of work righting it and climbing back in. Both of them were so exhausted by the time they returned it safely to the dock they never made love.

"Let's not do that again," he offered.

Rain laughed easily. Every time she went to see Jimmy, he took her out somewhere in his town, the two of them played the devoted couple, then most often he would get a motel room and they would have sex for hours. Jimmy was good, tireless, unless he was forced to spend almost an hour in water, and safe. In the years they'd known each other, not once did he tell her he loved her, and he'd never suggested she leave her job to be closer to him. Any other man Rain had tried getting close to inevitably suggested she quit her line of work to be with him.

"That sounds like a plan," Rain offered, glancing at the doorway when the shower turned off.

"So what is your week looking like?" Jimmy asked.

"Not good." She wouldn't tell Jimmy she was working undercover. They never talked about their work when they were together or on the phone. With Jimmy it was a fantasy. Both of them giving each other that special something without any ties or worries of one of them trying to crowd the other.

"Have you found someone else?" His question surprised her.

Rain figured it was fair enough for him to ask, though. It had been a good month since they'd last talked. "No," she said truthfully, shooting furtive glances toward the hallway. She pictured Noah stepping out of the shower, rubbing the towel over all that roped muscle. She hadn't found him, though. They'd been assigned to each other.

"I'm going to be busy with work for a while," she admitted.

"That job of yours," Jimmy said, sighing.

"What's that mean?" Rain glanced down at her hand and then twisted the simple narrow gold band around her ring finger with her thumb. She didn't hear Noah moving in the bathroom. Her heart picked up a beat when she wondered if he was listening.

"You've got to know how hot you are," Jimmy said instead of explaining his comment.

"You're not bad yourself," she offered, returning the compliment but instantly finding herself comparing Jimmy to Noah. There was no comparison. Where Noah was dark, mysterious, and brooding, Jimmy was easy, always grinning, and playful. Hands down, though, Noah was much better looking.

Jimmy chuckled, drinking in the compliment. "You're intelligent and easy to talk to. Any man would die to have you at his side, Rain," he added, suddenly sounding serious.

Rain didn't like where this conversation was going. The bathroom door opened and she straightened, feeling the urge to jump off the bed.

"Honestly, I would push this relationship to the next level if it weren't for your job," Jimmy said as Noah appeared in the doorway.

The look on Noah's face showed he'd been listening to the conversation. "We've all got to work," she said, and realized she still played with the ring on her finger.

"True," Jimmy offered. "Your job is a bit more intense than most. If a man weren't incredibly comfortable with himself, what you do might appear to be a threat to him."

"I wouldn't be attracted to a weak man anyway," Rain said, aching to end the conversation now. "I'm not sure when things will settle down," she added, hoping that would encourage Jimmy to let her go and agree to contact her later.

"Let me know when they do."

"Sure," she said, drinking in a deep breath while acutely aware of Noah leaning in the doorway, making no qualms of listening to her conversation. "Talk to you soon," she offered, needing to get off the phone. Noah's intense stare had chills rushing over her flesh.

"Sure thing, sweetheart. Call me as soon as you can."

"Okay. Bye-bye." Rain hung up the phone and dropped it on the bed next to her.

"I guess it makes sense you would have a lover," Noah said, his expression neutral as he studied her.

"He isn't a lover." Rain slid off the bed, already regretting taking the call.

"You've never fucked him?" Noah tilted his head, a challenge in his voice.

"Does it matter?" She moved over to the computer. His gaze followed her. She swore wherever he looked on her body it burned deep into her flesh, creating a swelling need that started throbbing deep inside her. "I'm sure you have a history, too," she added, praying that would end this conversation.

Noah had an uncanny ability to move in on her without making a sound. She barely registered him in her peripheral view before his strong arms wrapped around her waist and he pressed his half-nude body against her backside. Rain stilled, unable to breathe or fathom a thought when his mouth lowered to her nape.

"There's nothing wrong with history," he growled, raking his teeth over her flesh. "Yes, I have history. And it's nothing I wish to discuss. It's current events that matter. I'm not going to make love to a woman who is in love with another man."

"I'm not in love with him," she uttered, but then immediately realized that sounded like permission for Noah to fuck her.

When she tried walking out of his grip, Noah spun her around, damn near knocking her off her feet before he slid his fingers around her neck, tilting her head back slightly with his thumb under her chin.

"That's a very good thing," he rumbled, and then captured her mouth with his.

FIVE

Noah flipped over on the couch and then growled out loud. It was still dark outside. But if he lay there another minute, or even tried falling asleep, he'd wake up even stiffer than he was now.

And Miss Hot and Elusive Cop Lady rested peacefully in that large bed down the hall. Noah stood, letting the blanket that was wrapped around him fall to the floor, and stretched. Then scratching his bare chest, he stared through the gap where the front curtains didn't meet and into the darkness outside.

Somewhere out there, someone lived knowing they'd murdered at least four people. They knew they were being hunted. Were they sleeping right now?

It was the psychological part of a case that got him off sometimes more than researching and narrowing down the list. Why was each one of those people killed? And what kind of person possessed the confidence to keep killing?

Walking barefoot down the hall, Noah glanced at the closed bedroom door. Rain slept in there. He could open it, climb onto that bed, and seduce her until she forgot to tell him no. He doubted it would be that hard to do. Rain wanted him possibly more than he wanted her. But her stubborn streak glowed in those pretty baby blues of hers as strongly as her craving for him did.

Padding barefoot into the bathroom instead, he stared at his reflection in the darkness and then scrubbed his thick brown hair. He could stand for a haircut, but conforming to the standards of Bureau appearance didn't appeal to him. Most of his work was undercover, and the less he looked like a cop the easier it was to move among civilians and not make anyone jumpy.

He headed back to the living room and grabbed his cell to check the time, noted that it was almost 5:00 A.M., and decided that wasn't too early to start his day. Again temptation riddled him as he stared at his phone. It was hard saying what would happen at that potluck tomorrow night. He wasn't sure he wanted to watch Rain willingly allow someone else to fuck her, though, when she was repeatedly telling him no. Scratching his scalp some more, he glared at the closed bedroom door before stomping into the bathroom. If he closed the bathroom door loud enough to wake her, that was a damned fucking shame.

The clock on the computer screen said it was after seven when the bedroom door across the hall opened and he glanced at Rain as she ignored him and headed to the bathroom. Noah returned his attention to the list in front of him that he'd worked on for the past hour or so.

There was a sense of warped satisfaction when he picked up his coffee cup and sipped and waited for Rain to see that he'd finished off the pot of coffee and hadn't made more. He frowned when he heard the refrigerator open and then Rain popped open her can of Diet Dr Pepper. She seemed to be able to gather her caffeine fix from her soda as easily as a cup of coffee. So much for his warped satisfaction.

Rain appeared in the doorway a moment later, wearing her short, snug tank top that was damned near see-through and her loose-fitting shorts with a tie string that hung on her slender hips. Her being barefoot, with long, slender legs and perfectly shaped thighs, added to the sensual picture she presented. Noah glanced at her sleepy-looking face and her tousled dark hair that hung past her shoulders and down her back, ending with soft curls that rested against her waist. What he wouldn't do to experience all that hair tickling his chest while she rode him until she came.

"What are you doing?" she asked, and then sipped at her soda pop, watching him with sensual blue eyes.

"Going over that list of names your chief faxed over."

"I worked on that yesterday. I just didn't get it finished," she added, keeping her gaze focused on his.

"Now you don't have to." He pinned his attention to the screen when she entered the room, knowing as well as she did that if he'd continued with his seductions yesterday she wouldn't have had time to start on the list, let alone make any headway with it.

If he looked at her again he would touch her. Half the time his hands were on her before he even thought about it. Touching her just seemed so natural to do.

"Noah," she sighed, and then drank more of her pop.

He ignored her frustrated sound. "Have you ever bowled?"

"You want to go bowling?"

"Sure. Unless you suck at it. Might not hurt to just hang out at the bowling alley and see what we can learn about two of our victims. It wouldn't hurt to check out the racquet club, too." He looked up and caught Rain scowling at the computer screen. She shifted her attention to him and he let his gaze fall to her hard nipples that pressed against the pale pink material that stretched over her full, round breasts. "We need to buy you an outfit for tomorrow night also."

"An outfit? It's a potluck. What do you mean?"

His cell rang and Noah stood, intentionally pushing into her space while reaching around her for his phone. Rain tried moving, but he shifted so that he pinned her between his body and the desk.

"Move," she whispered, but didn't complain further when he answered his phone.

After acknowledging Brenda's secretary telling him that he now showed up as an employee of Computer Tech, Inc., he reached around Rain, jotting down the information on his new identity. If any of their new "friends" decided to get nosy and check him out, he would come up clean. Thanking the secretary and then hanging up the phone, he rested his arm on Rain's shoulder as he placed the paper and pen on the desk. Then placing his phone on top of his notes, he moved his fingers until they tangled in her hair.

"Are you having fun?" she snapped, bringing her can to her lips and glaring at him over it.

"I could be." He could prove to her how much fun both of them could have, and the more he thought about it, the better the idea sounded. Taking her can away from her quickly enough that she couldn't stop him, he placed it behind her, too, forcing her to lean backward or have his body pressed against hers. "Tomorrow night might be a potluck, but it's a swingers' party, too. The ladies are going to be dressed for the occasion."

"And the men?" she challenged him.

Noah shrugged and reached for a thick strand of her dark hair and watched it wrap into an adorable curl around his finger. "We mostly wear jeans, casual attire, that sort of thing."

"You're kidding." Rain put her hands on her hips, still standing with her back to the desk and him a few inches in front of her, and straightened so that her face was almost level to his. A challenge glowed in her eyes almost as strong as the desire he swore he saw there, too. "So let me get this right," she growled. "Swingers have their women strutting around in God only knows what. But the men do nothing to make themselves attractive."

Noah's initial thought that he would need to do some molding with Rain to prepare her for the party tomorrow night proved to be good thinking. His opinion of swingers needed to be buried. If she got even a whiff of the fact that he despised the thought of sharing what was his with others just so he could have a taste of what they had, they would never pull this off. At this rate, Rain would attack any man who tried touching her and chastise the women for flirting with all of the men. Noah didn't want to change her in that area. Again he reminded himself this was a case.

Rain wasn't a woman he could ever consider dating. They were undercover and all that mattered was that she play her part and be believable.

He untangled his fingers from her hair and placed his hands on her shoulders. Rain moved quickly. Slicing her hands up between them, she damn near karate chopped his hands off of her shoulders, slapping his forearms with the backs of her hands. Her expression hardened, anticipating, while she held her hands at her sides, waiting for his next move.

"Is that how you're going to act toward any men at the potluck if they try touching you?" he demanded.

"Nope. I know how to flirt with the best of them." Her eyes flashed a radiant blue as she bestowed him with the sweetest smile he'd ever seen on her face. It damn near stole his breath. "It's just how I'm going to treat you," she added in a softer, sultrier tone.

Damn her. Noah moved quickly, grabbing her by the waist and lifting her in the air, then turning and moving fast until her back hit the wall hard enough to make it shake. He pressed one of his legs between hers and pinned her with his own body as he grabbed her wrists when she tried striking out.

He knew his kiss was punishing. And as he parted her lips with his tongue and dove deep into her sweltering, moist heat, a small part of his brain argued that he wasn't being fair to her.

When he tasted her, and heard first her grunt when she hit the wall and then a soft sigh when he impaled her mouth, there wasn't any stopping. Noah held on to her wrists firmly, pushing her hands against the wall, and deepened the kiss, taking all she offered and craving more.

"Noah!" she cried out when he released her mouth and nipped at her lower lip.

One long bare leg wrapped around his thigh. It was smooth, warm, and strong considering she wasn't ripped with muscle. The more she pressed against the confines of his hands wrapped around her wrists, the harder he got.

When he leaned into her soft abdomen, his cock grew painfully, swelling and throbbing between them while the warmth from her body added to the torture he already endured.

As many thoughts attacked his brain, all arguing the pros and cons of his actions, one reality prevailed. If he backed down now, Rain would attack. And because he'd already seen how fighting turned her on, he wouldn't back down but would press her harder.

Noah let go of Rain's wrists.

"Why do you do this?" she cried, her frustration heavy as she yelled and balled her fists over her head.

Noah wrapped his arms around her waist and lifted her. He moved the few feet to the queen-size bed, set in the middle of the room against the wall. When he dropped her onto the bed, she looked beyond enticing, with blankets and sheets twisted around one other underneath her and several pillows scattered against the headboard above her head.

"Do what?" he asked, coming down on top of her quickly.

Rain pulled her legs up, trying to block him, but he grabbed them and spread them open. Her loose-fitting shorts didn't hide the fact that she wasn't wearing underwear. He almost missed the blow she aimed for the side of his head when he realized that Rain shaved—everywhere.

"Quit torturing me," she yelled, and aimed her fist for his head.

Noah had thrown off some hardened criminals in his time. On more than one occasion he'd taken down a man twice his size. Not that he was small by any means, and he wasn't slow. But Rain got damned close to knocking his ass out.

"Then quit telling me no," he hissed, emphasizing each word as he grabbed her wrist and held it firmly in the air between them.

Rain stared up at him, her dark hair spread out around

her head and her lips parted as she panted. Her legs were bent and spread open as he knelt over her. Slowly she brought her lips together and licked them.

He saw her expression strain as she worked to relax her fist in his hand. "This isn't about you and me," she said, her voice ragged.

"You don't want to fuck me." If he backed away from her now, he'd have to back all the way out. They could find their murderer, but it would be a hell of a lot harder pretending they were sexually active, and married, if they weren't having sex. "Because this ends now—one way or the other. You aren't the only one being tortured."

"Fuck you, Noah!" Rain yanked her fist from his hand and hit him in the chest—hard. "I don't want your goddamned ultimatums."

She pushed back from him, trying to do a backward crab walk. But with her legs spread and her shorts somewhat twisted on her now, the view was even more incredible.

Noah crawled over her, grabbing her tank top and twisting it in his fist. "But you want me."

It was like fire sparked in her blue eyes, turning them more intense than bright and pure rare sapphires. "I swear to God, I'll kick your fucking ass."

"Do it, princess. Fighting turns you on."

He wasn't ready for the fierce intensity that ripped through her. Rain came up hard with her legs and at the same time swung hard with one fist toward the side of his head and aimed at his neck with her other fist.

Noah held the advantage in his corner. Not only did he hold twice her weight in muscle, but he was easily twice as strong and he was already on top of her. Nonetheless, as much as he wouldn't let her put some unexplainable bruises on him, he wasn't going to hurt her, either.

Rain would spar and get off on it. He'd seen that quality in her since the first few minutes that he knew her. But this wasn't sparring. Rain went ballistic on him.

He grabbed her, holding her shirt when she sprang off

the bed and tried knocking him backward. As he grabbed her he heard material rip while dark hair flew in front of his face.

"Don't you ever, ever fucking call me princess again!" She still tried struggling against him when he finally got her wrapped in his arms tightly enough that she couldn't move. "Why the hell won't you listen?"

"Damn, Rain," he whispered, tightening his grip until he hugged her and buried his face in her hair. Pressing his lips to her neck, he felt the fierce beat of her heart against his lips. "It's like the word triggers something inside you into attack mode. Trust me, I'm not insulting you."

"I know," she whispered, going incredibly lax in his arms, as if not only did all fight leave her, but all energy she possessed drained right out of her, too.

When he relaxed his grip and laid her back on the bed, her body was relaxed, as if she were hurt. And for a moment he thought she was. He slid his arms out from behind her back and left her lying underneath him while he continued kneeling over her.

Rain's eyes looked moist when she slowly lifted her lashes. He felt her gaze burn over him as it traveled lazily up his chest, over his shoulders, to his neck and then finally his face.

Her tank top was twisted sideways and torn by one of the straps that hung off of her shoulder. The material flapped over one of her breasts, offering him one hell of a view that went way beyond sexier than hell. When she didn't say anything but simply watched him, not looking like she was waiting for any comment or action from him but simply taking a moment to stare at him, he watched something shift in her eyes. Maybe she needed this final moment to decide which way their undercover relationship would go, which was fine. The view lying underneath him tightened his chest, making it hard to breathe. And he wouldn't trade where he was for anything in the world.

Finally, accepting that round one was over and his wits

seemed somewhat in order, Noah slowly lowered his mouth to hers.

"Are you on birth control?" he asked when his lips brushed over hers.

She laughed out loud, offering him a mouthful of teeth to kiss. "Is this how you seduce all women?"

"I don't seduce women."

"Bullshit. Slut," she teased, her orneriness returning, although the fight in her had seriously subsided.

"Who told you that?"

Her lashes fluttered over her baby blues, which didn't look as moist as they did a moment before. Something about being called princess bugged the shit out of her. He would remember not to call her that again, but he ached to know why the term of endearment bothered her.

"I'm a damned good cop," she whispered. "And . . . yes."

He moved his attention to the side of her face, pressing kisses over her soft flesh and tasting her as he dragged his tongue to her ear. "Yes, what?" he asked, moving his hand between them and finding the bottom of her tank top. He latched onto her earlobe and at the same time dragged her top up over her breasts.

"Birth control." Her breath was tight. "*I'm on birth control*," she emphasized, and then hissed when he bit her earlobe and dragged his teeth across the soft, plump flesh. "Crap. Noah."

He'd found a spot on her. The way she tensed underneath him and her thighs pressed against his hips, Noah wondered what other spots on her body would make her sizzle like she did now.

"I'm going to fuck you, Rain," he whispered into her ear, and moved his hand over her breast. It filled his hand, firm and round, perfectly plump and so smooth and soft. He squeezed her nipple between his fingers, rolling the puckered flesh while he moved his mouth to her neck. "If you seriously don't want this to happen, say so now, or it's going to happen."

"Got rules, do you?" she growled, and then dragged her nails over his shoulders.

She dug in, too, creating a heat that pierced his flesh and tightened every inch of him. "Actually, yes. I do have rules."

He lifted his head, feeling the weight of his cock and the burning pressure that filled his balls. He watched her stare at his chest, take in his body, while the heat swelling inside him created a sheen of sweat over his body. There was no hiding how desperately he needed to fuck her.

Rain dragged her fingers to his neck and then to his face. Then pressing her palms to his cheeks, she held his face, staring up at him. "I've got rules, too, FBI man. This is sex. That's it. You forget that for one minute and you're going to get hurt. Hear me? We're doing a job. Nothing more."

"If this is part of our job," he began, pushing himself to his knees and enduring the pain in his groin while the throbbing of blood, pumping furiously inside him, made his ears ring. He stared down at her exposed breasts and damn near exploded. But if terms were being laid on the table, he would have his say in them. Rain wanted to play tough. But he'd bet damned good money her lecture applied to her as much as to him. "Then you better fuck me like a wife adoring her husband," he said, taking off his pants.

When her cheeks flushed, it confirmed what he already believed. Instead of waiting for her to challenge him again, he grabbed her shorts and lifted her hips off the bed when he pulled on them. Rain crawled backward, which aided him in sliding them down her long, thin legs.

"Not every wife adores her husband." Her response didn't surprise him. The wall around her emotions wasn't going to slip any time soon. "If I adored you, why would I want to go to a party to fuck other men?"

He met her gaze quickly. God, life seriously wasn't fair. A gorgeous woman lay underneath him, uttering the words he would have killed to hear Laurel say a few months ago. But Rain was right. This was their job. A murderer ran loose, possibly nearby, and it mattered more than keeping Rain's firm opinion on swinging intact that they find their guy and put him behind bars. "Rain, couples don't swing because they don't love each other. Most swingers are very happy with each other."

"Oh really."

"It's like the love of a sport. It's something they do together and enjoy together." An idea hit him and he tossed her shorts off the bed. "Before tomorrow night you're going to check out swinger Web sites. Read what real swingers have to say about what they do. I think you'll find, dear wife, that couples who swing do it because both of them love sex very, very much."

God. She was a vision to be adored. Rain moved to her knees and faced him, completely naked, or almost with her top pushed up above her breasts. There wasn't an imperfection on her. Noah wasn't sure he'd ever seen a more beautiful lady in his life. Laurel's body was covered with freckles and her skin very white. Any time out in the sun burned her painfully, so she avoided any outdoor activities and as a result was never tan. Noah didn't mind that about Laurel. She was gorgeous in her own right. He tried remembering when Laurel ever stole every thought from his head and made him forget to breathe the way Rain was doing right now.

Rain's breasts were more than a handful, her nipples rosy brown and big. Her body was firm, in good shape. Her waist was narrow and her hips round and perfectly shaped. But her shaved, smooth skin between her legs appealed to him, creating a carnal edge inside that burned hotter and with a rawness that would make it impossible for him to discuss the case or anything else with her as long as she was in front of him like that.

"The only thing I want to find is the murderer." Her gaze dropped as she spoke until it looked like she stared at the tent in his boxers.

"We're definitely going to do that." He pushed his boxers

down his legs and rose up on his knees, then stood at the edge of the bed and stepped out of them.

Her gaze didn't move and he saw her lips part when she saw him completely naked—again. This time, though, he was more than ready for her. She didn't comment, and didn't move her attention from his cock. Her silent praise caused the pressure inside him to swell to his chest.

Rain could talk all she wanted about this being just a job. Noah knew without any doubt that he couldn't fuck her if she didn't appeal to him. If there was no strong attraction between them, they would simply, and contentedly, pretend to be married, holding hands or putting arms around each other when the moment called for it. What hung heavily between them right now existed out of mutual attraction. Case or no case, he would find Rain sexy as hell. And from the flush that spread over her cheeks while she licked her lips and gazed at him with a raw hunger that matched the burning need inside him, Rain felt the same way about him.

Noah climbed onto the bed and watched her attention snap to his face. Once again she looked ready to take him on.

"We're done sparring," he told her, and continued crawling onto the bed until he pushed into her, and then eased her back on the bed. "Or can you only enjoy yourself if you make what you're doing into a battle?"

She sincerely looked surprised and pursed her lips together, although he saw quickly that she fought to hide a smile.

"Something funny?" he asked, adjusting himself between her legs.

Rain stretched out underneath him, with her head finding the pillows and her hair fanning around her flushed face. "No fight left in you, FBI man?"

"This isn't a fight," he whispered, pressing his lips to hers.

"As long as you try manipulating my thinking and actions, it will be," she said, turning her head to break the kiss before he could impale her. "I've read up on swingers ever since I took on this case. I'll act like one of them, and trust me they will believe I'm a swinger. But if you try your mind-play shit on me one more time, you won't have anything to swing with. I'm not changing my opinions, or values, for any man, regardless of the reason."

Goddamn, he didn't want to change a thing about her. His heart constricted dangerously and he closed his eyes, grabbing her jaw and turning her face back to his. Finding her mouth wasn't hard, and impaling her, plunging into her heat and quickly drowning in their kiss, seemed second nature. But with her strong, opinionated nature, letting her see for one moment how strongly he agreed with her would bring out the qualities inside her even more. He wanted to do that more than he wanted his next breath. For the sake of this case, though, he couldn't let her see his true nature.

Already Rain accepted how he said things would be. Even as he dragged his tongue down her neck and nipped at the soft spot above her collarbone, the fever raging inside him didn't prevent him from seeing when she willingly opened up for him. She might refuse to call it submission, and he'd be the last to point out to her that's what she was doing, but they were also bonding. A trust needed to exist between them that was strong enough an intelligent, psychopathic killer wouldn't see through them and grow leery in their presence, and satisfying a craving that would have interfered with their investigation if they didn't fuck each other soon eased them closer to that necessary level of trust.

As Noah tasted her, and caressed her soft, warm flesh, the debate as to why they were having sex faded from his mind and the intense desire to enjoy Rain, watch while she came for him, and experience her heat wrapped around him consumed his thoughts. It didn't matter anymore that they explored each other simply to appear familiar with each other in public. There wasn't any thought to keeping the pleasure they shared together at a physical level, or so that they wouldn't be obsessed with learning what it was like to be with each other. When Rain purred like a cat, arching into him as he sucked her breast into his mouth, all that mattered was taking her to the point where she exploded. Noah needed to see how she looked coming after he took her over the edge.

Rain opened up to him, running her hands over his arms, his shoulders, and then down his back. She lifted her legs, offering herself, shifting until she was right where he needed her to be. Their bodies moved together, molding against each other without any awkward motions or hesitations. Rain was tall and shaped so perfectly that he could be made to believe at that moment they'd been created for each other. When she grabbed his head and then tangled her fingers in his hair, her mutual excitement to feel the passion burn to its highest intensity between them melted something inside him.

"Kiss me, FBI man," she drawled.

"Bossy bitch," he whispered into her mouth, giving her a roguish grin.

"Don't ever forget it," she purred, rewarding him with a smile so genuine he would have done anything she asked of him at that moment.

Rain brought his mouth to hers and encouraged the heat to flow between them, kissing him while raising her hips and brushing her moist heat against him.

Noah growled, barely needing to shift before he pressed against her entrance. As he slowly slid inside her, sheathing himself with smooth, velvety warmth that instantly soaked him and created wave after wave of pleasure that about took him over the edge, a sensation hit him that he hadn't expected.

Noah filled her, burying himself deep inside her moist heat, and swore he'd come home. It wasn't even a thought that came to him clearly. So many soothing muscles constricted and stroked him, easing his way as he created a rhythm between the two of them. The realization slipped into his head, settling there. Fucking Rain made sense.

Not because they needed to appear familiar with each other. The act they shared wasn't just physical. Something slipped inside, a shield or barrier that was installed so securely for so many years that when it shifted, feelings spread throughout his insides that took over his strength to argue with them. Being inside Rain was where he belonged. Because they wanted each other. Because in the matter of a couple of days the sparks that flew around them every time they were near were the creation of something stronger than just lust.

It took him a moment before he realized he no longer compared her to Laurel. For three years he'd believed Laurel was for him. In a matter of less than a month, with a wedding date set, she'd exploded that reality in his face. But Rain, with her fiery temper and willful nature, her actions speaking louder than her words, was the woman he'd been looking for all his life. The swelling that threatened to implode around his heart made it impossible to take his next breath. He couldn't have Rain. He couldn't let her know how he truly felt. And he hated that knowledge as much as he loved sinking deep inside her pussy.

Noah broke off the kiss but didn't move his face from hers. She continued holding his head, her lips swollen and wet as she stared into his eyes. And that's when he saw it. Impaling her again, thrusting deeper and harder, he couldn't deny that she saw it, too.

He held on to her gaze, drowning in those baby blues, and for the first time in his life prayed that it might take them a while to nail their guy. Rain was perfect—and not just physically. This wouldn't be the only time he fucked her, it wouldn't end their fighting, and it wouldn't stop her from continually challenging him.

"Rain," he hissed, the knowledge that he wanted more from her, craved her even as she gave herself to him, exploded inside him.

"Yes," she whispered, tightening her grip in his hair, and opening her eyes wider as she stared into his. It was like she answered his thoughts, knowing and understanding what he felt.

This was about more than work. It just became personal.

SIX

If she dropped the soap one more time she'd scream. As good as the hard pellets of water felt pounding on her back, the knot in her gut refused to allow her to enjoy the hot shower.

What the hell did they do?

She didn't need to have sex with Noah to work this case. They could have easily played off being happily married during the investigation without fucking.

"Quit lying to yourself," she groaned, bending over and picking up the bar of soap. She stared at the gold band on her ring finger.

What was it about Noah that made him so different from any other man who'd entered her life? Even after her father died, she'd been able to keep all of them at bay. How did Noah so successfully sneak around the barrier that she kept around her heart?

"Rain?" Noah's deep baritone was on the other side of the shower curtain, and she didn't even hear the bathroom door open.

She jumped, dropped the soap again, and cursed. His rich baritone chuckle pissed her off even more.

"What?" she snapped.

"Sorry to startle you. I'm heading out for a while."

"What? Where are you going?" She glared at the soap, which was sliding in a stream of suds toward the drain.

"I won't be gone long."

"What?" Rain stepped into the water, scrubbing her head furiously to get the soap out. "Where are you going?"

"Stay here. Play the happy and satisfied wife. Paint or something."

"Wait!" she yelled, and then heard the bathroom door close.

Rinsing as quickly as she could, Rain turned off the water and grabbed the towel. Then hurrying out of the bathroom, she wrapped the towel around her naked body while creating puddles up and down the hallway as she hurried through the house.

"Noah?" she called out more than once. Like hell he would fuck her, telling her they needed to act married, and then walk out the door without as much as an explanation.

She grabbed the door off the kitchen leading to the garage as Noah headed around the rental. "Where are you going?" she demanded.

Noah turned. Standing in the garage with her still in the kitchen in the doorway put her an inch or so taller than him. His gaze traveled down her wet body, with only the towel wrapped around her, and her long hair dripping, creating puddles at her feet.

"Want some more already?" he asked, slowly raising his attention to her face.

When he reached for her towel, Rain stepped back but then grabbed the doorway to prevent herself from slipping. "I want to know where the hell you're going," she demanded. "Why are you leaving me here alone?"

Noah climbed the one step into the kitchen, quickly eliminating her height advantage. "Husbands don't take their wives with them to work," he explained, the sudden softness in his baritone making her wary.

He moved in on her, and again Rain stepped backward, not willing to relax and let him off the hook that quickly for attempting to leave without an explanation.

"But husbands say good-bye and where they're going," she informed him.

"I don't have a problem with that," he said, grabbing her before she could move out of his reach. His fingers wrapped around the top of her towel and he tugged.

"What are you doing?" she demanded, covering her

hand with his but knowing without challenging him she couldn't stop him from yanking her towel away if he decided he really wanted to do it.

"Saying good-bye," he offered, twisting the material, which tightened above her breasts, and then dragged her to him.

Noah pulled her into his arms, tilting her head and pouncing on her mouth before she could protest. What sucked was she didn't want to protest. And she didn't want him leaving her here alone all day while he went and did God only knew what while making a show of being at work. What the hell was she supposed to do without a car? It was impossible to present her case and argue it with him, though, when he damn near leaned her over backward, impaling her mouth with a kiss that robbed Rain of her ability to think.

"I could get really used to that," he warned her, his lips brushing over hers while he straightened her but kept his arms around her.

Rain didn't remember wrapping her arms around his neck but let him go and grasped her towel. It seemed the room remained tilted sideways when she stepped out of his grasp, grumpier than she was a moment ago now that he'd re-created a need in her as strong as it was right before he fucked her.

"Where are you going?" She ignored his comment, knowing anything she said would make him late to this "job" he planned on heading out the door and going to.

"I'm supposed to install computer systems. I figured I would stop in at the police station and talk to the chief." He tapped her nose with his finger. My cover allows me to go anywhere, but not with you. "I'll be sure and tell him you send your love."

This wasn't part of the deal. She didn't like him leaving her here carless and, worse yet, heading out to her stomping ground.

Turning to the bathroom, she waved over her shoulder.

"You do that," she said, closing the bathroom door at the same time the garage door closed.

Rain took her time getting dressed and then made the bed and straightened the house. There was no way she could paint, and not just because Noah had suggested she do so. It pissed her off he would leave without her. They were partners. Partners worked together.

Scowling all the way to the bedroom, she slumped into the computer chair and glared at the screen. There were the notes she'd taken the night before and information she'd added to their chart. She stared at the names of everyone going to the party. Beneath those were names of acquaintances, business associates, anyone who knew the victims and their families. Some of the blanks next to each name were filled in. Sheila Lapthorne was involved in a nasty child custody case twelve years ago. During that time George Lapthorne was charged with child endangerment, but it didn't stick. There was also a DUI on his record. It appeared they were trying to get all of his priors expunged when he was murdered.

Otherwise, Lorrie Hinders had a best friend, Nina Bogart, who had a criminal record—shoplifting and aggravated assault. Nothing showed up on any of the other names Rain entered into the system. She could head out to the pawnshops and find out who'd purchased a gun that would shoot .32-caliber bullets. Of course, they didn't know how long the murderer owned the gun. It could have been a weapon housed in the family for years.

"But with no car, it's kind of hard to do any investigating." She scowled at the screen and finally opened a new browser window. "Maybe I should learn more about this kinky world I'm about to dive into."

An hour or so later, Rain was lost in a world of perversion and kink that was professed by all who partook in it as normal and healthy. Some of the sites had stories, and although she quickly learned all of them weren't for her, she enjoyed reading a couple where two men enjoyed one woman sexually.

"That would be okay," she mused, clicking out of the site after finishing the second story. "I can see how reading these would help keep a marriage solid."

How would it pull off in real life, though? Rain imagined being in a relationship with a man and then sharing him. Or understanding the type of man who would willingly allow another man to fuck her. It would be damned hard not to get jealous. Focusing her thoughts further, she imagined watching Noah fuck another woman and enjoy her as much as he enjoyed Rain.

"Like hell." She cringed, and then noticed she was white-knuckling the edge of the desk.

She glanced at her notes, scribbled in an open spiral notebook next to the keyboard. "Motive," she whispered, staring at the word she'd written in block letters and underlined a few times. "Jealousy would definitely be a motive."

Blowing out an exasperated sigh, she leaned back in the chair, clasping her hands behind her head and closing her eyes. Immediately images of Noah above her appeared in her mind, his perfect body tense as he drove deep inside her again and again. The thoughts caused her insides to swell and tingle. In spite of having just fucked him and being pissed at him at the moment, she wanted him again.

And she didn't want to share him. "Crap," she grumbled, and forced herself to remember this was just a case. There wasn't anything between them, and there never would be.

The way he looked at her while making love to her sure implied otherwise.

"Fucking, not making love to," she instructed herself.

Rain looked up quickly, her insides tensing, when someone knocked firmly on the door. Sliding her chair away from the computer, she stood, patting her hip, and then hurried around the large bed to where her suitcase and gun were hidden under the bed. She wore shorts and a sleeveless button-down blouse with tennis shoes. There wasn't anywhere on her to conceal a weapon.

The doorbell rang and she turned around quickly in the room. She needed something she could slip on that would conceal a weapon.

"Shit. I hate this." Being unprepared in any way always irritated her. It was sloppy. Hurrying to the one window that faced the front of the house, she peered out and saw two ladies standing on the stoop, both staring with blank expressions at the door. "What the hell?"

Grabbing one of Noah's oversized sweatshirts out of his duffel bag, Rain yanked it over her head and then stuffed her handgun down the back of her shorts. It pinched her skin and was seriously uncomfortable. The sweatshirt hung well past her waist, though, and concealed it nicely. She'd have to live with the cool metal digging into her spine.

"We're so sorry to bother you." A woman possibly forty, with short brown hair and a stylish business suit, offered Rain a friendly smile when she opened the front door.

"What can I do for you?" Rain decided she didn't like the fact that there wasn't a screen door. Gripping the door handle, she stood face-to-face with two strangers. Although they were harmless looking, she would have preferred some form of safety net between her and anyone who might come to her door.

"Are you Rain Kayne?" The other woman, who was a lot younger, possibly in her early thirties, wore clean blue jeans and a pale pink blouse that showed off not only a fair amount of cleavage but also her nice, even tan.

"Yes. And you are?" Rain's radar cued in. The woman had called her by her cover name. The only people who knew that name were the butcher and his wife, Brandy, and the Gamboas whose party she and Noah were going to to-morrow night.

Which meant these two women knew either or both of those couples. Or maybe they were Brandy and Mrs.

Gamboa. Rain fought to keep her excitement concealed and forced down the urge to immediately invite them in.

"I'm Patty Henderson," the woman in the business suit offered, and then stuck out her hand. "I know this is terribly forward of us, but we heard you and your husband were new here in town and that you'd talked to Butch."

Rain shook Patty's hand, which was very warm and damp, a sign the woman was nervous about something. Her expression seemed calm and relaxed, though. Rain stepped backward, opening the door farther, and gestured for them to enter.

"We are new here. And I'm afraid we're still settling in. But please, come in. Are we neighbors?"

"We sort of are." The younger woman walked into the middle of the living room and turned around slowly, checking the place out. She had a small African violet in her hand and held it out to Rain. "I'm Joanna, Joanna Hill. Patty didn't think it would be a good idea for me to come say hello alone."

Patty scowled at her and made a show of rolling her eyes. "Joanna speaks her mind. But hopefully we all can. I came over on my lunch with Joanna because honestly, we wanted to check you out."

"I admit you're seeing me at my worst." Rain inspected the small plant in its clay pot and then nodded for the women to sit. "Let me give this some water. Thank you by the way. I love plants and we haven't had time yet to go shopping for homey things. This is so kind of both of you."

"A housewarming gift. Casseroles seem so clichéd, don't you think?" Joanna didn't sit but followed Rain into the kitchen, obviously inspecting as much of the house as she could. "Is your husband here?"

"He should be here soon." Rain turned on the water and doused the plant with a good soaking, then set it on the windowsill over the sink. Maybe it was normal for swingers to want to check out the member of the opposite sex of a new couple on the block. For some reason she didn't have any desire to keep the subject on Noah. Turning to face Joanna, Rain noticed that Patty hadn't followed her. "Thanks for the plant. I had to give all of mine away before we moved."

"Good. I'm not very good with plants myself, but they told me you were the artsy type, so I thought maybe you'd have a green thumb, too." Joanna gave Rain a thumbs-up with both hands, as if proving neither was green. "I'm not very artistic, either. But maybe we'll get along anyway."

"Why wouldn't we?" Rain asked, not missing a beat as she smiled sincerely at Joanna. "Can I get either of you something to drink? Patty?" she called, and held on to her relaxed smile when the woman appeared in her doorway. "I have coffee, soda pop, and bottled water."

"Coffee is fine, black," Patty added, her attention moving around the kitchen. "You know, Joanna is a marvelous interior decorator. She really fixed my home up. As bare as your home is, I bet she'd have a field day here if you allowed her to do your home."

Joanna gave Patty a worried look but quickly diverted her attention to Rain, her smile appearing sincere. "It's something I always have loved doing."

"You know it's funny, I was just thinking about that before you two showed up," Rain lied, and then turned to get coffee going. "We were in such a small apartment, and now with this bigger home I have all of these dreams."

"Wonderful!" Patty sounded almost too excited and clapped her hands together. "Joanna is a great decorator, and a really good friend, too."

Rain turned around, her back to the percolating coffeemaker, and studied Patty's enthusiastic expression. Joanna looked smug but not embarrassed by the praise. They were an odd mix, with Patty's conservative business attire and Joanna's casual, if not promiscuous, look. She wore light solid colors to Patty's bland pastels and way too much makeup, while Patty possibly didn't wear any. Both women were decent looking, but Joanna would stand out in a crowd easily, and it appeared that she wanted to do just that.

One thing reassured Rain. She was positive she didn't know either woman. Rain had worked undercover on another case a long time ago and had to do some persuasive talking to be allowed the chance to do it. As she had grown up in Lincoln, Chief Noble worried she'd be recognized. But Lincoln was a growing metropolis and few ever saw her in street clothes, with her hair down, and away from her squad car. She relaxed, taking her time studying both women, and wondered how long each of them had lived here in town.

"We'll get a chance to become just as good friends," Joanna offered. "Both of us will be at the Gamboas' party tomorrow night." Her grin widened as if she expected Rain to register shock at her knowing about Rain's personal schedule.

Rain did her best to give the reaction she thought both women expected to see. "Okay. How did you know we were going?" she asked, sounding stumped.

Patty beamed, her smile finally looking sincere. "We're a tight-knit group. Butch suggested we pay you a visit. Brandy said she spoke with you on the phone, but with kids at home it's harder for her to get out. We're very careful about who we allow to join us."

"Especially lately," Joanna mumbled.

"Why is that?" Rain noticed Joanna's immediate discomfort, as if she'd said something she immediately regretted.

"Nothing." Patty glared at Joanna, but the look faded so quickly Rain might have missed it if she weren't paying very close attention to their body language as well as what they said.

If only she and Noah could wire the rooms so what was said in here would be recorded. She turned around and stared at the coffeepot, silently blowing out a breath, and forced herself to keep her cool.

"What Joanna means is that we are a very safe group.

As with any club, organization, or just tight group of friends, there will be problems." Patty hesitated and Rain almost questioned her, wondering if pushing the subject would get her more information or cause the two women to clam up. "And honestly, I guess you could say that is why we stopped by."

The coffeepot was half-full. Rain wanted to keep them here as long as possible and so turned around instead of getting down coffee cups. She made her expression relax and her tone sound lighthearted. "So is this an interview?" she said, teasing.

"Of course not," Joanna insisted, waving her hand in the air.

"Well, in a way," Patty chimed at the same time.

Rain laughed, determined to keep the atmosphere relaxed and casual. "Perfect. This will be fun. I wish I knew you two were coming and I would have made a snack tray. But we can take our coffee into the living room. I'd love to get to know both of you better as well. I'm sure you agree that it will make tomorrow night easier if we all know each other somewhat before the party begins."

"Absolutely," Patty agreed.

Rain was glad she had enough coffee cups and made a little ceremony out of pouring coffee and handing the cups over to the ladies. Then leading the way into the living room, she took the couch, which encouraged Patty to sit in the upright chair opposite Rain. Joanna took the other end of the couch but didn't give any indication that she found it uncomfortable.

"So tell me about both of you. What do you do for a living? Are you married?" Rain put an excited edge in her tone purposely, appearing anxious and excited at the possibility of making new friends. Again she wished that at least she could record their conversation. As it was, she prepared herself to stay as focused as possible and remember everything they said.

"First things first," Joanna said, holding her hand up in the air. "I'm bi and Patty is straight. What are you?"

Rain blinked, her smile fading as she stared at Joanna's broad grin.

"Forgive her," Patty said, rolling her eyes. "With her, it's all about swinging."

"It is not," Joanna protested, crossing one nicely tanned leg over the other and balancing her coffee cup on her knee. "But I do believe establishing our sexual preferences out in the open leads to a better relationship. I mean, what if I made a pass at her husband? I need to know what her rules are."

Rain recalled some of the stories she'd read online before these two showed up, and the swinger lifestyle Web sites she'd visited. None of it seemed real, but now these two women, both appearing normal and educated, spoke just how people did on those sites, and as calmly as if they were talking about the weather.

Realizing both women looked at her, politely waiting for her response, Rain leaned back and sipped at her coffee. "That would be Noah's choice," she offered simply. "If you make a pass at him and he's not interested, he'll let you know."

Joanna grinned like she'd just been given permission to raid a candy store. Her long, radiant red hair flowed perfectly over her bare shoulders and down her back. Not one strand appeared out of place. Rain would guess she put some effort into her appearance before coming over.

"My guess is you're straight. Am I right?" Patty asked.

"I'm not bisexual. I enjoy men." She remembered the story about a woman enjoying two men at once. "The more the merrier," she added.

Patty's grin turned sincere. "Amen to that one, sister."

"You two don't know what you're missing," Joanna piped up. "There's nothing hotter than getting it on with a lady while the men watch and then having them join in."

"To each their own," Patty said, dismissing the topic with a wave of her hand in the air.

"Are you satisfied that she's for real?" Joanna's question shocked Rain.

And Patty's face immediately sobered. She gave Rain a furtive glance and Joanna cleared her throat.

"You'll learn that Joanna here is the sweetest lady you could ever know, but she'll never make a good detective. Anything on her mind comes right out of her mouth."

"Damn, Patty. Sorry," Joanna said, sounding wounded.

"Wait a minute." Rain straightened on the lumpy couch, scooting to the edge while shifting her attention back and forth between both women. "What do you mean, detective? If you want to know something about me or my husband, just ask."

"It's really not like that," Patty assured her.

"I know, I'm the blabbermouth, but I really believe being open and honest is always the best approach," Joanna said, focusing on the coffee cup that she gripped firmly in her hands. "Rain, we did come over here to check you two out. Our lifestyle seems very normal and everyday to us, but that doesn't mean people who aren't appropriate partake in swinging as well."

"I assure you we're very normal." Rain remained perched on the edge of the couch, aware that she'd tensed up but fighting for the right words and praying one of the women would say something to indicate they knew about the murders.

She stood and didn't add anything else before heading into the kitchen and grabbing the coffeepot. The two women remained silent in the living room, but Rain sensed their tension. She believed they had stopped by to check her and Noah out, but what was it they hoped to learn?

Rain walked into the living room with the coffeepot. If the women suspected someone they knew had committed the murders, it would explain their coming across as edgy and suspicious. Most people had a very hard time keeping information of that proportion inside without talking to someone about it.

"More coffee?" Rain asked, stopping in front of Joanna and holding the pot over her cup.

"Thank you."

Rain refilled Patty's cup, too, and then met her speculative gaze.

"We really do owe you an apology. I'm sure you were excited at the possibility of new friends showing up at your door when you've just moved here. And that is what we are: new friends. I promise. We heard you were from Washington, D.C., is that right?" Patty's smile was tight in spite of the softness in her tone. "And we didn't come over here to judge you, or decide if you met our qualifications for friendship. We aren't like that."

"We really aren't," Joanna piped in before Rain could confirm where they'd lived before here. "The group of people we hang out with have always been so wonderful, and easy to hang out with."

Rain turned, facing Joanna. "I'm sure Noah and I will like all of you," she said quietly. She hurried to put the pot back in the kitchen and spoke as she entered the living room. "You did make me worry for a minute, though. We don't want to be part of a group who screens their friends to make sure their income and wardrobe meet a certain standard."

"None of us are like that," Patty said, but her tone still sounded guarded.

Rain sat on the edge of the couch and rested her elbows on her knees, lacing her fingers and focusing on Patty and then Joanna. Both women shot each other furtive glances, like they were trying desperately to mentally communicate and determine what they should say next.

"Is there something we should know?" Rain asked.

"We're a great group of people," Patty offered quickly, straightening and clasping her hands in her lap as she pierced Rain with a determined look. "And like with every group, there's always drama even when you try hard not to make life too complicated."

Holding her tongue, Rain watched Patty and waited for what she would say next.

"How long have you been here in Lincoln?"

Rain immediately guessed Patty wondered if she'd heard about the murders on the news. "We just moved in the other day," she said truthfully.

"And I'm sure you haven't spent much time learning about Lincoln's current events."

Rain's heart started pattering harder in her chest. She strained not to move a muscle but smiled easily. "We moved here with the bare essentials," she again said honestly, and then waved her hand at the room around them. "As you can see, we don't even have a television out here yet. What current events are you talking about?"

"Tragedies," Joanna muttered. "Such terrible, terrible tragedies." She cleared her throat and Rain noticed her cup shook as she gripped it tight enough that her knuckles turned white.

"What tragedies?" Rain asked.

Patty stood and held her half-full cup to Rain. "My lunch hour is about over. Joanna, we need to leave."

"Yes. Okay." Joanna hurried to her feet and nearly shoved her coffee cup at Rain, then hurried toward the front door. "It was great meeting you."

"But," Rain blurted, trying to balance three cups while turning toward the door. Already both women were standing there. "What was it you were about to tell me? What tragedies?" There was no way she could let them leave when they were so close to telling her what they knew. Rain hated that she couldn't force them to stay.

Joanna pulled open the front door and her jaw dropped when she stared outside at something. Patty turned toward Rain, not seeing Joanna's suddenly surprised expression.

"I'm sure you and your husband are very nice people. So please don't take this the wrong way." Patty searched Rain's face, and concern caused wrinkles to appear around her eyes. She sucked in a deep breath and blew it out slowly. "You two would be smart not to go to the potluck tomorrow night. Find another group of swingers. For your own safety. I wish I could tell you more, but I can't. Just please, listen to me. Find another group to be friends with."

"Patty," Joanna whispered, and pressed her fingers against Patty's sleeve.

Rain stepped closer so she could see out the front door, ready to see Noah outside. But it wasn't Noah. She reminded herself that he would come in through the garage door off the kitchen. Rain saw a car out in the street that had slowed. As she watched, it accelerated and then disappeared from Rain's view. All she could note was that it was a dark silver Miata convertible, but it was gone too quickly for her to see if a man or woman drove.

"Why shouldn't we go?" Rain asked. As she did, another car slowed outside but this time pulled into the driveway. Noah was back.

Patty followed Joanna outside and Rain left the coffee cups on the floor by the couch, then hurried outside, bringing up the rear and leaving her front door open. Joanna glanced down the street in the direction the car drove off before turning her attention to Noah, who did stop in the driveway and looked at the three women curiously before getting out of the car.

Joanna turned to Rain. "Your husband is gorgeous," she whispered.

"We've got to go," Patty encouraged, wrapping her arm around Joanna's.

Rain doubted Noah would have heard Joanna's comment, but nonetheless, he approached her and the women with a slow, almost cocky strut that made her want to roll her eyes. It was like he knew he was on display and so strutted his stuff for their perusal.

"Ladies," he said in a deep baritone, and it appeared he puffed his chest out, too. Noah looked at her, raising one eyebrow in question.

"Noah, this is Patty Henderson and Joanna Hill." Rain returned her attention to the women. "Are you sure you have to leave? I'd love it if you came back inside and explained what you meant with what you just said."

"We can't." Patty stared at Rain and then reached out

and grabbed her wrist. "But please, I know you want an explanation. I can't give you one. Please do as I suggest. Maybe someday I can explain."

Noah had the good sense not to question Patty's odd farewell speech and stood silently next to Rain as the two women hurried across the street and got into their cars.

"You know, if you were really my husband, I'd kick your ass for strutting over here like some stud in heat," Rain said quietly under her breath while watching the women get into their cars. "Don't you think the two of them could tell just by looking what you have to offer?"

She waved when they looked her way, and Noah waved, too, then turned and, placing his hand in the middle of her back, guided her toward the car in the drive.

"Damn good thing I'm not your husband then, huh," he said, focusing over her shoulder at the departing women. "Because we know what happens when you try kicking my ass, now don't we?" he growled, his long nose and broad cheekbones giving him a regal, dominating look. But when he shifted his attention to her, his gaze smoldered. "Sounds to me like the more I flirt, the more you'll make love to me."

She slapped his arm, ready to remind him that they fucked and didn't make love. For some reason, the words wouldn't come out. "That was a very interesting visit," she said instead.

"Mind telling me what that was all about?"

"They're both friends of Butch's and the Gamboas', where the potluck is going to be tomorrow night."

"Oh really?" Noah's interest was piqued. "Do you need to debrief?"

"Probably." She glanced at the large box in the back of the car and tilted her head, trying to get a better view of what it was. "The two of them stopped by to check us out, I think."

"Do we pass?" he asked, his expression serious while he searched her face and waited to hear more.

"I'm not sure," she answered truthfully. "Both of them have information about the murders, though. So whatever it takes, we need to get closer to them."

"Whatever it takes?" Noah lifted an eyebrow, although he didn't look like he was joking.

"Well, besides fucking them."

"You don't want me to fuck them?"

The last thing she'd admit was how much she hated the idea of him being with another woman. He could wait until this case was over before he moved on to the next lady. Even that thought left a sour taste in her mouth.

"I really don't care," she said, straightening and swallowing the bitter bile that quickly rose in her throat. "But it's not exactly what I meant," she added, then shifted her weight while crossing her arms and forcing her thoughts to focus only on the case. That meant not looking at his virile body standing so close to hers. "I meant both of those ladies have firsthand information about the murders."

"Let's talk about this inside." Noah stepped around her and she watched roped muscle stretch under his shirt when he bent down and then dragged the box out of the backseat. It was obviously fairly heavy and his biceps flexed and bulged as he situated the box in his arms. He could barely see over the top of it.

"Mind guiding me to the door?"

"Is this a TV?"

"Let's say we earned a bonus today. From what I overheard, possibly we both put in an afternoon's work."

"What did you find out?" She brushed her fingers over incredibly hard, solid muscle as she touched the back of his arm and steered him toward the front door.

"Tell me about your conversation with the ladies first," Noah said, grunting as he hauled the large box into the front door.

"Okay," Rain agreed, holding the door while he entered the house and then watching muscles bulge everywhere, stretching against his shirt as he moved around the couch. "They showed up unexpectedly," she began, shutting the door behind her and then pulling her gun from inside the back of her shorts. After checking the safety, she continued. "Joanna was very open, willing to say her mind. But Patty was jumpy, on edge the entire time she was here, as if coming here wasn't her idea and she followed out orders she would have rather not done."

"What makes you say that?"

"A feeling I got." Rain glanced around the living room and met Noah's gaze when she caught him looking at her. "I think it would be a good idea to wire the house, or at least set up something so we can record conversations."

"Okay," he said slowly, prompting her to continue.

Rain remembered the Miata that had stopped in front of their house and the expression on Joanna's face when she saw it. "It might not hurt to put a camera system outside, either," Rain added, watching when he returned his attention to the box now in the middle of the living-room floor. "I don't suppose you noticed a Miata coming at you when you were coming here?"

"Where?" Noah straightened and pulled a small pocketknife from his back pocket, then began slicing the tape off the seams of the box. "What does a Miata have to do with these two women? Why don't you tell me everything that happened from beginning to end?"

"That's what I'm doing." It was hard not letting her gaze travel down his body when he twisted, popped his back, and then tugged on his shirt and stretched it over all that hard-packed muscle.

Rain shared the rest of the conversation, trying to remember word for word everything said among the three of them. "It was weird before they left. Patty was anxious to get out the door after Joanna said something about tragedy among them."

Noah reached inside the box and muscles appeared damn close to popping the fabric loose that stretched across his back when he lifted the television out of the box. "Patty didn't want to talk about it?" he asked, glancing over his shoulder at Rain.

"Not at all." Rain hurried around the couch, pulling the box out of the way while Noah carried the television to the corner near an outlet. "Right before she left she told me the two of us would be smart not to attend the potluck and to simply search for a different group of friends."

"Interesting."

"Very."

If he noticed her practically drooling, he showed no indication and instead headed toward the door, draping his arm over her shoulder and leading her back outside with him. "What's the big deal about a Miata?"

"When Joanna and Patty were leaving, or more like hurrying to scramble out the door, Joanna looked shocked, or possibly scared, when a silver Miata stopped outside the house in the middle of the street. It was only there for a moment and then it took off. Less than a minute later you pulled into the driveway."

"Convertible?" They reached the car and Noah let go of her, then reached inside the driver's side and popped the trunk.

"Yes." She glanced in the trunk, curious, and then accepted a file folder with papers stuffed inside it when he handed it to her.

"A man was driving it. Black hair, I think. I was focused on the three of you and not him." Noah lifted a box out of the trunk that appeared to be full of framed pictures and figurines. He closed the trunk and then led the way to the house. "So we've been warned to steer clear of this particular group of people, huh?"

"The warning was pretty clear."

"Sounds like tomorrow night might be more informative than I originally thought it would be."

"I'd have to agree. We're going to have to upset Patty and show up at this potluck anyway. I'll just tell her that one look at her and Joanna and you couldn't stay away."

Noah placed the box he'd just brought inside on the couch and then wrapped his arms around Rain's waist, staring into her eyes with an intense, brooding look that stilled her heart. She hated the thought of sharing him with anyone.

"Is that what you would really tell them?" he asked, searching her face as if he could learn her answer without her speaking.

Rain stiffened, clearing her mind of any emotion, or reaction to him touching her. It was damn near impossible to do. "We're here to solve a case, aren't we?" she whispered.

Whatever intensity glowed in his eyes faded quickly. "Yup. Sure are," he grunted, letting go of her.

Rain shoved the thought out of her head that her response disappointed him. They had something here. Joanna and Patty showing up, the Miata stopping out front—all of it indicated she and Noah might be closer to their killer, and possibly to people who knew who the killer was, than they realized.

Noah pulled several items out of the box, and Rain gasped. She tilted her head and stared in awe at the framed oil painting depicting a wild scene with three young men in white shorts doing acrobatics.

"Noah," she whispered, reaching out to touch it. "Tell me that isn't a Peter Blume."

She looked up, shocked, when Noah threw his head back and laughed. "I don't know a lot about art. But I was on the phone with Brenda after leaving the morgue and she said you would appreciate these." He gave her a wicked grin and walked toward the bare walls. "Where do we hang it?"

"You don't know how bad I wished the house was wired so conversations could be recorded." Rain stood next to Noah after they'd hung several pictures and surveyed how the living room was shaping up and coming to life.

Noah rubbed his knuckles along her jaw and she looked up at him quickly. His eyes glowed almost as dark as onyx while his thick lashes hooded his stare when his focus seemed to drop to her mouth.

"Do you really want everything that goes on in this house recorded?" he asked, his voice suddenly gravelly.

"Of course not," she snapped, making a face and then trying to slap his hand from her face.

Noah moved quickly, grabbing her wrist and then yanking hard. She damn near fell over the TV box, but he pulled her to the side and she collapsed into his arms.

"I bet we could work up something that we could turn on discreetly if the need arose where we wanted something recorded." He grabbed her other hand when she reached for his shoulder to brace herself.

Noah pushed her backward and, in spite of her struggle, tackled her to the floor. The carpet scraped her backside, making her flesh burn, which ignited fire inside her she couldn't extinguish. She put some effort into fighting him off but ended up laughing and cussing him out so much she couldn't gather enough strength to stop him from latching her wrists together over her head. He pressed them together, bound by his hand, and then stretched out next to her, leaning on his arm and holding her in place with one leg.

"There are definitely moments with you I don't want recorded, or shared with anyone," he growled, tracing a line down her face with his free hand.

"Do you want to share me with other men?" she asked, the question slipping out as she stared at his face. Rough-housing with him turned her on more than she wanted to admit. It brought back memories of playing rough with her father when she was a little girl. And although those moments were far from sexual, they were memories of a happy time, and made it impossible not to smile now.

Noah smelled good, the Old Spice he put on that morning still lingering around him. All the hard muscle brushing over her and against her, along with his very satisfied expression and tousled hair, added to his sex appeal and got her hot and wet instantly. She managed to finally catch her breath and blinked a few times to clear her vision while

Noah ran his finger down her neck to her collarbone and then traced a line from one nipple to the other.

"We're here to solve a crime, right? That's what you said a few minutes ago," he said, his husky whisper causing her insides to sizzle.

"Yes. We are." She noticed the brooding expression return and wondered at that. They wouldn't have met under different circumstances, but if they had, Rain couldn't help imagining how romantically involved she could get with Noah. He was everything she ever dreamed of.

"Then we have to go to that potluck and play the happy couple more now than ever," he said, sounding determined, and appearing as unwilling to answer her question as she'd been when he asked.

"Yes, we do." There wasn't any point in fighting him; she couldn't get free. Hissing a breath out through her teeth when he pinched one nipple through her shirt, she focused her thoughts on the case. "Those two women not only know about the murders, but something has them so scared they came over here to warn us, to warn strangers, to avoid their group and go find other swingers to get to know."

"Possibly talking to them again might give us a clue toward our motive." Noah let go of her wrists.

She didn't move at first, her body tingling from him touching and teasing her and her brain churning while she tried speculating on why Joanna had looked so scared when someone stopped out front yet had enough nerve to come over in the first place and talk to her.

Noah grabbed her by the waist and lifted her with ease, as if she weighed nothing. He wrapped his arms around her and then cradled her, this new position so intimate, so passionate, that it stilled her heart. For a moment he simply held her, until finally she let her head fall back against his arm and looked up into his dark, ominous expression.

"We should know the results on the murder weapon soon." He didn't look at her but stared across the living room. In spite of how intimately he held her, he appeared unaware of their positioning. His expression hardened, and he looked almost dangerous as he spoke slowly and quietly. "Every one of those murders was well plotted. Their aim was precise. One shot killed each victim. Whoever is doing this has an agenda. We've got to find out what it is before they kill their next victim."

"What makes you think they've lined up their next victim?" She liked watching him when he brainstormed. Fighting the urge to cuddle into him, she focused on a tiny muscle twitch just above his jaw while he pressed his lips together and continued staring across the room.

"Those two women wouldn't have come over here if they didn't believe danger still existed." Finally he looked down at her, searching her face. "We're going to find out where Joanna lives. You said she told you it was nearby. And you said she didn't mention needing to get back from her lunch.

"Good idea. Joanna spoke her mind more than Patty. If she knows something, I know I can get it out of her, especially if Patty isn't with her to warn her to be quiet."

"We're going to pay that sexy redhead an unannounced visit just like she did to us."

SEVEN

The murders were going to start garnering national attention. It would be known the FBI was involved. When Noah talked to Brenda earlier on the phone, she didn't need to tell him the media would destroy his cover in their effort to exploit the victims and the lifestyle they led prior to their deaths. Their killer would go into hiding or on a rampage, depending on his or her nature. And of course Brenda insisted on pointing out that he didn't even have a profile worked up yet on their murderer. In no few words, she informed Noah his time was up in molding his partner into his hot and compliant wife.

When he returned to the house, and the period of time that immediately followed, showed Noah how close he and Rain had become in the past two days. Her frustration and something akin to panic when he first showed up at the house and then later, after they decorated and unpacked the television, were as noticeable as the perfume she wore. When they wrestled, her fierce urge to win, as well as her sexual arousal, was as clear to him as the big grin on her face. The passion that ripped through her attacked him harder than he thought it would. Even as she fought it and forced the conversation to stay on the case, he felt her. They were becoming a team, good partners, and not just working partners.

As he stood next to Rain, staring at Joanna Hill's front door, he again felt her. She shifted her weight from foot to foot and then rubbed her hands against her hips. If he judged by her actions, he'd say she was anxious, eager to talk to Joanna and learn something, anything that would bring them closer to their murderer. He didn't need to watch Rain physically to know that about her. Noah felt the same way.

But it was more than her actions that helped him know Rain. Her emotions ripped him open and burrowed deep inside his gut until he felt them, too.

Rain was determined. Within thirty minutes of him suggesting this visit, she had pulled the address and phone number for Joanna Hill off of the computer. Then touching up her makeup and brushing her hair, applying some more perfume, and glaring at her wardrobe until muttering something he didn't catch, she was ready to go. In the car and standing next to her now, Noah easily grasped the level of her determination.

"Doesn't look like she came home." Rain glanced around the front yard and then turned, clutching the handbag that hung on a narrow strap over her shoulder and housed her gun. "I'm going to walk around back," she informed him, and then headed across the grass without waiting for his response.

He stayed right on her heels. "You forget, sweetheart," he whispered as they walked between Joanna's house and the one next door, which was no more than possibly twelve feet away. "We're a couple, not law enforcement. I'm not going to play eagle eye while you sniff out the backyard. We stick together."

"That's fine." She wore one of her sleeveless blouses that buttoned down the front. She'd tucked it into a straight-cut tan skirt that showed off her long, slender legs. Rain ran circles around the redhead in the sex appeal department. "Let's see if there's a car parked inside her garage."

"What do we tell the nosy neighbors?" He stayed close but enjoyed how Rain didn't hesitate and was quick to learn what she could at a scene.

She glanced in both directions and, like him, saw no one. "That I'm new in town, just met Joanna and wanted to see if this was her home or if I had the wrong address." She looked up at him, searching his face as she offered a cocky grin, but then brushed her hair over her shoulder and headed across the backyard to a single-car detached garage.

Rain stretched and leaned over short shrubs to see in a dirty window. "Holy crap. Mustang—'67, I think. Automatic. Leather seats." She cupped her hands on either side of her face and pressed them against the window as she stared into the garage. "Miss Joanna Hill does okay for herself if this is her weekend cruise-mobile."

The garage was built sideways behind the house and opened up toward an alley. Noah looked toward the alley when a car made gravel pop as it approached. He protectively put his hand on Rain's waist and pulled her away from the window.

"We've got company."

Rain nodded and backed away from the window. She pressed her backside against his front and he watched over her head as a small two-door Hyundai appeared. Joanna sat behind the driver's wheel and froze, letting the car idle a moment before angling it toward the garage door.

"Let me do the talking," Rain whispered, and then pulled away from him, waving as she walked to Joanna's car.

Joanna looked terrified, as if she considered turning tail and running. After a moment, though, she pulled her car in front of the closed garage door and cut the engine.

"What are you doing here?" she asked, her expression strained, although she sounded like she put some effort into appearing cheerful.

"Returning the favor of arriving unannounced?" Rain said cheerfully. Ignoring Joanna when she stopped in her tracks and frowned, Rain sidled up to her and slipped her arm around Joanna's. "Truthfully, you must have known I couldn't stand you leaving me without clarifying why you and Patty wouldn't want us at the potluck. We're good people."

"I'm really sorry. I'm sure we hurt your feelings and that does suck. I could say it wasn't my idea, but that would make Patty sound like a bitch. And she's pretty cool, actually." Joanna glanced at Noah several times with large blue eyes filled with more than curiosity.

"Are you busy right now? Make it up to us by inviting us inside." Rain didn't show any intention of letting go of Joanna's arm as they walked past him toward the house. "We're going to prove to you that we're people worth knowing."

"I'm sure you are. And that doesn't have anything to do with it." They reached the door and Joanna looked over her shoulder at Noah. "And of course you two can come in."

"That's a nice 'stang you have out there in your garage," Noah told her when they entered the house through the back door. As simple as the house looked on the outside, inside "modern" didn't describe the atmosphere. "And Rain looked first," he added, winking when Joanna dropped her purse on the bar in the middle of the kitchen and easily drawing a large grin for his efforts.

"I've never been accused of being shy." Rain shrugged and then ran her finger over the shiny chrome top of the stove. "This kitchen is magnificent. How trendy! What did you say you do for a living?"

"I'm an interior decorator. I did work for a company downtown, but we had a few differences of opinion. I started my own business two years ago and I'm doing okay for myself. I'll give you a tour."

Noah managed to get closer to Joanna while she took them from room to room, showing off a home that could be the feature of a magazine. Even the bathroom was spacious. Rain walked in farther than he did and admired the mirror-covered cabinets hung on the wall. She opened one and Noah caught a glimpse of a variety of massage oils. The headboard on a king-size bed in the bedroom had several different-shaped and -sized dildos, along with a few condoms.

Joanna didn't have a problem letting anyone know how much she enjoyed sex. As she moved around and definitely put some effort into showing off a fair amount of cleavage, Noah didn't wonder for a second whether her breasts were real or not. Joanna paid good money for the body she appeared eager to flaunt before him. He wondered if her breasts would even bounce during the throes of hot sex.

"Rain was really upset after you and your friend left," Noah told Joanna when they returned to the kitchen. "Tell us why it's in our favor to search for another group of swingers."

Joanna opened her refrigerator and pulled out several bottles of flavored water. Then plopping down on one of the wooden stools surrounding the bar in the middle of her kitchen, she pushed a bottle toward him and Rain.

"I started swinging when I was in college," she told him while sitting with a slight arch to her back, which was probably intentional to aid in showing off her large fake breasts. "And I moved here right after college, which was not quite ten years ago. Lincoln is a good town and there are a lot of good parties and swinger groups you can become part of around here. I moved in a few different circles until I met Ned and his wife, Brandy."

"The butcher," Rain interrupted, and untwisted the lid on her bottle. "He and I chatted the night we moved in." She looked to Noah for confirmation.

He nodded. "We went down and talked to him the next day and that is how we found out about the potluck."

Joanna's smile made her blue eyes radiant. Redheads never appealed to him much, but he'd have to say she was very beautiful. He wondered if she was beautiful enough to kill for.

"That's Butch." Joanna laughed and then wrapped her full lips around the bottle and took a long drink. She licked her moist lips and looked like she performed the act to get his reaction. "I met Steve Porter and his wife, Susie, next. For a while it was the five of us, but Butch found others to join our group. Steve is concerned about it getting much larger, but then he's always been a bit possessive."

"Possessive?" Rain asked before Noah could. "How so?"

"Maybe 'protective' is a better word. And I really do appreciate it," Joanna added quickly, the glow in her eyes dulling for a brief moment.

Rain glanced his way, and he'd bet she noticed something as well.

"Did Patty tell us not to go to the potluck tomorrow night because it would upset Steve if new people showed up?" Rain asked.

"No. Oh God, no. That never even crossed our minds." Joanna reached out and touched Rain's hand. "Steve is the kindest, most generous man I've ever known," she said, her tone softening. "And like I said, I appreciate it. I really do."

The action seemed almost too much when the suggestion was so petty. Joanna said she was appreciative, not that she liked Steve.

"Then why did Patty ask us not to go?" Rain demanded.

Joanna stared at her for a long moment. She shot Noah a furtive glance once or twice and then finally stared down at her water bottle. Slowly, she started peeling the label from the plastic, a sure sign of someone who was very nervous about something.

"Because we're jinxed, okay?" Joanna jumped up from her stool as if something bit her and then walked around the bar to the counter.

Rain shifted on her stool to watch Joanna, and Noah kept his attention on her, too, knowing she was seconds away from telling them what they wanted to hear. If he pushed her, she would shut up. He knew Rain kept glancing at him, but he wouldn't let his attention from Joanna be swayed. All he could do was pray Rain wouldn't say or do anything to spook Joanna.

"Jinxed?" Rain sounded in awe but didn't look his way when he frowned at her. "You mean as in bad luck happens to everyone who meets one of you?"

"People are dying," Joanna whispered, suddenly looking very terrified.

"What?" Noah said, knowing if she came this far, she would tell them everything she knew. The words had left her mouth. Now they could press for more information. "What do you mean, dying?"

"Oh, I don't know why everyone is throwing a fit that you not be told. It's starting to be all over the news. They did a piece on it last night." Joanna brushed her fingers over her thick red hair. She pulled several thick, long strands forward over her shoulder and started twisting them nervously between her fingers. "They aren't just dying. Someone is murdering them."

"These are people in your swingers' group?" Rain asked, jumping in once again before he could say a word. "I saw that piece on the news," she lied. "You've got to tell me what you know." Rain sounded like she had just stumbled on the best gossip in town, and when she grabbed

Joanna's arm Joanna jumped but then noticeably relaxed when she let out a long, slow breath.

"Is someone in the group killing them?" Noah asked.

Joanna's blue eyes were large and suddenly looked moist. "Yes. People I know, that I've played with—had sex with—are being killed. And no. Oh, no way. No one I know would do anything like this. You'll see when you meet them." She looked down at the floor and put her fingers over her lips. "If you meet them," she added quietly.

Rain put her arm around Joanna's shoulder. "We had no idea," she said, her tone soothing. "Why don't you tell us everything you know? Noah always says that it's best to get everything off your chest. Sometimes telling a stranger is easier than sharing your feelings with people you know really well."

Joanna looked at him at the same time that Rain did. Both were sexy as hell. While Rain looked at him pensively, Joanna's moist gaze regained some of its glow and she smiled.

"There's nothing better than a good-looking man who is a good listener, too." She smiled, the corners of her mouth barely turning up. "I admit I wish your first impression of me was something a bit more alluring."

Noah smiled and crossed his arms over the bar, continuing to shift his attention from one woman to the next. "You're beautiful, Joanna, and I can see that you're upset. I can only imagine that when you aren't upset you're breathtaking."

Rain's expression was suddenly masked. It didn't take much investigative skill to see Rain didn't like him flirting with Joanna. He wouldn't focus on what might happen, or not happen, after this case was over. But at the moment, something swelled inside him with the knowledge Rain wouldn't encourage this type of extracurricular activity the way Laurel did.

"Oh." Joanna turned to Rain and grinned so broadly

her entire face lit up. "I swear you have the best man on the planet."

"I think so," Rain said softly, and graced him with a smile that damn near made him hard. She patted Joanna's shoulder and then dropped her hand to her side. "Now please, tell us everything. I feel so out of the loop not watching the news for the past week or so."

"Moving is a bitch," Joanna pointed out. "I'm so lucky to have this place. I hope I don't have to move again," she added wistfully, making it sound as if she hadn't lived here long, although she appeared very settled in the nice, small home. Downing a few quick swallows of her water, she straightened and tugged at her sweater, showing off some distracting cleavage. "Like I said, I don't know that I buy into keeping you two in the dark, or discouraging you privately, without letting the group know, to stay away from us." She walked in between them, again pressing her hands over her clothes and smoothing them, drawing attention to her narrow waist. "We were a tight group, the Gamboas, Flynns, and Porters being friends forever, and then I came along. Patty joined us at least four years ago or so. And for quite a while it was the eight of us. We even went on a cruise together a few years ago. I think around two years ago or so the Lapthornes and Swansons started coming to all of our events." She stopped and made a show of clearing her throat. Then taking a minute to get into her refrigerator, she pulled out a chunk of cheese and moved to her counter, grabbing a knife and cutting board. "I don't know about you two, but a snack sounds good. Anyone for cheese and crackers? Or are either of you lactose intolerant? I have special cheese and milk in the refrigerator. Steve is lactose intolerant."

"No, we're fine." Rain glanced at Noah and raised an eyebrow when Joanna turned her back.

He nodded once, barely moving his head to let Rain know he had picked up on that, too. They might be a tight group, but apparently the single Miss Joanna entertained here as well. Noah wondered if she entertained Steve alone and, if so, did his wife know?

"The Handels and Hinderses only started coming to our parties about a year and a half ago," Joanna continued.

"So you had seven couples and then you and Patty?" Rain asked. "Why no single men? Are single women sought out the most in your group?" she asked, focusing on Noah, her expression easily read. Noah had no doubts he'd get an earful that she might have been able to crack this case alone if they'd known prior to now that a single lady would be welcomed.

"We were a good-sized group of partiers there for a while," Joanna said, glancing at her as she sliced cheese. "But no, no more single ladies. I'm positive the group wouldn't allow any other single women, whether they were bi or straight, to become part of our group."

"Why is that?" Rain asked again.

Joanna raised and dropped her shoulder lazily and then turned, with the cutting board and knife and half a chunk of cheese left over with a layer of neatly sliced squares lying over each other. She placed the cutting board on the bar and smiled at Noah. In a different atmosphere, he would swear her quiet smiles were an invitation. But here, and now, he simply gave her a comforting smile in return. Glancing past her, when Joanna turned, he caught the scowl on Rain's face that faded quickly when Joanna moved.

"We're like the hot commodity within our group, and most of the guys will do anything for us. But you bring too many single women around and you're inviting trouble. I know I would vote against any more singles in our group." She opened a cabinet and grabbed a box of crackers and then poured some of them onto the cutting board. "Is it too early for wine? That would go perfectly with these."

Noah guessed the wine would help her loosen up and possibly they would learn more.

"You really don't need to go all out for us," Rain said before he could say the wine sounded fine. Rain didn't look at him, though.

"It's the least I can do after upsetting you the way we did." Joanna sounded sincere.

Rain stroked Joanna's hair down her back. "And now you're upset. So who got hurt? Someone from your group?"

Joanna opened a door that turned out to be a pantry and walked inside the small closet and reappeared instantly with a couple bottles of wine.

"Which is better for the occasion?" she asked Noah, holding the bottles out for him to inspect.

He tapped the bottle in her left hand, noting both bottles were pricey brands. "The Cabernet Sauvignon would go well since we're eating cheddar."

"Good. I'm so terrible at knowing what wine goes best with what food." She again gave him that inviting smile, then turned and stretched, her sweater rising and showing off her narrow back and slender spine.

Noah pointedly looked over at Rain, who rolled her eyes at him. He didn't know why, but her apparent jealousy appealed to him. And although he knew it wasn't the reason for being here, pushing her a bit, giving her a feel of what she would be exposed to tomorrow night, sounded like not only a good plan but fun as well. He liked the idea of smoothing her ruffled feathers later.

"All it means is that I've eaten in restaurants way too much in my life," Noah offered, grinning when Joanna closed the pantry door and turned around.

"Oh, I see," Joanna said, and scowled at Rain as if trying to figure something out.

Rain cleared her throat. "He means before we were married," she pointed out, and Joanna quickly nodded. "Tell me where the glasses are," Rain offered, turning around and facing the cabinets. That skirt made her ass look incredibly good. "If you're going to all of this trouble, the least you can do is let me help."

"It's no trouble. I admit going over to your house really

upset me, too. Honestly, I don't like thinking about it. But Patty and I talk from time to time, you know? And when all of us were sent an e-mail announcing that new blood in our group would help pull all of us out of our melancholy state and then announced that you two would be at the potluck tomorrow night, well, she called me and we discussed whether this in fact was a smart move." While she chattered on, she pulled a corkscrew out of a drawer and turned to Noah. "Would you mind popping my cork?" she asked, batting her eyes at him while putting an extra kick to her tone to make the question ooze with underlying meaning.

"I'd be honored," he said, straightening, and accepting bottle and corkscrew.

"I bet you'd be good, too," Joanna whispered, and then turned around before she could catch the scathing look that Rain quickly wiped off her face. "And I know, instead of enjoying our snack here, why don't we take it out to the patio? I haven't shown you my hot tub yet."

"We didn't bring suits," Rain said.

"No suits allowed in my hot tub, darling." Joanna tilted her head slightly and studied Rain, who to her credit didn't bat an eye at Joanna's comment. "The guys are going to love you and it's a shame you aren't bi. You and I could put on a show that would make the men come in their pants. That black hair is your natural color?"

"All of me is real," Rain informed her in just as sweet of a tone as Joanna used. "And it's really not black. More like a dark brown. It's more obvious in the sunlight."

"Well, it's beautiful." Joanna didn't seem swayed about the "all real" comment. Instead, she looked down at herself and then placed her hand on her breast. "I was all natural until I got these last year. And they're perfect, too. They don't feel like Nerf footballs the way some fake breasts do. Here—feel."

Noah almost broke the cork in half when Joanna reached for Rain's hand and then placed it on her breast. Again, Rain was smooth as the skilled professional that he already knew she was. This move pushed her to her limits, though, although she didn't blush.

"They do feel real," Rain offered, sounding sincerely surprised.

When she didn't pull away but instead dragged her fingers over them until Joanna's nipples turned into hard nubs, Noah's mouth went dry. But when Rain slowly turned her attention to him, and then graced him with a wicked smile, all blood drained to his dick. He pulled the cork out of the bottle of wine with enough force that it made a loud popping sound and he almost dropped the bottle.

Rain looked more than pleased that her action affected him, and he wondered for a moment if he'd read her wrong. Damn, what if she actually got into women, too, and for whatever reasons had decided to play it straight?

"Should we let him feel them, too?" he heard Joanna ask Rain in a soft, tempting whisper.

Rain shifted her attention from Joanna's breasts to him and Joanna tossed her hair over her shoulder, arching slightly when she cocked her head and flirted with him with her eyes. If this was a sample of what he was in for tomorrow night, he might have been wrong in guessing Rain needed more preparation for the evening than he did.

"You should feel these, sweetheart," she purred, grinning mischievously at him, although the glow in her eyes would have him hesitating if they were dating for real. "They really do feel real and are so soft and big."

Noah narrowed his gaze on her. There wasn't any way he could bring them the bottle, let alone get up and go feel Joanna's breasts.

"Trust me, I'm having a damned good time watching you play with them," he told Rain honestly, and prayed his expression didn't reveal the strain he endured to stay on his stool and not attempt to begin something that he knew without a doubt would start more trouble than it would be worth. Not to mention, Joanna's breasts weren't going to help him and Rain crack this case. He repeated that in his mind more than once as he cleared his throat. "But by all means, don't stop on my account."

"Men are all the same." Joanna rolled her eyes and then pulled Rain into a hug, whispering something to her that Noah didn't catch.

Rain laughed easily. "That's no lie. And you better watch out; Noah might be better at it than any other man you know. At least that's been my experience so far," she added, winking at him and appearing to be very much enjoying herself. The jealous strain he'd seen on her face when they first arrived was gone. Either Joanna was a professional at loosening up wives or Rain was truly getting into the moment. It might be a bit of both. Either way, Noah knew well enough to allow them their moment and not try to intrude. His partner and "wife" had one hell of a temper, and they would both work this case better if Rain remained happy and relaxed so she could gather what info she could out of the voluptuous redhead.

"That wouldn't surprise me one bit." Joanna's gaze burned his flesh when she took him in with an almost animalistic glaze in her eyes.

He ached to know what was just said but wasn't foolish enough to ask. Instead, he placed the open bottle of wine on the island bar and then plopped a slice of cheese in his mouth, offering both of them a roguish grin.

Joanna took down three wineglasses and placed them in front of Noah. She didn't say a word when she hurried out of the room. He poured wine and watched Rain while she stared after Joanna. Letting his gaze travel down Rain, and enjoying the hell out of her profile, with her perky breasts and nipples that were very hard at the moment, he'd have to say hands down she was a hell of a lot prettier than Joanna. In spite of Joanna's intense sexual aura, with her thick mane of radiant red hair and her bombshell figure, Rain's elegant stance, and sultry, if not mysterious, air she carried so well had him guessing he wouldn't be the only man aching to choose Rain over Joanna tomorrow night.

Before Noah thought to ask Rain what Joanna whispered in her ear, Joanna returned and walked to the back door and locked it, then slid out of her shoes. "Come on," she said. Grabbing the cutting board and her glass of wine and leaving her shoes at the back door, she headed out of the kitchen and farther into the house. "Follow me."

Noah brought up the rear as they entered Joanna's bedroom. She pulled back thick, long curtains and then opened a sliding door and led the way out onto a patio with a tall privacy fence that he guessed was probably ten feet high and completely enclosing the intimate outdoor setting. Joanna didn't ask for help but slid the cover off her hot tub and leaned it between the house and the tub. Then placing the plate of food on the edge of the tub, she ran her fingers through the water.

"Perfect," she informed them, and then smiled at Rain as she started undressing. "Shall we get in?"

It surprised him once again when Rain followed Joanna's lead and stripped out of her clothes without hesitating. She laid them on the back of a chair with Joanna's and then skillfully took her hair out of her clasp and twisted her hair at the top of her head, then replaced her clasp so her thick dark hair pooled around her face, with several strands draping over her shoulders. He stood there, watching one woman climb into the tub and then the other, both giving him a view men would kill to see.

Suddenly he was all thumbs trying to get out of his own clothes, feeling anything but like a stud for being able to climb into a hot tub with two hot, naked women. Each of them took their own corner, and bubbles prevented him from seeing too far into the water. Not that he cared; the cleavage and occasional nipple shot when either of them moved was such incredible eye candy that it was all he could do not to climb in with a raging hard-on.

Thinking about the best way to bring the conversation back to the murders helped keep everything under control.

Rain broke the silence first. "Inside you said people you knew were dying. How are they dying?"

"Yes. Three of them." Joanna sipped her wine and stared at him over the rim of her glass. "First Roberta and Lynn, and then George."

Noah felt toes crawl over his feet when he relaxed in his corner, and guessed his hostess was making her move subtly. Possibly he distracted her from the facts and that was why she said three instead of four, or maybe she didn't know about the latest murder. He adjusted himself and stretched out in the water, only to run into another pair of feet. Rain glanced his way and smiled.

Her expression sobered quickly, though, when she looked at Joanna. "How did they die?"

"Shot to death—all of them." Joanna placed her wine-glass on the side of the hot tub. Then clasping her hands in front of her, she straightened her arms and aimed with her fingers pointed like a gun, aiming at Rain's temple. "Imagine it. One moment you're alive and healthy and the next moment it's done, all over. To have that kind of control and power over someone living, or dying. It really makes you think, doesn't it?"

EIGHT

Half an hour later, Noah pulled away from Joanna's house. Rain didn't stay in the hot tub much longer after having Joanna point her fingers at Rain's temple. After agreeing they most definitely wanted to get together with Joanna again, they said their good-byes.

The glass of wine and hot tub put him in the mood for a nap, or at least crawling into bed. Ravishing Rain sounded like a hell of a plan, too. He had a feeling she wouldn't tell him no, in spite of the contemplative look on her face at the moment. She stared straight ahead, chewing on her lip. He was getting used to being able to see her mind churn when she was lost in thought trying to figure something out.

Turning off of Joanna's street, he headed in the opposite

direction of his and Rain's home. That's when he knew she was really tearing into something in that brain of hers. Letting the silence continue between them, he glanced at the time on the dash. Five o'clock. They would make their meeting that he had arranged this morning. He looked forward to brainstorming their time spent with Joanna and learning how the hot redhead's attention toward him affected Rain. The kiss good-bye that Joanna gave him was passionate in itself, but when she whispered in his ear, "I can't wait to fuck you," he wondered if Rain over-heard.

"I wonder if Joanna is typical of all swingers or if her personality is unique, in spite of the lifestyle she indulges in." Rain's expression didn't change and she continued staring straight ahead.

Noah glanced her way for a moment before slowing for a red light. When she tugged on her skirt, he reached over and ran his hand over her smooth leg. God, he couldn't wait to fuck her again.

"Are you referring to how quickly she could go from being upset about something to acting like she couldn't wait to jump my bones?"

Rain glanced down at his hand and then looked up at him with those baby blues. "Either that or her ability to be upset yet never quit yearning to fuck you."

Leaving his hand on Rain's leg, he brushed his thumb against her knee as he accelerated, then turned onto a main street that would take them across town. He focused for a moment, trying to remember the way without asking for directions. He really was curious how distracted Rain's thoughts were and how long it would take her to realize they weren't going home.

Home. It wasn't home, he reminded himself, but simply a staged setting they would continue to use until they cracked this case. His home was an almost empty apartment in D.C. He remembered fond memories of spending evenings there with Laurel, in between cases, and dreaming of the future. She'd been his life, his reason for getting a case wrapped up as quickly as possible. They would talk on the phone every night after she got off work while he traveled, everything from political debates to phone sex. Laurel didn't start into him on opening up their marriage until he put a ring on her finger. And she didn't start naming names of who she wanted to fuck until she and Noah had their wedding planned.

"I've had a few encounters with swingers over the years," he began, hating to use any past experience to define Joanna. "But honestly, we'll get a better feel for how she is tomorrow night. That is, if you still want to go to the potluck."

"Definitely. Don't you?"

"We have to go."

"I agree." Rain looked away from him and out the window. "Where are we going?"

He smiled and gave her leg a squeeze. "That visit left you grossly preoccupied."

"You're intentionally going the wrong way just to see if I would notice? Do you honestly think that I can't handle being around women groping you, mister?" Her tone rose along with one eyebrow. She glared at him while her eyes turned a violent shade that almost looked violet. "This is a case, Noah. We fucked each other, and okay, it was incredible. But don't think for one minute that I'm some ill-prepared rookie who doesn't have a clue how to rein in her emotions and not keep her thoughts on her job. And where the hell are you going?" By the time she demanded to know their destination she was yelling at him.

Noah pulled his hand off her leg and placed it on the steering wheel. He focused on the road, watching street signs. "Excuse me for thinking your preoccupation had something to do with you sorting out the data we gathered on a possible suspect," he said tightly, fighting not to white-knuckle the steering wheel. It wasn't that he believed everything Rain just spit out at him. Maybe he needed to be more careful what he wished for in the future. If anything, her sudden tirade proved that not only did Rain get jealous, but it pissed her off that she did, and now she would berate him for it. Like he would put up with that. "And we've got a five o'clock appointment, if I can remember how to get where we're going."

Rain crossed her arms over her chest and leaned back in her seat, crossing her legs, which caused her skirt to ride up high on her thighs. He barely risked stealing a glimpse of her hot long, slender legs before forcing his attention on the road.

"Where are we going?" she asked coolly.

He rattled off the exact address that he'd been given earlier and committed to memory. "It's a strip mall and there is a flower shop there. We're heading inside and we'll meet someone there who will drive you to the morgue. It's just a precaution. I don't want anyone seeing the two of us going down there together."

"I see," she said, but then went silent.

She was right about one thing she had screamed at him. They weren't rookies, neither one of them. And they needed to discuss Joanna.

"Do you think we can debrief each other without any more yelling?" He knew he sounded condescending, but he didn't like his head being bit off and handed to him.

"Sure. Forgive me for yelling," she said tightly. "You looked so triumphant that I didn't notice sooner where we were headed that I thought you were suggesting Joanna's flirting with you bothered me. Because it didn't. I don't get jealous that easily and sure as hell not after knowing a man for two days. We're together to catch a killer and nothing else, right?"

"Right," he agreed easily, although he swore the tightness in her tone meant she was forcing herself to voice the words.

"Good."

"Good." He relaxed his hands on the steering wheel and slowed at a green light until he saw the street sign. "I commented on your distraction because I enjoyed watching your mind churn while you worked to analyze and search for clues from our meeting."

"Oh." She sucked in her lower lip and nibbled on it. She caught him watching her and then, to his surprise, reached out and ran her fingers through his still slightly damp hair. "Why do you think she said there were three murders and not four?"

"Maybe she didn't know about the fourth. You need to get your chief to assign someone to record any and all news clips that cover these murders on TV."

"Good idea. And any newspaper articles. Any discussion of this case at all by the media," she added, shifting to face him and forcing her seat belt to press against her heart and accentuate the round curves of her breasts. "I'm pretty sure the address you said is the Southern Hills Mall. There's a flower shop there. You better take a right up here."

He nodded, more than willing to let her navigate. "Either she didn't know about the last victim or she tested us to make sure we didn't know about the murders like we claimed."

"That crossed my mind, too. And what about her locking the doors? Possibly she has visitors comfortable enough to simply walk in when they stop by."

"It could have just been a safety precaution. I would have done the same thing, too, if I were getting naked in a hot tub with a couple ladies. I wouldn't leave my home unattended without locking doors."

"Turn there!" Rain pointed to the left when he'd almost driven through the intersection, and he slowed in time to make it without pissing off anyone behind him. "Sorry," she said, and patted his head roughly but then combed his hair with her fingers.

She didn't know how damn good it felt with her touching him. "So either way we can mark her down as cautious, whether it be concern of usually welcome guests showing up or possibly unwelcome ones."

"She does have company from time to time."

"Yup. The lactose-intolerant cheese. Mr. Steve Porter is there enough that she includes him in her grocery-shopping list. Makes you wonder how many she entertains. She's definitely got the house for it."

"Did you notice her comment right after we got there? She said she hoped she didn't have to move again. She is self-employed. Maybe she's not doing as well as she once was."

"I'll see if we can gather any information on her income," he said.

"What was your take on the wine?" Rain looked at him expectantly as if quizzing him and waiting to see if he'd get the answer right.

Noah grinned. "You mean that she buys wine but doesn't know what to drink it with? And expensive wine at that."

"If she's the one buying it."

"Sounds like we still have a lot to learn about Joanna Hill."

"It also sounds like she can't wait for you to know her better." Rain made a face and stuck her tongue out at him when he looked her way quickly. "I'm not jealous," she said, glaring at him. Then glancing out the front window, she pointed to a strip mall on the right. "There's your flower shop."

"Hinders' Greenhouse. Crap." Noah stared at the large sign on the building that was actually a greenhouse detached from the strip mall but used the same parking lot. As he turned into the lot, he noticed several buildings behind the store, which he guessed made the flower shop actually a nursery. "I don't know why I didn't put it together before. I bet you this might be the shop Lorrie Hinders and her husband owned. If it is, I'm surprised that it's still open."

There weren't any doubts when they pulled in front of the shop, parked, and noticed the display just inside the window. Done up tastefully, using a variety of different types of black flowers, a sign on the display said: "In memory of our beloved Lorrie."

"Damn." Rain got out and stood on her side of the car until he walked around and faced her. "Lorrie is the victim Joanna didn't mention. Granted she was just killed but she's been dead long enough for those who really loved her to do this. I wonder why Joanna didn't mention her."

Rain looked at him as if he would explain. More than anything he wished he could give her an answer that would wipe the lines of worry and frustration from her face.

"All we can do now is everything in our power to prevent anyone else from being killed," he whispered. Then because he wanted to, he cupped her cheek and felt the warmth from her skin seep into his palm.

She nodded, patted the back of his hand with her fingers, and then stepped around him. He turned, putting his arm around her waist, and headed into the flower store, which turned out to sell a hell of a lot more than just flowers.

"I've always loved these," Rain whispered, looking up at him with such a peaceful smile that instantly he felt a pang of jealousy over the stone birdbath she stroked with her fingers.

Which was idiotic. He glanced down at the carving of a small boy hoisting a jug over his shoulders. Water spilled from the jug into a large bowl. But it was the way her fingers moved over the stone that grabbed Noah's attention. At first she caressed it with three, but then she made a fist, extending her index finger, and appeared to be pointing at something.

Noah searched her face, the pleasant, relaxed expression that would honestly make anyone watching believe that all they cared about was how to landscape their yard. "Are you sure there isn't anything else you like better?"

He glanced around the store and then focused in the direction she pointed. A woman stood alone on the other side of the store, holding a gardening "how to" book. When he looked at her, she glanced up and then smiled. Placing the book back, she walked over to them casually like they were old friends. Noah was positive he'd never seen the woman before.

"Hi, Rain." She nodded at him. "Hello," she added, but then looked at Rain again. "Whenever you're ready," she said under her breath.

Noah glanced at the kid behind the counter, who seemed more intent on text messaging on his phone than trying to help customers. He guessed that Lorrie Hinders' husband was probably busy with family matters and funeral arrangements and had entrusted his store to hired help. There were a few other people in the store, all who appeared focused on finding what they needed. No one gave them any attention.

"We might have to come back and get this." Rain looked up at him, and although she no longer whispered, her soft-spoken words weren't meant to advertise their conversation.

"We'll see," he said, and reached around to grab her ponytail at the nape of her neck and gave it an affectionate tug.

Her smile didn't fade and she willingly remained at his side as they walked out of the store with the woman behind them. He'd have to give it to Rain: she was a natural at undercover work.

Once outside, she made little ceremony out of leaning into him and giving him a peck on the cheek. "See you in a bit," she said casually, and then turned and headed across the parking lot with the woman.

Noah didn't have a clue who she was, but obviously Rain did. Brenda simply had told him on the phone they would meet with a pickup who would take Rain to the station. Lincoln was a good-sized city, but the wrong person seeing them arrive at the police station and their cover would be blown.

He watched the women get into a minivan while chatting with each other. Neither of them looked his way as they drove off.

Noah climbed into his car, immediately finding himself bombarded by too many thoughts. Although he was alone the first half of the day, Rain was at the house, stuck there because he took the rental. For some reason her leaving now, with a co-worker more than likely, re-entering her own world, created an emptiness inside him he didn't like.

And this wasn't like him. Realizing suddenly that it would be a hell of a lot easier to follow them to the station than try to remember how to get there from this part of town, Noah started the car quickly and backed out of the stall.

This wasn't his first undercover case with a partner. And it wasn't the first time he'd worked with a woman. He'd slept with some of them, and others he hadn't. Once he started getting serious with Laurel, Brenda didn't assign him cases where he was put in an intimate situation with a woman. But even then, when he was alone he was content. It struck him as odd, now that he thought about it, that he never missed Laurel when he wasn't with her. They talked on the phone and that was enough.

Maybe he was getting older. Somehow he didn't keep his guard up at the right moment. Or possibly he'd slipped and let things get too personal. For whatever reasons, even after a couple days, Rain had crept under his skin. She might be denying it, at least to him, but he sensed Rain felt something similar.

Noah pulled into a stall next to Rain and the woman with her, relieved that he'd had these moments to come to terms with where his emotions were heading. It was best to see it now, before it got too late. From this point forward, he would keep his heart in check.

It was almost worth having a good laugh over. There were times when Noah worried a partner might get too attached and therefore hurt. Never would he have believed it would happen to him. Damn good thing he caught it early, before damage was done. Rain might be hot, with the feistiest personality he'd ever seen on a lady, and one hell of an incredible lover, but Noah wasn't available. He was married to the FBI, plain and simple. Never again would a lady rip his heart out the way Laurel did.

"Hey, Noah. Good to see you didn't get lost." Rain laughed and grinned broadly at him as she walked around the front of the minivan. "This is Detective Alicia Gomez," Rain continued, gesturing at the woman who pointed her key chain at the van until the lights on it flashed and it honked once. "Everyone calls her Al. She hates both her nickname and given name, so you can't go wrong with either."

"Special Agent Kayne, it's nice to meet you." Al didn't look like an Al. Although she didn't quite look like an Alicia, either. Her black hair was cut short and straightened so that it hugged the length of her neck. She was a bit more muscular looking than Rain but definitely not to the point where it looked unappealing.

Al made a face at Rain and then smiled up at him; being a few inches shorter than Rain, that meant she tilted her neck to look at his face. Bright white teeth and deep, forest green eyes contrasted nicely with her tan skin.

"Rain told me the two of you spent the afternoon interrogating one of your suspects naked in a hot tub. Hell of a way to earn your paycheck," Al added, her grin broadening as she turned and started toward the station.

Noah raised his eyebrows at Rain, surprised she would so easily share the story of their time with Joanna. Granted both of them would have to create reports, which meant many of their activities wouldn't be confidential. Nonetheless, Rain didn't strike him as someone who would so easily admit she'd been in a hot tub with a man and a woman naked.

"Al is in homicide with me. She's going to be my connection on the inside when I can't access files here at the station," Rain explained as they entered the station, and then placed her purse in a tray next to the metal detector and chatted easily with the cop on duty. Once they were through, Rain led the way to the stairs. "She's already working up a psychological profile on the evidence we have gathered so far."

"Good." He didn't bother adding that the FBI had a profiler working on the case. It wouldn't hurt to have two opinions on what made their killer click. He followed the women down the stairs and then entered a large room. A row of desks and computer equipment made the area look like many detectives' work areas.

Chief Noble looked up as the three entered. The chief stood, his attention on Rain.

"There you two are. Thanks, Al, for hauling our girl down here. Why don't you stay here and enjoy a good show."

"And miss *Sex in the City?*" Al sounded shocked.

"Last I heard you didn't even have a TV." The chief didn't wait for her to respond but walked over to refill his coffee cup. "We're here for an in-person brainstorming meeting. I want to hear everything you have right now. We have Brenda Thornton, Special Agent Kayne's supervisor, here on speakerphone. Brenda, you're joined by your special agent, Noah Kayne, Lieutenant Rain Huxtable, and Lieutenant Alicia Gomez, who is also in homicide."

"Hello, everyone," Brenda piped up through the box on the desk. "Get your coffee and get comfortable and let me know when you're ready." Even from across the country, Brenda was quick to take charge.

Rain nodded and headed back toward the refrigerator. Pulling out a can of Diet Dr Pepper, she popped the lid and then stood to the side, quiet and watching while Al started discussing the caliber and rifling of the bullets found in each of the victims.

"Looks like we're ready," Noah offered for Brenda's benefit when Al took a breath.

"Oh, sorry," Al said, grinning at the box.

"Let's get started," Chief Noble instructed, sitting behind the desk and adjusting the box so it faced Rain and Noah, with Al standing to the side, leaning against a nearby desk.

"We know we've got the same killer targeting a certain type of people," Brenda mused.

"We know each victim is being killed by the same weapon," Rain pointed out. She focused on Al. "If all the tests are in and conclusive."

"Each of our victims was killed with a .32-caliber bullet. Clean shot to the side of the head—dead instantly. Whoever our perpetrator is, they know how to shoot." Al stood facing all of them and rocked up on the balls of her feet and then clasped her hands behind her back. "Now I could speculate—"

"Speculate on your own time," Brenda interrupted. "Tonight I want to hear facts."

"Excuse me," Rain interrupted. "If we had facts, we'd have our killer. Speculation is part of a brainstorming meeting."

Noah was sure he saw Chief Noble wince. More than likely the older cop anticipated the fireworks in this meeting as much as Noah did. Noah leaned back in his chair, crossing his arms.

"Go on with what you were going to say." Rain glared at the speakerphone box for merely a moment before nodding to Al.

"I called this meeting to hear what you already have," Brenda's voice chirped through the speakerphone. "So unless you're trying to cover up the fact that you can't do the job—"

"How dare you!" Rain stood and reached for the speakerphone, as if she would shut it off.

"Oh, I definitely dare," Brenda barked before Rain reached the box. "Speculate on your own time. Give me the facts right now, if you have any. If not, this meeting is over, and Chief, we'll discuss how we'll proceed from here on out."

"You are not taking me off this case," Rain hissed, her eyes violet as she pressed her fists on the desk and glared at Chief Noble.

"Rain, that's enough," the chief barked.

"You're damned straight that's enough. I want her off this case right now!" Brenda yelled through the speakerphone. "I've already worried—"

"Everyone stop!" Noah moved in quickly, leaning forward so his voice would be heard over everyone else's through the speakerphone. "If she's off the case then so am I."

"Think carefully about what you're saying," Brenda whispered, her voice crackling through the small speaker.

Noah didn't hesitate. "I didn't want to work with local police on this any more than Rain wanted to work with me."

"And we didn't want the interference," Chief Noble piped in. "But we've got four murders. I don't want five."

"None of us do," Rain said, her expression still harsh as loose strands of dark hair fell free from her hair clasp at her neck and bordered her flushed face. "Noah and I have already made contact with two of the members of the swingers' group our victims were involved with. Even today, we spent time with a Joanna Hill, who knew all of the victims."

"And?" Brenda asked.

"And we'll share what she told us and our feelings on her reaction to the murders," Rain answered quickly. She then nodded to Al, who stood with her arms crossed, watching all of them as if it were the best entertainment she'd witnessed in a while. "First I'd like to hear what Al has to say, if that's okay with you?" Rain added, her question so weighted with venomous sarcasm it wasn't missed by anyone as she glared at the small box on the desk.

Silence weighed heavily in the room and finally there was a crackling sound through the speaker before Brenda spoke. "Fine. Impress hell out of me," she said flippantly. "You may proceed, Lieutenant Gomez."

Al looked to her chief for his consent, but Noah didn't focus on Noble. Turning to Rain, her defenses running high, Noah walked into her and forced her to back up and perch her pretty ass against the nearest desk. She sighed loud enough to show him she was still wound tight, but he didn't worry about keeping her in line. Once they got into talking about the case he had a feeling it would consume her thoughts and she wouldn't crave wringing his supervisor's neck anymore.

"All I planned to say was that I could speculate on the nature of our murderer from what we've learned about the murder weapon." Al hurried to one of the desks in the back of the room and shuffled through paperwork. "Give me one second."

Rain glanced up at Noah and he met her fiery gaze. She looked away first, turning to focus on Al, and he studied Rain's profile. Even with her thick dark hair pulled back in a bloodred velvet hair clasp, strands flowed free and caressed her milky complexion. Her back was slightly arched as she perched next to him, and the outline of her breasts simply added to a view of perfection.

Noah blinked, forcing his attention to Al as well. But he glanced at Chief Noble and realized he'd been watching him. Noah looked away slowly but wasn't sure what he read on the chief's face—disgust, disappointment?

"As you all know," Al began again, walking over to Chief Noble's desk and then spreading open several files and pulling out paperwork. "When a bullet comes out of a gun, the marks from the inside of the barrel are left on the bullet and that's our rifling. And everyone knows rifling is like a fingerprint." Al held up one of the pieces of paper. "Here is our rifling. Now of course the caliber also has to match the caliber the gun shoots."

Al fingered through the paperwork in her file, exhaling loudly, and finally pulled out some stapled papers. "We cross-referenced cases that have matched bulleting with different types of guns. Based on what we have on all four bullets from each crime scene, the rifling indicates we have one murder weapon." Al shot Noah a furtive look. "I've already cross-referenced what the FBI has worked up on this case, since we have murders in other cities. We aren't looking at the same murder weapon in the other cities as we are here in Lincoln."

"Are you sure about this?" Noah asked, leaving Rain's side and reaching for the printout in Al's hand.

She offered it to him and then shuffled through her files again. "I spoke with Ted Foreman in Kansas City and Gina Roper in Dallas," she offered.

"Both of whom are heading up the investigations in each of those cities," Brenda concurred through the speakerphone.

"So what do we have here then?" Rain asked. "Are our murderers in alliance with each other? Or do we possibly have a copycat murderer?"

"What do you mean by 'a copycat murderer'?" Noah faced Rain as she leaned against the spare desk in the corner of the office.

"The murders began in Dallas and spread to Kansas City," Rain explained. "The first murder here was three months ago, where Dallas first reported the murder of a swinger who was shot in the temple while sitting in their car six months ago."

"Why would someone copycat these murders?" Chief Noble asked.

"I would speculate to throw us off, make us believe the same person is murdering all of these people, or the same group."

Noah stared at Rain a moment longer when she finished speaking. He walked to her side, fighting the urge to brush her loose strand of hair from the side of her face. "Why would they do that?" he asked her.

Rain shrugged. "I've already confirmed who in our little swingers' group of friends has registered guns: Ned and Brandy Flynn, Steve and Susie Porter, and Joanna Hill," she finished, meeting Noah's gaze when she mentioned Joanna's name.

"That's not a lot to go on," Brenda said through the speakerphone.

Rain walked around Noah and once again rested her fists on the edge of the chief's desk. "We'll know more when Noah and I go to the potluck tomorrow. Everyone from that swingers' group where our four murders came from will be there. But right now, I would guess whoever our murderer is, they want to ride on the high-profile crime this situation has become. They want the fame, the attention, as they take out those they feel, for whatever reasons, no longer deserve to live. It's a power trip. And I have a feeling they are very pleased the FBI has stepped in to investigate them."

NINE

Patty Henderson secured the lock box on the doorknob of the house she'd just finished showing and backed away from the door slowly.

"Let's hope they buy you, sweetheart. Mama sure could use a cruise to the Bahamas. Or maybe Cancún. Anywhere that is far, far away from this town." She clucked her tongue along with the rhythm her shoes made against the stone-paved sidewalk as she headed to her car. It was already six thirty. "Looks like I'll be stylishly late."

The polite thing to do would be to call the Gamboas and let them know that it would be an hour or so before she got there. At least that way she wouldn't be snubbed. Damn it. She remembered when spending time with her friends used to be fun.

"If these are my friends, who needs fucking enemies?" she hissed.

She pulled out her keys and pushed the button on her key chain. Her car beeped once. Climbing in, she breathed in the new-car smell that still lingered inside. It was all about appearance. Her brand-new Mazda RX-8 was a statement. It said success, but it wasn't flashy. Not like

Steve Parker's souped-up Miata. Patty didn't want flashy. She wanted money. And although the payments on this sweet baby were a bit steep, they were worth it to show potential buyers that she was the Realtor who got the job done.

There were two showings tomorrow, and if she got into the office early enough, she could contact Ralph Hipp down at National Bank and see where she stood with a few of her clients. If she was in the office by nine, she should be able to get her phone calls out of the way and be ready for her first showing at ten thirty. There was no such thing as a five-day workweek in her world. Which was fine. Work hard—play harder. That was her motto.

Switching gears as she drove, she forced her thoughts off of work. It was Friday night, damn it. And she had plans. She didn't need to go by the office again tonight, just head home, shower, and get ready for the potluck. She hoped no one would cringe over her attempt at a fruit salad that she threw together over her lunch. At least she owned a pretty bowl to put it in.

"It's all about appearance, baby." She chuckled and adjusted her rearview mirror to catch her reflection. "Not bad for five o'clock." She wouldn't voice that it wasn't bad for forty-one, either. No reason to dwell on her age and bring herself down.

Maybe her friends weren't the best a person could ask for. Once, things were different. But something changed. She thought back, remembered when swinging was something casual and not a goddamned competition. But she'd gotten herself wrapped into this world, and now it was like a fucking addiction.

"And what's wrong with that?" She licked her lips and slowed at the stop sign, then accelerated out of the ritzy neighborhood where she'd already sold two houses. "Let Joanna think she's cream of the crop. Darling, you might be younger, but you sure as hell aren't better."

If she was, then why did Steve come to Patty all the time on the side?

"Because you're good, baby. You are so damned good. And you know it." Other men stopped by, too, from time to time. Not that Steve needed to know that. Not that anyone needed to know. "*It's my own damned business,*" she stressed out loud, feeling a twinge of nerves and forcing herself to suppress them.

That's what had changed with the group of swingers she was with. It was a control thing.

"And no one controls Patty Henderson but me!" she insisted. She would just let them think they controlled her.

Again the nerves twisted and tingled inside her, a rush of trepidation hitting that she didn't like. But there wasn't any turning back now. She was in way too deep and she knew it. It wasn't like her swinging life was all that bad. She had some really good times, and recently, too.

Maybe she'd call Elaine and Oscar. They were an awesome couple. It was a blast the last time she went over to their house. Although Elaine wasn't much into women, Oscar was one hell of a good fuck, and Elaine had filmed Patty fucking him. Then, sitting around and drinking beers afterward, she'd never laughed harder as they watched the film. My God, she sure as hell didn't look twenty anymore. All of them enjoyed the hell out of watching that film, almost as much as they did making it.

"Sell a few more houses, sweetheart, and you can get that boob job." A few nights at the gym and she saved thousands of dollars on a tummy or ass job. "You're looking good," she told herself. "And you're even better than you look." One final glance in her rearview mirror and she readjusted it.

So, a few phone calls, a shower, slip into the slinky dress she'd picked up at the cleaners, and it was off to party!

"Okay, Elaine and Oscar," she said out loud, and dug her phone out of her purse while keeping an eye on traffic. Early Friday night—traffic was a bitch. "When did I miss a call?"

She recognized Steve Porter's private cell-phone number, the one his wife didn't know about, and fought the urge to growl. He always got so pissy when she didn't take his calls immediately.

Fine. She'd call him back and then call Oscar and Elaine. At least then she could relax and enjoy their laid-back nature without tension building in her if she put off Steve any longer. She prayed that Oscar and Elaine remained fresh, didn't get tangled into the conniving, manipulative web that wound itself tighter and tighter around her group of friends. Maybe she should warn them the way she did that new couple who'd just moved to town.

Goddamn. It was a fucking mistake taking Joanna with her to their house. Joanna said she saw the damage happening, agreed that the murders were getting out of hand. But Joanna was a twit, a stupid bitch.

"And I know you're fucking her on the side, too, Steve Porter."

One thing about Patty's line of work: she was a pro at working a cell phone and dodging around traffic. Hell, she could even text message and drive, not that she would brag about that to anyone and hear their goddamned lectures.

She hated lectures, hated being manipulated, and, most of all, hated being judged, unless it was in her favor. The world needed to see her as a success, capable of taking on anyone, or any matter, and coming out on top. If someone didn't have something to offer her, she really didn't have any use for them.

"And that doesn't make me shallow," she reminded herself. "That means I'm strong, aggressive, a go-getter."

Pushing the button to return Steve's call, she let her mind wander to the last time he'd stopped by. Earlier this week, over lunch, and damn, did he fuck her! If Steve weren't so incredibly skilled, she'd probably tell him to go to hell. He was so stuck on himself. Hell, everyone's shit stunk every once in a while.

"Just not mine!" She laughed out loud and then adjusted her earpiece in her ear.

It rang once, twice, while her stomach slowly twisted in knots. There was something else about Steve, about his aura, his persona. His demanding, confident nature made him a man to reckon with—one to keep an eye on, and as well to keep on her good side. If that meant fucking him, then so be it.

More than once she thought he was probably the one murdering those in their group who weren't compliant. It would be just like him. There was a pattern creating here. And she couldn't be the only one seeing it. Anyone who didn't agree with the group majority's decisions, who tried calling the shots, or who ruined it for everyone else was dying.

Idiotic, yes. Insane, most definitely.

And a challenge that she could handle.

"God. I'm not a sick bitch, am I?" She hated the nerves that tingled furiously now inside her. "I'm not the one who decided to start killing people," she told herself, and drew in a soothing breath.

When it went to voice mail, she hung up. He would see the missed call, know she was returning his call. Good enough. She reached for her phone and scrolled down her phone numbers and then pushed to call Oscar and Elaine.

"Hello," Elaine's soft, almost girlish-sounding voice chirped.

"Hi, Elaine, it's Patty."

"Hi there, hon. Are you headed to the Gamboas'? We just pulled up here."

"Unfortunately, no. I'm headed home. I just finished a showing."

"Remember us when you make that first million." Elaine laughed.

Patty chuckled along with her but took the words to heart. "You'll be one of the few I remember," she said honestly. "I should call Ted and Jan. I'm obviously going to be a bit late."

"We'll let them know you're on your way. It looks like there's a few here already."

"Oh? Who is there?"

"Butch and Brandy."

"Of course," Patty said. "The perfect couple."

"What's that make us?"

"Also perfect," Patty assured her. "Is Joanna there yet?"

"No. And nor are the Porters from what I can see. There's a car here I don't recognize." Elaine kept talking about the style and make of the car, and Oscar said something in the background that made both of them chuckle.

Patty pulled into her driveway and didn't hear a word that Elaine said. She was distracted by the car parked out front. "I'm home, hon. Let me take a quick shower and I'll be there."

"Sounds good. See you then."

Patty didn't bother pulling into her garage. Turning off the car, she headed to the house, waving over her shoulder. "Come in if you like. I need to hop in the shower."

Hurrying inside and kicking off her shoes, Patty grumbled to herself, "It's not like we wouldn't see each other in a few at the potluck." But a hard, fast rule that she would never break—always let them see you smile. Even when she was tired, her feet hurt, and she was in a hurry. And even when that person was royally starting to get on her nerves. "Why the hell are you here anyway?" she whispered.

She stripped out of her clothes and tossed them on her bed, then headed naked down the hallway to the bathroom. Her alarm system buzzed once and she heard the door close.

"Just make yourself comfortable. I'll only be a minute," she called out, then closed herself in the bathroom.

What she wouldn't do to simply soak for an hour or so. And she would have, if she weren't already running late. She took time to shave, though. Not that she ever assumed anything, but it would be nice to get some tonight. She deserved it. She worked harder than anyone she knew, damn it. And she deserved her pick of men—several men, all at once.

Patty smiled at her reflection in the mirror, took her time with her makeup, and dried and teased her hair before heading back to her bedroom. "Where are you?" she called out.

There wasn't any answer, which was fine with her. She would never be rude, but it sure didn't bother her if others were. As long as they didn't step on her toes, she didn't care.

At quarter till eight, Patty grabbed her fruit salad, slipped into her comfortable sandals, and turned out the lights. Then keying in the code on her house alarm, she headed out the front door and closed it behind her.

"Fine. Show up, don't say a word, and then leave." She wondered how some people made it in this world without people skills.

Not that she fooled herself into thinking it was a perfect world. Hell, she knew better than many that it wasn't. How many times had she witnessed rude people trudging ahead in life?

Just look at the people she called friends. Steve was a prick. And if the IRS ever audited him, he'd go to prison. And don't even get her started on his lame excuse of a wife, Susie. What did he see in her? Patty definitely bought into the theory that Susie had entered that marriage with a lot of money. Not that Patty would ever ask. But Steve would marry for money. He sure as hell wouldn't do anything for love. Where was the gain in that?

That was about the only thing she and Steve agreed on.

Then there were Butch and Brandy. God, they sounded like names people would call their pet dogs. And in truth, their names fit. Patty saw right through the charade from the beginning. Butch played the good old boy routine to the hilt. And working at the grocery store as a butcher, he saw everyone, knew everything, and could pass on gossip in any shape or form that he saw fit. Patty wasn't stupid enough to think that only white-collars had power. Butch could destroy a person over a lunch hour while slicing meat and spreading false rumors. And Butch could add to anyone's small realm of power, too, if he was properly motivated. Patty would openly admit he'd sent more than one client her way.

Butch had his kink, though. Brandy didn't like anal sex. But Patty didn't mind it. Hell, if it was done right, she loved the hell out of it. So Butch got what he wanted, and in return, he gave Patty what she needed: more clients. That didn't fool her into thinking she was the only back he scratched, though. Butch was in it for Butch.

"And Steve, you better watch your ass, too," she said, and damn near grinned over the picture of Butch taking Steve down. What she wouldn't do to see that if it ever happened.

Brandy couldn't be head bitch, though. Not that anyone was in charge of her. Patty about puked, the way the women hovered around Susie. That little waste of a woman brought down every party she attended. She wouldn't give head, she didn't take it in the ass, and she never touched any of the women. Yet the men always fucked her.

Patty didn't get it. Not at all. Susie was a hundred pounds dripping wet, if that. There wasn't a damn thing appealing about her that Patty could see. Steve once told her that a man will stick his dick in any willing pussy. Men were sluts and they didn't care as long as the woman was willing. That didn't help Patty understand. She was willing. Why would anyone choose Susie over her?

Of course Brandy wasn't that much better. She had big tits, and maybe she was cute, for someone who'd had four kids. Who would want so many children?

Patty saw through her, too, though. The way Brandy kissed Susie's ass, like she actually liked her or something. Patty would bet that Butch didn't cheat on Brandy. He didn't strike Patty as that kind of guy. But Brandy? The jury was still out on that one. Patty would argue in favor of the probability that Brandy put out when it suited her.

There was that new boob job Brandy got last year. No

way could Butch afford that sort of thing on his salary. And Brandy sure as hell didn't work. All she did was stay home and watch her brat kids. Nope. Brandy probably put out where it counted. And Patty would bet Brandy told Butch about it, too, made him agree that her giving some on the side was worth him having a youthful-looking wife for a few more years.

"I'm starting to think I'm the only normal one in the bunch," Patty said, and headed across the lawn to her car in the driveway. "Everyone knows the Gamboas fight worse than cats and dogs. Tonight's party at their house should prove interesting." She would not allow herself to get down again over the fact that her house wasn't chosen for this month's party. "Why does Susie get to decide where the parties are every month, anyway?"

If Jan started into her heavy drinking, that would be the sign that the party would go to hell. She was a funny drunk toward everyone but her husband. And it was always that damned boxed wine. But once Jan turned to it full force, the rest was too easily predicted. How many times had Patty and Joanna sat back and counted down the minutes before Jan started attacking her husband?

It would start slow, little pokes, an innuendo dropped here or there, and then the insults would begin. Patty didn't get why Ted didn't see the signs as easily as everyone else did. One would think that after being married to Jan for so many years, and swinging for least as many, he would know once his wife started insulting him that he needed to keep his wandering hands off of the other women at the party.

Either Ted didn't care or he got off on his wife attacking him. Patty shook her head when she thought of Joanna's nice candelabra that Jan threw at her husband at the last gathering they had. Maybe it was just as well that the party wasn't at her house. Susie might think she was snubbing Patty by not selecting her to be hostess. But in truth, Susie was doing her a favor.

"Thank you, Susie!"

Patty opened the driver's side door and climbed in, setting the fruit salad on her passenger seat and then taking a moment to situate it so that it wouldn't spill. She'd paid extra for a leather interior. As much of a bitch as it was, it again made a statement.

The car rumbled to life and she shifted into reverse. "Well, hell," she growled as a car pulled up to the house again. "Some people care about being late," she mumbled to herself, and sighed, shifting back into neutral.

Patty placed her finger on the button to roll down her window when a sharp pain hit. It attacked her temple and then exploded in her brain, blinding her. The pain increased, racking every inch of her body. The steering wheel stopped her head from falling farther forward. She couldn't move. Nor did the blackness go away. Instead, everything faded away—everything. God. She was dead!

TEN

"I can only imagine how quiet life must seem for you here after living in Washington, D.C.," Brandy Flynn said, and popped a whole cheese cracker into her mouth.

"Noah and I love it here so far." Rain balanced her plate on her lap, not sure she could eat another bite, although the food was good.

"And you two don't have any children?" Brandy asked. "I can't even imagine that one."

Rain shook her head, grinning. So far, she might as well be at any of the many political parties her father used to throw a few times a year—just so the world wouldn't forget about him, or at least that's what he used to tell her. Rain knew he simply loved having everyone come over and swap cop stories. Once a cop, always a cop.

She'd answered this question enough times over the years. Tonight, though, a variation of the truth might prove more valuable. "No. We don't have children." She glanced down at her plate, letting the moment slide and sensing both Brandy Flynn and Jan Gamboa watching her with curious anticipation. Rain looked back up at them and went on quietly, although she would bet Noah was tuned into their conversation as much as he was the one he was having with the guys. "When we found out a couple years after we were married that I couldn't have children, I worried that I might lose Noah. He loves them so much."

"Oh, hon, how terrible!" Brandy reached over and patted the back of Rain's hand with crumb-covered fingers. "Well, you two can borrow my four anytime you want," she added, inserting her light comment with an easy laugh. "I swear every time that man looked at me for the first five years of our marriage he knocked me up."

"We've considered adopting," Rain added, remembering her notes on each couple and that Lorrie Hinders was trying to adopt before she was murdered. "I'm just not sure, though."

"What agency was Lorrie going through?" Jan looked at Brandy and then scowled when Brandy gave her a quick hard look.

"Who is Lorrie? Will she be here tonight?" Rain made a show of ignoring the looks the two women gave her and instead acted excited.

"She's not going to be here," Jan began, and hesitated.

"If we can find you information on agencies, we'll be sure and let you know, hon." Brandy patted Rain's hand again and then glanced over at the men. "I wonder what those fools are talking about."

"Probably which one of us they can fuck first," Jan offered, and broke out laughing.

Brandy laughed with her and, if Rain was to guess, she would say a bit too loud.

It grabbed the men's attention, though, and she looked over at Noah. He stood with Brandy's husband, Butch, and Ted Gamboa on the other side of the picnic table, where a handful of dishes were covered by clear wrap. The best Rain could tell, they were comparing the three women, and not being very discreet about it when she and the other women looked their way. If anything, it seemed the men's conversation grew louder when they realized they had an audience. Noah winked at her, but then Brandy made a humming sound of approval and Rain looked her way.

"I hope you don't mind my singing your husband's praises," she said, and then made a show of giving him the once-over. "You just got to love a tight ass in blue jeans."

"I don't mind a bit. And I agree," Rain said, silently concluding that Noah was definitely the best-looking man at this potluck. If they were supposed to trade or swap or whatever it was called, she was definitely not getting the better end of the deal. "I think the Midwest suits him. He seems happier since we've been here."

Jan sat next to Brandy on the wooden bench that belonged to the picnic table. They'd adjusted it so that everyone could move around the table more easily and help themselves to food, and now both ladies turned, looking at Rain, their shoulders brushing as they nodded. Rain considered ways of turning the conversation back to Lorrie, or any of the other victims, without appearing obvious.

"Ted and I love Lincoln," Jan said. "I guess it's got its problems like any city, but we're not going anywhere. We know everyone here. I tell him and the kids, there's nowhere you can go where someone isn't going to tell me they saw you. Keeps them on their toes."

"Lincoln is perfect," Brandy chimed in, glancing at her empty plate and then setting it next to her on the bench. "I've been back east before, although it was many, many years ago. You aren't going to find scenery like this in all of those crowded cities."

The setting was perfect, a large but cozy backyard. The huge tree behind Jan and Brandy offered shade to over half of the backyard. It reminded Rain of the trees in the yard at home, back when her dad was still alive. There were times when she regretted selling the house, but keeping it, without Dad, was too painful.

"This is a beautiful old tree," she said, and leaned back in her lawn chair, while crossing one bare leg over the other. She'd hesitated to wear her strapless minidress to a potluck, but Noah had damn near insisted on it.

"I bet they don't have trees like this where you're from," Brandy boasted with pride, and tugged on her fishnet shirt.

Rain didn't feel like she dressed in too revealing an outfit once she arrived and saw Brandy wearing her see-through shirt, with no bra on underneath. There was no way her firm, large breasts were real. It took a bit to get accustomed to looking at Brandy while she spoke without dropping your gaze to those large breasts.

"It sure is a beauty." Big old trees made it easy to forget all of her worries. Rain leaned back and adjusted her ponytail holder that fastened her hair at her nape, while gazing up at the many intertwining large branches. "If I were dressed differently, I'd be tempted to try and climb it."

"I think all three of you should get up there and climb it," Ted said loudly, obviously eavesdropping and grinning when the women looked at him. "It would definitely improve the view, don't you think so, guys?"

Butch moved pretty quickly for a stocky man when he made a show of diving toward his wife. She squealed and sent a few choice words in his direction that only made him and the other men laugh louder.

He leaned over her, cupping her breasts, and fondled them through her fishnet while laying a loud one on her neck until her cursing turned into laughter. Either the two of them knew how to put on a good show or they were pretty happy with each other. Brandy finally turned her head and kissed her husband but pulled away at the sound of laughter behind her.

"Sorry I'm late," Joanna sang out, holding a pan in her extended hand and doing a fairly decent job of walking across the yard in very high-heeled sandals. "The fun hasn't started without me, I hope."

"Everyone's late tonight," Jan informed her, fixing a

pout on her face. "I started thinking my party would be a dud. We're just hanging around out here eating. Nothing exciting yet."

"Thanks a lot," Brandy said, nudging her. "I guess we're not entertaining enough." She shoved Butch off of her and winked at Rain.

"I've got plenty of entertainment for you right here, baby." Butch puffed out his chest and held his arms out to Joanna.

Joanna plopped down her pan that appeared to have cake or brownies in it and sidestepped Butch. She wrapped her arms around both women, shaking her rear for the men while hugging Brandy and Jan fiercely.

"You're all that counts," Joanna told both women, and then kissed each lady on the lips. Turning around, she wrapped her arms around Rain, kissed her on the cheek, and then whispered, "I'm so glad you two are here."

"I'm not feeling the love!" Butch suddenly wailed, sounding like someone just took away his favorite toy.

Joanna let go of Rain quickly, leaving her in a cloud of musky perfume. "Oh, hon, you know I'd never forget you."

Joanna didn't bother tugging down her short dress that had crawled up her ass from hugging the women. She wrapped her arms around Butch's neck and kissed him. Rain stared at the bottom half of her bare ass. Joanna wasn't wearing underwear, not even a thong.

Rain looked away quickly and Brandy grinned at her and then rolled her eyes.

"He's such a slut," Brandy muttered.

Somehow, seeing Brandy's indifference to her husband kissing Joanna, right after Brandy and Butch acted so frisky together, relaxed the moment for Rain a bit. She didn't quite get it, though. If they loved each other so much, why would they want to share each other?

But if they were cool with all of it, then knowing tension wouldn't quickly develop in the air made it easier to handle.

Rain watched the incredibly sensual kiss and glanced

at Brandy again while her husband mauled Joanna. Brandy looked anything but annoyed. If anything, her expression was a mixture of amusement and boredom.

"Aren't they all sluts?" Jan asked.

"Yup. We sure are," Ted said, rubbing his hands together. "Where's my warm welcome, Joanna?"

Joanna looked pleased as punch to leave Butch's arms and fall into Ted's. The ritual continued, the kiss deep and sensual. Rain glanced at Noah, who stood facing the men with his arms crossed. When Joanna came up for air, she strutted toward Noah like he was the prize of the night.

"I have been waiting all damned day for this," she purred, acting like a cat in heat as she rubbed herself against Noah. "Come here, lover boy." She scraped her long fingernails over his shoulders and then wrapped her hands around his neck.

"Yup. They're all sluts," Rain said, parroting Ted, and looked down at her plate. She prayed she sounded and looked casual.

Not only was it paramount that she appear completely relaxed in this swingers' environment, but the last thing she'd let Noah see was her sweat it while they were here.

"Mmm, mmm, looks good. Tastes great," Joanna purred. She hung on him while glancing around, her gaze resting on Rain only for a moment before she looked at the rest of them. "So where is everyone tonight?"

"I'm not sure," Jan offered, and glanced down at her watch. "It's after eight. Elaine and Oscar were here for a few, but they left because Elaine spilled catsup on her dress."

"It was such a cute dress, too," Brandy added, and made a tsking sound. "They said they would be right back and that was over an hour ago."

"And Elaine said she'd talked to Patty and she was running late because of showings," Jan continued.

Joanna laughed and stretched her fingers over the middle of Noah's chest. "Patty will be late to her own funeral," she mused.

"I think we should grab these dishes and head inside. Anyone want to refill their plate first?" Jan looked to Ted. "It's almost dark. Should we head down to the family room?"

"I know what I want on my plate." Joanna turned and leaned into Noah again.

He backed away from her and Rain hid a smile.

"Let's get you a plate," he suggested, and reached for one of the plastic plates on the other end of the table.

He looked up at Rain and narrowed his gaze at her, as if somehow she should figure out how to get Joanna to quit hanging on him. Or maybe he was searching Rain's face, seeing if she minded if Joanna made out with him while everyone watched. Rain wasn't sure, but she stood when the other women did and offered Noah the most pleasant smile she could muster. When he scowled, something fluttered around her heart. He didn't like the attention Joanna was giving him.

"I'll help carry everything inside," Rain offered, turning her attention away from Noah and Joanna. Rain was pretending to be his wife. In truth, it shouldn't bother her one bit who hung on him. That's why this case should be easy for them to work. She should be able to act and feel just like Brandy appeared when Joanna hung on her husband.

"We'll set everything on the bar in the family room," Ted announced.

Minutes later they were in a finished basement that was nicely arranged into a comfortable family room. The dishes were placed on a bar, and Ted went behind it and started scooping ice into glasses as he played bartender.

Noah turned from the bar with two drinks, and Rain noticed Joanna's expression fall when he brought Rain her drink.

"Peach schnapps and Seven Up," he informed her, and handed her the cold, sweaty glass.

Rain barely managed to hide her surprise. But his pleased expression told her she didn't do a good job of it.

He put his arm around her neck and pulled her to him, the smell of Joanna's heavy perfume hanging all over him.

"I'm good, aren't I?"

"Apparently the natives are dying to find out," she whispered back, relaxing against his hard, solid, warm chest and glancing over his shoulder as another couple came down the stairs.

"The only woman I'm fucking tonight is you." Noah let his hands slide down her arms and then let go of her, then brought his drink to his lips and sipped, his gaze smoldering, and sealing his promise.

Rain drank as well, and then licked the taste of the sweet liqueur from her lips. Heat swarmed inside her, along with a wonderful sense of power when Noah watched the act before turning and acknowledging the couple who'd just joined them.

His hand remained on her hip when he focused on the two, whom Rain easily picked up on as Steve and Susie Porter, even prior to any introductions. And obviously this group didn't ride high on formalities. It appeared all of them were more concerned that they looked good to whomever they were addressing.

Rain watched the men do their backslapping, voice-bellowing rituals as they greeted one another. Brandy and Jan, on the other hand, seemed to prance around Susie Porter, repeatedly complimenting and singing her praises over anything they could think of.

"If that isn't just the prettiest dress." Jan swooned, circling around the very thin, pale blond woman who stood next to her tall, dark, almost intimidating-looking husband.

"Oh my, Susie, you must tell us where you got it," Brandy chimed in.

Both women wrapped their arms around Susie and swept her over to the bar, continually talking over each other. The frail-looking, pale blonde allowed the ladies to lead her, and almost appeared to float between them. As she moved past Rain and Noah, Susie turned her head and looked at Rain with large, round eyes. Susie didn't hold her head high with confidence but instead raised thin lashes slowly, as if intimidated at the thought of meeting new people.

But at the same time, when Rain made eye contact, she swore she stared into an empty soul, one depleted of all zest for life. It was a look Rain had seen before, often in seriously depressed individuals, beaten and abused wives, and criminals who'd given up hope of ever living their life anywhere but behind bars.

Rain tried picturing Susie Porter willingly fucking any man in the room. The woman looked like her own shadow would spook her. Susie didn't look like the kind of woman who would enjoy sex, although she didn't appear to mind Brandy and Jan stroking her, touching her, as they led her across the room. She just didn't return the affection or attention.

"Rain, Noah, meet Susie Porter." Jan played the happy hostess.

"I'm not sure who is the prettiest lady in the room." Noah's baritone dropped to a sultry whisper that grabbed more than Rain's attention.

When Noah took Susie's small, pale hand in his and brought it to his lips, Rain glanced toward Steve Porter. Her first reaction was that he looked like a very successful used-car salesman. She searched for a reaction to Noah giving his wife attention but didn't see one. What she did notice was a man sizing up another man, not out of jealousy, but a competitive edge still existed.

Steve's dark, sun booth–tanned skin almost seemed to glow against the light yellow polo shirt that he wore. His jeans looked like they'd been ironed, and Rain wasn't sure when she'd last seen anyone wear penny loafers. It amazed her that someone who stood out so dynamically in the room could live in this town and she'd never noticed him before.

His raven-black hair was combed back and the wave in it almost made him look like a young Elvis. But it was

Steve's black eyes, piercing, sharp, and pretentious, that grabbed Rain the most. When Noah took Susie's hand and kissed it, Steve looked at Noah and appeared for a moment like he might leap across the room and attack.

Oddly enough, though, Rain didn't get that sense of jealousy. There was a spark in the air, a sizzle that wasn't there before the couple arrived. If Rain could guess, she'd say that Steve viewed himself as alpha male of this group and didn't like the idea of another alpha strutting into his territory. The look in Steve's eyes was one of a conqueror, confident that he could knock Noah down, and he itched to do it.

Immediately Rain didn't like him.

When he shifted his attention to her, his expression changed to something darker, almost predatory. Rain felt herself straighten to her full five foot ten when he walked between Ted and Butch, with Joanna wrapped around his arm just as she'd been glued to Noah when they were outside. Steve didn't try to peel Joanna loose, though. Instead, moving with her at his side like she were some trophy, he swept across the room with a determined gait that damn near put Rain on the defensive before he said a word.

"Who do we have here?" he asked, matching Noah's deep baritone with one just as rich, if not even more booming.

"I'm Rain," she said casually, opting at the last moment not to offer a last name. When she reached to touch Noah's back and introduce him as well, Steve reached for her, freeing Joanna, and took Rain's hand before she could touch Noah.

"Rain. A compelling name for an incredibly compelling woman," Steve said, lowering that baritone even further. "Is it your real name?"

If she weren't so damned accustomed to being questioned throughout her life over her first name, she might have been offended. Instead, she offered him the story she'd concocted in the academy, which was a hell of a lot more entertaining than the truth.

"Yes, it is. My mother wished to get even with my father." She smiled, allowing Steve to stroke her palm with the pad of his thumb. "And you are?"

"Steve Porter, my dear," he said, sounding like he could pull off the commercial for that used-car lot where she pictured him working. "And why would your mother wish to get even with your father when he gave her such a beautiful creature like you?"

Rain smiled sweetly. "Because he wouldn't divorce his wife."

Stunned silence lasted a mere moment before Butch snorted and then the entire room burst into laughter. Although Rain gave herself credit for offering the punch line with a perfect beat, she had to give Noah as much credit for turning around gallantly and petting her hair.

"Isn't she the sexiest bastard you've ever laid eyes on?" he asked, cupping her ass and then giving it a good swat.

"She is definitely that," Steve agreed.

The men's comments were drowned with laughter and then everyone was talking. Ned again played bartender, getting drinks for Susie and Steve and refilling everyone else's drink.

The tone in the room didn't return to the relaxed state it held before the Porters' arrival. Steve and Susie's arrival brought life to the party and as well created a sizzle in the air that didn't diminish as the evening progressed. Where the conversation was calm, relaxed, and only mildly flirtatious before they arrived, now everyone talked, joked, and chided one another.

Steve didn't let go of Rain's hand and instead held it firmly when he walked to the bar. Ned quickly offered Steve's drink, obviously knowing the man's poison, and then leaned against the counter, nursing a bottle of Budweiser and grinning at her like a hopeful schoolboy. Butch stood next to Steve, backing anything the man said, but

Steve focused on her with those dark eyes as if his mission was to know everything about her before the evening ended.

"Butch, you didn't do this lady justice when describing her to me," Steve said, his back to the room, and if he pushed any closer, her back would be bent in two from the edge of the bar.

"Why do you think I invited her and her husband into our group?" Butch stood with legs spread, and his chest poofed out like a peacock ready to strut for the females. "And if I made her sound too incredible you would have raced to get here sooner. At least I got some time with her before you showed up."

"You're lucky you did," Steve said without looking away from Rain. "Because she is mine for the rest of the night."

Joanna wrapped her long, slender fingers tightly around Steve's biceps. "I knew you'd love her, Steve," she purred, her voice throaty as she moved in closer to him, appearing desperate to try to regain his attention. "Rain and I are already planning on decorating her new home, aren't we, sweetheart?" Joanna's gaze never left Steve's when she questioned Rain.

It was the most bizarre flirting session Rain had ever seen. A competitive cluster fuck that she couldn't imagine ending in anything passionate and fulfilling.

"Our home does need a lot of work," Rain admitted.

"But the layout, my dear," Joanna pressed. "I can already see it in my head. And I promise you it won't cost a lot of money, unless of course you have it to spend." Her shrill laughter bordered on sounding nervous.

The tension lining her eyes faded when Steve looked at her finally. She returned the gaze with such strong affection glowing on her face Rain wondered how anyone could miss it. Were these two in love?

"You've been over to their house?" he asked.

Joanna searched Steve's face as if she wanted to say

something but then thought better of herself. Her smile faded momentarily but then broadened wider than it was before. "As soon as Butch told me about the Kaynes, I stopped by. Rain and I are practically neighbors." Joanna let go of Steve and moved to lean on the bar next to Rain. She ran her fingernail down the side of Rain's head, combing her hair with one finger. "Rain's even been over to get in the hot tub with me." The invitation in Joanna's eyes was as obvious as her desire for Steve when she batted her eyes at him. "Maybe next time you can come join us."

Steve moved in closer, putting his arm between her and Joanna, until he'd pushed Joanna backward and blocked Rain's view of the room. Then lowering his mouth to her neck, he nibbled while his hand squeezed her breast.

It was hard as hell not to stiffen or push him backward but at the same time not to appear too anxious to have him maul her. Rain imagined Noah, the way she felt when he first touched her, how his expression darkened as he slowly seduced her. Steve didn't possess a fraction of Noah's charisma, or his ability to appear infatuated, instead of on a mission. It was a damned good thing that Steve wasn't the cop here. No one would ever buy into this man's sincerity. She honestly tried figuring out why the entire room sucked up to him when he was rude, arrogant, and smelled of cheap cologne.

"Do you play without your husband, Rain?" he whispered, speaking so quietly it was quite obvious he wished to arrange a tryst and possibly got off on doing it under everyone's noses, including his wife's.

Rain stared into those dark eyes and saw the cold-hearted bastard for what he was. "Never," she informed him, and then smiled at the instant disappointment on his face. "And I don't approve of anyone who does anything without their spouse knowing, either."

Steve's disappointment faded as quickly as it appeared. Straightening, which made him stand possibly an inch or so taller than she, he crooked his finger over the top of her strapless dress and between her breasts. As he tugged slightly, she felt the material stretch over her breasts and threaten to lower if he put more effort into it.

"Damn good answer, my dear." His crooked smile offered a bit of boyish charm. But he'd already shown his true colors, and his sudden relaxed nature and glint in his eyes didn't sell her at all that he'd been joking, or anything other than sincere with his question. Steve lazily shifted his attention to Joanna, although he didn't move his finger from Rain's dress. "No one likes a slut, right, darling?"

"I don't know," Rain said before Joanna could figure out whether she was being insulted or not. Rain wrapped her fingers around Steve's wrist, feeling his pulse thump strongly against her fingers, and then removed his grasp on her dress. "Sometimes a bit of sluttish behavior has its rewards."

Rain stepped around Steve, wishing she could see his reaction to her comment but not daring to give him a moment's more attention. Instead she walked around Butch, placing her hand on his shoulder. For the first time that night, and possibly since she'd first met him, he looked distracted, possibly worried.

"Are you having fun?" she asked smoothly and quietly. "Ready for another beer?"

"We can't have you waiting on me, gorgeous." Butch reached for her glass. "Allow me to freshen your drink."

Her cocktail was more watered-down than gone, but she relinquished her glass to Butch and moved to join the ladies. Susie sat on the coffee table, her back to Rain. Brandy and Jan were on the couch, though, and possibly could have witnessed Steve's bold moves. The women looked past Rain for only a moment, seeing what she wished she could see, and that was Steve's reaction to her snubbing him.

"Here you go, my dear," Butch said when he brought her fresh drink to her. "Ladies, refills?"

"Most definitely. More wine!" Jan held up her glass, her eyes already looking a bit glassy.

And as the alcohol flowed, so did the promiscuous nature.

Although curious whether everyone would end up naked in a pile or pair off and disappear, Rain wasn't in a hurry for that part of the evening to happen. She enjoyed talking to almost everyone here and wanted to learn as much as possible. And what she needed to know she would find out through conversation, not in how they acted between the sheets. As tasty as her cocktail was, she sipped slowly, and when she glanced Noah's way she noticed he was still on his first drink. He and Ted stood to the side in a fairly serious conversation. Steve didn't pursue her further, instead seeming content to molest Joanna at the bar. Rain made herself comfortable on the couch with the women, while Butch plopped his stocky rear on the solid-looking coffee table and wrapped his arm around Susie. She looked like a small child as she relaxed against him.

"I wonder what happened to Elaine and Oscar?" Brandy asked, and then finished off her wine.

"Maybe she couldn't find another dress to wear," Jan offered, and started giggling.

"Oh, hon, be nice," Brandy said, although she snickered, too.

"Elaine spilled catsup on her dress right after she got here," Jan told Susie. She got up and walked behind the bar, then returned with a box of wine. Refilling her glass and then Brandy's, she placed the box next to Butch at the edge of the coffee table. "She was so upset when it was obvious we couldn't wipe out the stain. I'm sure it was a brand-new outfit."

"It was a beautiful dress," Brandy added. "Do you think we should call and check on her?"

"No." Susie spoke so quietly that it seemed odd when she answered with such conviction. "We'll give her a call tomorrow and make sure she is okay. And when you do, be sure and extend the invitation to our next event."

"Oh!" Jan bounced on her side of the couch and Rain

almost fell over against Jan. "Have you decided where our next party will be?"

Rain straightened, confused for a moment but sure she hadn't missed any of the conversation. Both Jan and Brandy watched Susie like every word that might come out of her mouth needed to be put to memory. Butch rubbed Susie's bony shoulder with his thumb and looked down at her with fondness. Maybe Rain's first impression of Susie was premature. Her large eyes and gaunt, petite figure sure made her look like the mousy, neglected housewife. And although she still looked that way, along with her soft-spoken words, everyone looked at her like she was the decision maker of the group.

"I think it would be wonderful to have our next gathering at Rain's house."

Rain blinked and looked quickly at Susie. "My house?"

Susie's large eyes still looked spooked, but there was something else lingering behind her timid-appearing demeanor, something Rain swore wasn't there before.

"I'll have to get back with you on that," Rain offered politely. "We're still unpacking and organizing. I'm not sure we're ready for a party."

"It will be a month from now. That is enough time, don't you think?" Again those large eyes seemed to glow with something that was hard to label.

If Rain hadn't watched Susie all evening, seen how she almost jumped when her husband touched her, she would guess the look was sinister. Could this petite little thing aim a gun at someone's head and pull the trigger?

"Joanna helped decorate this room," Jan told Rain. Jan gestured by holding out her wineglass, but when some dribbled over her hand she brought the glass to her mouth and downed half of it. "She's an incredible interior decorator."

"And Patty can pull up homes on the Internet that are offering virtual tours. It's a wonderful way to get decorating ideas." Brandy frowned. "Didn't you say she told you she was on her way over a couple hours ago?"

"Elaine told me that when she first arrived. Patty called her right after she left a showing." Jan looked down at her glass for a moment and then focused on Susie. "Maybe Patty and Elaine and Oscar hooked up without the rest of us," Jan suggested, making it sound like to do so would be akin to a criminal act.

"You'll find out tomorrow when you call. Elaine and Oscar are new to our group. We won't take offense to any of their actions." Susie straightened and pressed her hands into her lap, almost looking pristine. "I can't imagine why Patty isn't here, though."

Brandy made a coughing sound and stood, and Butch looked up at her, frowning. She patted his head and then reached for Susie's empty glass. "Hon, may I get you another drink?"

"Yes, thank you." She rested her hand on Butch's leg when his wife left to go to the bar. "This is a very good party, Jan."

Jan looked like someone just handed her an award. "Thank you," she said on a breath, and drank more of her wine. "You're having fun, aren't you, Rain? And where is your husband?" She turned and looked at Ted and Noah standing over by the stairs. "Why are you ignoring me, Ted?"

Rain swore Jan's husband scowled at his wife. The two men walked over to join them, though. She glanced over at Steve and Joanna and noticed Joanna's dress was now hiked up and she was completely naked from the waist down. She sat on a bar stool with her legs wrapped around Steve. Rain didn't care enough as to what the two of them might be doing and returned her attention to those around her when Ted reached for his wife, pulled her to her feet, and then took her place on the couch. Jan looked ready to berate him some more, but he pulled her onto his lap. Rain wasn't sure whether she should move or stay put when she noticed Noah put his hand over his shirt pocket.

He met her gaze as he pulled out his beeper.

"Don't tell me you're on call or something," Ted said, looking up at Noah.

Ted ran his hand down Rain's bare leg and adjusted Jan on his lap. "Don't you dare let him drag you away from us so early," he said lightly.

"Hopefully a phone call is all I need to make." Noah pulled his cell off of his belt and didn't offer any more explanation as he headed up the stairs.

Rain itched to follow him. She couldn't think of any good reason why Noah would be paged, but if his supervisor was calling out of warped curiosity, Rain wanted to be there when he talked to her. Rain would swear Brenda felt a bit too protective of Noah, not only from what she'd overheard during their conversation after their first night at the house but as well from when Brenda grew so unreasonable during their meeting at the station. It was as if she searched for a reason to insist Noah be assigned to someone else on this case.

Rain patted Ted's hand and then stood, working her way around legs until she reached the stairs. She ignored Steve when he turned around, with a raging hard-on creating a tent in his pants.

"We'll be back down in a moment," she said, excusing herself and then hurrying up the stairs to find Noah.

ELEVEN

Noah glanced over his shoulder at the sound of someone approaching quietly behind him. It amazed the hell out of him how after he had moped over Laurel for months after canceling their wedding, Rain seemed to be creeping into space he swore no woman would ever get near again.

"What is it?" she whispered, her long dark hair sweeping over her bare shoulders. The strapless dress she'd tried on earlier and he'd insisted she wear tonight was by far the sexiest thing he'd ever seen a woman wear.

"I don't know yet." He looked over her shoulder, half-expecting at least the prick to show up and demand to know what was going on.

The light over the stove was on, and when he moved farther from the stairs to the basement, heading down a hallway, lamps in the living room provided the only other lighting on the main floor. He found the bathroom, though, and closed the door after Rain entered. Then lowering the lid to the pot, he sat on it, looking at her concerned expression while returning Brenda's page and calling her.

"We have a code blue," she said flatly, without bothering to say hello.

"Who? Where?" He glanced down at a heater vent in the floor. Voices from downstairs drifted through it. He didn't focus on what they said but instead tightened inside, waiting to hear the worst.

"The victim was identified as Patricia Sue Henderson. She was shot in the side of the head and found dead in her car at her place of residence."

"Son of a bitch," he hissed, and looked up at Rain, who stood with her arms wrapped around her waist like she would be sick. He knew he read concern on her face, though. *Patty is dead*, he mouthed.

"God damn it," Rain whispered, turning away from him for a moment and frowning at the wall. She glanced back at him, and he knew he read hope when she looked at him. "Are we going in?"

"We can't." He ached to scour the crime scene before the local police messed with it, but doubted they would make it in time. "There's no way we can be seen over there."

She nodded once and then walked out of the bathroom, leaving him alone when she closed the door.

"It appears the victim was just leaving," Brenda told him. "Her car was running and in neutral. She was shot once to the temple and was found dead in her driver's seat, head on the steering wheel, which kept the wheels from turning. But the car rolled out of the driveway and was blocking the road. The tires stopped against the curb across the street."

"And no witnesses? Have they matched a bullet?"

"Time of death is being marked at approximately eight this evening, pending the autopsy confirmation. None of the neighbors saw anyone unusual, or usual for that matter." Brenda sounded disgusted, but he felt her aggravation. People these days would run to their front porches to watch a fight, or a horrific storm, but ask them to notice anyone in their neighborhood who didn't live there and they were clueless. "There was a dish of fruit salad in the passenger seat and her cell phone shows she called two people within an hour prior to her being shot."

"Who did she call?" He glanced at the vent next to the toilet when a burst of laughter rang out downstairs.

More than likely, Rain had returned to the party, assuring everyone that Noah simply needed to take a call pertaining to work and would join them soon. He hated leaving her down there with those vultures, but so far she was holding her own pretty good. It was an odd group down there.

"The first number was a track cell phone, which can't be traced other than where it was purchased. That's being investigated right now. But the second number is registered to an Oscar and Elaine Phillips. Local police dispatched a car to their house to question them."

That explained why the couple didn't return to the party. And if time of death was around eight, both Joanna and the Porters showed up after eight. Everyone else was accounted for, except those names in the group who weren't here. Noah didn't know whether they'd planned to come, though, or not.

Noah glanced at his watch. It was almost ten thirty. "I'll touch base with you in about an hour."

"That's right. You're at your swingers' party tonight, aren't you?"

"Yup." He closed his eyes and pinched his nose, praying she wouldn't ask how he was handling it. Brenda hated Laurel for what she did to Noah, but then over the years Noah noticed Brenda didn't like any woman he al-

lowed into his life. It wasn't jealousy. There wasn't anything in Brenda's actions that ever suggested her interest
in him went anything beyond her claiming him to be one
of her best agents. But she was the protective mother hen.
"And I really shouldn't leave Rain alone too long with all
of them," he added.

"Anyone arrive after eight?"

"Several people."

"Is Rain enjoying herself in that environment?"

"About as much as I am. I need to go join her."

Brenda was silent for a moment. "Noah, be careful."

"I'm fine." He stood when music started downstairs.
"I've got to go."

"I know when you're fine and when you aren't," she
said quickly, her tone too smooth, too confident. "She's a
cop, Noah, from Lincoln, Nebraska. You're on a rebound
from a terrible falling-out. I worried putting you in this
atmosphere might be hard on you, but I needed my best
man for this one. Just don't let her get to you."

This time he hung up without saying good-bye, and
wondered if Brenda noticed that he'd picked up on her
lack of phone etiquette. He didn't want a lecture, though.
It pissed him off that she would cross that line and imply
that he'd done the same. There was nothing that he'd done,
or said, that could lead Brenda to think that Rain was getting under his skin.

Shoving his cell phone into his clip on his belt and
making sure the flat beeper in his shirt pocket was secure,
he opened the bathroom door. Steve Porter stood in the
dark hallway.

"Care to use my office?" Noah offered, stepping around
the cheap-looking man and heading toward the kitchen
and the stairs to the family room.

"Must suck to have to work on a Friday night."

"It's the price of success, I'm afraid, my friend," Noah
said all too cheerfully, deciding it would be more fun to
annoy the crap out of the pretentious pig than to release
his aggravation and get pissed at the creep.

"Success?" Steve wore more of Joanna's musky perfume than he did of his own cheap cologne. "Is that why you bought into a middle-class neighborhood?"

Noah turned in the kitchen doorway, and then wagging his index finger, he stepped toward Steve, taking his time in choosing his words.

"You know," he began confidentially. "I've learned that buying a home outright, instead of taking a mortgage, and then fixing it up and listing it again is a hell of a way to create extra income. Talk to me sometime if you're interested. Rain is excited to have Joanna help her with the redecorating, and I hear that Patty is a Realtor. I thought I'd let her list it here in a couple years. She's one hell of a hot lady, and successful, too, am I right?"

Steve stared at Noah a moment, obviously speechless. Then, leaning in the doorway, while music thumped loudly downstairs, Steve grinned in the darkness and started laughing.

"She's one hell of a hot little piece of ass. Just don't ever turn your back on her," he said, wagging his eyebrows. He rubbed his fingertips, which appeared nicely manicured, up and down the wedge in the doorway and glanced past Noah, as if someone else might sneak up just to eavesdrop on them. "I can arrange for you to spend time with her, or Joanna, whenever it fits into your schedule. I've been thinking about pulling some new blood into our group as well, so if you've got any kinks, let me know, and I'm sure I can find the perfect partner for you."

Noah nodded and turned again as if to leave. "The wilder and more submissive, the better. But in case you haven't noticed, I already have the perfect partner. Rain and I don't do anything without each other."

"I'd keep a short leash on her if she were mine, too," Steve added easily. "The hotter they are, the more coveted. And we're all human; sometimes sampling a delicacy is too hard to pass up, even if we aren't supposed to."

Steve nodded once, his expression sobering, and then turned into the bathroom, closing the door quietly behind him. Noah got the strongest urge to punch the guy's lights out. The epitome of a fucking creep, and with just enough balls to admit he was one.

Noah understood that Steve had just told him that if he had half a chance he'd fuck Rain, whether Noah was around or not. He wondered if Steve would rape her, and then pushed all doubt out of his mind. Anyone willing to openly confess they had no scruples would do whatever they wanted for their own gain. Possibly even murder.

Old disco thumped loudly, causing the banister to vibrate when Noah held on to it and paused at the bottom of the stairs. Brandy, Joanna, and Jan were dancing topless, with Ted and Butch gyrating around them and all of them laughing and appearing not to have a care in the world. Joanna would be the only one in that group who could be named a suspect in Patty's murder. He watched her until she spotted him and then pulled away from the group, sashaying toward him with her breasts barely bouncing as she held her hands over her head.

"See anything you like?" she yelled into his ear after practically falling into him when he stepped off the stairs.

"Plenty," he said, grinning at her pleased and satisfied expression.

Joanna wrapped her arms around him, pressing her bare breasts against his chest, but then looked over his shoulder. He watched her expression change. Was it fear, loathing, that he saw? Whatever emotion hit her when she saw Steve returning to the party, it disappeared quickly.

Noah didn't force her to choose but stepped to the side. He doubted she noticed him remove her hands from behind his neck and practically hand her to Steve. If Noah let her continue to cling to him, or even responded to her teasing, Steve would strut right on over to Rain. And that wasn't going to happen.

Rain sat on the coffee table next to Susie, and the two appeared engaged in a serious conversation. They were huddled close, their faces inches from each other, to be heard over the music. More than likely Rain had watched

Joanna meet Noah at the bottom of the stairs, even though she didn't look at him now. When he walked over to join them, she looked up and then stood.

"Susie wants this party to be at our house next time," Rain whispered into his ear.

Noah ran his hands down her back and then cupped her ass. He moved his mouth over her cheek to her ear, and then nibbled her lobe. The chill he gave her was so noticeable that he was instantly hard.

"Sounds like a blast," he whispered, and then pulled his head back far enough to stare into her face.

Her expression bordered on comical, and he fought the urge to laugh. If he didn't know better, he'd guess she wasn't having that much fun. Granted, they were among some of the most bizarre company he'd ever encountered. Picking a murderer out of this crowd was going to be one hell of a challenge.

It wasn't hard to convince Rain to leave. They'd stayed at the party to the point where fornicating was going to start at any moment. That wasn't why they were here. His ears were ringing when they headed to the rental car, and he desperately needed a shower to remove the perfume that clung to his clothes.

"I think the first thing we should do is create notes, writing down everything we know about each of these people," Rain said, speaking for the first time since they left the party.

"Sounds good." At the sidewalk, he glanced up and down the street and took Rain's arm when a couple approached. "How's it going?" he asked, announcing their presence.

Rain obviously was lost in thought, possibly already mulling over the mental list she'd created, because she looked up quickly.

"We're sorry if we startled you. I don't think we've met. I'm Oscar Phillips and this is my wife, Elaine. Is the party over already?" Oscar sounded weary yet smiled and glanced toward the house. "Honestly, I'm not sure why we returned."

As his words faded out, his wife, Elaine, looked up at him and then squeezed his arm. She offered Noah and Rain a pleasant smile. The couple were possibly in their mid-forties but attractive looking. If Noah didn't already know they'd had an evening from hell, he possibly wouldn't have guessed how distraught they were at the moment.

"No, the party isn't over," Rain offered. "If Noah didn't have to get up and head out to work in the morning, we'd probably stay longer."

"We know that one," Elaine said, smiling. "I'm sorry we didn't get a chance to visit with the two of you. Have they announced where next month's party will be yet?"

Rain shook her head, making a coughing sound. "Well, Susie suggested that it be at our house," she began.

"Wow. You must have made an impression. She hasn't chosen our home yet for the parties. And dear, that wasn't a suggestion. Susie says where the parties will be every month. We will all be at your home." Elaine actually looked envious.

"Well, we haven't confirmed yet," Noah explained.

Oscar scowled, looking at Noah like he didn't quite understand what Noah just said. "Are you not going to stay with our group?"

"Huh? No. That isn't what I meant. We had a really good time tonight. Both of us hated leaving." Noah studied the couple, noting when both of their faces relaxed at the same time and they again smiled. Their confusion when he said he and Rain hadn't confirmed next month's party was odd. But then the whole lot of them were odd. "We'll be at next month's party no matter where it is."

"If Susie says the party is at your house next month, it's at your house," Elaine said. "You don't tell Susie no."

"You're kidding, right?" Rain laughed and then crossed her arms against a swift breeze that brought a hard chill to the air. "What's there to say no to? Susie is so quiet, she barely uttered a word. You make it sound like she rules the roost or something."

"I wouldn't talk about her that loudly," Elaine said, fluttering her hands in front of her as if to hush both of them.

Oscar quickly wrapped his arm around his wife and tucked her in against him. "Don't let Susie fool you," he said quietly. "And please, please don't ever cross her."

Elaine looked up at her husband quickly, her lips parting as if she would speak. Oscar looked down at her and made a shooshing sound, then took her hand in his while still holding her.

"It's okay," he whispered to her. "We can say that much. I don't see any harm in that. They're new and we're helping them understand."

"Who's to say where harm lies?" Elaine whispered, suddenly sounding terrified.

"Is everything okay with you two?" Noah asked, wondering if they would bring up Patty.

"Fine. We're fine." Oscar answered too quickly, making it grossly apparent everything was far from fine.

"We should go in now," Elaine said. She glanced from Noah to Rain, her smile so forced it was hard not to press further as to what bothered them. But already she pushed her husband toward the house. "Hopefully we'll be in touch before next month's party."

Noah watched the two of them hurry toward the house, damn near running and then disappearing into the shadows along the side of the house as they headed around back.

"My God," Rain said, exhaling, and then walked out of his arms and around to the passenger side of the rental.

Rain didn't say much on the ride to their house, which apparently now they had a month to turn into a home. Noah prayed the case would be solved long before that.

He learned years ago never to assume the obvious was true. But if it was, there were only a few suspects who could have killed Patty. And the logical guess would be, find that killer and they had their murderer for the previous crimes. Then they would learn why the Swinging Killer in Lincoln was imitating the murders occurring in Kansas City and in Dallas.

Rain pulled out her phone and punched a number into it without saying anything. "This is Detective Rain Huxtable. My ID number is four-six-two-four-five. I need Detective Al Gomez's personal cell-phone number, please."

Rain shot him a quick glance before adjusting her phone between her ear and her shoulder. "Repeat that, please? . . . Yes. Two-five-five-four. Got it." Slapping her phone shut, she looked at him again. "Take me to the house so I can change, then let's see if we can't at least go take a look at Patty's car. It's already been impounded, so we should be safe."

It was midnight when they pulled outside a well-locked privacy fence to the wrecker service that had towed Patty's car. Rain jumped out on her side, now wearing jeans and a sweatshirt and tennis shoes. Her hair was still pulled back in the ponytail, though, and floated down her back when she walked ahead of him with the tow truck driver, who spit chew as he willingly rambled on about being called to go get Patty's car.

"We get calls like this every now and then," he told Rain, and then reached for the lock that secured all of the vehicles behind the large wooden fence. "I had to take this one personally, since I knew PD needed someone there ASAP."

"Where was the car when you got there?" Rain asked, stepping out of the way when he started opening the gate.

"It had rolled out of the driveway and was blocking over half the road. That's a pretty nice part of town over that way. You got the address?"

"Yes. We've got it," Noah told him.

The wrecker driver looked Noah's way, nodded once, and then aimed and spit behind Rain. Then flipping on a heavy-duty flashlight, the driver gestured with it as he headed into his lot.

"When I got there, the body was gone. There isn't much blood inside the car. You should see some of the suicides I've picked up. Blood and brain matter splattered all over the place. I reckon this lady wanted to go in style."

Noah didn't comment on the man's assumption that it was a suicide, and Rain remained quiet as well.

"You mind if we borrow your flashlight for a moment?" Rain asked the man.

"Well . . ."

Rain quickly pulled out her badge and flipped it open, then shoved it into the light from the flashlight. "We're not going to remove anything from the vehicle. We just want to take a look."

"That's fine." He smiled at Rain and let her take his flashlight.

He then looked Noah's way when Rain headed toward the car. A patrol car pulled up behind where Noah had parked their rental, and Al hopped out, then hurried to join them.

She held her badge up for the wrecker service owner to see but focused her attention on Noah. "You two are quick. When Rain called me to find out where the car was towed, I figured I had at least twenty minutes. Have fun at your party?"

She grinned easily at him, and he imagined that very little upset or got past the spunky, short cop.

"You should go with us next time," he said, and managed not to crack a smile when her eyes widened. He turned before allowing her response time, and followed Rain through the maze of cars.

"That's it." Al also carried a small flashlight and raced it from one end to the other of the pristine-looking Mazda RX-8. "New window and she'll be good as new."

"I'm sure her next of kin will be thrilled to hear that," Rain said dryly, and then turned to look at Al. "I need gloves."

The three of them traipsed back to Al's patrol car,

pulled latex gloves out of the trunk, and then, donning them, returned to the car.

"You all going to be that long?" The tow truck driver rubbed his head and then made a show of yawning loudly. "The cops have already been all over that thing. What do you have to do to it?"

"We won't be long." Noah only gave the guy a moment's attention. The three of them could take as long as they wanted, and there wasn't anything he could do about it.

Obviously the guy knew that. He mumbled something and then walked over to the gate, leaving them to their work.

Noah caught up with Rain and reached for the flashlight.

She clamped down on it. "You get to drive. I get to hold the flashlight," she grumbled.

"Fine," he told her, itching to stroke a loose strand of hair that had escaped her ponytail away from the side of her face. Instead he wrapped his hand over hers and aimed the flashlight at the driver's side door. "See how far the window is rolled down? Patty recognized her killer and started rolling her window down to talk to them."

"That or she simply already had it cracked for air," Rain said slowly, but then wrinkled her nose as she returned her focus to the car door.

"I'm betting I'm right." He held her hand firmly, both of them clasping the flashlight, and led them up to the side of the car. "You knew her better than I did."

"After a thirty-minute conversation," Rain added, and tugged on the flashlight as she opened the car door. Pulling harder while leaning into the car, she pointed with her free hand at the controls on the dash. "The air conditioner was on. Possibly you're right. She didn't strike me as a fresh air over air-conditioning kind of gal."

"I arrived at the scene," Al offered. She stood on the other side of Rain and scanned her light over the front seat. Glass particles were scattered over both leather seats. "And you're right. The car was still running when I got there."

"I want pictures," Noah told her.

"No problem. I'll e-mail them to Rain in the morning." She scanned her beam over the back of the car. "When I arrived, the victim was in the front seat with her head resting against the steering wheel. She wore a cocktail dress, and with the covered dish in the passenger seat," she added, shifting her flashlight beam to show the dish still sitting there, "it appeared she was leaving for a party."

"Yup. Anyone do measurements on the exact height that the bullet entered the window?"

"I'll check the report." Al studied his face. "Why do you ask?"

Noah pointed to the window. "She was shot in the side of the head. If the bullet entered here," he said, pointing his hand like a gun and aiming it at the window, "she would have been sitting upright."

"It didn't enter her forehead, but her temple. Whoever shot her . . . she wasn't looking at them."

"And the window wasn't rolled down very far," Rain added. "So either the conversation had ended or they were able to approach her by walking in her front yard, with her not noticing."

"If the bullet entered more around here." Noah moved his finger, drawing a circle in the air near the front of the window closer to the steering wheel. "She would have been leaning forward, possibly starting the car, adjusting mirrors. But if it entered back here, she would have been reclined in her seat, which is more of a position meaning the person is prepared to drive. What gear was the car in when you found it?"

"It wasn't in gear. When we found her it was in neutral and I'm pretty sure no one touched it prior to my arriving. Witnesses standing at the scene all concurred with that fact. They saw the car, that a violent act had just occurred, and called into nine-one-one on their cell phones. Two calls came in around the same time, more than likely once the car was spotted blocking the road."

"Why would she be sitting in her car, with it running, and in neutral, and not doing anything?" Rain asked.

"Maybe she was speaking with her killer, had just finished the conversation, started rolling the window up, and she was waiting for them to leave so she could leave. She was running late." Noah moved Rain's hand, training the beam on the interior of the car. He started around the car, taking Rain and the flashlight with him. "Looks like we missed out on a fruit thing," he added, aiming the light at the dish.

"Looks yummy," Rain said sardonically, her body brushing against his as he stood partially behind her and moved the flashlight with her over the interior, finally resting back on the dish. Other than the dish, the inside of the car was impeccably clean, shy of bloodstains, which were minimal.

Clear plastic covered a nice ceramic bowl that had some kind of fruit medley thing inside it. Other than glass flakes that appeared to have punctured some of the plastic, and the white powder that forensics used while checking the interior for prints, the dish Patty had prepared for the party was untouched.

"It looks like something someone would throw together who cares more about appearance than taste," Rain mused.

Noah bent over, letting go of the flashlight, looking inside the car, and Rain slowly squatted next to him. She pressed against his legs and her thick hair, which grew more and more disheveled as she continually tugged at it or combed it with her gloved fingers to keep it out of her face, touched his hair. He put his hand on the top of her head, ignoring the quick glance Al gave him when he touched Rain, and then stroked the back of her head.

"When I was upstairs at the Gamboas' and Steve Porter stopped me outside of the bathroom, he made a comment about parts of town."

"Yeah?" Rain balanced herself by pressing her hand against the floor of the car and glanced up at Noah. "What does that have to do with anything?"

"He said our home wasn't in a better part of town, but where Patty lived and apparently where he lives are the areas where the successful reside."

Al snorted. "Successful wannabes is more like it."

"Patty lives in a trendy part of town. The house we're in is stable middle-class, but certainly not a bad part of town by any means." Rain returned her attention to the interior of the car. "Patty probably lived the life of someone who was concerned the world saw her at the top of her game. This car, the bowl the fruit is in, the neighborhood where she lived, are all indications of a woman doing very well for herself."

"But Joanna's home, although simple on the outside, reeked dollar signs on the inside as well," Noah added.

"Where are you going with this?" Again Rain looked up at him.

"Maybe nowhere. I'm not sure. We're obviously seeing control issues with this group. We have one person who decides, with no need to create discussion, who will hold the next party."

"And it looks like whoever holds it is in a coveted position."

"Like you've fallen into good graces with the anorexic, brooding blonde," he said, and then moved the flashlight in Rain's hand so he could better see the dash. "As well, this group is very into appearances. Let's find out how much our Miss Patty was making annually. My hunch is she was living way beyond her means."

"Don't most people?" Al asked.

"Too many, probably," Rain answered before he could. "But if we have a competition going on over who rakes in the most, someone might not like it if they think someone else is passing them up."

"To the point of murdering?" Al shook her head. "Hell of a group of friends."

"You've got a point," Rain said, straightening and following Noah around the car. "It was very obvious tonight
at that party that everyone wanted to impress the Porters.
The couple who arrived when we were leaving almost appeared scared to voice any negative comments about
them."

On the way back to the house, Rain sat in the passenger seat, one foot propped up on the seat while she rested
her arm on her knee, chewing her finger while scowling
ahead.

"Any bets on who our guy is?" he asked, breaking the
silence and shifting his attention in the dark to take in her
contemplative expression and the way her dark hair draped
over her shoulder and parted, allowing him a very nice
view of the swell of her breasts.

She shifted with a start, as if she'd forgotten he was
next to her. "I was just thinking our motive might be a lot
simpler than we're making it," she said, ignoring his question. She scowled at him and still looked hot as hell with
shadows accentuating her facial features and her thick
lashes draping over her pretty blue eyes. Watching her at
work turned him on as much as seeing her in the skimpy
outfit she wore to the potluck. She kept going when he
didn't comment. "What if we simply have a case of a wife
who's been pushed too far?"

"Someone killing off her husband's lovers?" Noah
asked. "Then that husband must be going both ways. How
do we explain George Lapthorne's murder? And why would
these murders match the timing and profile of deaths occurring in two other cities?"

"That's what I was just thinking about," Rain offered,
shifting in her seat so she faced him, her seat belt strain-
ing down the middle of her sweatshirt and aiding in showing off her breasts. "If we have a pissed-off wife, why
would George have been killed? Unless maybe he knew
something. Maybe he caught one of the husbands in the
act of adultery and wanted to make a stink out of it. In a
world where image is everything, maybe he got himself

killed because he threatened to go public with what he'd seen."

"So we have an insanely jealous wife who would rather eliminate the partners in crime than prevent the crime from happening again."

Rain shrugged and then shook her head slowly. "The motive for murder is seldom any prettier than the act itself. But if it's true, we might also have an incredibly intelligent and sadistic wife who believed matching crimes occurring around the country might allow her to get away with her crime once the murderer was found in the other cities."

"There's another angle," Noah said, forcing his attention to the road.

"What's that?"

He was aware of Rain studying him while he stared at the quiet road ahead of them. "Maybe we're not looking at a wife, but a girlfriend. Possibly our murderer is a jealous lover, comfortable in her position, and unwilling to allow anyone to take that rank from her."

"Comfortable in her position, or *his* position," Rain said, and adjusted her body so she faced forward, once again assuming her brooding position.

TWELVE

Rain stared at the thermostat and seriously doubted the budget allotted for either her or Noah would cover sending someone out to look at the air conditioner. It was muggy as hell outside and twice as bad inside. She wished it would just rain and get it over with.

Noah squatted in front of the large-screen television, the manual on the floor next to him, and studied the remote while fighting to get the programming to work on the set. Rain didn't need to know him inside and out to know he was best left alone. God forbid she suggest he read the manual. And she was pretty sure it would be an even larger crime if she picked up the book and started reading it and advising him.

"Maybe when you're done with that you can look at the air conditioner," she suggested, staring at roped muscle, which rippled across his bare back. Or maybe she should just go up to him and slide her body against his. It might be tight and muggy in the house, but what better way to distract herself from the humidity than to enjoy his virile body? Spending time alone with him here in this house was becoming sheer torture.

"Hmm," he answered.

She turned, grabbing her hair and twisting it into a knot on top of her head. Then as she headed to the bathroom in search of a clip to get it off of her neck, her thoughts strayed to the night before. Noah had crashed before she did, leaving her to work on profiling each suspect. He'd made himself comfortable in the large bed, sleeping naked. When she finally crawled in next to him, he didn't move. Even though she'd stripped down and slipped under the cool sheet, she wasn't comfortable enough with him to cuddle up next to all that hard-packed muscle. Not that she didn't want to—Lord, it was torture not touching him. Rain was sure she'd toss and turn all night, and even prayed it would wake him up. But she'd been asleep in minutes. Noah was awake and showered before she got up this morning.

Rain stared at her face in the mirror, noting the glow on her cheeks and forehead from a sheen of perspiration. She contemplated applying a bit of makeup, some powder, to give her a fresher look, and then scowled as she adjusted her hair clasp behind her head. It felt a hell of a lot better with her hair off her neck.

Her father used to tell her repeatedly she was too pretty to hide under a mask of color and paint. She didn't need makeup, and any man who requested it was too shallow to see all the gifts she had to offer. Rain bought into it easily, never having been one to waste time primping.

She shifted her attention to the doorway, hearing Noah down the hall as he messed with the television.

"What would you have thought of him, Dad?" she whispered, returning her attention to her reflection in the mirror.

Boyfriends didn't hang around long while Rain was growing up. Her father held tight to strict rules, one being any boy, or man as she grew older, who wanted to take her out entered their home and faced the inquisition. No matter how many times Rain assured the men she was interested in who came around that her father didn't bite, eventually they quit calling. Her father always said good riddance. None of them met with his approval.

Heading down the hallway, she glanced in the empty bedroom facing the front of the house that they hadn't done much with yet. A car drove by slowly outside, looking as if it would stop at their house. Frowning, Rain walked into the room and stood in front of the window, then leaned to see the back end of the car as it reached the corner.

"Interesting," she mused, staring at the back end of what looked like a Miata. "Driving by to see if you can catch me home alone?"

She remembered then that the rental car was in the garage. Anyone driving by wouldn't know if either one of them was here. Rain hurried out of the bedroom and into the bathroom, applied the makeup she'd hesitated on a moment before, and then headed back to the living room.

"I'm going outside," she offered as she opened the front door, and then left it that way, not too surprised when Noah grunted something unintelligible.

She wore her pale yellow tank top and hip-hugging blue-jean shorts and was barefoot. She immediately felt awkward with the amount of makeup she'd applied.

"This is undercover work," she reminded herself, fighting the urge to run her finger over her eyelid and dull some of the eye shadow she'd applied. "You know damn good and well Steve Porter likes a good slut."

Which she wasn't. Not even close. One-night stands didn't exist in her world. Even after her father died. For the first time in her life at the age of twenty-eight she was living on her own. Work preoccupied her enough Rain didn't give a lot of thought to dating. She could count on one hand how many men she'd had sex with during her life.

Could Steve Porter even remember the names of all the women he'd probably fucked?

Noah would guess she had prettied herself up just for him, and it would be best for both of them if they kept their private time at the house on as much of a business level as possible. This was about saving lives, not creating a relationship. But if he questioned her, Rain's reasoning was sound. Steve Porter would expect (and be more impressed and more likely to continue talking to her) if she appeared the part and played the kind of woman he would chase.

"Okay, Mr. Porter, are you going to come around and double-check to see if the missus is home alone?" She walked barefoot down the cool sidewalk and tried to figure out what she could do out here to make herself look busy.

Halfway down the walk, she turned and faced the house, checking first and noting that the Miata, if that's what she saw, had already turned at the end of the block. Either he would drive back around the block or she came outside to simply allow the mosquitoes some free lunch.

She continued looking at the house, at the bushes growing alongside the front door all the way to the garage, and thought it would be smart to trim some of them back. Not that it would be a comfortable hiding space, but as thick and overgrown as they were at the moment, someone could hide in them and surprise anyone coming to the door.

The house was a simple ranch-style home, with a few others on the block having similar architecture. She hadn't noticed before, but as she looked now, there appeared to be three different types of houses on the block. She counted three two-stories, four that matched the layout of her house, and five that were like her home without the garage. Of those, three had built-on carports. It was all about keeping up with the Joneses.

Rain studied the four houses that looked like hers and then glanced back at the front of her house—or better yet the city's house, although paperwork had been adjusted to show Noah and Rain Kayne as the owners, just in case anyone got nosy and decided to learn whether they really owned their house or not. She pictured it with a fresh coat of paint, the bushes trimmed, and possibly shutters on either side of the windows, when a car turned onto the street at the end of the block—the opposite end of the block from where she just saw the Miata turn.

"Damn, I'm good," she muttered, turning slightly so it looked like she studied her home, but she could better see the silver Miata coming toward her.

As the car approached slowly, Rain walked over to the bushes and then bent over, offering him an enticing ass shot, and picked up a few loose branches that were underneath the bushes. There was more trash closer to the house, but she would have to go around the bushes to get it. She stood with branches in hand and headed to the garage.

The Miata pulled into the driveway as she reached the garage door. Steve got out, looking like he just won the lottery.

"Offer a view like that, sexy, and you're going to cause accidents." He was dressed similarly to the night before, still wearing his penny loafers and jeans. The wide-collared button-down shirt looked like something a tourist would wear on a trip to Hawaii: bright red, with orange and yellow birds printed on it. She wondered at the type of man who'd willingly put something like that on in the morning.

"Not on this road," she countered. "Only reason you'd

come down our street is if you meant to, or have a lousy sense of direction."

Steve laughed easily. "You're probably right about that." But then he didn't elaborate, as if his showing up obviously made her day.

Instead he followed her into the garage when she lifted the garage door. "Where's your husband?" he whispered, snaking his arm around her waist and pulling her backward against him. "You've got to be the hottest fucking lady I've seen in a long time."

"He's inside," she said, knowing if she said he wasn't here, then Noah would come outside.

She tried turning away from Steve, but he tightened his grip on her. "Sleeping?" he asked, and ran his hand up her front to squeeze her breast.

"Nope. He's setting up our new TV." She struggled in his grip and managed to point to the wall. "Right on the other side of that wall."

"Too bad," he whispered in her ear. "I'm dying to taste you."

She wasn't sure how to react. Her gut told her to elbow him hard in the stomach, force him to take his hands off of her, and possibly slam him to the ground just to make sure he understood how he was supposed to behave. More than likely doing that would send him away and she wouldn't have the chance to learn anything from him. Not to mention, she was supposed to be a swinger. Unless everything she'd read was fiction, swinging wasn't synonymous with cheating.

"That sounds good to me," she said, with her teeth clenched, and pried his hand off of her waist. She turned around to see amusement in his eyes. "But I don't play without my husband."

"Of course," he said so sweetly it was sickening. "Especially when he's on the other side of the wall," he added, whispering, and then winked at her.

The door from the kitchen opened and Noah stuck his

head out the door. "I thought that might be your car," he said, and stepped out so that all three of them stood alongside the car.

"I hear you've got a new TV." Steve didn't take his hands off of her but instead ran his hand down her hair. "I was just out here molesting your wife."

"I didn't hear her complaining." Noah's brooding expression wasn't readable when he moved closer.

"Neither did I," Steve said agreeably, and tried pulling Rain into his arms again.

She was ready for him this time and turned away when he reached for her. Noah's hands clamped down hard on her shoulders, pinching her skin and preventing her from moving closer to Steve. Unable to pull her to him, Steve settled on putting his hands on her waist and then moving closer to her.

"You're one of those greedy ladies, aren't you?" Steve said, once again using that sickeningly sweet tone. His hands moved underneath her arms and stopped at the sides of her breasts. "You want two men to yourself."

Rain blinked, suddenly incredibly aware of how close both men were to her, and their hands on her. In all truth, she'd known Noah less than a week. Granted she'd had sex with him and they'd accelerated and almost forced a relationship that she now fought from moving to a dangerous level. But Steve, regardless of whether he was a murderer or not, was a swinger. And he believed her to be one, too. She told him she wouldn't play without her husband, and Noah now stood right behind her.

She swallowed, and hated how dry her mouth suddenly was.

"Show me a lady who doesn't want two men to herself?" Noah mumbled from behind her, and then slowly caressed her shoulders with his thumbs.

"You've got that right," Steve said, looking past her at Noah. "Well, if you're interested, I'm your man."

Maybe she imagined it, but Rain swore Noah's body stiffened. Rain prayed silently Noah wouldn't push the situation. Just picturing doing anything intimate with Steve made her stomach churn. There had to be a better way to pry information from him without having sex with him.

Suddenly she needed to get out from between the two of them. She turned toward Noah but then pushed past him, using enough force when his hands moved down her body for him to back up.

"Today's not a good day," she announced, keeping her tone relaxed.

"You've heard already, haven't you?" Steve asked.

She turned around, her entire side pressing against Noah's body and the warmth from his bare chest scalding her arms and overheating her instantly.

"Have they come and talked to you, too?" Steve pressed, his attention shifting from her to Noah over her shoulder.

Rain focused on Steve, and realized possibly for the first time since meeting him she might be seeing the true man. His expression was hard, his black hair still impeccable but his dark eyes flat with something that looked a lot like hard-boiled outrage.

"Has who come and talked to us?" Noah sounded incredibly calm.

"The cops. I'm not going home until those bastards quit coming and sniffing around." Something changed in his expression and he focused on Noah, slow understanding making his mouth curve into an unpleasant-looking smile.

She planted a frown on her face as Noah guided her to the door leading to the kitchen.

"What do you mean?" Rain asked. "Why did the police come to your house?"

"Why don't we go inside," Noah suggested, continuing to push Rain through the kitchen door.

Steve came inside with them without hesitating. The television appeared to be working, with the news on the large screen and the box and manual lying spread out on the floor. Rain made herself busy picking up the dilapidated box while Noah and Steve stood around her watching.

"I guess you haven't heard then. Something terrible happened last night. We were all at the party, but Lincoln cops aren't the smartest tools in the toolbox," Steve offered, his voice again shifting and resuming its annoying sweet inflection.

Rain crunched the box, immediately aggravated by the man's presence and his dogging the local police. She was sure the stupidest man on the force probably ran circles in intelligence around this numbskull. She scowled at Noah, who had plastered a very neutral expression on his face while he stared somewhere at the floor in front of him.

"What happened?" Noah asked, not shifting his focus but ignoring Rain as she carried the empty box into the kitchen to the trash can just inside the garage.

"Patty—she's dead."

Rain turned around in the doorway to the kitchen, the box almost blocking her view of Steve. "What?" she hissed. "Patty, the lady who was over here the other day with Joanna?"

"Yup." Steve rocked up on his heels, as if proud to be the one to tell them the latest gossip. "Disgusting actually. She got shot in her car. More than likely she screwed someone on a deal on a house."

Rain turned and tossed the box toward the garage door in the kitchen. She couldn't throw it hard enough to relieve the irritation mounting inside her.

"That sounds pretty cold," she couldn't help saying.

"You didn't know Patty."

"Oh? Was she not a good person?" Noah asked.

"We're all good and bad, wouldn't you say?" Steve looked away from the two of them and glanced around the living room. "Why did Joanna and Patty come see you two?"

Noah glanced at Rain. She walked back into the living

room, moving around Noah, and then reclined in the corner of the couch.

"Butch told Joanna about us," Rain offered, shrugging. "They stopped by to welcome us to the neighborhood."

"Why were they supposed to come over?" Noah walked up to the TV and picked up the remote, which rested on top of it.

"They weren't," Steve said quickly.

Noah turned around, remote in hand, and studied Steve. Rain shifted her attention from one man to the other. If Steve just slipped and said something he suddenly felt he shouldn't have said, he gave no indication. That cocky, almost vindictive sneer was once again planted on his face.

"I don't know that they discussed coming over here with anyone prior to doing it," Steve added, sounding as if the two women acting without permission from someone broke some kind of rule. "So they welcomed you to the neighborhood?"

Rain nodded her head to the kitchen. "They brought me an African violet as a housewarming gift. Were they supposed to discuss that with someone prior to doing it?"

"We're a very tight-knit group and the single women are like family to all of us," Steve explained, sounding like he was repeating something to a child for the hundredth time. "Both of them have been told many times that if they're going to seek out swingers that we don't know, they need to let us know where and when they're going."

"For their protection," Noah added.

Steve turned around, pointing at Noah and nodding. "Exactly. Not that I'm saying either of you is dangerous."

"Of course not," Rain mumbled, imagining Steve ordering any woman he could get away with bossing around who she could see and when. More than likely it was why his wife looked like a beaten pup.

Steve didn't pick up on Rain's sardonic tone. "I'm sure

their coming over here had nothing to do with Patty getting killed."

"Why do you think she did get killed?" Rain asked, wondering if their coming over here might have broken a rule, which wouldn't be tolerated. She remembered Joanna's fearful look when she noticed the Miata in front of the house while they were here.

"Now, honey, I don't want you to go and start thinking that Lincoln is a dangerous town. You two have found a wonderful group of swingers. We're all like family." He turned to Noah, straightening and his expression hardening. "And like with any family, we aren't perfect. We all stick to the same rules and it keeps us close, happy, and comfortable with each other."

"What are those rules?" Noah asked.

"Nothing complicated. We stick to our group, no one strays, and that way there aren't any worries. There are enough of us in our group to keep everyone happy, even an old hound dog like me," he added, and then chuckled and turned to wag his eyebrows at Rain. "Now then, sweetheart, I don't want you getting all upset about this tragedy. I'll arrange for you to spend some time with Joanna. The two of you will make great friends."

"Honestly, as sad as it is that she's been killed, we didn't know her," Noah told Steve. "Of course we're upset. Someone is dead. That's horrible. If Joanna needs comforting, please let her know she's always welcome over here."

"I'm sure she is," Steve said coolly. Then tapping his finger over his lips, he stared at the floor for a moment, as if contemplating some deep thought. "They're trying to turn all of this into some sordid sex crime," he said quietly, sounding like he thought out loud. "Because Patty was a swinger, and with the others, the heat is on. But it's not because of us. Everyone who matters was at the party. You two were there. You know that and could vouch for all of our whereabouts."

Rain saw a hint of the pressure the investigators who

had questioned Steve obviously had applied. Because he speculated, either he wished to create alibis out of the two of them or he was innocent and needed answers to help him with his own mourning.

"She was killed while we were all at the potluck last night?" Rain asked, aching to pry more of whatever thoughts mulled around in that conceited brain of his.

"Yup. So none of the others did it. But since we're such a tight circle—"

"What others?" Noah interrupted.

Steve shook his head and then walked to the window. With his back to them, he stared outside. Rain and Noah waited out the silence with Noah glancing her way several times, although she couldn't read his thoughts.

"Several of our friends have been killed recently," Steve offered, his tone so flat he almost sounded remorseful.

"You're kidding," Rain whispered. "What's going on? Is there some serial killer in this town?"

"There must be!" Steve turned around quickly, as if Rain's question suddenly offered light to something he hadn't been able to figure out up until that moment. "You've met all of us. Do any of us seem like killers to you?"

"I've never met a killer before," she lied, but then offered a small smile. "But of course not. All of you were very friendly to both of us."

Steve's smile was so cold and dark it gave her chills. "Like a killer would tell you if he were one," he said, his baritone as disturbing as the heavy glare he gave her. "Patty and Joanna came over to warn you, didn't they?"

"Warn us about what?" If Steve thought he could intimidate her, he could damn well think again. She didn't look away from those dark eyes and wondered why Patty or Joanna would give him more than a second of her time.

"Not us, her," Steve told Noah, but then walked toward Rain until he stood over her. "You aren't going to upset me by telling me the truth. You'll see, sweetheart. Both of them can be so damn possessive. Well, I guess Patty isn't going to be too controlling anymore, now is she? But I know why they came over here. They wanted to check you out. And when they saw for themselves how drop-dead gorgeous you are, they warned you to steer clear of me. Didn't they?"

Rain fought the urge to laugh. "Neither one of them had anything bad to say about anyone," she said, and then feigned confusion and looked at Noah, as if seeking her husband's help in a situation she didn't understand.

Noah was there for her immediately. "You'll learn quickly that my wife doesn't have an ounce of jealousy or possessiveness in her. She's a gem," he added, walking over to the couch and then standing at the edge of it so that he could stroke her hair but still face Steve. "I wasn't here while the ladies were here, but if either lady threatened my wife in any way, I promise you, we wouldn't have been at that potluck. Rain has been swinging forever, and she doesn't waste her time with anyone who tries manipulating her good time."

"That's good to hear," Steve said, but then his face lit up, and as if the words slowly sunk through all that hair gel and finally reached his brain, he smiled and then nodded. "Very good to hear. I'm the same way, exactly. It's all about having a good time, right? Leave that goddamned luggage at the door, I always say."

"I promise you neither lady tried telling me who I could spend time with, or who I couldn't. Does that sort of thing happen in your group?"

"Not within the group. As long as no one strays, then we're all good. Other than that, we hold all of our events at each other's homes."

"I wondered about that. I hope it isn't rude to ask, but why does Susie decide where the party will be held each month?" Rain watched something pass over Steve's face. She swore he almost looked disgusted at the mention of his spouse. "Don't get me wrong," she added. "I was flattered when she suggested the party be here, but I'm not sure we're ready for socializing. Not for a couple months at least."

"It wasn't a suggestion. And believe me, anyone in the group would do anything to hold one of our gatherings in their home. Don't let her size fool you. When Susie says how something is going to be, that is how it is going to be. Joanna can help you get your home in order."

"I think what my wife is trying to say is that since she's here all of the time, holding it somewhere else would suit her better. Rain loves to get out of the house when she can," Noah said.

Although he made her sound like some kind of hermit, Rain guessed he pushed Steve to get more of an explanation as to the odd pecking order that seemed to be in place among these people.

"Brandy stays at home, too. I'm sure it would be fine to get to know her better. If you want to get out of the house, I know she would love the company. Jan works during the day, and Sheila works for an accountant. But both women would generously give you time on the weekend. We'll make sure you're out of the house as much as you want."

"Sheila?" Rain interrupted.

"Yes. She showed up after you two left last night. She needed to wait until her teenagers were home for the night before coming out. That's how she always is now that she's alone. Richard couldn't make it last night, but he will be here next month. Mark Hinders refused to attend the last party with no valid reason. He's not part of our group now and we won't have him at the next party."

"Some people can miss parties, but others can't?"

Steve's laugh sounded mechanical. "Of course not, sexy lady," he told her, his eyes not changing at all from their hard flatness as he explained party etiquette to her. "We're made of better stuff than blowing each other off, though. A blow job is one thing," he said, winking at her. "But if I plan an event, show the good grace to attend, or contact me and let me know that you can't make it, and why. Our parties are structured, and not just for anyone. If we invite you into our group, it means we see that you're made of the right stuff."

"I didn't know the cotillion existed in Lincoln, Nebraska," Rain muttered.

He wagged a finger at her and then turned and marched to the door. As much as they needed to get anything he might know out of him, Rain prayed he'd keep marching. But he turned again, and put his fists on his hips, giving her his undivided attention. With the top button undone on his shirt, the movement forced it open enough to reveal a glimpse of an incredibly hairy chest. Rain liked chest hair on a man, but the black curls only made Steve appear cheaper in her eyes.

"I'm sure things are different back east. I'm a Midwest boy myself, born and raised in Iowa and relocated here some years back. We pride ourselves on propriety. Only the best, and therefore a firm set of rules to make sure our group is always made of the top of the line. We don't accept white trash."

"We're hardly white trash," Noah growled.

"I can see that," Steve answered coolly, actually fool enough not to bat an eye at Noah's threatening tone. "And that's why you're now part of our group." He returned his attention to Rain and her stomach turned from the intensity of his cold stare. "Joanna will contact you and take you out so you don't grow restless and bored stuck here all the time."

He opened the door then, and closed it behind him when he left without uttering a good-bye.

"If he isn't killed next, then he's definitely our murderer," Noah said, walking around her to the door and then locking it.

"What an asshole," she muttered, and hopped up from the couch, every inch of her feeling itchy and dirty just from Steve's hands being on her. "And he didn't seriously just tell us if we don't go to their parties, then we're ostracized from their group?"

"Ostracized, but not killed," Noah said, turning around and pointing his index finger in the air. "Patty was headed to the party, and got killed. And Mark Hinders I believe is Lorrie Hinders' husband."

"I caught that. And I don't blame the guy for not wanting to attend these parties anymore." She rolled her shoulders and stared at the TV. "Looks like you got it working," she added.

"Yup. Nothing to it." Noah came up behind her and placed his hands on her shoulders, then started massaging, his fingers feeling like they were straight out of heaven. "You know why he wants you over at Joanna's, don't you?"

"Hmm . . . why?" She closed her eyes and let her head fall back as he continued rubbing muscles that she didn't know were sore until he applied his very skilled touch.

"Because he wants you alone, without me around, so he can fuck you without another man to have to share you with."

She opened her eyes and stared at him upside down. "Thanks for ruining my massage."

"Oh, you want him and you know it. Admit it, Rain."

She turned around quickly, aiming straight for the jaw. It surprised her that his reflexes were as fast as they were. And when he grabbed her fist, his fingers clamped down hard enough that she worried for a second he might break bones.

"You're good, Rain. Damn near one of the best." He pulled her to him so quickly she stumbled and then his arms were around her, his lips searing her flesh when he began feasting on her neck. "But my dear, you've met your match with me. If I catch you fucking Steve, or anyone, without me, I'm going to be pissed."

His last sentence broke the spell he'd too quickly put her under. And this time she didn't allow him a moment's notice to learn her actions. She spun around, punched him hard on his arm, hurting her fist when she hit incredibly solid muscle.

Noah straightened, and she quickly moved away from that virile body of his. His dark eyes burned with more emotion than she'd seen in them before.

"Suggest again that I'm low-life enough to allow such a despicable man to have his way with me and I'll kick your ass," she told him, and started for the hallway.

Noah lunged at her, his fingers scraping her back when she darted for the hallway. "I'm not talking about Steve Porter," he growled, making another attempt and managing to pull her backward into his arms.

All air left Rain's body when her backside slammed against Noah's chest. "I know what you're saying," she said, sounding breathless. "You think I would succumb to these married men's advances because in their world having sex with women other than their wives is allowed."

"Would you?" He held her in a death grip but then moved one hand up her front, between her breasts, until he cupped her chin and forced her to look over her shoulder at him.

"No," she whispered, her heart pounding way too hard in her chest, making it impossible to catch her breath.

Noah held her a moment too long, allowing her to drown in his gaze and see what she feared he possibly saw in her eyes. They were falling for each other. And after just a few days.

"Let me go," she added, and wasn't sure if she was relieved or regretted it when he obliged.

She felt light-headed when she hurried down the hall to the bedroom. They really needed to find their killer. Spending many more days under the same roof with Noah Kayne could very well prove more dangerous than hunting down a murderer.

THIRTEEN

Joanna was a hell of a lot more upset about Patty's death than Steve was. Rain hung up the phone and dragged her

fingers through her hair. It was tough consoling Joanna—
and understanding her while she cried over the phone. But
worse yet, now Rain knew the details concerning Patty's
funeral. She couldn't go back to Wright's Funeral Home.

"Patty Henderson's funeral is at the same funeral parlor—" She stopped, closed her eyes, and dropped her cell
phone next to the keyboard. "It's the day after tomorrow."

Patty's murder was terrible. There wasn't any such
thing as a good murder. But Rain didn't feel the sting of
loss for her the way she did for her father. She'd seen a lot
of dead bodies and investigated some atrocious murders,
but since her father died, talking to those left behind hit
her harder than it used to.

She cleared her throat and reached for her soda.

"I can't go to the funeral," she told Noah, feeling her
eyes burn from dryness when she looked up as he stood in
the doorway. She drank, willing the scratchiness in her
throat to disappear.

"Okay," he said slowly, tilting his head slightly while
watching her. "Do you want to tell me why?"

Rain drew a line with her finger around the name of
the funeral parlor. She'd written down the address also,
although she didn't need to. Rain knew exactly where it
was.

"I've been there before," she muttered, not really wanting to offer more.

"Isn't there a reception?"

"Yes." Her vision blurred as she stared at the information Joanna gave her. "Her family is actually holding
the reception at her home. Joanna didn't approve. She said
they're probably going to spend the entire time they're there
taking pictures off the wall and going through all of her
silver and other valuables."

"Funerals are a blast."

Rain picked up her pen and doodled on the notepad,
thinking just the opposite. They sucked. There wasn't any
greater pain than the person you loved more than yourself
being yanked away from you.

"What's wrong, princess?" Noah asked quietly.

For a moment, she almost thought her father had asked the question.

Rain stood up quickly, unwilling to allow the pain to resurface. "I told you never to call me that," she said, feeling deflated but then hugging herself when she started trembling.

Noah didn't move to her, which she silently thanked him for. He remained relaxed, his large frame leaning against the doorway, where he'd been standing ever since the call came through from Joanna. With his arms crossed over his bare chest, the sex appeal radiating off of him created a raw tingling that mixed with the agonizing pain inside Rain.

"Why don't you like me calling you princess?" he finally asked, his dark, probing gaze giving her the impression she was all that was on his mind. More than likely, he had bestowed many women with that look over the years.

She couldn't allow herself to fall for Noah. If her dad were still alive, he probably would have thrown a fit about her living with Noah in this house, even if it was undercover work. But then her father always kept her on a pedestal, especially since it was just the two of them. Rain didn't have a lot of memories from when her mother was still alive, other than her hugs were warm and comforting and she never yelled. Rain's father yelled all the time, but never at her.

Rain shook her head, willing memories of her dad to go back into the comfortable spot where she kept them, and where they wouldn't bring her pain. "Because I told you not to, repeatedly. It's not a complicated request. Why can't you follow simple instructions?"

She marched toward him in an effort to leave the room. Instead of moving, he tried taking her into his arms. But her insides were too raw. Memories of her father's funeral, of that funeral parlor, of all the people who showed up and told her again and again how wonderful he was, bit at her repeatedly until she just wanted to run.

Noah touched her bare arms and then stroked her flesh until he gripped her wrists. If she couldn't run, striking out worked, too.

"Stop it," she yelled, yanking her hands back and then pounding his chest.

Noah still didn't move. "Stop touching you? Or stop calling you princess?"

"Don't mock me. It just makes you look like an idiot." She shoved hard against his chest, knowing she wasn't making a lot of sense. But damn it, she didn't have to reveal to him the pain and loss she still endured over her father. She'd never shown anyone that pain. Just because she and Noah were forced to remain together 24-7 didn't mean she needed to open up to him that much.

When he still didn't move, she backed up a step and squared off, imagining throwing him backward. Anything to exert enough energy to cleanse her insides and free the rising pain that would make her cry if she didn't release it through anger. "Get the fuck out of my way, Noah."

"I don't think so. You're not making sense. Until you tell me what suddenly crawled up your ass, I'm not budging."

"It doesn't work like that. I don't have to tell you shit. Now move!" Again she went after him, shoving hard, and this time forcing him to move backward a step.

"Rain, stop," he said, his voice still annoyingly calm.

"Quit telling me what to do." She raised her fists and he grabbed her arm.

Rain couldn't hold it in any longer. She hated him at that moment. His calm resolution, his continual efforts to console and be there for her, and his stubborn refusal to quit calling her princess made him as strong as her father. As perfect as her dad. And she couldn't let Noah have that rank. If she did, he would replace her father.

And then she might risk loving him. Rain couldn't handle loving and losing again.

Noah forced emotions she would just as soon keep buried to come forward. And they did, like a goddamned avalanche. Rain was slightly aware of her hair clasp sliding down the back of her head when she spun around and tried kicking him.

She had training—a hell of a lot of training. At the moment, it didn't bother her a bit that Noah had at least as much knowledge in aggressive maneuvers and self-defense. If anything, striking out at someone who could defend himself, could fight as well as she could, and wasn't weak helped more than Noah would ever know.

Rain attacked furiously, blinded by rage, and feeling only a bit of warped satisfaction when she connected with hard flesh. Her adrenaline peaked quickly, and all of her buried feelings for her father surfaced. Beating the crap out of Noah, telling herself he needed to be put in his place, would show her he didn't have what it took to fill the void left from her father.

"Rain," he said several times, dodging her blows at first.

She didn't want nice. She didn't want compassion. "Fight back, motherfucker," she hissed.

"Damn it, woman," he growled.

"What? Going to let a cop kick your ass?" She pulled out of his grasp and directed a blow straight to the kidneys.

"Nope. But I'm not going to hurt you, either." Again he successfully dodged her attack.

"You've already hurt me." She leapt at him, using all of her weight to try to knock him backward.

Noah caught her in mid-leap and then threw her over his shoulder. Then lunging forward, he tried entering the bedroom. Rain let go of him to grab the doorway frame, but Noah didn't release her.

"We're not going there, asshole," she said, her teeth clenched while her fingers burned against the door frame that she fought to hold on to.

"We're going wherever we need to go so that you'll quit attacking me and start explaining."

He flipped her over, like he would throw her to the ground, and her loose hair blinded her. Before she could balance herself or grab ahold of him, Noah caught her, crushing her against his chest and damn near folding her in half as he entered the bedroom. And then not too lightly, he threw her onto the bed.

She bounced off of the mattress and barely managed to not fall off the bed. The adrenaline crashed inside her. His hard expression was lined with concern and worry, not anger, and that was her undoing.

Looking down and breathing heavily, she adjusted herself until she sat cross-legged and then dropped her head into her hands. Noah's strong, warm arms were around her in a second and he pulled her against him.

"How have I hurt you?" he asked gently, way too gently for a man with the strength to lift someone her size into the air and throw them.

"Stop it, Noah. It doesn't matter."

"Yes. It does. Tell me." He crawled onto the bed and tried pulling her onto his lap.

Rain backed away from him. The tears were there. She hated crying. Hated it more than anything. Her father didn't want her to cry. He probably hated it more than she did. The only time he ever walked away from her was when she cried. If she didn't cry, he would be there.

But he wasn't there. And he never would be again.

"My father." God. How did she get here?

She didn't want to talk about her father. Dad was gone. She was alone. That was simply how it was.

Noah touched her. His fingers were warm, soft, and she ached to curl into him, lean against all of that strength. But the tears . . .

"Just don't call me that anymore."

"Your father called you princess."

The tears burned her cheeks. They fell without invitation and wouldn't stop. Rain wanted to die. She wanted to disappear and flee to somewhere the pain wouldn't be able to touch her.

His arms were around her, strong, powerful, and comforting. Time flew backward and for a moment her father hugged her, taking the pain from some childhood agony away while saying soothing words that helped form her into the woman she was today.

But her father wasn't holding her. Noah's strength and unique smell, a faint aroma of Irish Spring and Old Spice, filled her lungs with every breath she took. His heart beat solidly against her while he wrapped her tighter into a hug that would make it hard to breathe, if she fought him. But there wasn't any fight left. The tears were here. And in spite of how much she loathed crying, they wouldn't stop.

It took a few minutes before she could quit crying, but humiliation and yelling at herself to get tough helped a bit. Her cheeks were damp and she knew her eyes had to be puffy and bloodshot, but when she tried pulling away from Noah he tightened his grip on her.

"The other morning when I checked in at the field office and morgue and talked to Brenda on the phone, she told me you were the daughter of one of the best detectives in the Midwest. Double H, huh?"

Rain attempted a laugh at the mention of her father's nickname. It came out sounding more like a loud exhale. "Hugh Huxtable. He thought his first name sucked, and a lot of people called him Double H," she said, and tried pulling away from Noah again.

He loosened his grip on her but then reached around and pulled out the loose hair clip. "I heard that in spite of his great track record, he continually fought with child services over you."

Rain felt a wash of embarrassment flood over her still too-sensitive psyche. "I was a pain-in-the-ass kid."

"Imagine that," he said dryly. "So it wasn't because he fought for you in custody battles?"

Rain looked up, surprised, but then quickly looked away again, imagining she probably looked like shit. "God, no. Dad worked long hours, and although he kept me in day care when I was younger, when I was in high school he thought chores would keep me out of trouble. I hated him during that period of my life for being a cop. I couldn't go anywhere, or do anything—or at least I thought—without the law breathing extra hard down my neck."

"We take care of our own."

God damn him for repeatedly saying things her father used to say. She managed to crawl off of the bed and headed for the bathroom. Noah was on her ass, though, and leaned, once again, in the doorway while she splashed water on her face.

"Dad used to say when it rained, it poured, meaning that I couldn't do anything without taking it to the extreme. If a bunch of us kids wanted to TP a house, I would be the one organizing the army, and arming us with not only toilet paper but chalk for messages on the sidewalk, and eggs, and anything else I could think of." She patted her face with the towel and then surveyed the damage in the mirror. Let him watch if he wanted, but she was going to put herself back together. She grabbed foundation and blush out of the medicine cabinet. "Mom died from cancer when I was pretty young, and although I remember crying forever, Dad kept us together, and wouldn't let anyone take me from him."

And it wasn't fair that he was taken from her. She found that spot deep inside where she could stuff her painful emotions, and promptly put them there. Then patting her face with powder, she managed to dull the puffiness under her eyes.

"So what about the story about your name?" Noah looked fascinated watching her apply makeup.

His eyes no longer looked full of pity when she focused on him but instead glowed with that intensity that would get her in trouble if she stared at him for too long. She returned her attention to the mirror and grabbed her brush.

"Story," she muttered, drawing a blank, but then it hit her. "Oh shit. You mean the one I told Steve about why I was named Rain?" The sudden urge to laugh hit her almost too hard. Noah would think her an emotional seesaw wreck if she didn't clamp down on her reaction to everything. "It was a lie. My dad loves rainy days, always has. They named me Rain because when it rained, it always made him happy."

Noah walked into the bathroom, crowding her between the sink and toilet. It crossed her mind to try to escape, but he was already there. She looked at his reflection, shocked when he took the brush from her hand and then started pulling it through her hair.

"I lost my dad a few years ago," he told her, glancing at her reflection while he brushed her hair for her. "We never got along and I hated going to his funeral. He was a true bastard, but I still wished it had been different. You're lucky to have such wonderful memories."

"They don't feel wonderful."

"How did he die?"

"In the line of duty," she said, finally feeling numb. Her scalp tingled, though, as Noah brushed her hair, and his free hand pressing against her shoulder was warm. She watched his face in the mirror. He looked so serious while he focused on brushing her hair. "He was so close to retiring. When the doctors told him he had cancer, I was positive he'd turn in his badge. But not Dad. Not Double H. He endured the pain, and I know it was becoming too much for him. But I liked him strong. Dad was invincible. No one could take him down. And, I believed, not even cancer."

She sighed, closing her eyes and enjoyed Noah brushing her hair. He didn't say anything, and he didn't stop brushing. Rain blinked, her eyes dry, the tears once again gone, leaving her empty inside.

"I was working on a different case and he'd wanted to meet for dinner. We did that a lot, bounce ideas off of each other and brainstorm while both of us tried solving our cases. Dad was growing more and more tired. I know others noticed. But no one dared try and stop Double H. He didn't sound good when he called, but he told me to meet him at his favorite restaurant, Montana Mike's. But

I'd just got a call, and couldn't meet him. He decided to return to a crime scene and ran into his perp while there. The guy fired first, but Dad fired last."

Noah met her gaze in the mirror. "He get him?"

She nodded, praying her dad died knowing he got his man. "Both were DOA."

"Damn." Noah put down the brush and then pushed her hair over her shoulders so that it tumbled over her breasts. "And you were his princess."

Rain couldn't decide whether her father would love Noah or think him a pompous ass. Oftentimes men who knew other men who acted just like they did hated each other's guts.

"I still am," she whispered.

"He was a lucky man," Noah told her, his voice suddenly more gravelly than it was a moment before.

She felt his cock stir against her ass and her breath caught in her throat. At the same time, her insides responded with a fierceness that matched the strength of her emotions. Instantly she swelled with need and his hands, which now caressed her arms, scalded her flesh as desire ripped through her.

All she needed to do was turn around and she could fuck him. As much as she knew having sex with him would complicate things even further, it wouldn't take any effort at all to gain the relief she suddenly craved.

It took a moment for her to realize her cell buzzed in the other room.

"Saved by the bell," Noah muttered, backing off and allowing her space to move.

"Fuck you," she grumbled.

"It crossed my mind."

His words sizzled in her brain and suddenly it was way too hot in the house. And it wasn't from a malfunctioning air conditioner. She hurried into the bedroom, grabbed her phone, pushed the button to answer, and turned around to run into Noah.

"Hello," she said, tightening her grip on her phone so it wouldn't go flying when she slammed into his rock-hard chest.

"Huxtable, I think I found something." Al's scratchy voice was brimming with excitement.

"Yeah? What do you got?"

"Are you secure?" Al asked.

Rain scowled. Her cell phone was department issued and had been on her every minute, other than when she and Noah were at the potluck, and then it was locked in the car. She made a habit of disassembling and reassembling it when she charged it.

"Go ahead," she decided, seriously doubting anyone would have been able to bug her.

"You're secure," Noah said quietly, giving her the impression she was more secure than she thought.

"Damn, sounds like he's on top of you," Al chuckled.

Noah opened his mouth to say something and Rain pointed a warning finger at him. "He's not. I assure you. What do you have?" she said, needing something besides his virile body and commanding presence to focus on.

"Although this isn't a surprise to anyone, ballistics came back today confirming there was a silencer on our murder weapon. You know that exit wounds are usually larger than entrance wounds," Al began.

Noah leaned into Rain, tilting his head with a faraway, relaxed expression on his face as he easily listened to Al speak through the cell phone.

"Of course. Are your entrance wounds too large?" Rain asked, and realized her palm was flat against Noah's chest. His chest hair tickled her hand and his heart beat with steady determination, pulsing with life as strong as the man.

"At first I didn't notice, but yes, exactly. Usually the entrance wound is smaller than the exit wound. With each victim, though, the entrance wound is at least the same size as the exit wound. Also, the inflammation and abnormal redness is indicative of a bullet fired through a silencer. The first two murders don't show a silencer was used, but then our next three do. And all the murders in Kansas City and in Dallas report a silencer used on their murder weapon."

"The muzzle imprints appear inflamed?" Noah asked.

"I think I just said that," Al said, and then chuckled. "You two should ask me next time before we do a three-way. I'm pretty open-minded, but a girl likes to feel respected."

"I respect you, my dear," Noah said too smoothly.

Rain shot him a curious glance and he raised one eyebrow, almost appearing to be challenging her. She looked away quickly. Right now wasn't the time to slip into a head trip game with him.

"So okay," Rain said, turning from Noah and barely able to take two steps before reaching the window. So much for pacing while she brainstormed. "Possibly our murderer learned a silencer was used on the other murders and so started using them here. Find out for me when it was first announced anywhere that a silencer was used on the murder weapon in either city. Also, get me all info you've got on the bullets. I know we're dealing with a semi-automatic shooting .32 calibers."

"Probably a sub-compact that someone's got in a purse or something," Al suggested.

Rain turned around and once again ran into Noah, who now had her pinned in the corner of the room. She glared at him and he straightened.

"Put it on speaker then, *sweetheart*," he whispered, but emphasized the word "sweetheart." Was he actually finally listening to her and not going to call her princess anymore?

Rain yanked the phone from her ear and then switched it to speakerphone while an odd pang of regret hit her. It didn't bother her that she was strong willed enough to make Noah submit to her demands, and she sure wasn't upset that he would choose another term of endearment. Nonetheless, the pang twisted inside her while she stared at his bare chest. There wasn't time right now to dwell on why it bothered her that he wasn't so strong, so bullheaded, that he would demand to call her the same name that her father called her.

Lord, what was her problem when it upset her that Noah adhered to her wishes? She didn't want a man who never listened to her or cared about her feelings.

What the fuck! She didn't want a man at all.

"What makes you think our perp would carry a purse?" Noah asked, pulling her back on track. Obviously he'd been able to hear Al even before she was on speaker.

"Just a hunch. And I don't have a perfect track record with hunches," Al added, laughing easily at herself. "But we don't have one single witness—and we've got five bodies now. The murder is taking place at close range. A reason for that could be lack of confidence in hitting their target at a further distance."

"It would appear our killer is capable of appearing on a scene without standing out. So either they're at the scene of the crime on a regular basis—"

"Or they are normally an inconspicuous person," Noah finished for her.

"Your hunch is a good one, Al. They're not overly confident in their ability to hit a target with a gun, so they're firing at close range." Rain raised her attention to Noah's face. "They somehow have the means to obtain a silencer, which is an illegal device."

"You can buy them off the Internet if you know where to look, though," Al pointed out.

"So although they're insecure about their firing abilities, they aren't that lacking in confidence," Rain added. "They have the will and the strength to walk up to people and pull a gun while aiming at their victim's head."

"Which could just make them insane," Noah threw in. Then turning and heading to the computer, his bare back a field of rippling, bulging muscles, he picked up her notepad where she'd jotted down the funeral information. "See if you can get someone assigned to be at the funeral. We won't be there. I think this would be a good opportunity for us to visit a few of the local hangouts without having to worry about anyone from our swingers' group being present."

"Ten four," Al said.

"Has anyone received confirmation yet on whether the murderer is the same person in Kansas City and in Dallas?" Rain asked, still holding the phone but watching Noah.

"Negative. Not at this end," Al offered.

"I'll get a positive on that one," Noah said, without turning around.

"I'll talk to you soon," Rain told Al, said good-bye, and hung up.

Rain paused at the end of the hallway a few minutes later, unable to take her gaze from Noah as he leaned over the new television.

"What are you doing?" she asked, focusing on his hard, firm ass.

"Making sure this works." He straightened, his dark, wavy hair in disarray when he turned around. "One of a few toys I prefer using on a case," he added, and pointed to the back of the television.

Curious and not sure what he was getting at, Rain walked toward him warily. He rubbed her arm, encouraging her closer, until she stood next to him and could peer around the back of the set.

"This is the latest audio jammer. Simply install it anywhere out of the way and it will jam all signals in a twelve-hundred-square-foot area." He spoke like a proud papa as he pointed at a small, unimpressive black box that was fixed to the back of the stand that housed the new television. "Anyone trying to listen in on anything we say inside this house, or on our cell phones, will be blessed with an annoying high-pitched squeal."

"The gadgets the United States government gets to play with," she said, sighing. "That's why you said it was okay to talk to Al."

"Yup. Everything shows it is working properly. I'd say you two could have conspired anything and no one but the two of you would know."

"And you," she said, straightening and grinning at him.

Noah cupped her cheek and then leaned into her, brushing his lips over hers. "Always me," he whispered.

FOURTEEN

Noah held the door for Rain as she entered Hinders' Greenhouse two days later. This time there weren't any other customers in the store and a man possibly ten years or so older than Noah stood behind the counter.

"Afternoon," the man said cheerfully, looking at them over his glasses. "Holler if you need help with anything."

"Thanks," Rain said, and once again ran her fingers over the sculpture of the birdbath she'd noticed last time she and Noah were here.

She pulled her hair up before they left the house, and he focused on her slender neck and the dark strands that glided over her nape as she walked in front of him, taking her time looking at various items. He got the oddest desire to run his finger down the slope of her neck. It was impossible not to touch her, and even though he kept his actions respectable, he found his hands on her every time they moved.

"Look at this," Rain said, her voice just above a whisper. She held up a gardening magazine and tapped the cover with her finger. "We could ask him about this."

Noah wasn't sure exactly what she meant to ask, but he nodded. "Just get a conversation going. I can lead it toward questions we need answered."

"If he has the answers." She looked into Noah's eyes with those clear baby blues but then diverted her attention to the guy behind the counter. "I have a question," she said, heading over to the counter.

Noah forced himself not to take a moment to adore that

perfectly shaped ass of hers in the blue jeans she'd opted to wear. The sleeveless sweater-vest she had on didn't quite reach her hip-hugging jeans, and the trace of bare back looked delicious. The entire fucking package was a feast suited for a king.

Noah couldn't waste time drooling, though. He ripped his attention from her and stared past her at who they believed to be Mark Hinders.

The man once again glanced up over his glasses, which he wore low on his nose, and offered her a pleasant smile. "What can I do for you?"

"Honestly, I'm not sure. My husband and I want to do something with our yard. We just moved in, you see." She sounded so sincere, complete with wringing her hands together as she spoke. And when she shifted, giving Noah an almost apologetic smile, he wasn't sure he'd ever seen anyone undercover slide so smoothly into their role. "The yard has so much potential. But we don't want to bite off more than we can chew. And well, some folks we've met here in town mentioned your store to us. Do you have a minute?"

"I have all day." He took his glasses off and left them on the counter, then walked around and stood next to Rain. "And it's good to see that word-of-mouth advertising is still alive and thriving."

Rain smiled but didn't say anything. Instead she walked over to the magazine she'd shown to Noah a moment ago. "You're going to think us dreamers, but is creating a yard like this really possible?"

Again Noah silently applauded her. Mentioning any names of who might have sent them here would upset Mark, if this was indeed their man. They needed to build a rapport with him first, establish trust, and show they were good people through conversation before pushing for information.

"And by that she means can two people, who aren't professional gardeners, pull something like that off?" Noah added.

"Of course you could do this, if you really wanted this. It's a gorgeous setting, peaceful and romantic. It depends on how badly you want it."

"It was the first thing she said when we bought the house," Noah offered, and sighed to show he'd been dragged into the project. "You know how wives are."

"Yes, I do. Or I did," he added.

They had their man.

Rain looked up from the magazine quickly, glancing back at Noah with concern in her eyes. After the emotional outburst she had earlier in the week, Rain showed Noah a side of her he would bet good money very few people ever saw. Her vulnerable side. Watching her now, Noah knew what he saw in her pretty blue orbs was legitimate. She understood the pain involved in losing a loved one and didn't want to hurt Hinders any more than he had been by plying him with questions.

"We saw the memorial in the window the last time we were here," Rain said quietly, and touched her fingertips to his shirtsleeve. "I can't imagine not having my husband in my life. What a sad tragedy."

"I wouldn't wish this pain on anyone," he said, and then coughed, stiffened slightly as he moved away, and did a damned good job of giving Rain a sincere smile. "And thank you for your condolences. But it wasn't a sad tragedy; it was an atrocious act of jealous cruelty."

Noah snapped his attention to Mark Hinders and saw the pleasant expression on his face had changed to something bordering on demonic. Blind rage burned across his face like a red smear.

"Jealous cruelty?" Noah questioned. "No offense, my friend, but that sounds a bit intense."

"Let's just say it was a matter of believing a certain group was our friends when in fact they were worse than enemies." He cleared his throat and made an effort to reach for the magazine.

Noah couldn't let it die yet. "Certain group of friends?" Now he lowered his voice, knowing they were alone in the store but glancing around to be sure. "I know we're strangers, but we're new to town. And we also were interested in finding special groups that were into the same lifestyle we enjoy. But then after one party, a lady who was supposed to attend is dead."

Rain moved closer to Noah and wrapped her arm around his. "And she was over at our house just earlier this week."

"Patty Henderson?" Hinders asked, and rubbed his forehead as he stared at them. It looked like he actually saw them for the first time, and took his time putting them to memory.

Noah extended his hand, hoping if they took this conversation to a more personal level, Mark Hinders would share what he meant by "atrocious act of jealous cruelty."

"I'm Noah Kayne and this is my wife, Rain. We've just moved out here from D.C.," he offered.

"Mark Hinders, owner and proprietor." He offered a firm handshake and then nodded to Rain.

"My wife was told by the butcher down at the grocery store in our neighborhood about a potluck where we could meet folks like ourselves," Noah began, intentionally baiting Mark.

"That would be Butch," Mark offered, nodding, but then returned to the counter and picked up his glasses.

"We enjoyed ourselves at the party, but then when we found out one of the ladies who were at our house just a few days ago didn't make it to the party because she was shot—," Rain began quietly.

"Well, now we aren't so sure about this group," Noah finished for her.

Mark slid the glasses up his nose and they immediately fell to the edge of his nose, where he left them. "I don't blame you. And my advice to you would be to find a new group of friends. Not that I would ever tell the police, but I know who shot my wife. And I'll get my revenge."

Noah glanced at Rain, who picked up the magazine with the nicely landscaped yard on it and ran her finger over the glossy cover. "Everyone seemed so nice," she murmured, but then looked up at Mark quickly, her blue eyes glassy with moisture. "Well, except for—"

She bit her lip, as if remembering suddenly that bad-mouthing others in public wasn't something respectable people did. Noah sincerely wondered how much of her presentation was an act and how much was sincere.

Mark walked toward her, pausing and adjusting a basket on the corner of a wooden table that was full of packages of seeds. "That's a pretty yard," he said, his voice thicker than it was a moment ago. "I could order in that fountain, have it here in a week if you want."

Rain looked up at him, smiling. "I bet your wife was a really neat lady. I'm sorry I didn't get to meet her."

"She was perfect. Or at least to me she was," he added with a wry grin. "I think she tangled with the wrong person, not that she deserved to die over it. We were talking it out." He shot Noah a furtive glance. "This lifestyle has been our social life throughout our entire marriage. Both of us have been tempted to go beyond the boundaries, you know? Almost always we managed to remain where we belong. But I wasn't always the ideal husband, so I couldn't blame her for slipping, either."

Noah guessed that Lorrie had cheated on Mark with someone in the group. But Mark was right: that wouldn't be grounds for shooting her, unless a person was grossly unstable. It might have led to actions, though, that would have ended in murder.

"Do you have a catalog on fountains?" Rain asked, dragging Mark's attention back to her. "I definitely love the rose garden bordering one side of the yard. We would need to find the ideal trellises to go with our setting."

"Yes. Yes." Mark turned, rubbing his forehead and heading around the counter again. "Give me a minute. Lorrie always kept all catalogs in order. But she had a system, and I never messed with it. She would have killed me," he said, his voice trailing off as he knelt behind the counter and fished through things on the shelves. "Let me check the back room. I'll be right back."

"If we see a variety of things, we can leave to make our decision, and come back in a day or two. It will help build a closer bond with him," Rain whispered the moment he was out of the room.

"I'd love to know more about what Lorrie was doing right before her death," Noah also whispered, and glanced toward the back room where Mark had disappeared and then at the front door. The display in honor of Lorrie wasn't there anymore. Instead, a nice flower arrangement filled the lower half of the window. Noah could see outside, and the parking lot was half-full, with most customers heading toward the strip mall next to Mark's store. "I don't know how long we'll be alone with him, though. See if we can fish for more details on what events transpired up to her death."

Rain looked up at Noah, and a slow grin appeared on her face. "Decided I'm not so bad at undercover work?"

He rubbed her chin with his thumb, enjoying how soft her flesh was. Her eyes glowed a deeper blue while he watched. Rain wanted him again, and that knowledge made it damned hard not to arrange their day so they could spend a portion of it naked and sweaty and intertwined with each other.

"You're definitely good under the covers," he growled, and loved how color washed over her cheeks when she glared at him.

"Here's a few catalogs," Mark announced as he walked out of the back room. "Honestly, I haven't looked through these two. They just came in a couple weeks ago and Lorrie always hurried to file them before I could even glance through them."

"Oh. These are perfect." Rain started flipping through one that he put down on the counter. "Did she do a lot of landscaping?"

"Not as much as she would have liked to," Mark said,

again the loss of his wife making his voice thick with emotion. "Good help is really hard to find. I'm afraid both of us have worked here day and night as long as we've had this place."

"How long have you been open?" Rain asked.

"Nine years. When we paid off our house, and with no kids, we realized we didn't need all the space we now owned. We sold the house and opened this store. There's been no looking back ever since," he said, almost proudly. But then his tone darkened. "The only thing I regret was becoming involved with that group of lunatics. I swear if I ever go to a party again and any of them are there, I'll walk out on the spot. If I didn't, I'd go to prison," he added, his expression pinched with anger.

"The way it's been explained to us, they prefer everyone in their group to only be sexual with those in the group," Rain offered, lowering her voice to a soft, sensual-sounding whisper, in spite of the fact that the three of them were alone in the store. "In fact, Steve told us that just the other day." She looked over her shoulder at Noah for reassurance.

"I think he has an agenda of his own," Noah growled.

Rain's eyes grew wide and she stared at him for a moment but then shifted attention to Mark quickly when he spoke.

"A snake in rat's clothing," he snarled, sounding fiercer than he looked like he could. True hatred made him shake, and he put the other catalogs he held on the counter. "I know he set my Lorrie up. That asshole gets off annoying his wife more than he does having sex with other women. I'd bet money on it."

"What?" Rain asked, echoing Noah's thoughts.

Mark waved his hand in the air and offered her a sincere smile. "Let's talk about your yard. It's a much more pleasant subject." Again he rubbed his forehead, pushed his glasses up his nose, and then looked at the catalogs after his glasses slid back to the edge of his nose again and stayed there. "Do you know how many square feet you're talking about?"

"There's already a deck back there." Noah wasn't able to picture the yard very well when his brain continued repeating over and over Mark's words about Steve and his wife. "I'd say the yard is about fifteen hundred square feet, but I don't know that she wants to use all of that space."

"It just gives me an idea of what we're working with," Mark told him, waving his hand in the air dismissively and then flipping pages in the catalog.

The door to the shop opened and a bell rang over it. Noah turned and saw a woman enter, possibly in her mid-forties, wearing faded jeans that were a bit too tight and a blouse with no bra. Her aggravated expression didn't change when she saw Rain and him talking to Mark.

"Nina, I didn't expect to see you," Mark said, his tone suddenly stiff.

"I'm sure, but I need to work." Nina placed her purse on a shelf behind the counter and then dragged a thin strand of bleached blond hair behind her ear before focusing on Rain and then Noah. She gave him a toothy smile. "You're in good hands with Mark. Whatever you need, he's the man to make your yard perfect."

"Nina," Mark said, sounding exasperated. Then glancing at both of them, his face looked strained with worry. "If you two will excuse me a minute."

Noah nodded, but Rain appeared engrossed in the magazine. At first he couldn't hear what the two of them said, but when Nina reached a shrill pitch she was easy to overhear. Noah watched Rain, though, curious as her expression hardened and she glanced up at him furtively before focusing on the back room.

"You and Lorrie complained all of the time about how hard it was to find good help. I've never done you wrong, never taken one damned dime from this store. And trust me, it hurts me as bad as it does you that Lorrie got murdered.

She made a mistake, but that shouldn't have cost her life. Don't punish me because she's dead."

Mark's low, angry tone was harder to hear, but Noah strained as hard as he could until finally he turned from the counter and moved to a display of cactus that was closer to the back room.

"One more outburst like this in my store and I'll get a restraining order against you, Nina. Now leave."

Nina marched out of the back room, grabbed her purse from behind the counter, and growled as she looked at Noah and Rain. The door closed firmly and Mark appeared, letting out a defeated sigh.

"I am so sorry," he said, and then looked for a moment like he might collapse.

"It's okay," Rain assured him. "None of us have perfect lives."

"If you two want to take your business elsewhere, I'd understand."

"No. No, you've got what we need," Rain said again. "Actually, though, I was just telling my husband while you were back there, it would be great if I could pore over these catalogs tonight and work up a diagram of what I'd like our backyard to look like."

Mark moved behind the counter and looked at the three magazines that were now spread open and overlapping each other. "That's fine. Take them. I'd appreciate it if you brought them back, though."

"We'll be back tomorrow," Rain promised.

Once outside, Noah watched Rain scan the parking lot. "Did you know that Nina chick?"

"The question is, would she remember me?" Rain offered. "She's been booked several times and I've seen her down at the station."

"Lovely." He didn't see Nina as he and Rain got into the car. "Well, it looks like you're safe where she's concerned. At least Mark doesn't want her working there, so hopefully she won't be in again."

"If memory serves, she's got a rap sheet for shoplifting." Rain rested the magazines on her lap and blew out a breath of air. "But today's visit wasn't completely unproductive. It sounds like part of our motive might have been cheating spouses."

"I agree." He started the car and backed out of the stall. When they reached the exit, he spotted Nina walking away from them on the sidewalk. "What would you say to opening a joint checking account with me?"

Rain glanced over at him, studying his face while he was sure the obvious thoughts went through her head. He'd have to check the statutes for Nebraska, but in most states creating joint accounts constituted a legal unity between couples, often referred to as common-law marriage, which in some cases held up in courts of law. He prayed she didn't take it that way but couldn't completely shove aside thoughts of trying to see her once this case was wrapped up.

"Why?" she asked.

He nodded up the street. "There's National Bank. Do you know how many branches it has?"

"It's not a large bank. That's the main office and there is a drive-through across town." Then she frowned and nodded. "Lynn Handel worked there. Okay, let's go open an account. I take it you've got cash? They would be thrilled but might wonder why I was transferring money from my bank to this one."

"I always pay on a date," he informed her.

"Some date."

"You don't think I know how to take a lady on a date?" The bank was just down the road, and he turned into the parking lot while glancing over at Rain.

She gave him a quick once-over. "When's the last time you took a lady on a date?"

He wasn't sure he wanted to share anything about Laurel with Rain. Her breaking down on him the other day wasn't intentional. Noah knew without any doubt if she could do it over again, she probably wouldn't share personal information with him about her past. It was inevitable, though, the longer they spent time together, the more they would learn about each other's personal lives. Lives that had nothing to do with solving this case. Her baby blues burned into his flesh as he put the car in park but left it idling for a moment.

"Just because it's been a while doesn't mean I don't know how to show a lady she's worth something." He knew he took the easy way out and didn't answer her question. There wasn't any reason he could think of, though, why he should share anything about Laurel with Rain. Laurel wasn't ever coming back. He'd made sure of that. After their final fight, and the few choice names he'd called her, Laurel would never see him again. Which was fine with him.

"That hardly answers the question," Rain said dryly.

"When was the last date you've been on?" Turning the tables was a hell of a lot safer than allowing Rain to analyze his relationship with Laurel. He could clearly imagine Rain's opinion of Laurel if he told her why he lost it on his fiancée and called off a wedding a week before it was to take place.

"Oh no," Rain said, laughing, and then leaning against the passenger door as she crossed her arms over her chest and grinned at him like a female predator, ready to pounce and go for the kill. "You aren't getting off that easy, mister. You said you always pay on a date. I say you're lying. I say you don't have a clue how to date. I bet your idea of a date is remembering names and phone numbers of willing, submissive bimbos who can't wait to spread their legs for Mr. FBI Man when he struts into their town to save it from destruction and demise."

"Is that the kind of man you think I am?" He didn't have to act shocked at her guess into his nature.

"Noah, however you act in your downtime really isn't any of my business." Rain allowed her gaze to stroll down his body lazily, making a show of sizing him up. When she lifted her long, thick lashes, her baby blues glowed with emotion. More than anything she wanted to know more about him. "I'm sure I don't have to tell you when someone answers questions with questions they are avoiding offering the truth, or confirming it as the case may be," she added, smiling triumphantly.

"If I agree to tell you about my love life prior to meeting you, then you're going to agree to do the same."

Her expression changed quickly, suddenly looking haunted, or possibly even pained. "Give me the goods, mister," she said, straightening, whatever emotion he tapped on a moment before now gone. Rain's expression turned tight, determined.

"Her name is Laurel Neiman." Noah watched the color wash out of Rain's expression and wondered how good of an idea it was to share his past with her.

"Who is she?" Rain asked, almost whispering.

"Laurel was going to be my wife." There wasn't any pain, he noticed, when offering the information. Not like he suspected there might be.

"Oh." Rain continued watching him while he stared at the bank in front of them. A few moments passed before she pressed him. "What happened?"

Noah searched for a way to summarize the fiasco his life became over the past six months. "Let's just say she showed me her true colors, and fortunately in time. I called the wedding off."

He'd much rather see Rain's defiance, or her expression flushed with desire, than the pinched-lipped, blank stare she offered him at the moment.

"Okay, there you have it," he announced, narrowing his gaze on her intentionally. "There are no ladies scattered around the country anxious for me to grace them with my presence. Sorry to disappoint you. So spill it, Lieutenant. It's your turn. Tell me where all your men are in this town so I can bulldoze them down one by one," he growled, doing his best to change the mood in the car and wipe that odd look off her face.

"I lived with my father until I was twenty-eight." She stared at Noah as if that answered his question.

"Okay, and?" He remembered her file saying she was thirty and her father had died a couple years ago, which meant she'd stayed with him until he died.

"Dad was very good at reminding me no one wants to be with someone who will jump when the phone rings and then disappear out the door, sometimes for days." Her facial features relaxed, but Noah was learning Rain well after being with her barely a week. She'd applied her mask to her face, successfully hiding her feelings from the words she offered him. "I think it stemmed from his inability to start another relationship after Mom died. Dad didn't like me dating, and was very good at sabotaging any relationship that might have had a go to it. After I learned he had cancer, and it became clear he wasn't going to listen to any doctor and seek treatment, or let anyone else besides me know about the disease, I quit trying to find a boyfriend. Dad didn't want to share me."

"I don't blame him a bit for that," Noah said easily, ignoring the tilt of her head at his response. Rain wasn't a virgin, but he would accept her answer. More than likely she had more one-night stands than he ever did. It was probably the only way she could maintain sexual satisfaction and keep her father happy. "It sounds like I need to show you I can take a lady out and give her a good time."

Rain reached for her door handle. "I'm not sure if that's a good idea, Noah."

Before she could open her door, he grabbed her arm, dragging her across the hard plastic console between the two seats. Rain wasn't a short woman, but her body was willowy. He opened his door and continued dragging her.

"Noah!" she complained.

"Quit fighting me, Rain," he said, keeping a firm grip on her arm until he'd pulled her out his side of the car. "Because you know what happens when you do."

Rain tugged her sleeveless sweater-vest when he let go of her and then swatted loose hair over her shoulder. "What?" she demanded.

"This," he said, closing the car door and then pinning her against it.

Her mouth was soft as her lips moved against his, and her breasts were full and soft against his chest when he wrapped his arms around her. Noah deepened the kiss and a growl escaped him. If he wasn't careful, they wouldn't be entering any bank but returning home. There weren't any answers concerning what would or wouldn't happen once this case was solved. There was too much of a connection between them, not only physically but as partners as well.

Rain rested her fingers against the back of his neck, stroking his skin in a soothing motion, and then let her hands fall, her nails dragging down his arms as she lowered her face, ending the kiss. He kissed her forehead, breathing in her alluring scent.

"I'm not going to let you deny something exists between us just because we don't know what the future holds," he whispered.

Rain slipped her hand into his and easily moved out between him and the car, keeping her firm grip as she began leading him toward the bank. "Fine, if that's how you want it. Come on, husband of mine. Let's go open that account."

Rain let go of his hand when they entered the bank and tugged on her sweater-vest as she walked up to the receptionist at the desk in the middle of the small bank. Noah patted his wallet and hoped Rain had remembered to carry the fake identification they'd been provided with. He let his gaze drop to the spot where her long legs met her ass. Her blue jeans hugged her, showing off how perfectly shaped she was. Rain was a woman among women, beautiful to a fault, and so damned dedicated to her work. He imagined that very few men ever got the chance to get close to her. Maybe taking her out on a real date, or as real as it could get for the two of them, would be a treat both of them deserved.

"Hi there," Rain said sweetly to the lady at the desk. "My husband and I are new in town, and we'd like to open a checking account."

"Sure." The lady left the magazine she'd been looking at open on her desk and stood, brushing her hands over her dress and then pointing to a couple of chairs along the wall. "Have a seat and an officer will be with you momentarily."

Noah followed Rain to the chairs, glancing around the bank as he did. He noted two cameras installed in either corner, both aimed at the tellers. Two ladies were behind a wooden counter, and there were three glassed-in offices where he guessed the officers worked. The receptionist walked over to one of them and said something to a man behind the desk. He glanced at Noah before looking at the receptionist and nodding.

She returned to her desk and sat down, licking her finger before flipping the page in her magazine. "Mr. Hipp will be right with you," she told Noah, and then returned her attention to her reading.

Noah didn't respond. She'd already dismissed them, her job complete. Instead he focused on the man, possibly in his fifties, thin and friendly looking, although the lines on his face indicated he carried a fair bit of stress in his life.

The man reached them and extended his hand to Noah. "Ralph Hipp," he said amiably. "How can I help you?"

"Noah Kayne," Noah said, and then nodded to Rain when she stood and moved next to him. "This is my wife, Rain."

"Nice to meet both of you. Come on back to my office."

Noah waited for Rain to sit in the chair that had its back to the glass wall and faced Ralph's desk. While Ralph closed the door, Noah scanned the contents of the desk, noting printouts that looked like mortgage paperwork and applications for home loans. Something caught his eye as he took the seat next to Rain. A card leaned against Ralph's flat-screened monitor. Noah read the name—Patricia Henderson.

"Did I hear that you're new in town?" Ralph asked, moving around his desk and then glancing at the paperwork spread out before him before sitting down.

"Just moved here from D.C.," Noah told him. "I've brought cash, though, so we don't have to transfer from another account."

"That makes it easy." Ralph sat down, glancing from Noah to Rain. "Welcome to Lincoln, Nebraska. I hope you love our town as much as I do."

"Honestly, we've had quite the interesting welcome," Rain said quietly, leaning back in her chair and folding her hands in her lap. The clasp holding her long hair had slid down her head a bit, probably from Noah forcing her out his side of the car. The effect was enticing, with the loosened strands pulled back but looking like they ached to be set free so they could fan over her narrow shoulders. As if she knew his thoughts, she raised one hand and slid a loose strand behind her ear. "We're welcomed to town by a local Realtor and then she is murdered."

"Patty Henderson." Ralph lifted the card that Noah had noticed and flipped it in his fingers. "I can't believe it myself. Lincoln is usually a quiet town, peaceful and friendly. I've lived here most of my life. One of our tellers here was killed just a couple months ago. Real shame." He offered them a reassuring smile. "I guess that isn't the best news to offer you, since you're new in town. But we do have incredible law enforcement here in Lincoln. You better believe they are tracking down that murderer as we speak."

"That's good to know," Rain said, and licked her lips.

Noah understood the sensation of being praised but not able to acknowledge that the praise was directed at him.

He cleared his throat. "We couldn't believe she was dead."

"I know," Rain interrupted. "One moment she's having coffee in my living room, and the next moment we hear she's been shot. And in her driveway? She didn't strike me as the kind of woman who has enemies."

"Neither woman did. Not that I know of." Ralph shook his head. "Unless there is some crazy bastard out there who believes that pretty women shouldn't work."

"The teller here was pretty, too?" Rain asked. "Patty impressed me, such a go-getter. She seemed to be doing so well for herself. She and a girlfriend of hers stopped by to bring me a plant and welcome us to the neighborhood."

"That's Patty." Ralph nodded, then glanced at his screen and put his hand over his mouse. "She always went the extra step, convinced that every move she made would bring her a step closer to closing a deal. There aren't many men out there with the craving for success like she had. The police never questioned me, but if they did, my money is on some delusional man who wants all women in the kitchen with frilly aprons tied around their waists."

It didn't surprise Noah that Rain didn't have a response for that one. "I don't see a thing wrong with that image," he said, just to fuel her fire, and grinned when she glared at him. "Or maybe they both had some distraught lover. Was the teller here as successful as Patty?"

"Well," Ralph began, laughing easily at Noah's intentional sexist comment and clicking his mouse as he spoke. "She was a teller. They don't make the greatest income, you know. But I would buy into the distraught-lover theory. Mind you, I don't partake in office gossip, but we're a small bank, a good place to be if you want to deal with people and not computers," he added quickly, not missing a breath when it came to plugging his institution. "But I did hear the ladies chatting from time to time about someone that she might have been seeing on the side. I guess he showed up here once. In Lynn's defense, though, she always denied it."

"Hardworking women who take lovers. I guess there are probably a few men out there who believe that is typical behavior only for the male gender." Rain smiled sweetly at him.

"Low blow," Ralph said, but again laughed easily. "Well, okay then, let's get your account set up here."

Half an hour later, Ralph walked the two of them out to the tellers, introducing them and announcing they were new customers, new to town, and needed to be shown that Lincoln really was filled with wonderful people. Noah heard Ralph whisper under his breath to the teller nearest him that the two of them knew Patty.

"She died just like Lynn did," the teller said to Ralph, although she glanced at Noah, giving him a quick once-over. "You know it's that terrible man who did it."

FIFTEEN

Rain about fell off the couch when her cell phone rang. Muscles in her back screamed when she slowly stood and then grabbed her phone from the coffee table. If she'd slept with Noah last night she would fuck him again, and things were already getting a bit too complicated between them. But damn, they needed to figure out something with the sleeping arrangement. This couch sucked.

"Hello," she said, her voice scratchy. She stared down the dark hallway, able to hear Noah's steady breathing as he slept soundly in that awesome large bed.

"Rain, Al here. Sorry to wake you, darling." Her anxious tone helped Rain wake up, and she padded barefoot to the kitchen and then squinted against the refrigerator light when she reached inside for a can of Diet Dr Pepper.

Something told her she needed it. "No problem. What's up?"

"It was damned near ten forty-two and I was ready to head home for some shut-eye when we got a domestic, along with an eleven six."

"Gunfire?" Rain scratched her head, then combed her hair with her fingers. Popping the can open, she gulped greedily. "Was anyone shot?"

"Doesn't appear to be. But we've got the weapon. And guess whose house it is?"

Rain walked to the edge of the hallway and stared into the darkness, focusing on the open bedroom doorway. She didn't hear Noah's breathing anymore. She pictured him lying there listening to her and she moved as quietly as she could closer to the open doorway.

"Whose house?" she asked quietly.

Rain reached the doorway and simply stared at Noah's bare chest. The blanket covered him to his hips and he was propped up on his elbow, his hair tousled as he met her gaze in the dark.

"Steve and Susie Porter's," Al told her. "I'm heading downtown to test this weapon now against the bullets that shot the others. But if we have a match—"

"Then one of those two is our murderer," Rain finished for her. "Damn, girl, you're going to solve this case all by yourself."

"Hardly." Al laughed off the compliment easily. "We got a lucky break. If these two weren't going at it, we wouldn't have gotten our hands on the weapon. I'll be at the station in fifteen."

"Sounds good. We'll meet you down there." Rain snapped the phone closed while Noah pushed himself to a sitting position.

"What's up?" His deep, sleep-filled baritone sounded warm and enticing.

"I've been sleeping on a fucking cruel couch and missing all the action," she grumbled, and grabbed her hair, slowly twisting it so she could put it up.

Noah stood, and the blankets slid off his body. He was completely naked. "There's room in this bed for two."

"I know." Her fingers quit working and her hair tumbled over her hands. Suddenly her mouth was too dry and then quickly too wet. She swallowed hard, staring at all of that perfect muscle that moved in slowly on her. "Noah," she began.

He grabbed her jaw, forcing her head back, and then devoured her mouth. If it was a punishing kiss for making him sleep alone, she didn't have the strength to defend herself. Not on two swallows of caffeine and with sore muscles cringing along her spine as he held her, making her back arch as he feasted on her.

He impaled her with his tongue while his cock sprang to life between them, pressing against her inner thigh. She swelled inside, immediately ready for him. Pressure built while the temperature in the room soared to dangerous levels.

Noah pulled away, leaving her in a haze while he rubbed his thumb over the edge of her jaw. "Who called?"

She blinked, fighting to regain the ability to speak. "Al. They had a domestic right before her shift ended. She took the call and it turned out to be at Steve and Susie's house."

"No shit." Noah walked away from her and grabbed his jeans that hung off the edge of the bed. Typical law enforcement—clothes always ready to jump into at a moment's notice.

"Apparently there was a shot fired, although no one was hurt, but Al's got the weapon. She's headed to the station now to determine if it's our murder weapon."

Noah kept his back to Rain and she stared at his hard, firm ass as he pulled out clean boxers and then stepped into them. Her insides were racked with turmoil. If she hadn't come in here, more than likely he wouldn't have kissed her. Now she ached and the need to mount him, ride him hard until she found relief, made it damned near impossible to move.

"Why did you do that?" she demanded, angry with herself and with him for kissing her.

He turned, holding his jeans, and stared at her, his brooding expression focused intently on hers. "Let's just say it helps knowing that I'm not the only one suffering here," he said simply, and then stepped into his jeans.

"Fuck," she hissed, and turned for the bathroom.

It was six in the morning when she followed him out into the cold, dark garage.

"What do you say we do a bit of our own investigation,"

he suggested as he pushed the button to open the garage door.

"What do you mean?"

"You ever want to do what you can't do as a cop?" He grinned at her over the top of the car and pushed the button on the wall to open the garage door.

"What are you talking about?" It was cold, and even colder in the car. She wrapped her arms around herself, wondering if she should suggest they go by her house to get a sweater, or even a jacket. "If I can't do it as a cop, then hell no, I don't want to do it."

"I bet you do." His mischievous grin bordered on evil. "Tell me you've never wanted to investigate further than what's allowed without a warrant. Or maybe sniff around places that haven't been authorized."

"Oh." She reached over and flipped the car to heat.

"I'll be right back." He jumped out of the car.

"Hey! It's cold. Hurry up," she snapped.

But he'd already bolted into the house. Granted, he did hurry. When he returned with a duffel bag that she hadn't seen before, she wondered where he got it. Noah slid behind the wheel, putting the bag in the backseat, but then handed her a thick, large black sweatshirt.

"We can't have you freezing to death, even if the view is to die for," he informed her, his gaze pointedly dropping to her breasts.

She snatched the sweatshirt out of his hands and slid her arms into it before pulling it over her head. "Thank you," she said, appreciating the gesture in spite of his crudeness.

Her nipples were hard and they hurt. More like ached. His staring at them didn't help ease the pressure. Need tore at her insides sitting this close to him, especially with a dark shadow darkening his chin and jaw, and his tousled hair only added to his damn near irresistible sex appeal.

"I was going to suggest we go by my home so I could grab warmer clothes."

"No time for that right now. We're fighting sunlight

here. It will be light out too soon, and the darkness is better for what we're going to do."

"What about going down to the station?"

"Al sounds like a competent lady. Besides, do you really want her cracking this case all by herself? It's time for you and me to do some digging." He appraised her after she'd pulled the sweatshirt over her head and tugged on it until it fell to her thighs. "You even look good in an oversized sweatshirt. Damn," he growled, and then turned to put the car into reverse.

Noah didn't ask for directions and they drove in silence, Rain's insides sizzling as she fought with thoughts of allowing their relationship to develop into something she knew would break her heart if she allowed it. Noah slowed when he turned onto a street in a very nice, pretentious neighborhood in town. After turning off the car, instead of getting out, he leaned into her and then reached for the duffel in the backseat.

Instead of pulling it to the front with them, he easily unzipped a side compartment and pulled out two small objects.

Noah handed one of them to her. "Insert it in your ear. These babies are every good spy's best friend."

Rain did as instructed and pushed the small oblong cream-colored object into her ear. Noah reached for her, and his knuckles were warm when they pressed against the side of her head. His expression was focused and serious as he adjusted the object until a slight ringing filled her brain.

"How is that?" When he spoke, it echoed in her head.

"I think it's working."

He nodded, then turned for the duffel again. Now she was fascinated and adjusted herself, taking a moment to scan the quiet street for any morning joggers, or anyone else who might see them and get too curious.

Next he handed her a gun. "It's loaded."

She checked the barrel and then the lock before lifting her sweatshirt and stuffing the gun into her jeans. The hard, cold metal bit at her flesh but nonetheless offered a sense of security. She quickly focused on what he pulled out of the duffel next.

"What's that?" she asked, holding her hand out to take the small cylindrical objects from Noah's hand.

"Greedy," he teased. "You want all of the best toys."

"Damn right." She tried taking them from him and he gazed at her, causing her heart to do a triple beat that hurt and stole her breath.

Noah didn't pull his gaze away but held out his hand, palm up. "They're GPS tracking devices. Each one has a magnet on it. Simply place them in a tire well. Nothing to it."

She picked up the two small black devices, each one no longer than her finger. "A woman would catch hell trying to cheat on you," she murmured.

"I wouldn't stay with a woman who would," he growled, his eyes growing darker than midnight while his expression tightened.

Rain wondered if his sudden hardened features had anything to do with the woman he was going to marry. In spite of her curiosity being piqued, she wouldn't take the conversation there. Noah already intrigued her more than he should, and prying into his personal life would probably result in getting hurt in the end even more.

"What else do you have?" she asked.

Noah didn't say anything else but used both hands to lift out what looked like a small laptop from the duffel bag. He flipped it open, and it did appear to be some kind of computer. It only took moments to boot up, though, and he pulled a Velcro black bag from it and removed wires from inside. Once it was plugged into the cigarette lighter, he plugged another gadget into a USB port and then placed what looked like a small satellite dish on the dash.

"This little baby not only detects any movement in a three-hundred-foot range, but we can pick up sound as well. So here's the game plan," he said, talking as he typed on the small keyboard. It was amazing how his big fingers managed to hit the exact key on such a miniature pad. Noah had skills in many areas, all of which impressed the hell out of her. "The Porters live at Twenty-three Fifteen Malibu Drive. We're on Malibu," he said slowly, typing still and then running his finger up the screen. He glanced out the front window. "It's that house over there, across the street."

Rain followed his gaze and took in the large, if not gaudy, stone home. There was one car parked in a circular drive and another on the street in front of the house. A two-car attached garage had separate garage doors that were oval at the top—not very practical to park anything in other than a compact car. Rain didn't see Steve's Miata and guessed it might be in the garage. There was a door next to the garage doors, and then a stone path that led from that door to the large front door. Stained-glass windows covered the top half of the front door. There weren't any bushes or flower gardens, just neatly trimmed grass that looked a darker shade of green than their neighbors' yards.

"Looks like a goddamned mausoleum."

Noah snorted. "It definitely sticks out compared to the other homes around it."

"Steve's Miata might be in the garage. I bet all the doors are locked. I'd love to put one of these tracking devices on it." She looked at Noah when he turned again and pulled out a black rod that wasn't quite a foot long.

"The LockBuster Hydraulic One-Man Forcible-Entry Tool," he said proudly. "Ever use one of these?"

"No, but I've read about them." She took it from him, holding it for a moment as she figured out by looking how it worked. "It's lighter than I imagined it would be," she mused, and then ran her finger over the top and around the end of it that would be placed against a lock. "Wouldn't it be easier to just wait until Steve goes to work, and then place the GPS device on his car?"

"Once both of them go to work, wouldn't you love to do a bit of snooping?"

Rain looked at Noah. "If we get caught."

"We won't," he informed her, making it sound like even if they did, the repercussions would be mild.

"I could lose my badge."

"You don't trust me?"

She stared at him a moment longer. More than anything, she'd love to go through the Porters' house. If she and Noah found what they needed, evidence of any kind that pointed toward the murders, they could nail Steve. It wouldn't take anything to push him into a confession. And what she wouldn't do to be the cop in the interrogation room with that creep.

"I trust you," she said slowly. "But if you cost me my badge—"

"I thought you said you trusted me," he interrupted, his attention on the screen. "We've got movement in the house, upstairs, back room. Let me see one of those GPS devices. I can get it on the car parked in their drive before they move further through the house."

"I'll do it." She put one of the GPS trackers on the seat next to her, and then set the LockBuster down, too. Holding the other GPS device in her hand, she rolled it between her fingers while energy charged through her. She needed to get out of the car to do something, and this would sure give the adrenaline pumping through her an outlet, not to mention hopefully sizzle out the burning need that was still enflamed deep in her womb. "We've got maybe fifteen minutes before the sun comes up. I'll be back in a second."

"Rain, I will do—"

She didn't wait for him to argue but hopped out of the car and closed the door quietly.

"You don't listen very well," Noah's baritone purred into her ear.

She damn near jumped out of her skin, having forgotten she still wore the communication device in her ear. "Watch my back," she whispered, wondering if the device would pick up her voice.

"I'm watching every inch of it, *sweetheart*."

She scowled but then pushed his comment out of her head. There was work to be done, and truth be told, Rain loved doing this shit. Some thought her crazy, and she'd learned over the years not to share this with many, but Rain loved the high she got from sneaking. In another life she would have made one hell of a cat burglar.

Rain kept the GPS device in her hand as she hurried across the street to the nicely paved sidewalk. There wasn't a house in the lot in front of her but instead a gazebo with flower arrangements that would soon come into bloom, which created a small neighborhood park. There wasn't any playground equipment, and Rain imagined the people living in these homes on this street cared more about appearance than the happiness of their children. That is, if any of them had sex with each other enough to procreate.

Darkness surrounded her and morning dew was heavy in the air. It clung to her flesh, mixing with the smooth sheen of sweat that broke out all over her. She was overheated and the chill in the air felt incredible.

"Just move up the drive and bend over and slap it on the tire well, then keep going," Noah instructed.

"You don't have to speak so loudly," she whispered.

"Your earpiece probably needs adjustment." He spoke quieter this time, although his baritone still filled her head.

It also made it seem as if he were right behind her and that at any moment those confident hands might touch her.

She hurried past the next house and came up on the Porters' home. Heading up the circular drive, she dropped low, shifted the GPS device from one hand to the other, and bent lower to slap it on the tire well of the car. It made a clinging sound when the magnet secured it to the vehicle. Rain let go, her hand wet from dew off the car, and then headed down the other end of the driveway.

Her heart pumped with life. She fought the grin that ached to spread across her face. God, she loved doing this shit!

Rain picked up pace, breaking into a jog, and headed toward the end of the block.

"Where are you going?" Noah asked.

"Thought I'd take a jog," she answered, feeling the icy chill in the air make her cheeks burn. "I'm going to head around the block," she decided at that moment. "If there's an alley, I can get a look at the back of the house."

"Damn it, Rain. If you get spotted you'll blow your fucking cover," he hissed.

"Lay off, Kayne," she ordered, the chill rejuvenating her and adding to the thrill of doing some snooping. "Trust is a two-way street, *sweetheart*," she said, emphasizing the last word like he did with her.

It was damn near impossible not to smile when he growled into her ear. But the neighborhood would be waking up, and anyone staring out a window, half-awake, would look twice at a jogger who was grinning from ear to ear.

"There is an alley." She turned onto the brick-lined alley, wondering how many neighborhoods in Lincoln rated such a clean back entrance.

Most alleys were no more than dirt and gravel, with huge potholes. God forbid Steve or Susie had to drive their precious vehicles over such weather-worn roads or alleys.

"Okay. There's movement in their house. Someone's coming downstairs. The stairwell is in the middle of the house." There was a clicking sound, as if he typed while speaking. "They're probably on opposite sides of the house, not speaking after their fight."

Rain walked along the edge of a privacy fence, grateful that this neighborhood was into their privacy. Tall fences lined either side of the alley. Her tennis shoes squeaked over the bricks, which were almost slippery in spots. It seemed the dew was heavier this morning than usual for this time of year, which possibly meant it would rain later today.

"I'm behind their house, and guess what?" she said as she stood at the edge of the fence.

"What?"

"The Miata is right here."

"Rain," he growled into her ear. "Be fucking careful. There is someone downstairs in the back of the house."

Rain peeked around the fence and stared at the house. With it still dark outside, when a light went on inside she could at least tell where someone might be. But there weren't any lights coming on.

"They're walking around in the dark then."

"Trust me. Someone is there."

She glanced up and down the alley, at the house on the other side of the alley. No one's lights were on in any of the houses she could see. Must be nice to sleep in past six.

Rain made her move, deciding it was better not to announce her actions, and damn near crawled toward the Miata and slapped the small magnetic cylinder to the tire wall. Then backing up, she sprinted down the alley.

She barely reached the end of the alley when her cell phone buzzed.

"I'm coming around to get you," Noah informed her.

"I've got a call."

"Who is it?"

Rain pulled her phone free, feeling her gun press hard against her flesh as she did. "It's Al." As Rain stood at the end of the alley, a car turned the corner, and Noah slowed as he approached her. She answered her phone as she got into the car. "What's up?" she asked.

"Where the hell are you?" Al snapped.

"Huh? Damn, girl. I didn't know I had a time limit to check in." She wasn't going to tell Al she had just placed tracking devices on private citizens' cars. She glanced at Noah. "We're headed that way now."

"Don't bother. Obviously you're having enough fun with your sexy FBI man not to be down here and defend our force when the government comes in and takes over."

"What?" Rain leaned back in her seat as Noah accelerated slowly and then turned in the opposite direction of the Porters' house. "Al, you aren't making any sense."

"They took it!" Al yelled loud enough that Noah glanced over at Rain.

"Who is they? And what did they take?" she asked coolly.

"They are the fucking FBI. And they took our weapon. They are going to make sure they get the goddamned credit for solving this case. And just maybe, if you'd bothered to get out of bed with your new play toy, your being present down here could have stopped them from taking the gun."

"Now you wait one goddamned minute."

"It's cool." Al sounded like it was anything but cool. "It's not like this will hurt your or my record. Neither one of us will get commendations, nor will we get credit for solving this case. I'm sure that doesn't matter to you, Detective Huxtable. Your daddy was the great Double H. You're good to go."

"Al, stop it." Rain rested her forehead against her palm and sighed heavily. "We made a slight detour, but we weren't—"

"Don't justify yourself," Noah hissed under his breath.

"Don't bother," Al said at the same time. "It doesn't matter. You call your own shots. I'm simply trying to catch a killer."

She hung up on Rain, and the compilation of emotions that ransacked Rain made her shake. "That's not fair," she growled, dropping her phone in an empty cup holder in the console between her and Noah and then leaning back farther to remove the gun from her waist. "Apparently the weapon picked up this morning at the Porters' has been confiscated by the FBI," she told him, anger and frustration mixing with pain at Al's obvious low opinion of her.

"We can head over to the field office." Noah signaled to turn right at the next intersection.

"No." Rain held out her hand and then pointed to the left. "Head to the station first."

"You're going to confront Al?"

"Hell no." She crossed her arms, fighting to chill out her anger. It wasn't working very well. "Any issues she's got are her own problem. But I am going to find out why they released that gun to the FBI."

"You already know the reason, Rain," he said calmly, but turned left as she instructed. "Local law enforcement agencies don't outrank FBI. More than likely we've got the equipment to handle ballistic fingerprinting better than you do."

Noah followed her direction and parked on the back side of the station. When Rain entered, she headed straight for the commons.

"Good morning, Detective." Betty, their dispatcher for the front desk, bent down and grabbed a candy bar out of one of the vending machines.

Rain let her purse drop from her shoulder and opened it to fish out change. "Hey, Betty Boop," she said, doing her best to smile.

Betty always appeared cheerful, and the general consensus was that she had the least stressful job in the department. Rain remembered the rumor getting out that Betty always smiled from lack of stress. A full-fledged bulletin and berating by the chief resulted. He dared any of them to sit at her desk all day and handle the calls that she handled. From that day forward a new rumor spawned, one that entailed the chief and Betty Boop getting it on, although cops weren't idiots. This second rumor was whispered and kept very under the wraps.

"You just missed all of the fireworks." Betty didn't hide the fact that she gave Noah a very scrutinizing once-over.

Her eyebrows shot up when he dropped change into the machine that Rain stood by, pushed the Diet Dr Pepper button, and then pulled out the cold can and handed it to Rain.

"Thanks," Rain said, looking over her shoulder and glaring at him. She turned and watched Betty as she headed toward the door. "What fireworks?" Rain asked, although she was willing to bet she didn't miss them as much as Betty thought.

Betty glanced at Noah, who moved across the room and helped himself to coffee, and then wagged her dark eyebrows at Rain as she moved closer.

"Impressive," Betty whispered, and then cleared her throat as she tugged on her uniform shirt. "Right after I clocked in this morning, an FBI field supervisor called informing me she was sending her people over. She talked to me like I answered to her," she said a bit louder. "The FBI pranced in less than an hour later, just as our officers were returning from a domestic, and took evidence from Detective Gomez. I thought Al was going to throw her out the window."

"Damn, we did miss a show." Noah blew on his coffee as he approached.

"Well, I got to get to work. Night dispatch always leaves my station a wreck." She rolled her eyes and then looked at Noah. Humming her approval, she turned and left the break room.

"I guess it's good to know not all cops hate me," Noah said, draping his arm over Rain's shoulder.

Rain shrugged away from him and headed out the door. "Just because she likes buns of steel doesn't mean she likes FBI."

Noah caught up with her at the elevator. "I've got buns of steel?"

Rain stared at the closed elevator doors, listening to the elevator groan and squeak as it approached. Noah didn't need his ego stroked, and besides, she wasn't in the mood. At least not in the mood to assure him that all women would find him drop-dead gorgeous.

"Let's go find out if ballistics managed to do anything before they lost their evidence." Rain entered the elevator when it opened.

Noah stayed put. "Go do what you want to do," he told

her. "I'm heading back to the car and going to monitor our tracking devices, see if we learn anything new."

The doors closed before she could ask why he didn't want to go up with her. "Your equipment will record what it finds," she grumbled, and then watched the numbers light up above the door as she headed upstairs.

SIXTEEN

Noah stared at the steaks grilling and then gazed through the rich-smelling smoke that drifted and was caught by a breeze in front of him. Ever since they got back to the house yesterday, Rain seemed more reserved, lost in thought. Monday morning, tomorrow, they would probably know if they had a match with the bullets and the Porters' gun. His bet was on the match; then it was just a matter of bringing the two of them in, questioning them, and making an arrest. In a few days he could be back in D.C. Not quite two weeks to wrap up a case; pretty good timing. He wished it would take longer.

"Do you have any more steaks?" Rain walked onto the deck smelling of the same perfume she'd applied for the potluck that last weekend. It was a wonderfully enticing scent.

"There's a few more in the freezer, but they aren't thawed. Why?" He turned around and then stared at the corset-type blouse she wore and blue jeans that hugged her like a second skin. "Damn, woman. What's the occasion?"

Rain raised one shoulder lazily and let it fall. Her shirt pushed her cleavage together and made it swell over the snug shirt. What she displayed looked a hell of a lot more appetizing than the steaks. And a moment ago, they looked damned good.

"I just got off the phone with Joanna. I thought she just called to check in, but she mentioned she had a date with a friend." Rain's hair was down, which made her look very sultry. "Then she mentioned Jan Gamboa was fighting with her husband and Joanna felt guilty that she couldn't ask her over and get her out of the house for a bit."

"Subtle hint, huh."

Rain smiled and then moved to stand next to him. She breathed in the smell of the steaks, which pressed her breasts against the form-fitting shirt. He focused on where they pressed together, and ached to run his finger down the inviting curves she displayed.

"I took the hint. And anyway, after I called Jan and learned that Sheila Lapthorne was with her"—she offered him a small smile—"they're on their way over."

Noah nodded. "Hopefully we can get more steaks thawed out in time. I don't suppose you're game to make a side dish of any kind."

"You make it sound like I don't ever cook." She held her arms out. "Do I look like I'm starving to death to you?"

"You look like you want something, or possibly are offering something."

Rain turned around and headed back into the kitchen. "Damn. I was just trying to look nice. Is there something wrong with wanting a bit of downtime? This case will be wrapped up in no time, and I don't feel like I've done shit to help get it there."

Noah followed her into the kitchen and grabbed her arm, spinning her around to face him. "You look incredible, Rain. Gorgeous." He pulled her closer, even when she stiffened. Her blue eyes grew large, and she licked her lips, then opened her mouth, her body language suggesting a protest was on the tip of her tongue.

Noah didn't want protests. Maybe it was selfish of him. In a few days they might part ways and never see each other again. But he wouldn't be going into another woman's arms, and something about Rain appealed to him too damned much to just ignore her during their time together.

He tangled his fingers in her silky hair and held her in place while devouring her mouth. Rain stiffened further, and her fingers dug into his shoulders, like she would push him away. When her tongue moved around his and the heat she offered soaked over him like an aphrodisiac, he growled, instantly needing her more than he needed to breathe.

Rain sighed into him, and instead of pushing away, her fingers drew lines up his neck, and then she massaged his head while a soft, yearning sound escaped her.

Noah got so fucking hard that he damn near came. The sound she made matched the craving burning feverishly inside him. Breaking the kiss, he nipped at her lower lip, then dragged his tongue down her neck, nipping at her soft flesh. Rain hissed, and the temperature in the room got even hotter. He inhaled and filled his lungs with her perfumed scent.

"How much time do we have before they show up?" he growled.

Rain dragged her fingers through his hair and then rested her hands on his shoulders. "Not enough."

"A quickie?"

She laughed. "A quickie wouldn't work with you." She stepped back and adjusted her shirt, cupping her breasts and straightening her clothes.

Noah reached in to help. The least he could do. "I messed you up," he said, grinning at her while he fondled her, knowing he did damn little to fix her clothing.

"You didn't mess me up," she told him, and walked toward the hallway. Then as she turned and looking over her shoulder, her blue eyes smoldered even as her expression hardened. "I won't let you mess me up," she whispered.

Noah let her go without commenting, although he understood her words. As much as he hated admitting it, it was exactly what he'd been thinking outside. There was

something between them, something he'd like to understand. Rain wasn't going anywhere. Once this case
was solved he'd be on a plane to D.C. Unless Brenda had
another pending case, and then he'd be shipped off to God
only knew where. Either way, it would be impossible to
say when he'd see Rain again. He didn't want a relationship with a woman he only saw a couple times a year.
Rain wouldn't want that, either.

Grabbing several more steaks out of the freezer, he got
busy thawing them out. From the bits of information
they'd shared with each other, Noah knew Rain's father
kept a tight leash on his daughter. As bullheaded as Rain
was, Noah knew she wouldn't do anything she didn't want
to do. But Rain loved her father a lot. Noah saw that. She
didn't press dating because it upset her father. Hugh
Huxtable was selfish, keeping his daughter to himself.
Noah would give the deceased man this much, though: he
had brought up an incredible lady, with scruples and enough
guts to take on the world and get what she wanted.

There was one flaw, though. Rain wanted him. Her
loyalties to her dead father were still so strong she wouldn't
admit it was okay to want him. And that was where Noah
was torn. If he pushed her, Noah could have what he
wanted. But would it be fair to instigate something neither
one of them was sure they could handle?

Noah continued brooding over this while preparing the
steaks and adding more steaks once they were thawed. He
glanced through the open door from the back deck when
he heard women laughing inside. But when he heard a
man's voice, Noah put his tongs down and headed inside.

"You haven't eaten until you've had my man's barbecue," Rain sang out, grinning broadly at him, as she walked
into the kitchen from the living room. She held a wine
cooler in her hand and her face was flushed with color,
which added to her incredible sex appeal. "Come here and
meet everyone," she said, wrapping her arm through his
and guiding him into the living room.

"Sure hope you don't mind us crashing your private

party this evening." A man probably close to fifty, with a box of beer under his arm, stepped away from Joanna's side. "Richard Swanson. I've heard good things about both of you."

"I'm glad to hear it," Noah said, falling into the role of happy and carefree husband quickly. "Let's get those in the refrigerator."

"So you two are new to town?" Richard asked, following him into the kitchen. "Joanna gave me the full rundown on both of you on our way over here."

"Joanna is a nice lady," Noah said, opening the refrigerator and moving items to make room for the beer. "And yes, we are."

"Make room for my wine," Jan sang, and grabbed his ass when she came up behind him. "I am getting drunk tonight!"

"We've always got room," he told her, winking and accepting the boxed wine. Her glazed-over eyes showed she was already well on her way to accomplishing her mission. "And I hope you all are hungry. Rain is right about one thing: I do love to grill."

"Everything smells so good. Although you know Steve and Susie are going to blackball you if they think you're throwing a party behind their back," Joanna announced.

Her words sent a noticeable chill through the room, and for a moment everyone was quiet.

"Don't be silly," Rain said, breaking the silence. "This is completely impromptu. People don't really blackball anyone, anyway."

Jan made a loud snorting sound and then started coughing.

"Joanna's right, but fuck them," a woman Noah guessed was Sheila Lapthorne announced, and then raised a fresh bottle of beer in a mock salute. "They don't care about anyone but themselves anyway."

"I doubt they care about each other that much, either," Jan said, and grinned at Rain. "Do you have any wineglasses, hon? And you will drink with us, won't you? I brought enough for all of us. That little wine cooler won't give you the buzz this wine will."

"Of course." Rain moved through the group who'd congregated in the kitchen.

Richard tilted his head and looked like he might start drooling as he stared at Rain's ass when she opened one of the cabinets and stretched to pull down wineglasses she and Noah had purchased along with a lot of the other kitchen items he'd bought and charged to the FBI.

Noah turned to catch Joanna scowling at Richard, but the moment she noticed him watching her, she winked and then grabbed her breasts, squeezing them as if that was an invitation for him to come do the same.

"They sure as hell care about what all of us do, though," Sheila said bitterly. "And I tell you what, you two will learn, don't cross them."

"And don't be deceived by Susie, either," Jan said, grinning when Rain handed her a wineglass and then turning to Noah, who still stood in front of the refrigerator. "I've never known such a small woman to have more power."

"What do you mean?" Rain handed Noah her glass, too, and then crossed her arms over her chest, creating an incredible distraction with the cleavage she displayed. "I mean, I only spent some time with her at the potluck at your house, Jan, but she seemed pleasant enough."

"That means she wants something from you," Richard offered, and then moved in, smiling wickedly when he put his arm around Rain and pointedly stared at her breasts. "And I know Susie Porter well. She doesn't want what I want."

Everyone started laughing, and quick work was made of getting everyone's drinks poured or beers offered. Noah was shocked when Rain checked the oven and he realized she'd wrapped potatoes and had them baking. But his shock was noticeable enough to render him busted when he gawked at the casserole dish she pulled out with hot pads.

"Accuse me of not being able to cook again," she

snarled under her breath when he managed to reach her side.

"Oh, that's right!" Joanna announced, and hurried out of the kitchen and then back a moment later, holding a can in the air. "One can of French-fried onions."

"You're a lifesaver." Rain set the casserole dish on the back of the stove and popped open the can. She sprinkled the crispy onions over the bubbling green beans and grinned at him triumphantly. "Green-bean casserole."

"I'm impressed," he whispered, and leaned into her, nibbling on her ear. "How did you know green-bean casserole was one of my favorite dishes?" he whispered so only she would hear.

Although with the loud chatter surrounding them he probably could have said anything to her without them being overheard. And there were a few more things he would like her to hear. One of them being, he would do his damndest to fuck her after everyone left.

"Are you going to share some of that tonight?" Richard asked, coming up on the other side of Rain and running his hand down her hair.

Noah caught his meaning immediately. "Rain makes her own decisions in that department."

Rain looked up at him quickly; her surprised expression that quickly turned to a blush of embarrassment showed he'd caught her off guard.

She looked over to Richard. "You never know what the night might bring," she said flirtatiously. "But we sure wouldn't want to do anything to upset Steve and Susie. I hate the thought of anyone feeling left out."

Richard's expression hardened so quickly it was almost shocking. "Promise me right now that you won't ever let that bastard manipulate you," he hissed. "And don't trust Susie, either. They want us to have sex with who they say, and damn us if we don't comply. But I'm here to tell you, doing as they say isn't the answer. They pushed and pushed, for the sake of simply seeing how far they could manipulate." He took a breath and forced his expression to relax, searching Rain's face as he did. "My wife, Roberta, was murdered three months ago. The cops don't have a clue. But I do. The Porters pushed her too far, and when she tried pushing back, it cost her life."

Joanna wrapped her icy cold fingers around Noah's arm and snuggled against him, pushing her way between him and Rain.

"I told her not to try and take them on," Joanna said, almost a bit too coolly. "Didn't I tell her?"

Rain shifted and ended up a bit closer to Richard. She glanced at Joanna, and for a moment it looked like Rain didn't appreciate being pushed away from Noah. If he detected irritation in her face, it faded too quickly for him to confirm. Once again she displayed how well she pulled off undercover work when she didn't take Richard's wandering hands off of her but instead patted his arm and gave him a reassuring smile.

"I can't imagine how hard it must be losing your wife and knowing, or I guess feeling pretty sure you know, why she died," Rain said very quietly, although not so much so that Noah couldn't hear her. "I bet you want to go after them and get revenge."

"That won't stop anything. Richard knows that," Joanna offered.

She looked up at Noah and nodded once, but Richard exhaled and then finally took his hands off of Rain long enough to open his beer.

"It won't stop until they figure out they aren't in charge," Sheila said from behind Richard, proving their conversation wasn't discreet even though they spoke quietly while the women behind them chatted among themselves.

Jan hummed her agreement and downed her glass of wine. "Steve just wants to know that every woman in his world will put out for him whenever he wants them to."

"He's not that bad," Joanna chirped, and then nudged her cold, wet bottle of beer against Noah's arm. "Open this for me, please?" she purred under her breath. "I can't ever open bottles of beer without breaking a nail." Batting her lashes at him while turning enough that her large, fake breasts pressed against his arm didn't sell him on her attempt to appear helpless and vulnerable.

Noah seriously doubted Joanna was either.

"You'd bad-mouth him, too, if he weren't padding your bank account," Jan added.

"Jan," Joanna wailed, and took the open bottle Noah offered her.

He met Rain's concerned look and knew the only way to keep them going, and possibly learn enough to nail the bastard, was to allow the women to battle it out. Richard looked Noah's way, too, raising one eyebrow as if silently suggesting a diversion would be a good idea.

"Rain," he said. "Do we have enough chairs for all of us to sit out on the patio?" He knew she probably didn't have a clue, and there definitely were enough, but it was enough to distract the women, and for Jan to leave Joanna alone and head for the refrigerator to help herself to more wine. Once he had everyone situated, it would be a damned good idea to record their conversations.

"I can help take chairs out," Richard offered.

Noah nodded and turned to the garage door, but Joanna grabbed his arm again. She actually pinched his skin when she held him where he was and leaned in close.

"The truth is that those who don't listen to Steve and Susie pay, not the other way around." Joanna searched Noah's face when he looked at her. Her tan face offset her blue eyes, which at the moment glowed fiercely. "Steve is an incredible man. Don't listen to them. I know you'll agree when you get to spend more time with both of them."

"I'm sure," he told her, focusing on the intense glow he hadn't noticed in her eyes before as she spoke. Possibly she had stronger feelings for Steve than she should have, especially if he was helping her out financially.

"Even though you're a man, I'm sure you've got it a lot like I do," she continued, and then pulled a strand of her red hair forward and toyed with it while licking her lips and looking up at him suggestively. "Every woman here wants to fuck you, even your wife," she added, and then giggled. "You understand when temptation grows so strong you can't ignore it. Not everyone is strong enough to fight it. But those who don't even try, who give in and fuck absolutely everyone, those are the ones who ruin it for people like you and me."

Not only did he not have a goddamned clue what she was talking about, but the way she kept pressing into him, rubbing her boobs against him, began annoying the crap out of him. But it was her eyes, a much different shade of blue from Rain's, that worried him. In all of his years of interrogating, he'd learned to recognize the psychopaths, those mentally off or criminally hardened. If he didn't know better, he'd swear that Joanna had lost a few screws on her way over here.

"Here you go, sweetheart." Rain interrupted his conversation with Joanna, if it could be called that, and handed him a couple wooden folding chairs from the garage.

He turned away from Joanna quickly, and enjoyed the hell out of the view Rain offered with her corset top and her cleavage swelling as she handed him the chairs.

"Thanks, darling," he said, pulling his focus from her breasts to her face.

Rain didn't scowl, or show any sign of frustration or even jealousy over him talking to Joanna, but her blue eyes were as dark as thunderheads ready to explode. Rain didn't like other women hanging on him, and that about made him swell like a peacock, proud as hell that "his woman" looked ready to fight for him.

"If the food in here is ready to go, the steaks are good." Noah stuck to Rain's side, opening the chairs on the deck and then holding one for her to sit. "Enjoy your drink and chat with everyone. I'll bring the food out here and we'll make it a serve-yourself type of dinner."

"I don't mind helping," Sheila announced, opening her chair but then standing behind it.

"We'll all help." Jan struggled with her chair and her glass of wine. She was getting drunk quickly, and he knew she would need a ride home later.

It took more time than it should have taken to get everyone served. Noah ended up standing back by his grill and placing steaks on plates when they were brought to him. Rain didn't seem to mind the chaos surrounding her with everyone drinking, shuffling around one another to put food on their plates, and seeming determined to cop feels off of everyone in the kitchen, and then again on the back deck. It was more of a blessing than whoever had picked out this house for use in undercover work might have guessed that large bushes grew down the property line on each side of the yard. If anyone saw the antics going on, they would call the police. Rain would have Noah's head for that.

Noah stood with the grill as his shield from the antics and knew without any doubt Laurel would never have tolerated the lack of organization he watched. She would have created an assembly line, barked orders. Noah shook his head. Laurel, on the one hand, wouldn't have allowed an impromptu party, and she would have had it catered. Rain, on the other hand, appeared from the kitchen, watching everyone once they appeared with their plates of food and settled in their chairs on the deck, and grinned. Her smile didn't fade when she walked up to him, holding her plate for the steak he'd saved for her. She held another plate in her other hand and offered it to him.

"Extra green-bean casserole," she informed him, looking very relaxed and at ease.

"Save me a seat," he said, pulling her close and kissing her affectionately while she still held both plates. He nibbled her lower lip and loved how her moist, swollen lips formed a small circle as she stared up at him with sensual blue eyes when he straightened. "I'll be right back."

Noah didn't take more than a minute when he entered the empty house and confirmed his recording equipment was on. He managed to sit next to Rain and enjoyed the food and the conversation, which had shifted from anyone in their group or swinging and varied from local politics to popular movies playing right now.

"That was incredible food." Richard placed his plate on the ground by his chair and then grabbed Rain's knee. "I'm really curious if there is anything you aren't good at."

"You are such a slut," Jan said, her words slurring as she fell sideways against Richard.

"It takes one to know one," Joanna said, sitting across from Noah and stretching her legs so that her toes touched his.

"You should know," Jan retorted.

The two women broke into a fit of giggles and Sheila met his gaze and rolled her eyes. For being possibly the oldest woman present, she was very attractive. She looked a bit gaunt in the face, but her light brown hair, which looked good trimmed short around her face, and the casual tank top and shorts she wore helped show off a tanning-booth tan that was damn near as dark as Joanna's.

"This is probably the best evening I've had in a long time," Sheila told him, and then glanced at Rain, who sat next to Noah. "I can't remember when I didn't feel tension in the air while with everyone."

"That's because Noah and Rain are so perfect," Joanna purred. "They wouldn't try and manipulate or change how everything is supposed to be."

"My husband didn't try to change anything," Sheila said quickly, looking stricken by Joanna's words.

"Honey, don't put yourself through this again." Joanna reached out and touched Sheila's knee. "You just said tonight was perfect. We're going to keep it that way."

"Ted would kill me if I played without him." Jan pulled her knees up to her chest and started giggling.

Jan's short skirt slid up her thighs and she wasn't wearing underwear. As well, she was completely shaved between her legs. Jan was drunk and married. She lifted her gaze and stared at Noah with glazed eyes and then offered a small smile. There wouldn't be any way he could tap that, in spite of Jan's obvious invitation.

"Only if he caught you first," Richard told her slyly.

"Your husband is the least of your worries. God forbid you do anything without Steve's blessing," Sheila said. "Or you know what." She held her hands together like a gun and then made a popping sound with her mouth when she pulled the trigger.

"Sheila!" Joanna hissed.

"What are you going to do? Tell him I said that?" Sheila demanded.

"I don't understand." Rain held her hand up, causing both women and the others to look at her. "If all of you are so convinced Steve is killing your spouses and friends, why don't you go to the police?"

"We can handle our own affairs without intrusion of the judicial system," Joanna said, straightening and tugging on her shirt so that it stretched over her large breasts.

"When my husband was shot several months ago," Sheila began quietly.

"Sheila," Joanna said with a warning in her tone.

Sheila ignored her. "No one else had been shot. There were some things from his past, and honestly, I thought an old ghost came forward. I didn't know then that Lynn was dead. It wasn't until Lorrie and Patty were killed I realized they all died the same way."

"That's not true," Richard said, and then stood, turning and pointing at empties, gathering them up, and then pausing before entering the door to the kitchen. "My Roberta was shot and killed in her car before Lynn. I knew she was cheating on me and figured a lover was pissed that she wouldn't leave me."

"Any woman would be a fool to leave you." Joanna handed him her empty bottle and then ran her fingernails up his arm, smiling suggestively up at him.

"So how many are dead?" Rain glanced at him and then around at the others, her expression shocked. "And they all died the same way?"

"This is not something you can discuss with anyone." Joanna pointed a finger at Rain but then looked at Noah with an expression so hard and cold it changed her entire appearance. "Because I promise if you do, you'll be the next to die."

"Joanna, that sounds terrible," Jan whispered, covering her cheeks with her hands.

Noah wasn't sure he'd ever seen blue eyes look so cold and demonic as Joanna's did before she slowly pulled her attention from him and focused on Jan. But then everything about Joanna softened, like sweet butter melting, altering her entire appearance. Hard edges disappeared, and her eyes once again glowed with life and mischief.

"I just don't want anyone else to die," she said softly, and scooted closer to Jan, then put her arm around her. She kissed Jan's cheek softly, but then she adjusted her head and Joanna kissed her on the lips, a slow, passionate kiss that two lovers might share.

"Man, I leave for one minute," Richard complained, reappearing with a handful of beers and also managing to balance Jan's glass of wine.

Noah jumped up to help pass out drinks. "I was enjoying every minute for you," Noah assured him.

"I'm sure you were," Richard told him with a wry grin.

Noah took one of the beers and handed it to Sheila. Rain stared, head down, at her wineglass, which she turned slowly, causing the wine to swirl against the rim. She appeared lost in thought, and he sat down, ignoring the others while they chatted, and placed his hand on her wrist. Her tense expression didn't completely fade when she looked up at him. Several of the comments could have upset her, or all of them for that matter, and he hated guessing what put that look on her face.

It faded quickly and she masked her expression, giving him an adoring look he wished was real. As if she'd been doing it for years, she moved her hand, and squeezed his.

"I'll get the plates cleaned up," she said quietly.

"I can help." He let her stand first.

Rain bent to pick up Jan's plate. She was so grossly preoccupied with stroking Joanna's face and telling her she would never do anything to hurt her that she didn't notice Rain move around her.

Sheila offered her plate to Rain and then smiled at Noah. "You have no idea how relaxing it is spending time with you two," she said, sounding sincere.

"There's no pressure. We don't have to worry about being watched," Richard added.

"I'm watching you," Joanna said.

Jan jumped, almost spilling her fresh glass of wine, looking like she'd forgotten that anyone besides her and Joanna was there. Noah watched Joanna carefully, looking for that intensity he saw in her eyes earlier. It wasn't there. Instead they glowed, almost glazed but nothing like Jan's. Joanna shifted her attention to Noah when she caught him studying her and the corner of her mouth lifted as she slowly winked at him.

"Excuse me, please," he said, getting up and moving around Joanna, brushing his hand over her coarse long red hair.

It wasn't smooth and silky like Rain's but instead was almost rough, and held in place with enough gel that a hard wind wouldn't lift it off her shoulders. Ironically, the touch of her matched her nature. Joanna appeared the perfect seductress, almost pretty if you didn't stare too long. But the truth he was quickly learning was that she possessed a biting cruelty about her. He knew that was what he saw when her blue eyes hardened and glared at him earlier.

"How are you doing?" he asked Rain, pausing next to her while she loaded the dishwasher with rinsed plates.

"Good, you?" She glanced up at him, offering a very professional smile, which told him a very different story from what she voiced.

"Curious," he told her honestly, and then brushed his knuckles down her cheek.

Rain glanced past him at the group out on the deck. "They are all terrified of Steve and Susie," she whispered, and then looked into his eyes. "I wonder why. It can't just be because they're bossy. Those are a relatively normal group of people out there, but two of them have lost their spouses and won't share anything they feel with the police. What kind of manipulative behavior would it take for you to lose the love of your life and then do nothing to see their killer brought to justice?"

"We'll find out and you're right. It's not normal behavior, yet it seems to be coming out of normal people." He pondered the type of stimuli that would cause an individual to go against the grain of what they believed was right and wrong. He leaned against the counter, focusing on everyone lounging in their chairs, with Joanna and Jan once again kissing each other. "Unless of course, they've all redefined what they claim to be normal."

"Do you mean because they're swingers?" Rain closed the dishwasher and picked up her wineglass. "Have they shifted into a world slightly altered from what most deem as the accepted norm and therefore are able to tolerate what most would abhor and view as unacceptable?"

"I don't think it's because they're swingers." He focused on the moisture from her wine, clinging to her lips, and ached to taste her. "Swinging isn't as abnormal as those who don't swing wish to believe. It's a silent society, so discreet that those who aren't part of it don't realize how many people actually swing."

"You sound like you approve of it?" she asked, whispering and licking her lips while studying his face.

"I didn't say that." It sure as hell wasn't for him. That much he knew. The thought of sharing the woman he loved with anyone made his blood boil. But he wasn't closed-minded enough to not acknowledge others felt differently. His best man, Pete Compton, did his best to explain how he wouldn't mind fucking Noah's fiancée, but in no way would he do it without Noah's blessing. At the time, Noah fought the urge to punch his best friend in the face.

"I could possibly buy into that theory. But what can we use to defend these people? As it stands now, every one of them is going to be accessory to a crime if they continue to remain silent when they know who killed their loved ones."

"We don't have proof on Steve yet."

"You think he did it as much as I do." She narrowed her gaze on him, searching his face, and brought the glass to her lips again. Then, placing the glass on the counter, she crossed her arms over her chest, causing her cleavage to swell and create a sight distracting enough to make it hard to focus on her next words. "I want to know more about Steve and Susie Porter. What do you say to having them over for dinner? Let's see what makes these two so terrifying yet completely in control of the group they obviously have a stranglehold on."

SEVENTEEN

Rain stared at the monitoring equipment. The screen glowed in the dark room, burning her eyes. She rubbed them and reached for her Diet Dr Pepper. Noah's slow, steady breathing that she'd grown to know meant he was sound asleep called to her. She pressed her legs together, somewhat chilly after just waking up, and also willing the pressure that built inside her to go away. They had a lot to do today, typical Monday, and it would rock to start the day out with some hot and sweaty sex.

Getting out of the office chair, she left the monitoring equipment in the small second bedroom and padded barefoot over the cool floors into the hallway. Since they'd installed the GPS devices on the two cars at the Porters', there hadn't been any surprises. Trips to the grocery store, a liquor store, and two visits to an office building over on

O Street. The car parked in the front drive didn't move all weekend.

The cold hardwood floor added to the chill that rushed over her body. She paused outside the bedroom door where Noah slept, again enjoying the large comfortable bed by himself while she stubbornly endured the self-torture of the couch. Noah refused to sleep on it anymore, telling her he was too old to suffer the lumps and flat cushions. He argued they could both sleep in the bed and he wouldn't do anything she didn't want to do.

That was the problem. She wanted it. Wanted it so damned bad that she possibly would be an ice cube right now if it weren't for the raging need swelling from her womb and keeping parts of her way too warm. She stood where she was for a moment, focusing on the dark wave of hair that fell over one eyebrow. Long, thick lashes draped his eyes, and his pronounced cheekbones and long, straight nose gave him a regal, dominating look. There wasn't anything about this dark, brooding man that didn't appeal to her. No matter how hard she tried staying away from him, she was falling hard for him.

Almost two weeks. Two damn weeks. Rain never would have guessed herself the type of woman who would fall in love so easily.

It's not love. Maybe a seriously dangerous case of lust and infatuation, but not love.

Rain turned away, forcing herself to focus on the case. A hot shower would help, more caffeine, and then checking in down at the station. Plus, soon possibly ballistics would confirm the gun confiscated from the Porters matched the bullets found at each crime scene.

Rain closed the bathroom door quietly and stripped out of her nightshirt she always slept in. Dropping it to the floor, she tried picturing Steve Porter working at a small printing press. It wasn't the type of work she pictured him doing. It even surprised Noah when they verified Steve's employment at Hardister Press, his title simply Production Supervisor.

Since Hardister Press was a newer company, having been in Lincoln less than three years, Rain didn't know a lot about the business, other than no complaints existed against them. The business, registered as sole proprietor and not incorporated, didn't strike her as the type of company that would enable the Porters to live as they did and drive the cars they drove. Yet another mystery about the enigmatic Steve Porter.

Rain stepped into the hot shower and hummed her approval as the pelts of water hit her shoulders and front. Turning around, she leaned her head back and soaked her hair, then reached for shampoo and lathered, scrubbing her scalp, and enjoyed the steamy water that quickly filled with the orange scent of her shampoo.

Rain blinked, her eyes instantly burning, when the shower curtain moved and Noah stepped into her space.

"What the fuck?" she hissed, turning around quickly and ducking into the stream of water.

"I just got a phone call," he said, his voice deep with sleep.

"That's nice." She rinsed quickly, her heart suddenly pounding furiously.

How dare he violate her perfect shower and then stand right behind her, naked, and not touching her. Rain went to so much effort trying to keep her mind off fucking him and Noah wasn't helping her a bit. She spit water out of her mouth and pushed her hair back out of her face.

"We've got a confirmation on the murder weapon. It matches the bullets."

Rain turned around quickly, almost slipping. He grabbed her waist and she froze, blinking a couple times and then focusing on his face. His hair was slightly damp from the water that sprayed off of her and hit him, and it made the dark strands almost black in spots as it clung to his forehead. Tiny curls pressed against his muscular chest, too.

Goddamn, he was sexy as hell.

Her gaze lowered, and she closed her eyes, wishing she

hadn't looked. Noah was hard as stone, and her body responded to the view she had just inflicted upon her suddenly frazzled brain.

"You couldn't have waited to tell me?" she asked, her voice cracking as need swelled inside her so painfully she doubted it would go away until he relieved her of the craving he had just instilled inside her.

"I thought you wanted to know." He let go of her waist but then moved closer, his body pressing against hers as he reached over her shoulder and picked up her conditioner.

"Noah," she sighed, needing to voice a complaint. Rain didn't get how for years it was so easy to keep men at bay, but with Noah she didn't even want to try. She could just imagine what her father would have to say. Not that she ever would have told him, if he were still alive, that she was being intimate with her FBI partner while working a case. Just thinking about it helped sober her a bit.

Noah's gaze met hers as he opened the bottle and poured an ample amount into his hand. "Figured I'd put myself to use since I'm in here."

"You joined me to put yourself to use?" She hated how her voice sounded husky. Every inch of her shook with the amount of need coursing through her.

"Why? Is there something else you want?" He pressed his hands to her scalp, and then slowly massaged the conditioner into her hair.

"Umm, this is good," she breathed as he gathered her hair off her shoulders and worked the conditioner until suds dripped over her face.

His hands left her scalp and blocked the water behind her briefly. He was close, so damned close, with his muscular arms on both sides of her head and his chest brushing against her nipples. She couldn't open her eyes, but she didn't need to. Seeing him wouldn't help matters at the moment. As it was, every inch of her tingled and she fisted her hands on either side of her, determined not to lift them and touch him.

His fingers touched her face and she jumped; then confident hands held her while he wiped soap from her eyes. She blinked, and found herself staring into his eyes.

Noah's gaze smoldered with so much heat she couldn't breathe. Her heart hurt as she continued holding her breath when his focus dropped to her mouth.

"It's supposed to feel good, Rain," he said, his mouth barely moving.

She wasn't the only one suffering here. Somehow, that bit of knowledge eased the pain inside her a little, but not very damned much.

Noah reached for the soap, but there wasn't any way she'd be able to handle him touching her everywhere. She tried grabbing it and he raised an eyebrow at her.

"Don't want to be cleaned?" he asked, sounding too damned innocent.

"I can clean myself."

"Fine." He handed her the soap but then grabbed her, crushing her against him while he switched positions with her and completely blocked all water. "You do that."

He let his head fall back and soaked his hair until it pressed against his scalp. The curve of his Adam's apple, the tendons stretching in his neck, and the broad length of his collarbone appealed to her as much as his rippling chest. Muscles bulged everywhere as he made quick work of shampooing his hair and then rinsing.

Rain watched suds stream over his chest, around his belly button, and lower, catching in the dark curls that surrounded his still rock-hard cock. She didn't realize she gripped the soap so hard until it squirted out of her hand and fell to the shower floor.

"Shit," she hissed.

"Lose your soap?" he asked, blinking water and looking down with her.

Rain didn't answer but squatted and reached between his legs to grab the soap. He was so close to her, so damned close. She licked her lips, the steam in the shower only adding to her already-overheated system. Noah's fingers brushed over the top of her head, and she closed her eyes, losing the soap again.

"This isn't fair," she whispered, blinking soapy water out of her eyes and searching again for the soap.

"It's not fair for either one of us." His voice was gruff.

And his fingers moved over her head, pressing, encouraging, until she raised her lashes and let her gaze travel up his body. She didn't get far, not with the length of his shaft thick, swollen, and hard so close to her face.

"Don't talk like that," she complained, forcing her heart back down her throat and lowering her head while searching the bathtub for the soap.

Noah grabbed her, sliding his hands under her armpits and lifting her before she could react. "Do you think I don't know why you're stubbornly sleeping on that godforsaken couch? You can't get near me. And darling, when you do, the need radiating off of you is so charged it makes it damn hard to focus on anything other than burying myself deep inside you."

"Maybe you should request another partner?" she said, clenching her teeth and willing herself to hate him—hate him for being right—and hating herself for her inability to camouflage her emotions better around him.

"I wouldn't have guessed you a quitter."

"I'm not the quitter. You just said you can't handle working with me."

"No, I didn't."

The smoldering need in his eyes erupted into something darker, more dangerous and predatory. She barely had time to focus on a small twitch that started in his jaw when he, once again, moved faster than she had time to react.

His arms were like steel and his body harder than stone when he pulled her into an embrace that damn near suffocated her. Before she could complain, or acknowledge the need inside her swelling to the danger point, his hand tangled in her wet hair, tugging her head back, and he claimed her mouth.

The craving that threatened to explode inside her a moment before erupted with a ferocity that made her weak in the knees. Noah growled into her mouth while his fingers pressed into her spine and then created trails as he stroked her flesh down her back to her ass.

Wherever he touched her, fire ignited yet again until she was more than sure that she would burn alive, keel over from simply a kiss. In spite of the part of her brain that managed to hold on to a bit of rational thought, she couldn't master the strength to make him stop. Worse yet, not only did she not want him to stop; she also wanted more.

The hell with that. She needed more.

"Noah," she gasped.

Her lips tingled and felt numb and swollen. Noah's mouth seared her cheek with fire that damn near melted any coherent arguments left in her brain that supported reasons why she should stop this.

"Hmm?" He sucked on her earlobe while grunting his response.

She held on to his shoulders. His smooth, warm, and wet skin covered solid muscle. Every inch of him was hard, in control, and overwhelming her. He didn't seem to be shaking or hesitating. Noah came into her shower knowing what he wanted and had every intention of taking it.

And damn it all to hell and back. She wanted it, too. There was no argument left inside her that could justify why she should stop him.

The last thing she would ever do was beg, though. "Is this a new way of cleaning a person?"

His deep chuckle sent shivers rushing over her. He blocked a fair bit of the water, but it wasn't a chill she felt. The pressure he released when he first kissed her swelled inside her again, growing and throbbing, aching with every breath she took.

Noah left her ear and stared at her for a moment before dropping his attention to her breasts. "If you don't want this, you better tell me now," he informed her, and at the same time gripped her ass and pushed her, against his hard dick.

Her breasts smashed into his chest and for a moment she swore their hearts beat the same.

It wasn't the sex she didn't want, and she opened her mouth to tell him that. But voicing her concerns that being intimate with him repeatedly would become more than physical, and that she didn't want to get hurt, would complicate things. Already she wasn't sure she understood the glow in his eyes, the confidence with which he held her, and his incredible ability to find the exact spots on her body that made her smolder with an intensity she'd never quite experienced before.

"How are we going to do this in the shower?" It wasn't what she planned on saying, but as she willed the words of caution out of her mouth, what was on her mind most tumbled over her tongue without hesitating.

Noah's intense expression didn't change. His hands moved to her hips and he turned her around. Then pressing his hand in the middle of her back, he pushed her against the shower wall.

Rain pressed her palms against the wet wall and looked over her shoulder as his hard shaft nudged between her legs.

They were the perfect height for each other. She arched her back and, with the slight movement, granted him access. Noah slid inside her, stretching and creating even more of a burning need as he pressed deeper and deeper.

"The water makes you not as wet. Does it feel okay?" His baritone whisper crept into her fogged brain.

"It feels wonderful," she answered truthfully. In fact, it was better than wonderful. Rain was wet, soaked. But the shower water rushed over them, washing the thick cream seeping from her pussy and allowing her to feel every vein, his thickness, and his full length. The way he pressed deeper inside her, the soft flesh over his rock-hard cock like smooth suede. He was rough yet soothing her so in-

credibly perfectly she wanted to cry from the sheer pleasure of it.

He pressed one hand against her stomach and she covered it with her own. Immediately he slid his hand out
from under hers but then put his hand on top, intertwining
their fingers. She closed her eyes, holding his hand and
feeling him burrow farther inside her. He didn't stop until
he was to the point where he could break the pressure that
soared out of control inside her.

"God," she hissed, feeling him so close to where she
needed him.

Yet he stopped. Her world was seconds from shatter-
ing, the weight of need finally appeased. Yet he stopped.
He fucking stopped.

"Damn it, Noah," she cried out, dragging her nails
down the shower wall and then twitching her ass in an effort to get him moving again.

"You need this as much as I do," he said, his soft whisper too calm.

His voice raked over her nerves and did nothing to
soothe the fever that burned inside her.

"Fuck me," she demanded.

"That's what I thought," he said, the edge of triumph
registering, but a moment too late.

Noah thrust forward, breaking the dam that released
the pressure. He impaled her with enough force she damn
near passed out. And as intense as it was, she needed more,
craved more, cried out, unable to form the words to beg
him to do it again.

She grabbed at the slick shower wall, gripped his hand
at her waist, and held on for dear life.

"Noah, yes," she cried, finally finding words.

Nothing ever felt better. He glided in deep, reaching
that spot again and again that needed him so desperately.
His thick, long dick felt perfect, stroking tortured muscles,
relieving pent-up desire she'd tried ignoring for too long.
Nothing had ever felt so perfect, so incredibly satisfying.

Rain arched into him, causing him to go deeper with his next thrust, and she howled.

"You're perfect, Rain. Do you know that?" he growled over her, his hands holding her waist, his fingers long and his grip tight.

Rain opened her mouth to answer him, not caring what words came out. There weren't words to praise the intensity that he delivered, carnal and rough yet so incredibly soothing and perfect.

"Yes," she gasped. "Perfect."

She felt herself tighten around him, was acutely aware of his thickness, the length, and every time he spasmed inside her. Noah fought to hold on, to keep up the momentum, and it made her aware, also, that he needed this as much as she did.

Maybe even more, since he instigated it. That created a spark of hope inside her. Possibly this was more than sex for him. If it was?

"Rain, sweetheart," he growled, running his fingers down the length of her arm until he stretched his fingers over hers, both of them pressing against the shower wall together.

As he moved his other hand, gripping her shoulder and almost pinching her skin while creating friction between them she doubted all the water coming from the shower could extinguish, his lovemaking turned almost brutal. And God, she loved it. Needed it. Prayed it would never stop.

"You're so tight, so goddamned fucking perfect."

He swelled, thrusting one last time, and then roared next to her ear, bearing down hard while he spilled everything he had deep inside her.

Rain's world shattered, lights exploding before her eyes when she climaxed along with him. She heard her cries, knew she uttered words, but for the life of her didn't have a clue what she said. When he eased out of her, leaving her feeling empty, stretched, yet so incredibly satisfied, Rain didn't fight him when he held her close as he straightened. Nor did she care when he took great care washing her, making sure she was thoroughly rinsed, and then held her in his arms, cradling her while the water pattered over her back. There were things they needed to do. Lives depended on it. Yet Rain didn't have any desire for this moment to end, feeling one with Noah, completely relaxed, and possibly for the first time in her life not worrying about preventing someone from getting too close. Because it was too late. Noah had seeped deep inside her, and she felt him there still.

Half an hour later, Rain considered blow-drying her hair a bit before they headed out. She pulled ankle-length socks onto her feet and then slipped into her tennis shoes while Noah talked on the phone out in the living room. He continued talking as he headed back to the bedroom and sat in front of the computer where she could see him.

"We've still got usual movement, or at least the pattern remains the same since the GPS devices were put on their cars," he told Brenda, his supervisor, whom he'd been on the phone with since Rain came out of the bathroom.

She tucked her shirt into her shorts and stared at Noah, who sat in the chair without a shirt on. The top button of his jeans was undone, and the sprinkles of dark hair on his chest were curled tight, having dried that way after the shower.

He ran his fingers through his dark, damp hair and rested his elbow on the edge of the desk, hiding his face from her. "His car is parked at his work, a press located over on O Street. And Susie Porter's car, or at least the second car registered in their name, still hasn't moved from in front of the house. Hell, for all we know Susie might not drive." He paused and then, as if sensing she watched him, lifted his head and looked in her direction, his expression ragged. He'd been drilled, answered the same questions over and over again, as if he were the suspect in this case and not the investigator. "Yes, it's possible she uses another car, but we didn't see one at their home." Again a pause while he rolled his eyes at her. "Yup. We'll be down at the field office here in a few."

Rain fought the urge to yank the phone from his hand and disconnect the call. Noah's supervisor was a pushy bitch and a pain in the ass. Her questions were redundant and the sooner she backed off, the sooner Rain and Noah could get to work.

Returning to the bathroom, she stared at herself in the mirror when Noah came in and then moved behind her, wrapping his arms around her waist and then clasping his hands over her gut.

"We're heading down to the field office, getting the report on the weapon, and then we're supposed to get a warrant." He rested his chin on the top of her head.

She stared at him through the mirror. Even though she was well sated, with his arms wrapped around her and his body pressed against her backside, every inch of her tingled.

"Sounds like it's all wrapped up," she said, contemplating the thought of trying to fuck him again.

He continued studying her, not making any effort to let her go. "What's on your mind?" he asked slowly.

There wasn't any way she could talk to him about the two of them. Technically, there was no "two of them." Blowing out a sigh, she forced her attention to her own reflection in the mirror. There wasn't anything she could do about her hair with him resting his head on top of hers.

"I'm not sure we're ready for an arrest," she offered instead of sharing the thoughts that plagued her.

"I agree." He lifted his head but pulled her back against him. "Go on," he encouraged.

"I'm sure your supervisor won't put any merit on a cop's hunches."

"She doesn't put any merit on my hunches," he said, continuing to watch her in the mirror with a gaze so intense her insides fluttered, making it damn hard to organize her thoughts. He brushed his thumb over the underpart of her breast, his eyes growing bright when she sucked in a breath. "Tell me your hunch," he encouraged.

"Last night," she began, sighing and relaxing in his arms. It felt so good with his strong arms wrapped around her. "Everyone seems to have quite a resentment toward Steve. If you ask me, it almost makes him more the victim than the criminal. I just don't think we have this all the way figured out yet."

"What's your take on the gun that is registered to Steve Porter being the murder weapon?"

Rain frowned. Damned good question. "I say there is still something we don't know yet."

Noah nodded and backed up, then released her and headed out of the bathroom. When he paused in the doorway, corded muscles stretched and flexed in his arms and bare chest when he faced her, his expression tight. "Do you hate the fact as much as I do that we can't be the ones to question those two?"

Rain looked at him and grinned at his brooding expression. "I would kill for the opportunity to interrogate either one of those two."

"That's my girl," he said, and headed down the hallway. "You about ready to go?"

Rain stared at her reflection. She managed to straighten her hair with her fingers where Noah tousled it, and then quickly grabbed a hair clasp. Twisting it into a quick bun at the top of her head, she secured the clasp and then called it done.

"Ready!" she announced.

In spite of spending the first half of the day working on paperwork and then the latter part of the afternoon down in the detectives' lounge bullshitting with several of the officers and listening while Noah and a few of her co-workers swapped war stories, Rain was surprised when the chief showed up.

"We've got Steve Porter in interrogation room two, and his wife is in three," he said, not entering the room but standing in the doorway. He looked tired and squinted like he did when he had a headache. "You can come up and listen and watch if you want."

"Let's go," Rain said, turning to Noah, who already stood from the desk where he'd sat for the past hour while chatting with one of the older detectives on the force.

The chief stopped at the elevator, but Rain was wound too tight. "Want to take the stairs?" she asked Noah. She smiled when Chief Noble raised an eyebrow. "Sorry, Chief, nothing personal. I've got a lot of energy to burn."

"Come talk to me before you leave," he said, and then turned when the elevator doors opened.

Rain envied the hell out of Al when the detective entered the interrogation room where Steve sat waiting. He looked up, taking her in with a slow, curious gaze, as he made a show of letting his attention trail down her body.

"Where's my wife?" he asked, leaning back in the chair and crossing his arms. He glanced toward the two-way mirror where Rain and Noah sat on the other side. "And who's over there watching me? I have rights, you know."

"Yes, you do." Al was a pretty decent interrogator.

Rain knew Al could do her job well. Nonetheless, she chomped at the bit.

"Ever been on this side before?" Noah asked when she jumped out of her chair.

"No, and I don't like it." She stood with her back to him and crossed her arms, listening as Steve's and Al's voices came through the speaker over her head.

"You want me to remember where I was three months ago?" Steve laughed easily. "I don't remember where I was every minute of last week, let alone yesterday."

"What kind of relationship did you have with Roberta Swanson?"

"Roberta and Richard were good friends of ours. You aren't questioning my wife about her, are you? She was destroyed when Roberta died. I don't want her hurt all over again."

"Answer the question, please, Mr. Porter. What was your relationship with Roberta?"

"Are you asking if she was my lover?" Steve's cocky expression would nail him to the cross, and as shrewd as he liked to come across, obviously he wasn't smart enough to realize that.

"I'm asking what your relationship was with her."

"She was a friend. A good friend. And one that I miss," he added, almost as an afterthought.

"And Lynn Handel?"

"Wait a minute. You think I killed them." Steve pointed at Al and then looked at the two-way mirror, for the first time appearing serious. "Well, you can just tell everyone right now that I didn't kill anyone. Not one of them," he shouted.

A police officer stood just inside the interrogation room behind Al and stepped forward when Steve started yelling. Al held her hand up for the officer to stay where he was and kept her attention on Steve.

"Mr. Porter," she said, sounding annoyed. "Saturday morning the police were called to your house over a domestic dispute."

"I'm sincerely sorry that the neighbors were bothered. Every married couple has their moments." He held his hands out in surrender. "That doesn't make me a killer."

"You're aware that a gun was fired during that argument."

"The gun going off didn't have anything to do with our fight." He sounded exasperated. "I was cleaning it and didn't realize it was loaded. Susie wasn't even in the same room when it fired."

"Good thing," Al said dryly. "And that gun is registered to you, yes?"

"Of course it is. It's perfectly legal."

Rain shook her head and turned to see Noah resting his head on his palms and staring at the glass. He looked up at her when she glanced down at him.

"I agree," he grunted.

"You don't know what I was going to say."

"Sure I do." Noah stood and stretched. "He didn't do it."

"I don't think he's smart enough to have pulled it off." She turned and scowled at the glass.

"You aren't asking my wife about that gun, are you?" Steve demanded. "She hates that it's in the house. I always keep it out of sight, and believe me, she threw a bloody fit when I accidentally fired it. Put a hole through the kitchen cabinet, which she's making me pay for out of my check. And I told the police that."

"Yes, you did. I have your report right here." Al looked at her paperwork in front of her and then put her hands on it and stared hard at Steve. "Mr. Porter, I'm going to be very clear with you. I want you to think carefully before you respond to what I'm going to say."

Steve didn't respond but looked at her. Not only was his cockiness gone, but his serious expression teetered on nervousness now. Rain kept a close eye on him while Al spoke.

"When your gun was confiscated, several tests were run on it. Ballistics has the ability to determine if bullets found at a crime scene match a gun when it's brought in later."

Steve didn't say anything but stared at her, not blinking, as if waiting anxiously for what she would say next.

"Your gun is the gun that fired the shots that killed Roberta Swanson, Lynn Handel, George Lapthorne, Lorrie Hinders, and Patricia Henderson."

Steve jumped out of his chair, for a moment looking like he would leap over the table and attack Al. Noah was on his feet just as quickly, and the cop behind Al flew forward, grabbing Steve's arm and forcing him down into his chair.

"I want a lawyer!" Steve screamed. "Give me back my fucking cell phone right now! I'm calling my lawyer! Do you hear me, god damn it? I'm calling my lawyer right now!"

EIGHTEEN

Susie Porter smiled at James, her chauffeur, or at least that was the label she used for him, when he opened her car door and reached for her hand.

"Are you going to be okay tonight?" he asked, searching her face, and then grinning when Susie handed him a fifty.

It was amazing what money could buy. Barely twenty-one, with a perfect, youthful, well-toned body. James was her boy toy, her chauffeur, or whatever she wanted him to be.

"I'm better now, as always." She stood outside the Navigator and watched muscles flex in James's arm when he reached over her and closed the door. "Are you sure you need to go home? I'll be alone all evening tonight."

"It will probably be the best evening you've ever had," he said, winking at her. Those bright green eyes were prettier than rare gems.

And so what if he was a pretty boy? She already married Rough-and-Ready, and he turned out to be spoiled and stupid.

"I have an exam in the morning at seven thirty or you know I would love to spend the night with you here." James glanced around them and then bent over, kissing her quickly and straightening with a mischievous glint in his eyes. "Of course if you need anything in the morning after nine, I'm at your beck and call, my lady."

"Damn right you are," she snapped, and then wagged her eyebrows until he gave her that knowing smile that she loved seeing. He had fucked her as soon as she got the hell out of that nasty police station and already he wanted more. That's the way all men should be. None of this five-

minute "wham bam thank you, ma'am" for her. "I'll text
message you if there is time in the morning. Now be a
good boy and walk me to my door."

James nodded and gallantly turned, hurrying to open
the gate for her, and then walked along the stone path to
her back door. The motion-sensitive light turned on before
they reached the house. She hated that thing and all of the
other ridiculous security precautions that Steve insisted
upon. Like anyone would want to steal any of his crap.
Hell, she'd pay good money for someone to steal his wardrobe. Maybe she should have it all packed up and shipped
off to Goodwill while he spent the night in jail.

"Did you say your father was sending over some of the
servants to keep you company tonight?" James looked up
at the house warily.

"He said he would if I called for them." Susie walked
onto her back porch and then turned, holding the screen
door and smiling down at James. God, he was the epitome
of perfection. "Go make those good grades, my boy toy.
Maybe when you graduate, Daddy will give you a nice job
and an allowance to keep you happy for a lifetime."

"Works for me." He gave her a quick salute and then
turned and jogged back to the Navigator.

Susie entered her quiet house, exhaling as she closed
the door and then leaned against it. Most of the time she
didn't mind a bit leading a completely false life. Well, it
wasn't false in her mind. The rest of the world didn't need
to know shit about how her life really was. If she wanted to
have a rich daddy, who owned corporations around the
world and had enough servants at his disposal that he
could send some over to her on a whim, then that was her
business. No one needed to know she didn't have parents,
rich or poor. Hell, Steve didn't even know until they'd been
married a few years. And more than once she'd kicked
herself in the rear for her moment of weakness when she
thought she actually loved him and could confide in him.

"I can't believe it!" She laughed out loud, staring at
the clock hanging on the wall. Steve got his ass thrown in

jail, and all because of that stupid fucking gun. What an idiot.

Although the cops were even bigger fucking fools if they believed for a moment that someone as dense as her husband could pull off five murders. Hell, he couldn't even pick up his goddamned gun without hurting something. She stared at the hole in the cabinet and started laughing again.

"Probably the best shot you've ever made in your life, you moron." Susie shook her head and headed through the kitchen toward the back stairs, not bothering with lights.

After soaking in her garden tub, which she had to fill with water by herself since her stupid husband wasn't here to do it for her, Susie wrapped her silk bathrobe around her and headed into her bedroom. She knew she was alone, but even so, she glanced around the room before sliding the small wedding picture that hung on their wall to the side. After all these years, she didn't need to see the pad to push the correct buttons. Her closet door buzzed, indicating she'd unlocked it.

Steve might have thrown a fit hundreds of times that he didn't know the combination into her personal office, but tonight was proof she'd made the right choice there. But then, how often did she make a bad decision?

"I hope you rot in prison for life," she mumbled, entering her closet and hitting the light as the door swept closed behind her, locking her in.

Susie pushed the button on her scrambler that prevented anyone from detecting her inside her own piece of sanctuary. It was no one's business what she did while in her own home, or anywhere else for that matter. The only difference between her and the rest of the fucking world was that she had the brains to outsmart all the fools who purchased those spy contraptions and believed they could learn what everyone else did with their own time.

After typing in her password and then pulling down her favorites, Susie popped over to one Web site after another, checking hits first, making sure links worked properly. She was killing time and she knew it, but building up the anticipation always made the moment of discovery all the better.

"Well, I'll be, I almost forgot." She grinned and leaned across her desk where she'd placed the CD earlier this morning. "Susie, you truly are the smartest person on the planet." She kissed the CD case and then opened it and slid it into her D drive.

How many women figured out how to make a million, or two, on their cheating husbands? She meant to create a new Web site when she had time, maybe when she got older and was content to sit at the computer longer. She would design it specifically for those poor pathetic souls who needed to be counseled when they discovered the man they loved cheating with someone younger, prettier, and with more energy to get their man off.

But until that time, she wouldn't be greedy. For now, uploading movies of her husband fucking the little tramps he enjoyed and then selling them for fifty dollars a pop on one of her several Web sites that members could join for thirty dollars a month and then pay fifty dollars for the good stuff. Susie shook her head. If she had an ounce of scruples, she might feel guilty for how much money she drained out of some poor saps. But then if she didn't, who would keep her in the lifestyle she enjoyed? She glanced at the hits and then at the download figures.

"They definitely prefer it when you fuck them in the ass, my dear." Susie couldn't wait any longer and pulled open her personal account to see how much money came in while she'd been down at that pathetic police station. "Come to Mama, baby!" she purred, and grinned from ear to ear at the balance from her shopping-cart Web site.

Clicking to transfer the money out of the account and into one of the several bank accounts she had around the country, she leaned back while the computer hummed. Once her cash was transferred, she probably needed to transfer some of the money from one of her out-of-state accounts into her local bank.

"Idiot is going to cost me some money." She scowled.

Susie stared at her monitor but didn't focus on the screen when it changed and told her the transfer was complete. Instead, it hit her. What the hell had she been thinking?

"My God," she cried out, pushing her chair back and standing so quickly she almost tripped over her own feet. "Crap," she hissed, and then looked distractedly around the small room. "Okay, think. You've got to think."

There wasn't a shred of doubt in her mind that Steve didn't kill any of those fools. Letting him take the fall for it, and praying in fact they would actually press charges and not simply keep him in a holding cell while they gathered their evidence, would be an answer to a prayer. But in the meantime, the real killer was still out there. And she knew who it was. Granted, she wasn't positive. And a shred of doubt was something she hated having. She needed to know for sure.

"Proof yet again as to how damned smart you are, girl." Maybe the cops were stupid, but she sure as hell wasn't.

Susie pushed her chair into her desk but then finally saw her screen. "Okay. Take a deep breath." Not a good sign. Susie almost walked out of her office with her computer still booted up.

Maybe all of this mess had her a bit more frazzled than she wanted to admit. Not that she would ever let a soul know, but it scared the crap out of her, being hauled down to that station. If they searched her and Steve's home, discovered the code pad under their wedding picture, her life would be over.

Not that owning and maintaining a handful of pornography Web sites was against the law, but selling movies of people who didn't know they were being filmed was a minor crime. And it wasn't against the law to make a killing selling videos, or photographs, or live webcam footage, which wasn't really live, but again, it was not a crime. But moving the money around the country, laundering it until it arrived home safely and clean as a whistle, would give the IRS a field day. Susie hadn't reported a dime of income in the past ten years and didn't want to start doing so now.

She took her time closing out her programs and then turning off her computer. Then looking around the large walk-in closet that she'd converted into her own private office so many years ago, she made sure everything was in order. Satisfied that it was, she turned and punched in the code to unlock her bedroom door, turned off the light, and then let it close behind her.

Okay, now for a game plan. Susie paced her bedroom floor, nibbling at her fingernail, while carefully thinking over what had transpired so far.

Steve's gun was the murder weapon. She didn't doubt it, although she knew he couldn't have killed those people. Therefore, he had loaned it to someone, which was probably why he was trying to clean it himself the other morning. Whoever borrowed it had just returned it. Of course, idiot that Steve was, he more than likely had wiped all fingerprints off of the gun other than his own.

She continued pacing. She was smart enough to know that if she left the house, went anywhere for that matter, she would be watched. Susie didn't doubt for a moment that the cops watched her ride James the moment she left that lame excuse for a station.

Grinning, she continued nibbling on her fingernail, remembering how she put some extra show into it tonight. Usually she made James do all the work. Why should she build up a sweat just to get off? Tonight, though, knowing someone had binoculars pinned on her, and probably the equipment to see through the heavily tinted windows of James's Navigator, she got off even more imagining them getting a woody watching her fuck.

She even fantasized about some young, buff thing in uniform coming to the car with his long black stick and handcuffs. Crap! She got wet all over again just thinking about it.

"Damn it, woman," she hissed, banging her fist against

her forehead and then planting her butt on the edge of her bed. Once again her mind was wandering. This wasn't like her. "I guess even you react to a traumatic situation." And getting called into a police station because she had married a moron definitely qualified as trauma.

The questioning she had endured was beyond preposterous, although she deserved a goddamned Oscar for her performance in that interrogation room. Like she would exert the effort to kill any of those people. She didn't care enough about any of them to waste her precious time murdering them.

But someone cared, and it sure as hell wasn't Steve. The only person he cared about was himself.

Again she focused on how to go about finding the real murderer. It was up to her, and worse yet, once she got her confession, she would have to make sure they didn't kill again. At least not while Steve was in jail. That would absolutely ruin everything.

Somehow she needed to get out of the house. There was only one thing she could think of. The cops would know. There wasn't getting around that. They were watching her and she knew it. But if she simply called Joanna, asked her to come get her because she was distraught and didn't want to be alone, when the law listened in and heard her phone call and then saw her being picked up it would all look perfectly legitimate.

"You are good, my dear." She slapped her palms on her knees and grinned. "Too damned good to be wasting your time with so many losers."

Susie dressed simply, choosing her jogging outfit, although she sure as hell didn't jog. Then heading into her bathroom, she took care doing her face. If she had to spend the evening with the redheaded bimbo, she would at least look good while doing it.

The stage needed to be set properly before she made her phone call to Joanna. Susie entered her kitchen, imagining she had servants doing this while preparing one of her finer blends of coffee and then taking her silver set out of her cabinet. Once the coffee was in the silver coffeepot and the saucer, cup, cream, and sugar were placed perfectly on the tray, Susie carried it to her parlor, placed it on the small end table, and then sat in her large reclining chair, sighing as she leaned back to make the footrest come up and reached for her coffee.

"Thank you, my dear," she told her imaginary servant, and waved her hand in the air to dismiss her invisible hired help as she prepared her own coffee. "Crap," she groaned when she realized her cell phone was still upstairs.

It really sucked that her imaginary servant couldn't bring it to her. "One of these days," she mumbled, although she knew she would never hire real servants. That would mean allowing servants into her home to go through her things. No one could be trusted that much.

Getting up, she sprinted upstairs, grabbed her phone, and then hurried quickly, like she was in a race, back to her chair in the parlor. When she reached her chair, she skidded to a stop and then slowly turned, held herself gracefully, and reclined like the royalty she should have been back into her chair. She prepared her coffee, a drop of cream and one scoop of sugar, and then sipped slowly. Good. It was still hot.

"Excellent as always, Jeeves," she called out to her imaginary servant. Then picking up her cell phone, she placed the necessary call.

When that damned alarm system Steve insisted on wasting money on beeped twenty minutes later, Susie knew Joanna had let herself into the house, just as instructed.

"Hello?" she called out, her heels clicking as she walked slowly across the kitchen floor.

Damned bimbo. Did she hurry to put on something sexy to come over, hoping to spend a moment with Steve drooling over her?

"I'm in here," Susie called out, and then waited while the heels clicked until Joanna reached the carpeted part of the house.

"Hi, Susie," Joanna said, definitely dressed to the hilt in a dress that was so fucking tight on her it showed off the thirty pounds she could stand to lose.

Not that Susie cared. Although fashion leaders claimed the world adored anorexic women, Susie knew from experience that when it came to watching them get the shit fucked out of them, most men loved a bit of meat on their sluts.

"Thanks for coming over, sweetheart," she said in the smoothest voice she could master. "Please, have a seat. Coffee?"

Joanna glanced around at the quiet setting, obviously not what she expected. Susie fought a smile.

"Sure. Thank you." Joanna again looked at her warily before smiling easily and accepting the seat offered, an intentionally incredibly uncomfortable, stiff upright.

Susie let Joanna squirm a bit while taking her time preparing her coffee. The silence spread out, with only the grandfather clock in the hallway clicking away each second. Susie swore she could hear Joanna's heart thudding along with it. The bitch ached to know where Steve was.

Susie extended her hand, holding the cup out to Joanna, but made her stand and come get it. Now to lay her trap.

"Steve isn't here right now. I thought you could keep me company. Every now and then I let him go over to his little girlfriend's house to get a piece of young action." Susie watched with amusement when Joanna almost choked on her coffee. "But mind you," Susie continued, keeping her tone as sweet and placid as she could muster. "He only is allowed to go fuck her when he gives it to me very, very good. I swear, I'm absolutely exhausted after fucking him. But my Steve, he will come up with the energy, no matter what, to go spend time with his young college student, sweetheart. She's such a precious young thing."

"Oh really," Joanna said, her gaze darkening on Susie

as she stared at her over the rim of her cup. "And that's where he is right now?"

Susie glanced at her watch, then laughed, loving how melodic she made herself sound. "I'd say right about now he's got her spread-eagle and is riding her hot and hard."

"I see." Joanna put her coffee cup down, her hand noticeably shaking. Damn good thing she didn't spill any of the coffee on the cherry end table. "How long has he been seeing this college student?"

"Oh, I don't know." Susie pretended to think about it. "A few months or so. He picked her up online. But you know how it is. We all behave so well, staying with our group. I don't want you to think I allow him to do this all of the time. This is the first. And he wasn't complaining. My Steve never complains. You know that. But the little comments he dropped."

"Like what?" Joanna tried to look like she was comfortable in that too-tight dress she wore and the uncomfortable chair she sat in. She picked up her cup, sighed, and made a noticeable effort to relax.

"I'm sure it was only comments that a wife would notice," Susie said, and then sipped at her coffee. She wondered if Joanna had a clue how expensive and perfectly brewed the coffee was that she was drinking. "Things like it would be nice if we had some new blood in the group. I sure do know he can't wait to fuck Rain Kayne. She sure is a hottie, wouldn't you say?"

"Most definitely." Joanna looked so venomous it was priceless. It should have been obvious sooner, but now she stared with eyes that glowed with a rage ready to boil over. "So he is tired of all of us, then?"

"Oh heavens, dear. All of you are wonderful friends. Steve will never tire of having fun with you." Susie sipped her coffee and then placed her cup on her silver tray. Then lowering her footrest, she eased to the edge of her seat. "You realize I wouldn't have told you this if I believed you would tell anyone else about it."

"I wouldn't talk to anyone about Steve," Joanna said, sincerely looking offended. "And you know I'm the only one who defends both of you when all the others start going on their trashing binge."

Susie sipped her coffee; then once again wishing she could call her imaginary servant to refresh her cup, she sighed and accepted that she would have to do it herself this time. Joanna wouldn't understand Susie's need to have others take care of her. No one understood.

Joanna misunderstood Susie's sigh as meaning she cared what anyone else thought of her. "You know I always protect you the best that I can," she added, scooting forward on her own chair. "If you only knew, Susie, what I go through."

If Joanna thought Susie would get up and wait on her, she could just go without more coffee. Susie took her time, watching the dark amber fluid pour into her beautiful coffee cup. She added her spot of cream and one spoonful of sugar, then stirred, listening as the silver spoon clicked against the side of the cup.

"What exactly is it that you believe you're going through?" Susie asked, and continued stirring her coffee.

Joanna finally got up and took a step toward Susie. "The coffee was very good," she said slowly.

"Yes. It's one of my favorite blends." Susie pulled her spoon out of the coffee and placed it gently on the silver tray, making sure it was placed exactly in the middle of the folded cloth that was placed there specifically for that purpose. "You may have some more while you tell me what trials you are going through on my behalf."

Joanna's high heels made muffled thudding sounds in the thick carpet when she walked over to the other side of Susie's chair and poured herself more coffee.

"Just the other night, over at Rain and Noah's house," she began.

"There was a gathering at their house? Why wasn't I informed?"

"It was impromptu." Joanna once again sounded like her usual pathetic ass-kissing self. "Jan was fighting with Ted, and Richard was lonely."

"Jan is a pathetic drunk. Ted would do well to find himself a hot little college girl, too." Susie wondered if she could possibly arrange something. Ted was well built, and was huge. Put him with some skinny girl and film that! She'd make a million. "And Richard is probably better off alone. Roberta was always whining. Didn't you think?"

"Most definitely." Joanna used way too much of the sugar and damn near took all of Susie's real cream when she refilled her coffee.

The selfish bitch only cared about herself. Trusting anything she said would be a fool's mission. Fortunately, Susie was no fool. She knew how to work Joanna, and she was just getting started.

"So tell me all about this impromptu gathering at Rain and Noah's, my dear." Susie smiled pleasantly and fought to keep her expression from changing when Joanna gave her a quizzical look. Always keep them sweating. It made people flustered, and made them slip. Exactly what Susie wanted.

Joanna held her coffee in her lap with her fingers wrapped tightly around the cup. She sat up straight and pressed her feet together and looked very much like the schoolgirl getting ready to suck up to her teacher.

"Admittedly, I instigated it." The cruel harshness in Joanna's blue eyes was gone. Her gaze drifted around the room, focusing anywhere but on Susie. "Richard has been begging to take me out, but Jan was calling and crying about how cruel Ted was. I figured it would do the Kaynes good to start taking their share of the load so they can get used to our group." ·

Susie doubted seriously that Joanna thought any such thing. "Good, my dear. Very good. Keep going."

"Rain was all for having everyone over. She started praising her husband's ability to barbecue to the point where she was making me hungry." Joanna laughed, then placed her cup on the end table without using a coaster.

"Joanna," Susie said softly, knowing the plastic coating over the end table would prevent any water stains from damaging the wood. But if the end table were really expensive cherrywood as it appeared to be, placing a coffee cup on it without a coaster would be positively sinful.

"Yes, Susie?" Joanna asked, her voice so pleasant it was nauseating.

Susie stared at the coffee cup, imagining her servants leaping across the room, lifting the cup before it could damage the outrageously expensive piece of furniture. She hated that there were no servants, that the furniture wasn't priceless, and that she was forced to deal with a slut too stupid to behave while being entertained in a parlor with fine, quality coffee. At least the coffee was high priced.

"What is it, Susie? Are you okay?" Joanna suddenly sounded worried.

"Remove your cup from my table," Susie hissed, wondering if there was anyone on this planet she didn't have to completely think for.

"Oh crap!" Joanna lifted her cup, which was dry and didn't leave a mark. "I'm so sorry, Susie," she wailed.

"I'm sure you know how to use a coaster," Susie said, keeping her tone low and firm and loving how Joanna squirmed uncomfortably in that too-tight dress she was about to burst out of.

"Of course," Joanna said, but then looked around the room.

Susie wasn't sure she knew anyone with enough brains to pull off murdering five people in cold blood. Hell, the only person intelligent enough to accomplish such a feat was her. Like she would do such a thing. Blood was sticky and had such a foul stench to it.

"The coasters are right there," Susie said, pointing to the stack of coasters on the buffet along the wall.

Joanna got the coaster and placed it next to her on the side table, then smiled sweetly at Susie.

"You were telling me about this impromptu party. Were Rain and Noah good hosts?" Susie ignored Joanna's disgusting attempt to suck up to her.

Joanna pulled her long red hair over her shoulder and began twisting the strands around her fingers while shifting her attention to the kitchen door and then the hallway. "She really is a good cook. Rain threw together some casserole stuff, but Noah seemed surprised that she did it." Joanna laughed and gave Susie a shrewd look. "They play the perfect couple, but I can tell he finds her spoiled and annoying. And you can tell she is by looking at her, do you agree?"

"I'm not sure," Susie said slowly. "Go on." Truth be told, Rain and Noah were a couple she hadn't figured out yet. That wasn't usual for her, but it certainly wasn't something she would try explaining to a twit like Joanna.

Joanna cleared her throat and reached for her coffee, then gulped, made a face—probably because she ruined the great coffee by taking too much of Susie's real cream. Would serve the bitch right.

"The rest is simple to figure out. Jan got drunk off her ass and tried making out with anyone nearby. Richard obviously wants to fuck Rain."

"Did he fuck her?"

"No one did. Noah managed to get us all to leave and drove Jan home, alone, I think. I'm pretty sure Rain went to bed when he left." Joanna stared at her painted toenails in her open-toed shoes. "But everyone started complaining about how mean Steve is, and how he demands to know what everyone is doing. They even accused him of cheating on you and said that you didn't even know it. I told Noah that they were wrong, and that you two were wonderful."

"But Steve does sleep around with all of those women. He loves them thinking that I don't know. It makes him hot, and when he comes home and tells me all the details he can't wait to fuck me next." Susie chose her words carefully, waiting for Joanna's gaze to harden again.

"Why, just the other day, when he fucked you in the ass. You should have seen him when he came home. You really are a prize, my dear."

"He talks about me to you?" Joanna asked, and then pressed her lips together in what probably was supposed to be a smile.

"He talks about all the women he fucks," Susie said easily, but then waved her hand in the air as if none of it mattered. He might as well talk to her about all of them. It wasn't like she didn't know. Steve was such an idiot. "As for him being mean, or demanding to know what everyone is doing or where they're going, my husband is a bit possessive of those he cares about. You should see how he is with his new little college girl. He got her a cell phone, and insists she call his private phone number so that he'll never miss her calls. And now he wants to help remodel the small apartment she's living in. Maybe you can help with that?"

There it was. Susie had hit it. Joanna's blue eyes darkened to a dangerous midnight color. She didn't blink but simply stared at Susie while her pallor turned so white Susie swore it would glow in the dark if she turned off the lights.

But she needed to take Joanna even further. Obviously the woman stewed over the knowledge, however fabricated it might be, that she wasn't the only one who knew Steve's secret phone number. It pissed her off royally, thinking she was having a hot affair with a married man and then to find out that Susie knew all about it and didn't care. That took the passion right out of it. Which served the bitch right.

After a moment it appeared Joanna wouldn't lose it over any of this information. Susie needed to find that one special little trick that would push the stupid slut over the edge.

"Oh. There is something I wanted to ask you about," Susie began, and then stood, placing her coffee cup on the silver platter. Later her imaginary servant would clear it away, but he couldn't do that while Joanna was here. "Come into the kitchen with me."

"Steve doesn't see anyone on the side other than me and this college girl, right?" Joanna got up and followed Susie into the dark kitchen. "I mean, I'd like to know who he's having sex with. I have a right to know that about someone I'm sexually active with, don't I?"

Susie pressed the light switch and then walked across her modern kitchen, deciding it would be nice if the oak cabinets were polished sometime soon. Possibly she could get James over here in the next few days, dress him up in something sexy, maybe a loincloth, and make him dust. She grinned at the thought, her back to Joanna and ignoring her ramblings as Susie walked over to the cabinet that had the bullet hole in it. It didn't surprise Susie at all that Joanna didn't notice it. The little bitch was hopelessly lost in her own delusional state of mind. Sometimes it seemed the entire world lived in an isolated state of pure insanity. Susie was the only sane person walking this planet, which meant she needed to tread carefully. Taking her time, manipulating and coercing the person she was with, always ended up in her getting exactly what she wanted out of them. It was incredibly ludicrous how easy it was to control someone, or push them to where they were out of control.

"I wonder, do you know anything about guns?" Susie asked, turning around in time to catch Joanna's expression.

"About what?" Joanna had been rambling but interrupted herself and frowned at Susie. "What do you want to know about guns?"

Susie pointed to the cabinet but then made a show of being surprised. "It's not here. But this is where Steve always keeps it. I thought it would be nice to have it cleaned for him. I wonder where it is."

Joanna came forward and then squatted and stared into the empty bottom cabinet that usually was locked. A square red piece of velvet was on the top shelf where the handgun was usually kept.

"My father taught me to shoot when I was a kid," she told Susie. "I'm a pretty good shot. Steve asked me about his gun, a Bobcat, because he didn't think it was working properly. I switched the barrel on it for him, but that was it. I don't know where he put it."

Susie fought the urge to jump up and shout. It wasn't too often that something got her that excited. She then found it odd that news that her husband wasn't the killer impressed her. She already knew he wasn't. Except now she *knew*.

"You swapped the barrel from your gun with Steve's?" Susie asked.

"No. I picked up a gun at a pawnshop and used that barrel."

NINETEEN

Noah leaned against the wall while Rain paced in front of him. Chief Noble sat behind his desk, his chin resting on his folded hands as he glanced past her to Noah.

"I'm all about wrapping this up, folks." He squinted at Noah as he spoke, then rubbed his temple, showing all the signs from the weight of a case that was wearing on too damned long. "We've got our murder weapon, enough motive to satisfy any jury—"

"And what motive is that?" Rain demanded, spinning around and causing her twisted hair to slip farther down the back of her head. "We've just touched on the intensity of friction flying around in this swingers' group. But that doesn't mean we can pin the fact that Steve hated these people enough to kill them. It was more like they all should have murdered him. You didn't see that group last night." She waved her hand at herself and Noah. "We did."

"Rain, the AP wire has picked this up. We're starting

to appear in newspapers around the country. Not to mention someone did a spoof on it on YouTube this morning. This isn't the kind of publicity that Lincoln wants, or can afford to have."

"Aaron," she said, putting her hands on her hips with her back to Noah. "This is my town, too. Hell, my father is buried here. My roots don't get any deeper. But I swear to God that Steve Porter isn't our man."

"Then who the fuck is?" Chief Noble barked.

"Possibly our man isn't a man," Noah said. He ignored Noble when he groaned loudly. "I think we can wrap this up in the next few days. In fact, I'm sure we can."

He stepped forward when Rain looked at him. She looked as exhausted as he was after brainstorming the hell out of every angle to this case; the strongest urge to pull her into his arms hit him like a blow to the gut. Noah didn't fight it but reached for her, as if the act was a normal thing to do.

"You've got twenty-four hours." Noble pointed his finger at Rain, scowling at Noah's hand resting on her arm. "I've got everything I need to get a warrant and arrest Porter. If you don't give me good reason why I shouldn't by tomorrow night, we're charging him."

"I need a couple days," Rain complained instantly.

"You can't have it. I can't hold Porter longer than another day, and he's a serious flight risk if we let him go." Noble stood slowly, pinning Noah with a watery stare. "Not to mention your supervisor is threatening to book him if we don't."

"Are you scared of the FBI bitch?" Rain teased, a smirk appearing on her face that didn't fade when Noble stood.

His intimidating glare didn't faze Noah, either, although he waited silently for the chief to reprimand his detective for her insubordination.

"Get the hell out of my office," he growled.

Rain laughed and then turned into Noah, almost walking into his chest. Noah shook his head, silently agreeing with the frustrated look on Aaron Noble's face. Rain would be a challenge to anyone, no matter their relation to her. Noah's hand slid down her back as he led her into the hallway. It hit him hard how badly he would welcome that challenge in his life. If he could figure his way through the warped group of swingers they were associating with and nail their killer, then he could figure out a way to keep Rain in his life.

"You know what we've got to do," Rain pointed out, shifting in the passenger seat and pulling one knee to her chest while giving him a determined look.

They'd parked a few doors down from the Porter house and cut the engine. Noah couldn't risk someone overhearing them if they cracked any of the windows. It was tight in the car and he tugged at his T-shirt, surveying their surroundings as darkness settled in around them.

With the murders hitting national news, not only were reporters hitting Lincoln in droves, but pressure was coming down everywhere that an arrest be made immediately also. The news was having a field day with the knowledge that Porter was being held but not yet charged with even one of the murders. Newscasters around the country were speculating on whether Porter had killed all those people in Kansas City and Dallas. The nation would have him on the gallows before the case even went to trial.

"What's that?" Noah had put his phone on silent and looked at it when it lit up. It was a Kansas City area code. He didn't know the special agent assigned to the case down there, but he had a few buddies in that area. Noah sent the call to voice mail and focused on Rain.

"We need to get together with Joanna again." Rain let her attention drop to the monitors that showed the activity going on inside the house. It was a bit of a surprise to both of them to learn that Joanna was spending time with Susie.

"Again?" He remembered soaking in the hot tub with both Joanna and Rain, naked. Under different circumstances, watching her get it on with another woman would be hot as hell. He wasn't too cool with Rain being intimate with a possible murderer, though. "What do you have in mind?"

"Not what you're thinking." She gave him a lazy smile.

"Suddenly I'm an open book?"

"Sometimes." She shrugged and looked out the windshield. "But maybe something close to what you have in mind."

His blood pressure damn near shot through the roof. Suddenly feeling cramped, he adjusted himself in his seat and leaned forward to check the equipment on his dash. He loved this little contraption. It didn't have any lights on it that would glow in the dark and draw attention to them. And sitting in the dark right now was a damned good thing. Rain couldn't see how her comment affected him.

"And what exactly is it that I have in mind?" he asked, keeping his attention on the screen. It showed two people in a room downstairs. They weren't moving, so he guessed they were sitting. He watched as one of the dots on the screen, which indicated a person, started beeping, indicating movement.

"I would say you'd imagine watching two women getting it on, and then when every ounce of blood was completely out of your brain, you'd jump in and fuck both of us."

He narrowed his gaze on her. "I have no desire to fuck Joanna, or anyone else for that matter."

Rain straightened, looking down her nose at him. "No one else?"

"Just you," he growled, grabbing her by the side of the neck and pulling her face to his. "Does that surprise you?"

"No." Rain covered his hand with hers but then slipped out of his hold on her. She then nodded at the screen between them on the dash. "What's happening?"

"I'm not sure." He glanced up at the house. The people inside appeared to be moving toward the back door. "Looks like they might be leaving together."

"We've got a patrol car parked right around the corner," she reminded him. "What are they doing now?"

"It looks like they're just standing outside." Noah reached over, stretching over the seat, and pulled out the electronic listening device.

Rain took it from him when he straightened, and placed the small satellite dish in front of her on the dash. Noah untangled the headphones and slid them over his head while Rain adjusted the dish toward the house.

"You hear anything?"

"As if they were in the car with us," he told her, grinning. He nodded at the listening device. "It only records a couple minutes of actual time. Be ready in case we need to capture anything."

Rain nodded and turned the knob next to the small screen that also allowed them to see what they were hearing. Except that the house was in the way. She focused the device on the edge of the house and then looked at him.

"I want to hear, too."

Noah reached for her and pulled her up against him. She turned, adjusting herself, so that her back leaned against his chest and her face was next to his. Then moving the headset, he turned one side so that she could hear, too.

He couldn't stop thinking about what would happen after this case was over. Noah didn't mind his life. Showing up at a crime scene and entering an investigation when no one else could nab the perp were highs that he lived for. Not once during the three years he was with Laurel did he consider changing his line of work to be with her more. Laurel never suggested it, either. He never felt a moment of regret even when he jumped on a plane and went straight to the next case.

Which was why the longing to figure out a way to keep Rain in his life should really be bugging him. But it wasn't. With every hour, every day, that he spent time with her, he knew beyond any doubt he didn't want to let her go. Worse yet, he didn't want the type of relationship with Rain that he had with Laurel, calling each other every night, going days, often weeks, without seeing each other.

Noah had trusted Laurel, and it turned out he shouldn't have. If she hadn't approached him about entering into an open marriage, she would have cheated on him. Laurel pretty much made that clear with her proposition.

But Rain wasn't Laurel. Without knowing she was doing it, Rain had made it very clear to him that having sex with anyone, just for the sake of fucking, wasn't her style. And she didn't fuck Noah; she made love to him, passionately and with every inch of her soul. Noah rubbed his thumb over the curve of her shoulder, imagining working case after case with her. They were the perfect team in more than one way.

"They aren't saying anything," Rain whispered, pulling him out of his thoughts.

He leaned forward, keeping his arm around her so that she stayed secure at his side, and looked at the equipment on the dash. "They're still standing in the backyard."

"There they go." Rain didn't fight when he adjusted her closer to him.

"Why are you hesitating?" Susie demanded, her voice crisp and clear through the headphone. "You know that I'm going to give him grief about switching the barrel on the gun, don't you?"

Rain almost snapped forward. Noah was right there with her. He quickly grabbed the headphone, turning one side out so that they could both hear. Rain turned to look at him, her eyes wide in the darkness and her face close enough that he felt her breath on his cheeks. She placed her finger on the record button and he nodded.

"I never gave a thought to switching the barrel," Joanna said tightly. "Steve thought the gun was wearing out, so I helped him by picking up a new gun and fixing it for him. Would you rather he'd used new parts?"

"Guns don't impress me," Susie said in her usual tone.

"They are for people who are too weak to fight their own battles."

"Sometimes they are very effective."

"What times are those?" Susie demanded.

"When the only way a battle can be won is by eliminating someone."

"Eliminating someone means you aren't strong enough to control them." Susie sounded annoyed. "Are you going to open my door for me, or do I have to do it myself?"

"What is it about controlling people that turns you on so much?" Joanna spoke with a harsh edge to her voice that she didn't usually use, especially with Susie. "Don't you realize that most people do what you say because they want you to be quiet? It doesn't have anything to do with them being intimidated by you, or you controlling them."

Noah waited for the response, imagining it would be a good one, and knew Rain held her breath as well. They heard a car door shut and the sound of shoes crunching over gravel. Another door opened and closed and then an engine started.

"Well hell," Rain said, and leaned forward.

Noah moved with her, taking his arm from around her shoulder and holding the headphones to his ear in one hand while messing with the equipment with the other.

"I can't pick up their conversation in the car." Which really sucked. That conversation had the potential to go places.

"But they're in the Miata." Rain pointed to the screen that tracked the GPS device that she'd put on it the other day. "I'm going to notify backup to hold off. If they or one of them are planning anything, I don't want them thinking they're being followed."

"Joanna might not suspect anything, unless Susie's told her that Steve is in jail. But Susie will have her eyes peeled to her mirror. What do you want to bet?"

Rain nodded and pulled out her cell. After a quick call to dispatch, she again focused on the screen. "We need to be within at least a few blocks of them, wherever they're going."

"Yup." He finished wrapping the cord around the headphones and then placed them in the console between them. "Pull down everything but our GPS detection screen."

She gave him a mock salute. "Aye, sir!"

Noah started the car and then reached over and yanked on her already-loose bun behind her head. The clasp came out in his hand, and he held on to it, keeping it in his fingers while putting the car into gear and pulling away from the curb.

"I need that," she informed him, but didn't have time to tuck the wave of hair that fell over part of her face while she pulled down the small satellite dish that tracked activity in the house.

"I don't know. I might prefer it down." He grinned over at her while she struggled with equipment while managing to shove her hair behind her shoulder.

"And I might prefer it up," she countered, pursing her lips into one hell of a sexy pout as she glared at him. "Not to mention, some of us don't have the liberty of breaking dress code just to prove we're rebels."

"We'll see." He focused on the round green light that slowly moved along an outlined road map detailed out on the small monitor fixed to the dash.

Rain grumbled something as she turned and placed the other equipment on the floor of the backseat. Then pulling her seat belt around her, she gave him her attention.

"I can't chase after anyone with my hair blinding me."

Noah handed her the clasp and watched her when she took it and then twisted her hair at her nape.

"Then you can wear it down when we aren't working." He wasn't sure why he said that, since technically they were working every minute they were together. Her long dark silky locks were so captivating, he hated seeing them wrapped up and hidden behind her head.

"We'll see."

"I figured they would be headed to Joanna's," he said, changing the subject before it entered waters they weren't ready to explore yet.

"Same here. That's weird. They're headed toward campus."

"Why would they go on campus?" he mused, knowing Rain didn't have the answer any more than he did.

"Oh crap!" Rain grabbed her phone and at the same time pointed ahead of them. "Hurry up. Get to that booth and then stop."

"What's up?" He scowled, accelerating slightly, but not following why Rain suddenly punched numbers on her phone. "What the hell are you doing?"

"They just ran the campus booth. They'll get their stupid asses pulled over by campus police and we really don't want to have to make a scene and get the cops up here to back off." She leaned forward as she explained and then tightened her grip on her phone when dispatch answered. "Betty, put a call into campus PD. A silver Miata, soft top, just ran the booth on the north side off Salt Creek Roadway. Advise: do not interfere. Inform campus police to stand by but, I repeat, do not interfere."

Noah stopped at the booth and pulled his badge. The kid at the booth gawked at him, his eyes damn near bugging out of his head as his jaw dropped. Noah didn't wait for explanations.

"Better let them know we just passed the booth." He glanced at the monitor and then slowed at the next turn. "Looks like they're headed toward those dorms."

Rain hung up the phone with Betty but then groaned when campus police slowed in the intersection and stopped, waiting for them to go through.

"Better stop for just a second. We might be smart to just relay information firsthand here."

Noah frowned at the officer, who waited, not proceeding through the intersection, but watched both of them closely. "Wait," Noah hissed when Rain jumped out of the car. "God damn it." He slammed the car into park, then shot a quick look at his rearview mirror before hurrying after her.

As Rain hurried to the rent-a-cop, Noah watched the young man's expression change. He obviously recognized her and rolled down his window.

"Detective Huxtable," the campus cop said, shooting Noah a wary look but then focusing on Rain.

"Hi, Robert. We've got a possible situation here. I just requested dispatch to advise."

"What's going on?" Robert again shot Noah a furtive glance.

"Not sure yet." Rain backed up and started to turn back to their car. "We're watching a silver Miata, convertible with the top up. Female redhead driving and passenger is female, petite, and blond. Both in early thirties. If you could put a call in that we need a bit of space, I'd really appreciate it."

"You bet, Detective." He grinned at her like he had a hard case of puppy love. "Just holler if you need me. I've got your back."

Rain waved at him and turned to jog back to their car. "He better stay back," she grumbled, jumping into the car.

"Looks like they've parked." Noah decided not to give her shit on the obvious case of infatuation that the young cop had with her. Instead, Noah nodded to the cop, who gave him a stern look and quick pop of the head in response. The kid wouldn't get anywhere near badass for the next ten years at least. "Let's pull in here and see what we've got. I'm not sure yet if I want us on foot."

"If they get out of the car at least we can figure out what they're about." Rain already reached behind her, disregarding her seat belt, and pulled the small satellite forward. She held the headphones in her other hand when she balanced the listening device on her lap. "Why in the hell are they up here?"

"We're about to find out."

He watched Joanna park the car and then the Miata

lurched forward and died when she took her foot off the clutch too soon.

"Come on, you two, get out of the car, open the door, something," Rain encouraged, and turned the listener on as she placed it on the dash. Quickly unwrapping the cord from around the headphones that were between them, she lowered her head, anxious to hear the first thing they might say.

And Noah was right there with her. He parked along the street, grateful for a large tree offering a dark shadow and protection from the bright streetlights that flooded the area with light.

"Have you been here before?" Joanna sounded nervous and looked it, too, as she got out of the car and glanced around them. For a moment she stared in Noah and Rain's direction before looking down into the car. "For crap's sake," she hissed as she shut her car door.

Joanna marched around to the other side of the Miata and opened Susie's door for her.

"What is that woman's problem?" Rain whispered.

"God only knows." Noah stared at the Miata, waiting for Susie to get out of the car.

"And to answer your question," Susie began in an almost bored tone. "I haven't been here before."

"How do you know where to go?" Joanna stood back from the car and scowled at Susie.

"She told him on the Internet, my dear. We've got it in writing forever."

"Who is he?" Noah whispered.

Rain shrugged, but her focus was glued to the scene in front of them, as if she had been dragged into a great movie and the climax was about to happen.

"And he knows that you know that he's here?" Joanna continued, again looking around them and then twisting her hair over her shoulder and playing with the ends with her fingers.

"I was sitting right next to him at the computer when

he agreed to meet her," Susie snapped. "How dare you imply that I would tell you something untrue."

"I'm sorry." Joanna sincerely sounded it. "This just all seems a bit strange to me. Would Steve really want the two of us showing up while he's banging some girl?"

"What?" Rain and Noah whispered at the same time.

"Would you like to call and ask him?"

"No. I would not," Joanna hissed, and put her hands on her hips. "And why aren't you getting out of the car? Do you want me to hold your hand for you, too, while you stand?"

Rain let out a snort, then covered her mouth so she wouldn't laugh more.

"You belittle me one more time and you'll walk home in those high heels of yours." Susie sounded colder than ice.

"You've got me standing outside, and it's cold, and dark."

"Goddamn. I swear I don't have a clue what Steve sees in you." Susie slowly stood, ignoring the fact that Joanna looked like she wanted to belt her one. "I take that back. He sees you for what you are, a little slut and a damned good fuck."

"Susie, why are you being mean?" Joanna's tone hit a dead calm that sounded almost borderline hysterical. "I've never done anything to hurt you."

"Oh really," Susie hissed.

"What?"

"Nothing." Susie waved her hand dismissively. "Steve is inside that dorm there, second floor, third door on the left."

Rain glanced at Noah, confusion written all over her face. He didn't have a clue what was going on, either, but hoped to hell that neither one of them stormed in on some poor college kid.

"You're not going in?" Joanna's hands dropped to her sides.

"This is your show, darling."

"No way." Joanna turned and looked at the dorm, then back at Susie. "I can't walk in on Steve while he's doing someone else. He'd kill me." But then her jaw dropped. "That's what you want, isn't it? You want him pissed off at me."

"You're starting to create a scene." Susie slipped back into the car. "Never mind then. Let's go."

Susie closed her door and Joanna stared at her for a moment before sucking in a breath loud enough that it sounded like she inhaled in the car right next to them.

"What the hell is going on?" Rain sounded as exasperated as Noah felt. "Why would Susie bring her all the way out here for nothing?"

Joanna opened her car door. "You know I really don't get you," she said.

"That makes two of us," Noah whispered.

"I tried to give us something fun to do." Susie's calm tone was barely audible.

Rain lifted the headphones and Noah placed his hand under hers, bracing it, so they could press their heads together and hear what was being said.

"Maybe I'm being selfish, though. Steve and I share special pastimes that others might not appreciate."

"I see," Joanna said, sounding cold.

"You said that pawnshop where you bought that gun for the barrel for Steve's gun was the College Pawnshop. That's right down the road. Why don't we go there?"

"What did she just say?" Noah felt an icy chill climb his spine. Every muscle tightened and he gripped Rain's hand. She looked at him wide-eyed. "She bought a gun for the barrel for Steve's gun?"

"From a pawnshop," Rain finished. "Holy fucking crap!"

"Why in the world would you want to go to a pawnshop?" Joanna asked, climbing into the car. She closed her door and the audio disappeared.

"Okay. Wait a minute." Noah straightened, staring into Rain's blue eyes.

"Duck." Rain didn't elaborate but instead wrapped her arm around Noah's neck.

He understood, though. Joanna turned around at the end of the street and drove straight toward them, her headlights glowing in their faces. Noah pulled Rain toward him and kissed her, dragging her over the console between them and raising his arm, draping it over her shoulder, and blocking her face as he devoured her mouth.

A second, maybe two, or five, passed before he stopped impaling her mouth. They were shrouded in darkness and silence. The Miata was gone. His heart thudded heavily while his body screamed for more of her. His mind cleared quickly, though. Glancing at the GPS monitor helped. He turned and looked at Rain and her swollen, moist lips.

Reaching for her, he brushed his thumb over her bottom lip until she looked at him. "Sometime here soon we're going to talk about how those are starting to not feel like we're acting."

Her jaw would have dropped if he weren't bracing it with his hand. But the color that appeared in her cheeks, visible even in the darkness that shrouded them, told him what he wanted to know. They weren't acting. He meant something to her, too.

"It's just because—"

He pressed his finger over her lips. "No excuses. Now let's go." He turned on the car and pulled a U in the middle of the road.

They passed the college cop, who apparently had parked himself at the end of the block, and Noah saluted but then kept driving. Let the cop wonder who in the hell he was and how he rated being with the hottest cop in Lincoln, Nebraska.

Turning the corner, though, to leave campus, he slowed quickly when the little Miata pulled in front of a pawnshop that was across the street and at the end of the road. If he pulled to a stop at the intersection, they could be spotted.

"Pull over right here," Rain instructed.

But he acted as she spoke, pulling quickly to the curb and letting a car behind them pass. The driver flipped them off, his stereo loud enough to violate any noise ordinance, and then gunned his engine so that he could skid to a stop at the intersection.

Rain grabbed the equipment still set up on the dash as Noah stopped the car.

An explosion of street noise filled the car from the headset when she turned on the switch. "How do we cut this out? Susie is getting out of the car . . . by herself."

"Damn." He tried aiming the satellite directly at her and adjusted the volume.

The car whose driver had flipped Noah off skidded his tires when he took off. His sound faded and Susie's voice broke through the speaker.

"I'll be right back," Susie said, slamming the car door and moving faster than he'd ever seen her move as she headed into the pawnshop.

"Crap," Noah hissed. "Stay here. Call for backup."

"Wait one minute," she demanded, grabbing his arm when he opened the door.

Noah pulled out of her grasp quickly but then looked into the car at her pissed-off expression. "Scoot into the driver's seat. Call for backup. I'm heading around and if there's a back door, I'm going to hear what is going on. Either way, if Joanna purchased a gun here, we need information on that gun."

Rain stared at him and he knew she understood. Depending on who was working at the pawnshop, they possibly would need a warrant to go over the store's records.

Noah closed the car door and then sprinted down the street, thankful that Joanna's attention was pinned on the store and not watching the other direction. He ran past her toward the end of the block. If he was lucky, the pawnshop had a back door that was unlocked. If not, it was time to play cat burglar.

TWENTY

Noah pulled his cell off his belt as he hit the dark alley. A dog or cat, or maybe even a rodent, crashed through a few trash cans when Noah violated its dark sanctuary. He jumped at the crashing sound but then ignored it and broke into a run, counting the buildings as he held his phone out in front of him.

He started to call Brenda but then canceled the call and called Rain instead. Knowing she was safe would make all of this a hell of a lot easier to do.

Rain answered on the first ring. "I don't appreciate being left behind," she hissed into his ear.

He grinned in the darkness, at least now knowing she wasn't hurt. "Next time you can play in the dark with raccoons and cats and trash, okay?"

"Deal." There was a clattering noise in the background and he frowned, trying to figure out what she was doing while slowing as he came up on the back side of the building. "There's two doors," she said quietly into his ear. "The second door is the one you want."

"What?" He stared at two unmarked doors, both of them identical, spaced evenly apart on the building in front of him. "How the hell did you know that? And how did you know where I was?"

"I'm good," she purred into his ear. "That and I put one of your little toys in your cell phone and I've pulled up our Google Earth program that we use at the station."

"Son of a bitch," he cursed, impressed as hell and stunned that she had managed to bug him without his knowledge—not that he would let her know either. "I'm going to remember how good you are, my dear."

"You better." She sounded pleased as hell. "Go inside. There's a back room. Two people are in the store, probably Susie and the clerk. Both are up front."

Noah stared at the back of the building and the two doors, both of them identical and unmarked. Shaking his head, feeling an odd sense of pride at Rain's abilities, he walked across the uneven pavement, glancing up and down the alley. There wasn't anyone else around as he reached for the door. He turned the cold, wet knob and pulled. It opened easily, not even squeaking, and a glow of light spread over the damp, broken asphalt in the alley.

"I'm going in," he whispered.

"I've got your back."

"What?" Noah started to walk in the back door and froze, putting his hand over his forehead as he scowled at the dull wooden floor. "Don't leave that car."

The line went dead and he cursed, then stepped inside and held on to the door so that it closed quietly. A terrible sensation twisted in his gut that Rain had a plan running through that pretty head of hers that he wouldn't like. But dwelling on it would only make matters worse. All he could focus on right now was what was going on inside this store.

Standing with his back against the door, Noah stared at the doorway leading into the shop, not daring to move while listening and deciding where the best spot to hide might be. There wasn't much that impressed him as he took in his surroundings: shelves with a variety of supplies, lightbulbs, register tape, some cleaning supplies.

As solid and well-built as the old building was, when he stepped around several boxes, the floor squeaked. He could hear Susie and the clerk talking but wanted to see them without being seen. Unfortunately, it didn't appear that was going to happen. If he moved around too much, the squeaky floorboards would give him away.

Strong, bright light flooded half of the storage room from the front half of the store. If he stepped into it he'd be seen. But as he stood in the dimmer shadows, he could see the layout of the store and the shelves behind the counter where the clerk paced. As Noah watched, the clerk came into view.

"We don't get a lot of college kids in here. Some of them trail in, but they want more money than what their

shit is worth, usually." The clerk, a tall, heavyset man
wearing a T-shirt that hung loosely on his large frame and
fell damn near to his thighs, stopped with his back to Noah.
With his legs spread, holding a stance like he was ready
for action, the clerk turned his head, apparently watching
Susie move through the store. "Your kid hock something
that you're looking for?"

"Do I look old enough to have a kid in college?" she
snapped.

"Couldn't say," he grumbled. "I don't even try guessing
ages. That's what IDs are for."

"You make people show their IDs on all purchases?"

"What are you? A cop?" he sneered.

"Have you had cops in here lately?"

"Damn. What do you want to know for?" He rubbed
his closely shaved head, and wrinkles creased in his thick
neck when he turned and looked down the counter. "If
you want one of those guns you'll definitely be giving me
your ID."

"I don't want one of these guns; I want to know about a
gun you already sold." Susie sounded like she believed
the sales guy should already know this.

The clerk put his hands on his hips, obviously oblivi-
ous to the fact that Susie expected the world to treat her
like a goddess.

"Why do you want to know?"

A buzzer sounded and Noah felt a rush of cold air
when someone walked into the store. High heels clicked
across the floor and Noah knew who entered the store
even though he couldn't see.

"I told you to wait in the car." Susie's tone was venomous.

"It's scary out there." Joanna wasn't whining. In fact,
she didn't sound like she was scared, either. If anything,
her flat tone implied she simply had said the first thing
that came to mind. "What are you doing?"

"I'm having a conversation with the clerk. A conversation I thought was private. Thanks for respecting my

wishes," Susie added, her tone dripping with enough sarcasm to make it weigh heavy in the air.

"Go right ahead," Joanna said, sounding way too sweet. "Why are you looking at guns? If you wanted another one because yours is missing, you should have told me."

"What I want is for you to return to the car," Susie demanded in a low whisper.

"Why don't you want me to be in here while you buy a gun?"

"Do you want to buy a gun now?" the clerk asked.

"I'll talk to you in a minute," Susie hissed.

"If you didn't want to buy a gun, why can't I be in here?" Joanna demanded.

"What I'm doing is none of your business."

"Then why did you make me come with you?"

"Joanna, go sit in the car."

An uncomfortable moment of silence followed. Someone moved, walking toward Noah. He straightened against the wall next to the doorway, his hand instinctively reaching for his waist where his gun was. Patting the cold, hard metal always added reassurance during life-threatening situations. He realized the action was habit, especially since he wasn't in any danger. Nonetheless, Noah fingered the weapon, his gaze fixed on the light flooding into the dark back room, watching a shadow grow and slowly steal the light away.

A tall, thick man, somewhere in his early twenties, filled the doorway, his expression disgusted and subdued. Noah didn't move, holding his breath as half of his body hugged the wall next to him, and watched the man's profile until he stepped completely into the darkness.

Waiting out the moment for the store clerk's eyes to adjust to the darkness seemed to take forever. Slowly, the clerk turned his head, his expression remaining placid, until he spotted Noah.

And Noah was ready for that point in time when he would be spotted. He pulled his hand off of his gun, reached for his badge in his back pocket, and pulled out the slender leather case. As the man's mouth opened, ready to speak and blow Noah's cover, it was time to move quickly.

But if he moved with too much haste and made noise, the ladies out front would grow suspicious. Especially when both of them were already so close to the edge. It was imperative this scene play out if he was going to learn exactly why they were here in the first place.

Noah held up his badge with his right hand and put his finger over his lips, indicating the man remain quiet. The clerk cursed under his breath, walked farther into the room, then turned around, glaring at Noah.

Obviously either working in the pawnshop enabled the man to adjust quickly to unique situations or his nature was one that he was able to handle himself without losing it under extreme circumstances.

"Go back out there," Noah ordered, whispering. "Don't reveal that I'm here."

"You better have a warrant," the man hissed, and then left Noah standing in the darkness as he stalked back behind the counter.

"I don't appreciate being walked out on," Susie snapped the moment the clerk reappeared.

"You don't like it, you can go somewhere else," the clerk informed her, his voice on edge.

"I can't go somewhere else. Unless you keep your paperwork somewhere other than in your store."

"Paperwork?" Joanna asked. "Paperwork? Oh my God, Susie. Don't tell me you're trying to get paperwork on these guns. Who owned them before doesn't have anything to do with how good the gun shoots."

"I want to know who owned the gun that you used to switch barrels with my husband's gun," Susie said, her voice suddenly so flat that the silence that followed seemed normal.

"Why in the world do you care where that gun came from?" Joanna's shrill tone sent shivers down Noah's spine.

The bell rang on the door and he strained his eyes,

willing the ability to allow him to see through the wall to come forth. It didn't happen, but nonetheless, the slow-paced stroll, with steps confident and quiet and paced far apart, proof the individual who entered wasn't a heavy person or short, gave Noah a mental picture of the new party on the scene.

"What are you doing here?" Susie demanded.

"I was going to ask the same of you." Rain spoke calmly.

But hearing her voice shocked the crap out of Noah. He dropped his badge, then cursed under his breath when he squatted, picked up the leather-bound badge, and straightened, shoving it into his back pocket. What in the hell was she doing?

Noah imagined the glare Susie blessed Rain and Jo-anna with before speaking. "You two will leave this store so that I can speak with this clerk."

"What paperwork do you want to see?" the clerk asked quickly.

Susie made a gasping sound. "You will wait," she hissed. "Don't speak until I'm ready to talk to you."

"You want to see paperwork? On a gun?" There was movement that sounded as if Rain walked to the counter next to Susie. "Why do you want to see paperwork?" Rain asked. "Is there a problem with something? Maybe I can help you."

"You can't help me if you don't work here." Susie sounded resigned to dealing with others knowing her business.

Noah still didn't get why Rain came into the store, though. He'd keep his position and play this out, but she better have a really good reason to getting close to blowing her cover. They were too near the end to get sloppy. As frustrating as it was that he didn't know her mind, he would deal with her later; right now he had to cover her ass and make sure whatever harebrained idea she'd come up with didn't get both of their asses into deep shit, or worse.

"What exactly do you expect to find out?" Joanna asked. "Is something wrong with your gun? I thought you didn't even like it in the house."

"I didn't. And I don't," Susie added. "But there is something wrong with it. Do you know what that is, Joanna?"

Again Noah stood, pressed against the wall next to the door, and waited out the silence. His skin started itching, anticipation making it damned hard to stand still.

"Do I know what what is?" Joanna asked the question slowly.

"Do you know what's wrong with Steve's gun?"

"If something's wrong with your gun, why do you want to see paperwork?" the clerk asked. "Did you buy the gun here?"

"No." Susie moved, her small feet barely making a sound as she walked farther from Noah. He still heard her clearly when she continued in her condescending tone, "She bought a gun here, and replaced the barrel on my husband's gun with the barrel on the gun you sold her. I want to know who owned it before she bought it."

"Good grief, Susie," Joanna immediately complained. "If I'd known you would throw such a fit about a used barrel—"

"I don't remember selling you a gun," the clerk interrupted.

"And if you'd listened to me like you're supposed to, you wouldn't hear me *throwing a fit*," Susie hissed, emphasizing her last words and sounding very pissed. "Now if you're going to stand there, be quiet and stay out of my conversation."

"Do you know how to put a new barrel on a gun?" Rain asked.

"Sure," Joanna said, sounding like it was nothing. "But I didn't know she would get so upset."

"Lady, when did I sell a gun to you?" the clerk cut in. "I would have remembered seeing you in here."

One of them cleared her throat, sounding disgusted

with the sales guy's comment. Noah listened carefully, though. He agreed. Joanna wasn't a lady whom a guy would forget easily.

"It doesn't matter. I'll go wait in the car."

"It's about time," Susie snorted.

"Wait a minute. Are you telling me that you bought a gun from here and then used the barrel from that gun and replaced the barrel on Steve's gun?" Rain pressed. "How long ago did you buy the gun from here?"

"Lady, this woman hasn't bought a gun from me." The sales guy sounded very sure of himself. "I haven't had help in here in well over a month. I might be working long hours, but I know who I sell guns to. Paperwork or not."

"I did, too, buy a gun from you," Joanna yelled. "See, I'll prove it."

Noah inched closer to the doorway, fingering his gun while his skin itched and adrenaline started pumping hard and furious inside him. There was something in Joanna's tone that unnerved him. Without looking, he knew that hateful glint was in her eyes, a piercing glare that totally changed her image from that of a sultry seductress to that of a deranged possible killer.

He heard papers rustle and his heart pounded harder when someone slapped the counter.

"There. My fucking receipt."

"Hey," Susie snapped. "What are you doing?"

"You bought a gun in here two months ago?" Rain questioned. "This barrel wouldn't fit on Steve's gun. How long did you have his gun? You had to be pretty creative to put a new barrel on."

"I'm out of here." Joanna made a squealing sound.

"Oh my fucking God," Susie wailed. "You're a goddamned cop!"

"You're not leaving yet." Rain sounded colder than Joanna did a moment before. "You're going to answer my questions. And if I don't like the answers, we'll discuss it further down at the station."

"Susie!" Joanna wailed. "Do something!"

"Good girl," Susie said, and slowly started clapping. "Take her and release my husband."

"Release your husband?" Joanna said, sounding breathy. "What do you mean? You said he was at the dorm. Where is Steve?" she demanded, practically screaming her final question.

There was a quick shuffle and Noah flattened his hand against the wall, ready to jump into the next room.

"Not in my store, damn it!" the clerk bellowed.

"Steve is in jail." Joanna suddenly sounded deflated. "That can't be true. Tell me it isn't true," she wailed. "He can't go to jail. He can't."

Noah needed to see expressions, read body language. There wasn't much point in staying put if Rain just blew her cover. Not to mention, he was pretty sure he agreed with her. Something deep in his gut didn't feel right, though. He would sort it out here soon enough. One thing he sensed: Susie somehow had set Joanna up.

He stepped around the corner, narrowing in on Rain's guarded expression first when she shifted her attention from Joanna to him. Susie's hand slipped off the counter, her jaw dropping when she saw him.

"Noah?" Joanna asked, spinning around and looking beyond shocked.

The salesclerk frowned, his expression guarded, and then studied each of the women. "Want me to close the store?" he asked Noah.

"Might be a good idea."

"You will not close this store." Susie glared at the clerk when he came around the counter, pointing at him while shaking her head. "I will not be locked in here like I'm some kind of criminal."

The clerk glanced at Noah, who nodded once, which was good enough for the guy. He wasn't going to give Noah and Rain any trouble.

"What did I just say?" Susie snarled, lowering her voice

to a growl while she pressed her fists into her narrow waist.

"Susie, shut up," Rain said.

Noah swore Joanna's jaw would have dropped to the floor if it weren't attached. She gawked in disbelief while Susie turned slowly before walking up until she was inches from Rain. Noah moved closer, although Rain didn't look nervous. He was more than confident she could handle herself against Susie and in fact probably welcomed the opportunity to put the spoiled little blonde in her place.

"I'll disregard that you lied to me, and to my friends, about what you do for a living," Susie hissed. "But you will not cross me. I donate to your charities, and I pay taxes, which I'll remind you provides you with a paycheck."

"Susie, you'd be smart to—"

"I am smart. You're the one who is stupid." Susie raised her hand, interrupting and daring to stab her finger in Rain's chest. "I'm guessing you lied to all of us so you could figure out who is murdering everyone."

Joanna gasped and covered her mouth, her eyes wide as she glanced from Susie to Rain. She didn't look at Noah, though, or the clerk. And although she covered her mouth and her fingers spread over her face, Noah saw her cheeks burn with some emotion strong enough that she couldn't hide it.

"Are you familiar with the Miranda rights?" Rain's cool tone matched the fire in her eyes, showing she fought not to toss the little bitch across the room.

Susie staggered back as if Rain had just slapped her. The clerk flipped the sign on the door, indicating the store was closed. When he pulled the first blind over the barred windows, Susie jumped and then grabbed her heart. Joanna took a step toward her but then stopped, looking unsure what to do next.

"This is ridiculous. I ask for a few minutes alone and end up with a goddamned party." Susie obviously bounced back quickly. Her frail, surprised expression a moment ago was quickly replaced with a hard, disgusted glare. "Unlock that door. I'm leaving."

Rain glanced at Noah when Susie marched to the door. Noah walked over to her, passing Joanna, who almost tripped to get out of his way. The clerk stood by the door, watching Susie warily, and then looked nervously at Noah.

Noah held up his hand, indicating the clerk should wait a minute. "Why did you want to see the records on a particular gun? What did you hope to learn, Susie?"

Susie spun around, her eyes narrowing into outraged slits as she turned her attention on Noah. "That cops are as idiotic as I already suspected them to be," she informed him, her words pouring out of her like rich syrup.

They were so sweet it turned his stomach. "And why are cops idiots?"

"You don't know your own kind?" she snapped.

He saw no reason to enlighten her on who his kind was.

"If you're going to call me an idiot, you better have damn good proof, my dear," Rain said calmly enough to make Susie snap her attention to her. "Because from where I stand, it appears you're trying to cover tracks that possibly got overlooked."

"Looks like I don't have to do anything to prove your idiocy," Susie said, crossing her arms. "Keep going, Miss Know-it-all, and my husband will sit behind bars for a crime he didn't commit. Although truth be known, I haven't decided yet if that is a bad thing or not."

Rain raised an eyebrow but kept her attention on Susie. "You believe knowledge of a barrel being switched out on a gun might prove your husband innocent. And you might very well be right." Rain walked over to the counter toward the receipt.

Joanna moved just as quickly and grabbed the crumpled piece of paper and stuffed it back into her purse. "You're not going to pull me into this," she said, her voice shaking with emotion.

"I don't have to do a thing," Rain told her calmly. "You're the one who controls your actions. Let me see the receipt, Joanna." She held out her hand.

Joanna shook her head once but remained quiet.

"If it's two months old, I should have a copy here in the store," the clerk offered.

"Whose side are you on?" Joanna looked at him, her eyes large and full of terror. "You're going to try and make it a crime that I bought a gun," she accused Rain.

"You borrowed Steve's gun, and then returned it, claiming you repaired it for him. If you've got the knowledge to replace a barrel, then surely you know that gun," Rain stated, pointing at Joanna's purse, "doesn't have a barrel compatible with Steve's gun."

"Maybe they filled out the receipt wrong," Joanna said, and her shoulders slumped. "What does it have to do with anything anyway?"

"Nothing. Not a goddamned thing." Susie walked behind Rain and pressed her palms against the counter, ignoring the rest of them as she stared at the clerk. "Please pull up the records on who owned the gun that she bought prior to your selling it to her."

The guy studied Susie, obviously sorting out his options and probably trying to determine how deep he wanted to wallow in this sordid affair. "It would take some time to pull out any file on a previously owned gun that has already been sold," he told her smoothly. "And I'm not busting my ass to do that unless someone shows me a warrant."

Susie turned around, glaring at Noah and then giving Rain a condemning look. "You've really fucked things up," Susie snarled.

"Susie, let's go," Joanna said, but then shot a furtive look at the clerk, who still stood with a determined look on his face and his arms crossed over his barrel chest. She then looked questioningly from Rain to Noah. "You don't have any reason to keep us here." She made it sound more like a statement than a question.

There wasn't any way they were going to walk out of this store without knowing beyond any doubt whether Steve was guilty or not guilty. Noah walked slowly toward Joanna, noting that she looked very nervous, but that the evil glint he'd seen in her eyes before wasn't there now.

"Why did you borrow Steve's gun?" he asked.

"Are you a cop, too?" Joanna asked.

"Nope."

"If he is and you tell him anything, he can't use it against you or that's entrapment," Susie announced, pointing her finger at him and grinning so broadly one might think she'd just won the fucking jackpot or something.

"Very true," he told her, nodding once before shifting his attention back to Joanna.

"Are you really married to her?" Joanna asked under her breath.

Noah smiled at Joanna, searching her face when he saw a glint of hope spark in her bright blue eyes. "That, my dear, is none of your business," he told her just as quietly. "I would like to know why you had Steve's gun."

"So I could fix it for him," she said, shrugging and glancing at Susie. "He can confirm that, you know."

"He never said a word to me about it being broken." Susie looked at the guy behind the counter, who now leaned against it on his elbows. "Unlock this door. If you can't show me what I want to see, then we're leaving."

"Sounds good to me." Joanna hurried to the door and tried unlocking it herself.

"Tell me something." Rain moved next to Noah as the clerk came around the counter. "Why one bullet through the temple? Were you that concerned that it was all very clean?"

Joanna let go of the doorknob and turned slowly, looking first at Susie and then at Rain. "Do you really think if they're dead that they care if they're clean?"

Noah wondered if Rain saw it, too. Joanna's expression changed, and not just indicating another emotion but something darker, sordid if not demented.

"I wouldn't know. I think it would be more to the preference of the killer," Rain said softly, her tone having a deadly chill to it that damn near matched Joanna's glare. "Don't you think?"

Joanna shifted her attention to the clerk when he approached the door. "I've already unlocked it," she snapped at him, and then looked at Rain. "And I wouldn't know how a killer would think."

She opened the door and walked outside. Noah grabbed Rain by her arms, moving her so he could catch up with Joanna. Something was rubbing him wrong, and he'd be damned if the conversation would end by these two walking away before he had answers.

"It's all rather funny when you think about it." Susie sounded like a child talking behind him. "I come down here to gather information that would prove my husband innocent, and you successfully manage to clear the woman who probably killed all of those people."

Noah wasn't quite sure how she figured that. But she wasn't going anywhere without Joanna. And he wasn't done with her, either. He stepped outside with Rain by his side. She touched his arm and he looked down into those compelling baby blues.

"I want that receipt that Joanna pocketed," she whispered.

He frowned. Glancing over his shoulder, he saw Susie was finally getting her wish and talking to the salesclerk alone. Joanna had marched around to the driver's side of the Miata and climbed in behind the wheel. He wasn't convinced she wouldn't leave.

"What's up?" he whispered.

"Did you notice it?" she asked, resting her hand on his arm. "It's handwritten and torn out of a receipt book. This store uses register receipts. The clerk didn't even comment on that."

Noah stared at her and then turned and marched back into the store.

"As long as we understand each other," Susie said.

Noah marched up to the counter. Glancing over his shoulder, Rain met his gaze quickly. "Call for backup," he informed her, and then turned and pointed toward the door. "And don't let her leave. Arrest her if you have to."

"I thought you said you weren't a cop," Susie said warily.

"I'm not."

"He's FBI." The clerk, who five minutes ago appeared to be on Noah's side, now straightened, eyeballing him with a flat, unimpressed stare.

The look told him one thing. The guy would sell out to the highest bidder, and something told Noah he'd just been outbid.

Susie, however, rested one arm on the counter and let her gaze travel slowly up him, looking more turned on than he'd seen her look since he met her. It wasn't anything new. More times than he could count, a woman suddenly showed interest when he muttered those three letters.

"I'll be damned. Who would have thought the deaths of those losers would merit the interest of our federal government. Or is it simply the incompetence of our local law enforcement that brought you here?" Susie shot a disgusted look at Rain.

Rain's expression appeared bored when she glanced at Susie while speaking on her cell. She pressed her earpiece to her ear, speaking quietly. Noah bet she used more self-control at that moment than possibly she had in quite a while.

"There isn't anything incompetent about Lincoln's law enforcement," Noah growled, which simply got him a raised eyebrow and look of comical disbelief from Susie. He really didn't care what jabs she tossed out at them. Instead he focused on the guy behind the counter. "It would probably be a good idea for you to produce the history you have on the sale of any gun sold to Joanna Hill, or to Steve or Susie Porter, for that matter."

"Excuse me?" Susie gasped.

"You can show them to me, or I can put in a phone call and more than likely your store will be closed down so the FBI can go through your records. Obviously, it's your choice."

"Look, man," the guy said as a sheen of sweat broke out on his forehead. "I haven't had help in here for a couple months now. And as much as I'd love the vacation, there's no reason to close me down. I haven't sold a damn thing to either of these ladies. I can do a search on the gun if you want me to."

"What did I just say to you?" Susie asked curtly.

"I suggest you go outside and wait with your car." Noah was about sick to death of her mightier-than-thou attitude. "You interfere with an investigation and it's not going to go well for you or your husband."

"You can't touch me." Susie didn't budge and stuck her chin out as she glared at Noah defiantly. "I have connections that easily surpass anything you or your Bureau can manage."

"Pull up the records." Noah pointed at the clerk and glared at him for only a moment before the guy waved in an act of surrender and walked to the end of his counter where a dusty computer sat. Leaving the guy to his task, Noah turned on Susie, who still was idiotic enough to dare him with her eyes to do anything to her. Grabbing her too-skinny arm, he marched her out of the store.

He stopped in his tracks. Susie stopped next to him, not even trying to pull away. Rain didn't look up as she shoved Joanna against the car and yanked her wrists behind her back, then began reciting the Miranda Act.

TWENTY-ONE

Rain was too aware of Noah standing right behind her. Her skin prickled, electric charges dancing off her flesh, every time he adjusted his stance or sucked in a breath. If it weren't bad enough that he distracted the hell out of her, knowing several forensic officers and Chief Noble stood on the other side of the two-way mirror had her entire body wound tight.

She put all of them out of her head. But focusing on the smoldering pressure growing inside her as Noah shifted, moving closer to her, somehow added to the strength she needed to see this through. And she would see it through, even if it meant Noah would leave when it was over.

"Joanna, the evidence against you right now is insurmountable."

Joanna looked at Rain, tears making her blue eyes glassy. "I thought you were my friend."

Rain nodded. "Being friends would be nice. And if you're innocent, it's something we can work on. But if you're guilty, you're going to prison. And honestly, right now, Joanna, it's not looking good."

"I didn't kill anyone," Joanna sobbed, her shoulders shaking as she lowered her head. Her breasts actually jiggled when she broke down in tears, and when she looked up, glancing at first Noah and then Rain, her mascara made her tears black as they streamed down her face. "I took Steve's gun to fix it for him. It wasn't shooting right, he said."

"But you didn't switch the barrel. The receipt you have is not for the store you said it was from, and it's not the right barrel." Rain leaned against the table, opposite of where Joanna sat, and stared hard at her. "You had his gun and returned it after Patty was killed. You didn't make it to the potluck until after Patty died."

"I went to the store. Susie called me," Joanna cried out, her tearstained face desperate. "Damn it, you've got to believe me. Ask Susie."

Joanna straightened and then closed her eyes, dropping her head into her hands before slowly looking up at Rain. "Did she tell you otherwise?" she asked, sounding scared to hear the answer.

"Joanna," Rain said softly. "We've pulled all cell-phone

records for you, Steve, and Susie. No one called you before the potluck."

Joanna looked at Rain, confusion creating wrinkles alongside her eyes. It was like she didn't understand what Rain said to her for a moment. Rain noted that the venomous side to Joanna seemed completely dormant. Almost as if that part of her had died. It made her appear very innocent.

Rain hated it. If the mean glint would appear in Joanna's eyes, if something could be done or said that would trigger her darker side, Rain would be sure of Joanna's guilt. Her current actions and behavior were really starting to piss Rain off.

"She did call me," Joanna said, and then looked at Noah. "I went to the store for her because she didn't have anything ready for the potluck."

There was a tap on the door, and Al stuck her head in. "May I talk to you for a minute?" she asked.

Outside, Rain felt the aggravation inside her grow even further as she walked past the chief, who was busy talking to several officers and a few men she didn't recognize but guessed might be FBI.

"I don't quite understand this," Al said, and paused outside the interrogation room where Susie sat inside, just down the hall from where Joanna was.

"What?" Noah asked.

Al ran her fingers through her thick black hair and tucked the ends behind her ear. Nibbling her lower lip, she then stuck her thumb out toward the two-way mirror in front of them.

"Susie told us she wants her lawyer."

"Okay . . . ," Rain prompted, studying the petite, pale blonde who sat so rigidly in a chair in the small interrogation room that a board could be strapped to her back.

"She told me he's on his way here." Again Al paused and frowned at the two-way mirror. "But she hasn't called anyone, and refuses to speak until he arrives."

"I don't understand."

"How can a lawyer be on his way if she hasn't called anyone?" Al asked, looking puzzled. "And watch her; she talks to herself. I don't think a lawyer is coming and I think she is more than just delusional."

Susie didn't look toward them; instead, she continued sitting, her hands folded in her lap and her small feet crossed over each other while she tilted her head and glanced upward. A small smile played at her lips and she nodded once. Then it appeared she started speaking.

"What's she saying?" Noah asked.

Rain stepped in front of him, and his hand rested on her hip when she turned on the sound in the room. She didn't move when the audio began and they could hear the soft sound of Susie speaking, her tone placid, if not humorous sounding.

"I completely agree," Susie said, her hand steady when she reached up and patted her hair on the side of her head. "Please send for my driver so I can get home. I have my sites to check, you know. There will be money to transfer to accounts." Her laughter was melodic. "I'm sure you would like more money, which is why you aren't real. I'm not sharing my cash with anyone—especially Steve. It's all his fault I'm in this incredibly disturbing room anyway. Have you noticed how terrible it smells in here? And this table," she added, scowling at it as if it were the most despicable thing she'd ever seen. "It's so disgusting I'm afraid to touch it."

Rain glanced over her shoulder and slipped into the warm gaze that Noah offered her. He didn't say anything, but she felt his wonder, confusion, and speculation over what they witnessed in Susie's behavior. He was as puzzled and intrigued as Rain was.

"I need my lawyer, and my driver. As soon as I'm home it's going to be very important that I up security. They cannot find what I'm really about." Susie was not only talking gibberish, but for someone who appeared intelligent and professed knowledge of the judicial system she spoke so openly—to no one—without appearing concerned or acting like she knew at the moment that everything she said was overheard and recorded.

Rain snapped her head back to the window. Susie leaned back in her chair, crossing her legs, and rubbed her palms down her thighs. "I know you understand. You're my most trusted servant."

"Let Steve go," Rain decided, turning to Al.

"What?" Al raised her dark, penciled eyebrows and shook her head. "The chief won't agree."

Rain walked between Al and Noah, heading back to the chief. Noah grabbed Rain's arm, stopping her and flipping her around to face him. He was too damned close when he looked at her. As close as he was, though, she couldn't back away. His nearness, his presence, added to her determination, the power she'd already mastered to make sure they wrapped up this case without fucking it up.

"I don't have a problem with releasing Steve. You're right. I don't feel that he did it, either. But something is more than wrong with Susie." Noah's deep baritone flowed over Rain like a warm rush that made her throb inside, aching to touch him. When he placed his hand on her shoulder and brought his head closer, speaking so only she could hear him, his firm grip seared her skin through her shirt. "I want in that house. We're going to do a clean sweep through and learn why she wants security upped in her home."

"Because she's completely insane." Rain wondered, though, how insane Susie actually was. "Noah, she is in an interrogation room that she must know is bugged, talking to herself, and mentioning money that is only hers and upping security for whatever reasons."

"Do you really think right now she knows we're listening to her?" His gaze traveled over Rain's face, dwelling on her mouth for a moment.

Her lips were suddenly too dry and she ran her tongue over them. His eyes darkened as he watched, and when he looked at her eyes the heat he saw there damned near burned her alive.

"That or making a show of it now would make it a hell of a lot easier to obtain an insanity plea if she's charged."

Noah nodded and rubbed Rain's shoulder with his thumb. "We'll get that search warrant and I bet we get this wrapped up."

There was a sky full of stars when Rain followed Noah up to the Porter house. He walked with steady confidence, as if he knew exactly what he wanted out of the house and exactly where he would find it.

"Steve has a lawyer who's shown up at the station," Rain told Noah when they entered the dark, still house. She clipped her cell to her waist after hanging up with the chief and felt an empty chill while staring at the large foreboding living room.

"Should give us a bit of time." Noah was all business, pointing at the dining room as he directed the crew with them, and then turned the other way and headed into the living room.

Rain walked around a formal dining-room table, complete with silver candleholders adorning the center of the table, each one holding a long, tapered candle that had never been lit. She paused, not bothering to turn on the light, and stared at a china cabinet with a complete set of dishes, dessert bowls, coffee cups, and serving dishes neatly arranged inside. Tugging on her latex gloves, she opened the cabinet and picked up the top plate. It was covered with dust.

Rain moved on, glancing under the table and then leaving the dining room and entering a small dayroom. She met up with Noah in the kitchen and then headed for the stairs in the hallway. Upstairs they split in the hallway and Rain entered first one bedroom and then another that appeared to be unused. Closets were empty, and although there were dressers, there weren't even mothballs in them. All of them were empty. The entire fucking house appeared no more than a facade, a front for something that didn't exist.

Noah followed her into the master bedroom. "Finally a room that's had some action."

She turned around, disgusted. "Do you really think so?"

Rain studied the bed and almost cringed at the thought. The bed was made with incredible care, the blankets smoothed over it so that there wasn't one bulge and hanging off each side as if they had been measured.

"Not the kind of action I meant," he said, tapping her nose. "Not like our bedroom."

"Our bedroom?" She shouldn't let that sound personal.

"Yup." He squeezed her shoulders and guided her farther into the room. Every inch of her sizzled from his touch, and she sucked in a breath, more than aware of how desperately she needed him inside her. "There's something in this room. I can feel it," he whispered over her head.

Rain walked away from him, needing to cool the sizzling lust that damn near burned her alive. Forcing herself to take in the contents of the room, she willed thoughts of him away and searched for anything odd about the bedroom.

"You would think people who live like this would have a cleaning service," she grumbled, and ran her latex-covered finger over the lip on a frame that was covered with sticky dust.

"Unless they're living beyond their means."

"Possibly." She didn't get how anyone working at a piss-ass job like what Steve did would make close to the amount of money to afford a home like this. "But did you notice how well-stocked the kitchen was? They can afford to go shopping."

"You'd think with all of these brand names, he'd hang a few of these up," Noah commented, closing one drawer and opening another in a dark mahogany dresser on his side of the king-size bed.

Rain stared at the bed, noting two pillows, one on each end tilted slightly against the headboard. Between both pillows was a larger designer pillow that was overstuffed and didn't look very used. There were no head indentations and the fringes around it were neatly straightened, as if someone took meticulous care to make them look that way. "Looks like they don't even touch each other when they sleep."

"Marriage isn't for everyone." He stared across the bed at her with dark brooding eyes.

"No. It isn't." Rain couldn't tell whether he made the comment out of sheer observation or was making a more subtle statement. She looked away before he could see any worry in her eyes. No regrets. There would be no regrets. He'd already told her he almost made it to the altar, but after his engagement had fallen through, possibly getting serious with anyone else didn't appeal to him.

"Her dresser is the same," Rain said, changing the subject as she pulled out heavy drawers that held neatly folded jeans and T-shirts and all of Susie's dresses. "Clothes you would assume they'd hang up are all folded in their drawers."

Rain glanced over at the closed closet door. Or what she assumed was the closet. "It's locked," she said when she tried turning the handle. "I wonder what's in there if they have all their clothes in dressers."

She noticed the small eight-by-ten hanging next to the door: a wedding picture of Steve and Susie. They looked so young and scared, or tense. It was an odd picture; neither one of them was smiling. It reminded Rain of the famous painting of the farmer and his daughter with the father holding the old-style pitchfork and both looking so stern.

Rain adjusted the frame, which was slightly crooked, and tilted her head, looking at it closer. There wasn't dust on this picture frame. Maybe it hadn't been hanging as long. She glanced around the room.

"I wonder why they would hang this picture more recently than the others?"

"Huh?" Noah turned around from where he ran his hand along the windowpane under the curtains. "What do you mean?"

"Those other pictures hanging on the walls. The frames are all dusty. In fact, the entire house is dusty, as if everything in it was for appearances' sake only and has never been used." She pointed to the picture behind the bed, those over the dressers, and another by the door but then returned her attention to the closet door and the wedding picture hanging at eye level next to the door. "It looks like they just hung this picture, since it's not dusty. But why hang a wedding picture after all these years? They've obviously been married awhile," she added, gesturing at the two young people in the picture.

Noah rested his hand on her back when he moved in next to her. He eased the picture off the wall and Rain sucked in a breath. "Holy crap," she hissed.

"Explains why they don't use the closet." Noah hurried to put the picture on the bed and returned to examine the combination lock hidden in the wall behind the picture.

"Got any toys to make that baby open for us?" She grinned when he looked at her, his gaze traveling over her face while his dark eyes smoldered.

She saw a hunger that matched what she felt inside her, a craving to crack open a mystery, to learn what they didn't know and piece together a puzzle until the picture was clear.

At that moment, Rain feared she would have a hard time moving on after Noah left. Never in her life had she met a man who turned her on physically as well as intrigued her. His enthusiasm for his job, nailing the bad guy and stepping out on the edge to do it, matched how she'd always felt about investigative work. Her dad used to tell her many could train to be cops, but it was those few who were naturals and were born to ensure the safety of others who made the best cops. Hugh Huxtable claimed to be one of those cops, and he'd told Rain more than once that she had the same fire burning in her blood. She believed Noah was one of those few special people who also lived and breathed solving the mystery.

Noah looked away first, returning his attention to the lock in the wall, and ran his gloved finger along the bottom where the brand name was. She stared at his serious, intense profile and the way his dark hair bordered his face. Noah was a tall man, taller than most, and there wasn't an ounce of fat on him. Any woman would look twice at him, wondering if they stood a chance. It wasn't often a man entered a lady's world who not only was drop-dead gorgeous but also possessed intelligence and a well-rounded personality. Honestly, Rain couldn't think of a single fault he possessed, other than the fact that he loved pushing her beyond her safety margins. Her father would have liked Noah, she decided. Maybe not at first. But as determined as Noah was at insisting she accept her need for him, he would have been equally resolute with her father.

"Let me call in the brand name on this," Noah said, tapping his finger under the name of the company printed on the bottom of the keypad. "I'm sure we can get it open, one way or another."

Rain blinked, diverting her attention to the pad built into the wall. Swallowing the lump that suddenly emerged in her throat, she nodded. "Sounds good," she managed to say. Somehow accepting the revelation that her father would approve of Noah threw her off-kilter. She was light-headed when she made a show of once again looking around the bedroom.

It only took a couple of minutes to place a few phone calls. Rain paced the bedroom, returning to the combination keypad lock several times and trying her hand at cracking it. All attempts were futile.

A door opened downstairs and heavy footsteps bounded through the house. The crew downstairs exchanged words with the irate Steve Porter, who didn't hesitate hurrying up the stairs and into his bedroom, as if he knew that was where he would find Noah and Rain.

"Get the fuck out of my room," Steve snarled, his hair tousled and stress lines accented around his eyes and mouth as he glared at the two of them. "Fucking cops. I can't believe this shit." He turned a hateful glare at Rain and made a show of lunging at her. "You little cunt. Trying to get down my pants just so you could nail fucked-up charges against me and my wife."

Rain barely had time to react before Noah grabbed Steve by the back of the neck and flung him against the wall by the door. Steve hit the wall hard, shaking the pictures hanging there and letting out a howl when Noah lunged at him.

"You talk like that to her again and you'll be praying to be behind bars," Noah threatened in a tone so deadly Rain's heart stopped beating.

"Get out of my house." Steve didn't sound half as threatening as he did a moment ago.

Noah pressed his hand into Steve's neck, pinning him to the wall and looming over him while his entire presence seemed to grow as quickly as Steve's diminished.

"I've got a fucking warrant, and you're treading on ice so goddamned thin that you say another word and you won't have a home, or a bedroom, or even a bathroom that you don't share with a handful of new fuck buddies."

Steve pressed his lips into a thin line, not saying a word, but his eyes grew so bloodshot that they glowed red with anger and unadulterated hatred.

Noah didn't flinch or even back down. "If you know how to open that lock, I suggest you do it right now. If you don't, I'll arrest you for assault on a police officer, slander, and sexual-harassment charges that will keep you behind bars until we nail your disgusting ass for murdering five good people."

Steve stared at Noah, not blinking, while his entire face grew as red as his eyes.

"Speak now and tell me how to open that closet door."

Steve didn't say a word.

"Open the fucking door now."

"I don't know how."

"Fucking liar!" Noah lifted Steve by the neck, forcing him to stand on tiptoe. Steve grabbed Noah's hand and made terrible gurgling sounds.

"Noah!" Rain hurried over to him, grabbing him by the shoulder although his body felt harder than steel. "I believe him. He's not man enough to stand up to you. If he knew it, he would be blabbering how to do it without hesitating."

Noah released Steve and stalked away from him, walking over to the front window and moving the curtain to stare out into the darkness. Rain glared at Steve, who bent over, coughing profusely, while rubbing his neck. When he looked up at her, his pathetic stare made her stomach clench with revulsion. He didn't appeal to her before, but now, as he showed his even weaker and obviously quite ignorant side, Rain believed for the first time that he possibly was innocent.

"How long has that wedding picture been hanging in your bedroom?" she asked, pointing to the picture lying on the bed.

"As long as we've been married," he said, sounding defeated. "I've never paid attention to it, though."

"Now that I believe," she muttered, doubting he paid much attention to anything about his marriage. "Do you even know where it was hanging?"

"I'm not an idiot," he complained, and waved at the combination pad in the wall alongside the closet door. "I'm sure it was covering that thing."

"Why don't you use your closet to hang your clothes?" she asked.

Steve frowned at her and then quickly focused his attention on Noah when he moved to stand next to Rain.

"I don't know," Steve admitted, sounding exasperated and whiny as he threw his hands up in the air. "Susie always put my clothes in the dresser. I never gave it any thought."

"You've never wondered why you can't get into your own bedroom closet?" Noah asked, sounding like he didn't believe a word of what Steve said.

"Don't patronize me." Steve sounded more confident but nonetheless took a step backward, showing his first sign of intelligence in wanting to keep distance between himself and Noah. "Some things aren't worth fighting over. Susie didn't like me messing with the closet, so I didn't. For all I know she closes herself in there and wallows in fucking self-pity. You have no idea what it's like being married to an insane woman."

"Tell me what it's like then," Rain said softly, putting her hand on Noah's arm and praying he would get her silent message to stay quiet for a moment. Steve wasn't that unpredictable and possibly was no saner than his wife. "Explain Susie to me."

Steve snorted and walked around the bed, staring at his dresser as if by looking at it he could tell that Noah and Rain had gone through every bit of his personal possessions. "She's absolutely out-of-her-head mad," he said so quietly he was hard to hear. "She talks to herself and refuses to talk to me. She won't fuck me and then acts like it's a big deal for me to get some from someone else. One minute she acts like sex is the greatest gift from God and the next she'll convince you she's a virgin and doesn't have a clue about shit."

"Virgin?" Rain asked. "When's the last time you've had sex with your wife?"

"When's the last time you fucked Noah?" Steve countered, looking over his shoulder at her with an appraising stare.

Noah growled and moved in front of her. Rain really didn't need the testosterone-charged macho act. Steve backed down too quickly, which didn't surprise her. He bullied women but didn't have the stomach to stand up to a real man. She glanced at the window when she thought she heard a car door.

Brushing her fingers down Noah's back before she gave thought to how natural and good the act felt, she caught Steve watching her very carefully, his attention fixed on her hand that now rested on Noah's arm.

"Sounds like our locksmith might be here. Maybe you should go check and let me talk to Steve alone for a minute," she suggested.

"Like I'm leaving you alone with this fucking prick." Noah's charged anger wasn't going anywhere any time soon.

"Trust me, darling. He tries anything and he's going to wish it was you manhandling him. I'll kick his fucking ass."

The glint that appeared in Noah's eyes was amusement, or something else. Rain couldn't say. But she wasn't ready for him to lean forward and brush his lips over hers. In fact, it shocked the hell out of her, and if it weren't for years of experience covering her ass to prevent exposing her cover, she was sure her jaw would have dropped in disbelief. Noah made a clear and very distinct statement with his kiss. When she had time, she would analyze that bit of knowledge more carefully. Right now, if she didn't keep her mind better focused on every detail going on around them, she might miss the moment of truth. And she felt it in her bones, rushing through her veins. They were so close to learning beyond any doubt which one had murdered all those people and why, she could taste it.

"If backup is here, I'm running out to the car for a moment," he told her quietly. "Keep dipshit here in line and maybe I'll let you play with my toy when I get back."

His double meaning wasn't missed by her or Steve. Rain also tasted Noah on her lips when she licked them. She ignored Steve's wary look when she nodded to the bed. "Sit," she instructed, deciding putting him in his place physically would make a conversation between the two of them easier. It didn't surprise her when he obeyed without hesitating.

"You two really married?" he asked, sounding sincerely curious.

"No." She wasn't sure why she told him that, other than it was the truth. She and Noah didn't need to be married to feel how they did about each other. And if his kiss and the way he touched her, looked at her, and acted around her when anyone got out of line with her was all an act, then he was the best damned undercover agent she'd ever seen in her life.

Which he might very well be.

"How could you not know that your closet was locked?" she asked, studying Steve's frazzled appearance and hoping he was distracted and bewildered enough that she might actually get some form of truth out of him.

"I knew it was locked." Steve shrugged and stared at the closet door. "Susie keeps this whole fucking house under lock and key. I'm surprised she hasn't locked the refrigerator yet."

"She's paranoid?"

He shrugged. "She doesn't trust anyone and everything is hers. I can't touch anything or use anything unless she says it's okay."

"That doesn't sound like the kind of home life you would enjoy."

"It's not."

"Then why do you stay with her?"

He didn't look at Rain and didn't answer for a moment. "This is my home," he finally said, as if he'd given the answer some thought. "I've got nine years of my life invested in this place. It's not something I'd expect you to understand."

"Okay. But if she's so possessive about everything that is hers, then why the swinging? It would seem to me that a couple who swaps would have some sense of trust established in their relationship. If Susie doesn't trust you to the point where she locks you out of everything, how is she comfortable with you having sex with other women?"

"Hell if I know, but she is." He glanced at Rain, his gaze traveling down her quickly. "Seems to me that Noah is pretty fucking protective of you, too."

"Only when jerks get out of line and say things they shouldn't." She shrugged like she was used to it and could explain any action Noah performed with confidence. Maybe she'd confessed that they weren't married, but something told her it would go better if Steve believed they were in a seriously committed relationship. "He's very, very good at what he does. But for that matter, so am I. Steve," she said, grabbing his attention and locking gazes with him. "Did you murder those people?"

"You really do think I'm an idiot, don't you?" He sounded hurt. "Just because I stay with Susie, and I have my reasons for doing that, none of which have anything to do with anyone being alive or dead, doesn't mean that I don't know that you can't get away with murder."

"Five people are dead over three months. One might think they have gotten away with it when they weren't nailed after the first murder."

"Have you been on this case all these months?" He ran his fingers over his black, gelled hair, pressing it back into place and then patting it until it once again appeared as it always did, waving back Elvis-style. "You must have started thinking you were dealing with a criminal who might be smarter than you."

Rain listened to everyone talking downstairs. Noah was down there but for whatever reason wasn't hurrying back up here with the lockout kit or a locksmith to get them into the closet. She also noted that Steve didn't answer her question. It did piss her off that she couldn't say without a doubt that Steve was innocent. And it ticked her off even further that Steve, Susie, and Joanna all appeared equally guilty. God, what if all three of them were in on it?

"That's never crossed my mind," Rain said calmly. "Anyone who kills in cold blood isn't smarter than I am. Every one of those victims was approached, spoken to, and then shot without hesitation. They were killed without mercy, when they hadn't done anything wrong, by a coward with such little faith in their firing abilities they had to be at very close range to ensure they hit their target."

Steve noticeably bristled. "Maybe they were killed at such close range for saying something they shouldn't have. Or possibly each one of them did something so despicable that it was necessary to kill them."

She focused on Steve and listened to solid, steady footsteps coming up the stairs. "What could be so despicable?" she asked.

"If Susie killed them, then it could be something that wouldn't make sense to you or me, like them accusing her of not being sane, or suggesting she wasn't as important as she believes she is. If Joanna killed them, then she would have done it out of jealousy."

"Jealousy of whom?"

"Of me." Steve flashed Rain a toothy smile while shifting on the edge of the bed and puffing his chest out a bit. Or maybe he believed that repositioning himself made him look more appealing. God, like that was possible. He intentionally let his gaze travel down her body and licked his lips when he searched her face. "Joanna loves me and has for several years now. She tolerates Susie because she has to, but she would do anything to be in Susie's place."

Rain shook her head, trying to appear confused, but spoke quickly when Noah and someone else carried on a hushed conversation out in the hallway. She lowered her voice, wanting it to appear to Steve she didn't want anyone else hearing her. "Joanna is hot as hell. She's supernice. Why not leave Susie for her?"

Steve cocked one eyebrow. "Because Joanna isn't loaded and Susie is," he informed Rain, and at that moment, without him realizing it, revealed to her the true side of his disgusting nature.

"Susie came into your marriage with a lot of money."

"Some, not a lot. But she makes shitloads of money. She doesn't know that I know, but I've seen her bank statements. She has accounts all over this country. I've been married to her for nine years and I'm not walking away without my fair share. That might take time, but believe it or not, I'm a patient man. I've endured what no other man could possibly have tolerated. I deserve my cut and am not walking away without it."

Noah walked into the room with another man behind him whom Rain didn't know. He didn't bother with

introductions but pointed to the lock. The man walked up
to it with a fingerprint kit and dusted it quickly, then went
to work lifting the prints off of the lock.

"You better pray your prints aren't on that lock," Noah
informed Steve.

TWENTY-TWO

Noah parked in front of Rain's house and turned off the
engine. Draping his forearm over the steering wheel, he
took in the simple home that he'd been inside once, and
that was simply to clean it out so that he and Rain could
set up housekeeping to snag a murderer. It seemed ages
ago that he'd started this case.

In fact, it was just over two weeks ago. Two and a half
weeks that were a new life for him. If someone told him
a couple weeks ago he would meet the woman who
would make everything perfect in his life, Noah would
have ignored them, believing it impossible. He studied the
bungalow-style brick home, with its small front porch,
unadorned front yard, and narrow gravel driveway that
ended at the side of the house. She didn't have a garage,
and a small two-door newer green Toyota was parked in
the drive. He knew so much about Rain, yet there were so
many things he still didn't know.

Which wasn't a bad thing, he decided. He'd been with
Laurel for three years and didn't know everything about
her. Already, though, Noah knew enough about Rain to
believe in his heart, his gut, and his mind that she was
worth fighting for.

The FBI was poring over the files found on the computers in the Porters' bedroom closet. Steve was as ignorant as he appeared, even to the fact that he was an
Internet porn star. Noah didn't even want to dwell on that
one. The Porters were damned near the most fucked-up
couple he'd ever met. In spite of the fact that Susie did appear to show all signs of multiple personality disorder and

Noah doubted a judge anywhere would make her stand trial in her current condition, she had pulled off laundering money and running more illegal Web sites without paying taxes or adhering to any existing Internet laws for over five years. For that alone she'd do time, if they could try her.

Noah pushed his large frame out of the rental and walked around the car and up the paved walk to Rain's house, glancing up and down the street at the other nondescript homes on her block. A simple neighborhood, with hardworking people who'd long since pulled out of their driveways and headed out to work.

Rain wasn't at work, though. She'd taken a personal day from what he'd been told by her chief, and Noah didn't blame her. They still didn't have their murderer. Every test, every interview, had been combed over again and again. Noah swore at times Steve, Susie, and Joanna were all guilty as sin.

Worse yet, two days ago they had arrested a man in Dallas on charges of murder for all the deaths in that city. Last Noah heard, it appeared the man they had arrested traveled a lot from Dallas to Kansas City and possibly would be charged with all those deaths. Noah wasn't surprised to learn the man had never been to Lincoln, Nebraska. He was to the point where he doubted they'd get a confession. But he would trap one of the three into admitting they had killed those who had died here in town. And when he did, Noah would bet he'd learn they'd copied the murders committed in those other cities. It wouldn't be the first time it had happened.

Climbing the front-porch steps, Noah found himself pulling open Rain's screen door and letting himself inside without announcing himself. He couldn't ignore the oddest sensation that he was coming home. Rain's home. Rain was his woman.

The screen door hit his backside when it closed, but he didn't move. Rain lay on the floor facing him, her legs spread slightly, wearing spandex shorts that hugged her thighs and ended at her hips. A matching tank top stretched over her breasts, and her cleavage bulged when she raised her torso off the ground, her hands locked behind her head, and blew out a puff of air as she met his gaze.

"FBI doesn't know how to knock?" She didn't sound mad when she closed her eyes and brought her forehead to her knees. Sweat clung to her body, dampening her outfit and making her hair curl in tight ringlets around her forehead. She brought her torso back down to the floor, completing her sit-up, in a fluid, tight movement.

"Knock, knock," he murmured, moving to her feet and then kneeling, pressing his hands over her shoes when she came back up for another sit-up. "Who do you think our murderer is?"

Rain increased her pace, blowing out her breath when she came up and touched her forehead to her knees. Her blue eyes were bright against her dark hair and flushed complexion. "I've been thinking about something that Steve said to me the other night."

"What's that?" Noah wrapped his fingers around her bare ankles, holding her in place when she came up again.

"He told me that Joanna loved him." Rain remained in a sitting position, her breathing coming hard, while a bead of sweat pooled at the rise of her breast. "I belittled the murderer, commenting on how their shooting skills probably weren't that good since they shot at such close range. And that they were a coward for killing defenseless people who'd done nothing wrong."

"To see if you'd get a rise out of him." Noah nodded and brushed his fingers up her legs, instantly growing hard as he enjoyed her smooth, warm skin.

Rain nodded, dropping her gaze to his hands and chewing her lower lip. "He noticeably bristled at the comments. But I don't know if it was due to defense or because he took what I said personally."

"Defense?"

Her thick lashes fluttered over her gorgeous baby blues.

"I think he knows who is committing the murders. He's protecting them."

"Who do you think it is?"

She studied Noah a moment, her gaze traveling over his face while she nibbled her lower lip. He craved doing the same thing. In fact, it took more strength than he wanted to exert to not push her backward and take her right here on her living-room floor. Blood rushed from his brain, draining down his body and straight to his cock as he struggled with the desire.

Rain closed her eyes and lowered herself back to the floor. "Who do you think it is?" she asked, coming back up and this time bringing her elbows to her knees.

"My gut says it's Steve or Joanna, or maybe both of them, but damned if I can prove it. I'll admit it, princess, this one has me stumped."

She froze, her eyes darkening for a moment as she stared at him. But then as he watched, they softened, turning milky until she let out a sigh and shifted her attention to the other side of the room.

"Steve didn't do it," she said, her voice rough with emotion. "Joanna fought too hard to create a forged receipt for a gun that she claimed to buy. Her only mistake was not actually buying a gun that could have been used to match the barrel on Steve's gun."

"So he's protecting her." Noah watched Rain continue to do her sit-ups, while giving the matter some thought. "It would make sense. If she loves him, and maybe if he loves her, they would confide in each other."

"That's what they say people in love do," Rain said off-handedly.

"Yes, it is, princess."

Noah remembered her getting upset about being called princess. It was her father's name for her. He was obviously a man she adored and loved more than anyone else in her world. But her father was gone now, and he was here. Rain was his princess.

"I want to talk to you about the case." He gripped her chin and turned her face toward his. "But it's not all I came over here to discuss with you."

"Oh?" she asked, her voice cracking so that the question came out a whisper. There wasn't a more gorgeous sight than the way her dark hair frizzed from her workout and fell in thick strands, clinging to her neck and brushing over her chest. Not even the clasp at the base of her neck could maintain the thick hair, any more than her stubborn nature could conceal the many emotions that raced across her face while she waited for him to elaborate.

"You might have been your father's princess," he began, suddenly feeling shaky waters. Proposing to Laurel had been so easy, like it was simply the next step in a long process called life and not something he gave much thought to other than that. But with Rain, stating how he felt, showing her what she meant to him after just a couple of weeks, meant so much to him he would risk his heart to do it. "When I call you princess, it isn't out of disrespect for him."

"I know." Her long, thick black lashes hooded her sultry blue eyes and she licked her lips before trying to lean back and pull free of Noah's grip.

Noah stretched his fingers down her neck, keeping his hold on her. Then cupping her cheek with his other hand, he leaned in and kissed her. Her full, moist lips parted, greeting him willingly. And he couldn't help but feast like a starving man. There was no getting enough of Rain.

He dipped his tongue inside her, tasting her and feeling every inch of him harden as need coursed through him at a maddening speed. Tilting her head so he could go deeper, Noah brushed his fingertips over her hair, loving the thick silky texture and imagining it stroking his bare chest while she rode him until she collapsed.

"Noah," she whispered, turning her head slightly and allowing him to kiss and lick her neck. "Noah. God."

Noah growled and then pulled her into his arms, forcing her to her knees before dragging her over his lap and then grabbing the strap of her top with his teeth. He pulled it off her shoulder, then sucked and nipped at her flesh, his cock swelling painfully while more blood drained from his brain until he swore the room tilted to the side.

"Damn it," she hissed, dragging her nails down his arm and creating a fire inside him that immediately burned out of control. "If this is good-bye, then please stop. Noah . . ."

He lifted his head and watched her lashes flutter over her heated gaze. "Does this feel like good-bye to you?"

"No."

"Good." He ran his finger over the swell of her breast. Her nipple hardened, puckering and trying to poke through her top. "I'm not stopping, Rain."

He needed her to understand that. There wasn't a shred of doubt in him when it came to Rain.

"You're leaving." She didn't make it a question.

"Like hell." He had her on his lap but grabbed her hair and came down on top of her, almost throwing her to the ground and then pressing his body over hers. "You don't want me to leave."

She stared wide-eyed at him without blinking. If it weren't for the rapid beat of her heart against his chest and the way her breasts swelled and nipples poked against him, he'd question her mind. As hard and neutral as she tried making her expression, Noah was starting to see Rain as an open book. It wasn't anger that laced her pretty face but fear. Fear of him going away and hurting her.

"Tell me that you don't want me to leave," he demanded.

"Why? Lincoln isn't your home."

"I don't have a home," he growled, raising himself off of her enough to grab her arms. He wasn't sure why he didn't see it over the past few years. He'd never been anxious to return to D.C. just to see Laurel. It didn't make him crazy in the head when he went days without being with her. "But I do have you."

Her cell phone buzzed and Rain pushed against him,

looking away from him quickly. If she was going to denounce that fact he'd pounce on her in a second, challenging her until she admitted to the truth he saw on her face, in her actions, and in how she made love to him.

"Let me up." She pushed hard against his chest, the small muscles in her bare arms bulging and flexing under her smooth flesh.

Noah shifted, sensing her irritation and noting that admitting something existed between them that was stronger than just an affair that would last the duration of the investigation was harder for her to do than it was for him. Rain had lost her father and Noah imagined the wall around her heart was in place solidly to prevent her from feeling more pain from loss. He wasn't the most patient of men, but he was always up for a good challenge. He reminded himself that he already knew Rain would always challenge him.

Pulling her back into his arms, he sat up and then leaned and grabbed her phone. Rain took it from him but then pushed her way out of his grasp and stood. She attempted straightening her hair while answering the call.

"Hello?" When she turned around and looked at him, her expression was all business. "Who is this?"

Noah stood and moved closer, able to hear the stressed tone of a woman on the other end of the cell but not quite grabbing what she said.

"No, it's okay. We'll be right there." Rain hung up her cell and hurried out of the room.

He was right behind her when she raced up the stairs and into her bedroom. "What's going on?" he demanded.

She didn't have any qualms about yanking off her workout clothes and re-dressing in front of him in a pair of jeans and tank top with no bra. "That was Brandy Flynn. She showed up at the Gamboas' and said that Jan had been shot but was refusing help. Brandy called me because she'd heard we were working undercover and said we needed to get over there right away."

Fifteen minutes later, Rain cursed when they walked

across the yard to the front door of the Gamboas' and stared at the car in the driveway. The driver's side door was opened, and there was blood in the seat. He guided Rain away from the car when the front door opened.

"We'll get a team out here in a few," he let her know under his breath, but then straightened when he saw Butch standing at the front door. "Is this where she was shot?" Noah asked, not bothering with salutations.

Butch nodded stiffly once and stepped back to allow them into the house. "Show me your badges," he said after closing the door behind them.

Rain produced hers, holding it at his face without releasing it, her attention on the rest of the house. "Where is she?"

"Upstairs. Stupid twit wouldn't let us call an ambulance. Go on up," he added after nodding at her badge. "She's going nuts that we don't call nine-one-one. She's about to piss me off whether she's shot or not."

Rain didn't wait but hurried to the stairs, bounding up them without another word.

Butch took Noah's badge from him and glanced at it a moment and then turned it over before returning it to Noah. "I'll be fucking damned," Butch swore under his breath, giving Noah a hard look. "I don't know if I'm an idiot or to be praised for allowing you two into our group." He rubbed his thick fingers over his short hair and studied Noah with that all too familiar query on his face that Noah had seen more times than he could count over the years.

"It would probably depend on if you're guilty or innocent."

Butch's serious expression lasted a moment longer before he smiled and laughed dryly. "Good point." He rubbed his head again and then looked away first, nodding at the stairs. "I was sure as hell that Ted and Jan finally had that fatal fight when Brandy called me."

"You aren't so sure now?"

"Brandy said Jan was in her car, slumped over the

console between the seats, when Jan found her. Ted's been at work since five this morning. He didn't do it." Butch gave Noah a strange look, his expression growing paler. "I think our Swinging Killer struck again," he whispered, anger and fear hardening and darkening his expression.

"That's a pretty harsh accusation." Noah watched Butch straighten, his strength and resolve showing in his face. "Did you see anyone or anything that would give you an idea as to who it was?"

"I just got here about twenty minutes ago. Left work when Brandy called me in a panic about Jan. I guess she's absolutely refusing medical attention or any involvement with the police." Butch shot another worried look at the stairs. "I told Brandy that Jan might talk to Rain, since she views her as part of the group. You know, man, it still blows me out of the water that you two are cops—and you're FBI. Shit."

"I wasn't called in until the case started receiving too much news coverage. Otherwise, we usually let local law enforcement handle matters like this."

"And Rain? Is that her real name? I would have remembered seeing her in a uniform here in town."

Noah headed to the stairs when he heard Jan cry out. "Yes. It's her real name. She's a detective and it says a lot that you haven't seen her. Means you're keeping your nose clean."

"Well, we know each other now," he said seriously.

Noah glanced over his shoulder at the stout man. Butch didn't look pleased about any of this. But then, he shouldn't look pleased, not if he was innocent. Noah didn't think for a moment that the local butcher had anything to do with these murders.

"Did Jan say why she didn't want the cops called or to go to a hospital?" Noah asked, pulling out his cell. They needed forensics on that car ASAP.

"Not that I've heard. My guess is she saw who shot her and doesn't want her arrested. She's not sober, but then lately, she never is."

Noah placed a quick call while Butch listened silently. Regardless of what Jan wanted, it was imperative they gather all information while it was fresh in her head, even if she wasn't sober.

" 'Doesn't want her arrested'?" Noah put his cell back on his belt and started up the stairs with Butch in tow.

"Brandy has been trying to get Jan to tell us who did this to her since she arrived. Jan told us again and again that it wasn't Ted. I put a call in to him, though. He will probably be here soon."

Noah didn't say anything. The women were in the bathroom, and when Rain glanced over her shoulder when he approached, her tight expression told him what he feared. She didn't have any information to offer.

"She needs to go to the hospital," Rain told him quietly.

"I'm not going anywhere!" Jan announced. "This is my house. I'm staying right here."

"Let me talk to her," Noah whispered, taking Rain by the arm and guiding her out of the bathroom. He saw Brandy give her husband a worried look but then focused on Jan, who sat on the closed toilet. She wore a short dress with spaghetti straps and a bandage was wrapped around her left shoulder. Blood soaked through it and she looked incredibly pale.

Noah backed into the hallway, pulling Rain into his arms. "I've put a call in to have the car dusted and photographed. I'm sure your chief will be notified and have a crew out here as well soon."

"Good thinking." Rain leaned into Noah, placing her arm on his shoulder and then pressing her lips to his cheek. "She knows who shot her," she whispered, using the intimate moment to share the news with him. Then relaxing and putting some distance between them, she turned to Brandy. "Give Noah a minute with her."

Brandy glanced at her husband, who nodded and gestured for her to come to him. Brandy's cheeks were stained with tears when Butch led her downstairs.

"Go stay with them and I'll be down in a minute," he told Rain, and brushed his knuckles along the side of her face, pushing her hair away from her eyes while she stared up at him. Something tightened inside him, fierce and demanding. It was so overwhelming that it stole his breath and hardened every muscle in his body. "Be careful," he added, and finally managed to move and allow her to pass.

Then putting the strong emotions out of his mind, or at least on a back burner where they continued simmering, he moved to the bathroom doorway.

"How are you feeling?" he asked, keeping his tone soft and nonthreatening.

"I'm getting a headache." Jan's mascara spread down her cheeks, making it look like she had black eyes. "And it's really cold in here. I don't know why it's so cold."

He walked into the bathroom and opened a cabinet in the wall next to the medicine cabinet. Finding a washcloth, he soaked it with warm water. Then squatting in front of her, he gently applied it to her face. She closed her eyes, allowing him to wash her face.

"I know why you won't tell them who shot you," he whispered, and placed his hand on her noninjured shoulder. Noah moved the washcloth, having gotten most of her eye makeup wiped off, and saw her bloodshot eyes and the panic that brewed in them. "There's so much to lose. I know."

Jan licked her dry lips and moaned when she tried straightening. "I'm just in the way. Ted is going to be so pissed when he gets home. He'll know I was already late to work when . . . it happened."

Noah nodded as if he already knew everything. "Does coffee sound good?"

"With Baileys in it." Jan smiled, and dimples appeared in her pasty cheeks. It would take some work, but Jan could be a very pretty woman. Right now her wavy brown hair was in strings and clung to her face where he had wiped it with the washcloth.

"Do you have any?" The alcohol would numb her pain a bit and possibly make it easier for her to talk to him. Not to mention, making her feel he was on her side was imperative. Jan had the one piece of information they needed to close this case.

"In the kitchen. I should get out of this bathroom. I just don't understand why it's so cold in here." She put a fair bit of her weight on him when she tried standing.

When she started falling, Noah scooped her into his arms easily enough, being careful not to touch her injured shoulder, and then headed for the stairs. Jan wasn't light, but he made it downstairs.

"I remember when Ted used to hold me like this," she said, her eyes watery when she looked up at Noah. "That's back when he would make love to me. Now the only time we have sex is if others are there, too. Maybe you and Rain should join us. I bet you're really good."

"Sounds like fun." He entered the kitchen and glanced over at Rain, who stood in the doorway to the rest of the house when he entered from the stairs. "Think you can get some coffee going?" he asked Rain.

If she overheard any of Jan's ramblings, she gave no indication but nodded and started searching cabinets until she found coffee and then poured water into the coffeepot.

"We're going to have to change this bandage soon." Noah tried placing Jan in one of the kitchen chairs, but she stiffened and ended up standing in his arms. "It's got to hurt like hell."

"It does."

She collapsed against him and for a moment he thought she'd passed out. Rain moved quickly, apparently drawing the same conclusion. Noah noticed that Butch and Brandy weren't around and glanced toward the front of the house.

"Maybe some wine while I'm waiting for coffee," Jan muttered, her words slurred while she grabbed his shirt.

Noah nodded to Rain, and although she frowned, she

complied and found a box of wine in the refrigerator. When Rain brought a glass of the cold peach-colored alcohol to her, Jan let go of him and found strength to stand on her own while downing the wine, at least as much of it dribbling down her chin as she managed to swallow.

"There are two special agents outside with Butch and Brandy," Rain informed him.

He acknowledged her with a slight nod but then managed to help Jan into a chair. "You know I can protect you," he told her, pulling another chair from the other side of the table around and sitting facing Jan. "I get why you don't want to squeal on her, but do you really want her trying to shoot you again? She might be more successful next time. What would happen to your children if you died?"

Jan held her glass to her lips but didn't drink, instead staring at him while she appeared to digest his words. "If she doesn't, then Susie will. Steve won't, but only because he'd rather fuck me than kill me."

Noah's heart stopped beating in his chest. Joanna! Crap!

Already Rain left the room, pulling her phone from her hip as she went.

"You'll be protected, but if we don't get you to the hospital, with the amount of blood you're losing you're going to pass out."

"I don't feel very good." Jan's hand lowered and the wineglass almost fell.

Noah grabbed it, placing it on the table, and moved fast enough to catch Jan when she crumpled out of the chair. As Noah was lifting her again into his arms, Jan mumbled something before he carried her to the couch. Rain stood in the living room, her thick dark hair twisting down her back in its ponytail. She stared out the front door while speaking quietly on the phone.

"I'm positive," Rain said. "I need a warrant and I'll bring her in. But we need an ambulance here . . . ASAP."

Noah placed Jan on the couch while she continued mumbling incoherently. She was fading fast. She didn't hear or didn't have the strength any longer to argue when Rain demanded an ambulance arrive at the scene.

"As soon as medics show up, we're out of here," he told her, deciding he wanted to stay with Jan just in case she was more coherent than she appeared. He'd told her he'd protect her, and he would. "After we bring in Joanna, we'll head down to the hospital. Hopefully once they have Jan cleaned up and on pain pills we can get more details out of her."

"Good idea. I'm getting a strange feeling here." Rain brushed a stubborn strand of hair out of her face that didn't want to comply and stay in the ponytail holder. "Something tells me this isn't going to wrap up easily."

Noah stood outside the house a few minutes later, listening to the forensics team leader explain their findings while glancing at the yellow tape that now enclosed the Gamboas' property. Two women stood down the block, whispering to each other while watching the circus act take place in their neighborhood. He and Rain needed to wrap this up by the end of the day; nothing else would do. He could almost count the minutes before the first news-channel van pulled around the corner and stopped across the street.

"The warrant is ready." Rain walked over to him after standing by as Jan was loaded into the ambulance, her husband by her side, acting anything but how she had described he would act.

"Let's go." Noah didn't have any desire to shield reporters, and the Gamboas' marital problems were their own.

After grabbing the warrant and dealing with the annoying minutes of paperwork, Noah and Rain headed over to Joanna's house. Rain sat next to him, alert and tense, her energy rippling off of her and charging the air around him. He understood how she felt. They were closing in on the kill, and the final moments mattered as much as all of their investigating did.

Rain glanced over at him, obviously sensing him

watching her, and sucked in her breath. Then nibbling her lower lip, she didn't look away. There wasn't any need for words. He sensed her emotions as strongly as he did his own. Not only did their next actions matter, but other feelings, thoughts, and concerns weighed heavily between them.

The thought of leaving Rain made him sick. For the first time in his life, someone mattered to him more than his own life did. In a way, he owed Laurel a lot for craving a type of relationship he wasn't capable of having and for being woman enough to admit it. As much as he originally hated her, he was now in her debt. If it weren't for his relationship with Laurel, Noah wouldn't understand today what love truly felt like.

"Are you ready?" He stroked Rain's face with the backs of his knuckles, ordering himself at the same time to worry about their relationship later.

"More than ready," she whispered.

He accepted that putting Rain completely out of his thoughts was impossible to do. Noah swore it was the same with her. The way she looked at him now, answering him but not moving, allowed him to see deep into her soul, into those sensual blue eyes that glowed with emotions he also felt sizzling in the air between them.

And because she didn't move but continued staring at him, Noah leaned into her and kissed her, tasting her and growling when she sighed softly.

"Let's go," he said, and got out on his side the same time Rain opened her door and then waited for him to come around before walking with him to the front door.

"I knew she wouldn't answer," Rain grumbled when they'd both taken turns knocking.

"I'm going around back," he decided. "Let's see if her car is in her garage."

"She won't be here," Rain mused, again glancing at him with those baby blues. "Sucks we didn't put a tracker on her car, too."

A quick search showed Joanna's car wasn't there. He

led the way around the house, glancing in windows, and decided Joanna wasn't home. Not that he was too surprised.

"I have an idea," he said when he and Rain were again sitting in the rental, and pointed to the equipment in the backseat. "Pull it up and let's see where Steve is right now."

"Okay. What are you thinking?"

"That after so many murders life might just go on par for the course at this point."

"You think they're together?" Her arm brushed against his when she leaned into the backseat, and her perfectly round ass bobbed in front of him when she stretched to get the equipment.

Noah gave her rear a slight slap, unwilling to resist enjoying her when she was so close.

"What are you going to do when one of these days I smack you back?" she demanded, her hair falling over her shoulder when she adjusted herself in her seat and placed the laptop on her lap.

His insides hardened at the thought of getting rough with her. "Try me and find out," he growled.

Rain hummed but didn't comment as she launched the site that would show them where the Porter vehicles were right now.

"What do you have?" he asked while driving around the corner and then idling in the alley and glancing past Rain at the back side of Joanna's quiet home.

"Interesting." Rain tapped the small monitor. "If I'm reading this right, Steve's Miata is parked at Seventieth and Normal Boulevard."

"Where's that?"

"It's Holmes Park." She studied his face for a moment with a brooding expression. "Possibly a rendezvous point?"

"Let's go find out."

Rain navigated while Noah drove to the large park.

"This is where our Fourth of July fireworks are held every year." Rain played tourist guide for a minute when they entered the large park. "Fishing and swimming are over there. The monitor says he's parked that way," she said, pointing to the right.

Noah kept at the 20-mile-an-hour speed limit and followed the road into the park and toward the lake. He glanced at the monitor, which showed the small solid circle. It wasn't blinking. Steve was parked.

"There he is." Noah pointed over his steering wheel and felt a surge of adrenaline kick in. Joanna's car was parked next to Steve's.

"Let's go get her." Rain reached for her door handle and opened the door before Noah had the car in park.

He stopped his car behind both Joanna's and Steve's parked cars, leaving his running and at an angle, just in case he and Rain needed to leave quickly. Hurrying out, he reached her side, when both of them froze.

Joanna's and Steve's silhouettes were easily seen in the front seats of Joanna's car. But the gun that Joanna pointed at Steve's head reflected the sunlight and damn near blinded Noah.

TWENTY-THREE

Rain unclipped her gun from her waist and rubbed her palm against her jeans before pulling her weapon free. Whatever the two of them were talking about inside the car, it had them so wrapped up they were too distracted to notice another car had pulled into the small parking lot. Or that Rain and Noah now stood on either side of the back end of it.

"Backup's in place," she whispered.

"Ten four. It's your show," Noah responded in her ear, and winked at her when she looked at him standing less than twenty feet away on the other side of the car.

Noah held her gaze and nodded once. Rain took the signal, her heart pounding while a bead of sweat tortured her flesh between her breasts. This was it, the moment they'd been waiting for and the moment she'd craved for the past few months. Everything would be wrapped up in a matter of minutes. She acknowledged the high adrenaline rush peaking inside her and wiped her hands on her jeans, shifting her attention from Noah to the car. Rain stood planted where she was for another moment, just out of view from all car windows, and then made her move.

"It's over, Joanna," she yelled, running to the car and grabbing the passenger door handle with one hand while aiming her gun with the other. "Put down the gun."

Steve screamed when Rain announced her presence. The two of them weren't smart enough to have locked their doors, thank God! Rain yanked the door open on her side at the same time Noah pulled open the driver's side door.

"What the hell?" Joanna twisted in her seat, her red hair already tousled and flying around her face.

Although not too surprised to see Joanna's shirt completely unbuttoned, Rain focused her attention on the gun. Joanna lowered her right hand, which held the gun, and Rain grabbed that arm, dragging her backward.

"Get out of the car, now!" Rain dug her grip into Joanna's arm. As long as she kept a hold on Joanna's arm, Rain prayed, no one would get hurt.

"What's going on? Stop it!" Joanna sounded more than bewildered and fell out of the car, hitting her knees on the asphalt.

Rain waited for the pain to register, for Joanna to cry out. Her knees had smacked the ground pretty hard. But criminals come in all shapes and sizes, with all types of mental stability. Joanna jumped up, trying to twist Rain's arm off of her own.

"Let me go!" she hissed. "You have no right."

"Actually I do," Rain said, but anything she said right now would fall on deaf ears. "Drop your weapon."

"It could break." Joanna twisted again and almost elbowed Rain in the gut. "I tell you what, you drop yours and I'll drop mine."

Joanna was ripped out of Rain's hands so quickly she

didn't see Noah until he lifted Joanna in the air. With a quick, solid movement he slammed her against her car, sending Joanna's gun flying.

Rain ran over to the gun while Joanna flew into a wild rage, screaming and kicking while her red mane flew around her face. She was a mess of legs and arms, struggling furiously to get away from Noah.

Two police cars and a third unmarked brown car pulled into the parking lot. Noah's expression was fiercer than Rain had ever seen him. He barely moved while holding the hysterical maniacal woman but successfully pulled her arms behind her back and cuffed her with skills that put Rain's to shame.

"You've got the wrong person." Joanna doubled over and started coughing furiously. "I'm hurt and you're hurting me more," she wailed.

Rain gestured to Al when she hurried out of the patrol car. "Gloves," Rain yelled, and tapped the gun with her foot.

"Got it!" Al hurried toward her while pulling gloves onto her hands.

"If you quit fighting, it will quit hurting," Rain told Joanna when she reached Noah's side.

"Fuck you! I thought you were my friend."

"And I told you already that I can't be friends with a murderer because they would be in prison," Rain answered calmly.

"I'm no murderer. He's still alive, isn't he?" Joanna straightened, tossing her head so that wild strands of red hair flew over her shoulder. Her blue eyes were demonic, filled with rage and hatred so strong the emotions charged the air around her.

"What?" Rain asked, still keeping her tone calm and quiet and focusing only on Joanna and not on Noah, who continued holding her. "The others don't count?"

Joanna's lips looked dried and cracked when she pressed them into a thin line and glared at Rain. "No one counts but Steve," she hissed, barely moving her mouth.

"I know now that you killed them," Rain said, just as quietly. "It's over, Joanna."

Joanna's entire body deflated, her jaw dropping as she sagged against Noah. "They said the dead couldn't talk."

"You've got the right to remain silent, Joanna," Rain began. "Anything you say right now can be used against you in a court of law."

"And I have a right to an attorney." Joanna looked over her shoulder to where Steve stood, talking to several officers. "Steve, I need a lawyer."

Steve wouldn't look at her and, if anything, ducked his head and shifted, blatantly ignoring her as he continued speaking to the officers.

"Steve!" Joanna cried out.

"If you can't afford a lawyer, one will be provided for you." Rain took Joanna's arm. "Let's go."

"You're not any better than they are," Joanna said, her tone relaxed and her red hair frizzy as she met Rain's gaze with watery blue eyes. "You think you're better than me just like they did, but when it comes down to it, you're playing, too. None of the life you showed me about you was real. I bet Noah doesn't even love you. That makes you so incredibly the same as everyone else."

"The same as who?" Rain asked.

"As Steve and Susie, as Patty, Lorrie, George, Roberta, and Lynn." Joanna allowed Rain to guide her into the backseat of Al's patrol car. "We're all playing a game, dodging reality to make life more pleasurable. The only difference is that some of us are better at it than others."

Rain leaned back in her office chair as her stomach growled loudly.

"You did a damned good job," Chief Noble said as he approached her desk and tugged at his tie. "I'm sure you know that, but I wanted to tell you anyway."

"Just doing my job." She dropped her pen on top of the forms she'd finished, wishing they would scan themselves and she could just go home. A hot bubble bath and her slippers sounded good. Seeing Noah sounded better, but she pushed that bittersweet craving to the back of her mind.

"Tell me something." Noble relaxed on the edge of her desk and studied her for a moment. When she finally looked up at him without saying anything he went on. "How much of it was a bluff?"

Rain thought of the hours of interrogation she'd finished before starting in on the paperwork. She'd gone in alone with Joanna, and although it was hardball at first, Rain learned a few things in the time she'd spent with Noah. Pretending to have all of the facts oftentimes managed to get them all laid out before you a lot sooner.

"None of it, Chief," she said, leaning back in her chair again and ignoring her tummy when it growled. She laced her fingers behind her head and felt the muscle soreness that was setting in. "I admit it took us some time to sort out which one of them did it, but when we were ready for the arrest there wasn't any doubt."

"Good to hear." The chief stood and looked at the clock on the wall. "Where is that FBI partner of yours? He hasn't headed out already. I thought I heard his flight didn't leave until the morning."

If it weren't for years of undercover work she wouldn't have managed a straight face at his comment. "I'm sure he headed out to pack. Who wants to hang around for all of this fun?" she added dryly, tapping her pen over the forms she'd completed.

Chief Noble pursed his lips, his watery eyes studying her before he looked away slowly and headed for the door. "Go get some sleep, Rain. It will be here for you when you come in tomorrow."

"Yes, it will," she grumbled. And as much as that hot bath called to her, going home and being alone didn't sound appealing at all.

"That's an order, Rain," he added, and turned into the hallway, his heavy footsteps echoing slightly as he headed for the stairs.

By the time she let herself into her dark, quiet, and very empty-feeling home, the bath had completely lost its appeal. Running her hands over her body, knowing Noah had touched her everywhere she would touch herself, was a bitter reminder she wasn't in the mood to experience. She headed for her bed, kicking off her shoes as she entered and not bothering with the light.

She froze when she reached for her blankets and focused on her bed for the first time, and the lump under the covers.

"I'd hoped you would get undressed before crawling into bed," Noah said, his voice gravelly.

"What are you doing here?" Rain's heart stopped, her ability to register excitement, or bitterness, that Noah would assume she'd want one last moment with him too much for her to dwell on at the moment. "You scared the crap out of me," she admitted, her mouth almost too dry to speak.

"You should pay more attention when you walk into a dark room." He pulled back the blankets for her and revealed his bare chest while his dark eyes gazed up at her.

"I guess I was a bit distracted," she whispered, but then wondered why she told him that. It was too late and her brain too fried to get into a discussion over the relationship they didn't have.

"Then come to bed." He continued holding the covers for her. "Without clothes," he added, his dark brooding gaze traveling down her slowly. "I need you."

The way his tone dropped with his last comment sent chills rushing over her and at the same time created a flush of heat that settled deep in her womb. Her body responded to him even if she hesitated with the words.

She needed a minute, just some time to get her head on straight. This was the last thing she expected when coming home and jumping into bed, into his arms. Being with Noah sounded better than sleeping, or the hot bath she'd already given up on.

"Is this how you say good-bye?" She turned away from

him to her closet and peeled off her tank top. Suddenly she was more nervous than if this had been her first time. And more than anything she didn't want to hear that it was her last time with Noah.

"No." His one-word answer made her heart explode.

But she needed to know more. Telling her he wasn't saying good-bye didn't tell her anything. She let her tank top fall to the floor, not even trying for her laundry basket. Strong, warm hands took her arms and turned her around.

"I'm not saying good-bye, Rain. Neither of us want that." He stared into her eyes only for a moment, long enough to show her the heat burning inside him matched the passion tearing her apart.

His mouth captured hers and he pressed his naked body into her, forcing her back up against the wall. Noah was rough, demanding, and determined as he devoured her mouth. There weren't any soothing caresses or soft kisses. Nor were there affectionate, reassuring words.

Noah grabbed her arms, pushing her backward so that her back pressed against her cool, hard wall, and then impaled her with his tongue. The fever rushing through him filled her, burning her alive, and making the need that had simmered inside her all day and evening swell to a point where she swore she would pass out.

His fingertips rubbed hard into her flesh when he cupped her breasts, growling into her mouth while continuing to kiss her. Noah pinched her nipples. Sparks ignited in her, then took a fiery path straight down her body to between her legs. Again he didn't hesitate, didn't offer slow, soothing touches, but took what he wanted with an aggressive nature that turned her on more than she ever thought it would.

He pressed his bare leg between her, pushing hard-packed muscle against her pussy and damn near making her come. Rain twisted her head to the side, needing to breathe, fighting desperately to regain control when she felt herself slipping further and further into a warm pool of lust and desire that seemed to be bottomless.

Worse yet, she wanted to surrender to him. It made no sense. There wasn't any ignoring the overwhelming urge to allow him to take her, respond to his demands and submit. Doing so went against everything she was, her nature, how she'd been trained and raised. My God, her father would roll over in his grave. When she'd finally come to terms with her father liking Noah, which made it so damned easy to fall in love with him after that, accepting behavior her father would raise a holy fucking fit over didn't set right inside her.

"I want your clothes off," Noah demanded, dragging his fingers down her front and grabbing the waistline of her jeans.

Now wasn't the time to be thinking about her father, or anything else. Noah demanded every ounce of her attention. He twisted her pants at the waist, forcing the top button to unbutton. She wasn't sure whether he popped it off or not but knew if she didn't assist, the zipper would be broken in the next moment.

Noah scraped his teeth down her neck, grabbing her hair with one hand while attacking her zipper with the next. Rain intervened, pushing her hands underneath his determined fingers, and pulled down the zipper. Immediately he tugged hard enough that she almost staggered to the side.

Instead of helping her regain her footing, Noah stepped backward, leaving her breathing so hard she felt the room shift to the side. He pushed her pants past her hips and let go when they fell in a pool around her ankles. She tried stepping out of them, but Noah moved quickly, straightening and pulling her jeans free of her body.

"Turn around," he insisted, moving her as he spoke.

"Noah, I can—" She tried saying she could undress herself, but he flipped her around so her back was to him and grabbed her panties at her hips. "You're manhandling me." She didn't quite pull off the right tone to make it sound like a complaint.

"I'm handling you." He shoved her underwear down

her legs until she stepped out of them. Noah lifted her into his arms, his hand sliding down her back as he carried her to the bed. "And I don't plan on stopping."

She sunk into the rumpled blankets, feeling the warmth from his body wrap around her as the covers pooled against her.

"If this isn't good-bye, then what is it?" She needed to understand.

As much as she loved the attention he gave her, craved more of it with every breath, she needed to know the reason he attacked her like a starving man. And as she contemplated in her mind every reason that might exist behind his motives, her heart swelled, a mixture of pain and excitement creating a strange sensation inside her.

Noah bent over her, his cock swollen and hanging low between them as he parted her legs and then ran his hands over her flesh to her face.

"This is me loving you." His face was so close to hers when he spoke that she saw slivers of green streak through his dark eyes.

She opened her mouth, shocked at his choice of words and scared to put meaning behind them. He pounced on her, pressing their lips together, and once again sent her over the edge with a kiss.

He was loving her. His words. They repeated themselves in her brain like a mantra.

Noah leaned on his side, pulling her up against him. So many rock-hard muscles pressed against her, from her toes to the tips of her fingers. One hand was firm against the middle of her back, with his fingers stretched and his warm, confident touch searing her flesh. His other hand gripped her chin, keeping her face at the angle he preferred so that his tongue could dance with hers.

When Rain surrendered to him, a feeling washed over her that she'd never experienced before. It was like bathing in a waterfall, except the water was warm. It was like knowing life without any worries, any problems or fears.

She drowned in the sensation and was too far gone before she realized what it was.

She loved him.

God! She loved him more than she ever loved anyone before.

Rain had loved her father; even now that he was dead, she loved him with all of her heart. But this—what she felt for Noah—wasn't the same as the love for her father. Without a doubt, she knew she'd never felt like this for any other man, and doubted any other man could make her feel the way Noah did.

"I've needed this all day," Noah whispered into her neck, tickling the sensitive flesh just above her collarbone with his breath.

She needed this for the rest of her life. "Uh-huh," she whispered, feeling the swelling inside her move to dangerous levels.

"Watching you work that arrest, maintain Joanna when she lost it, and even down at the station," he continued, his hands moving down her body, gripping her hip, and turning her to her side. "You're one fucking hot cop, Rain."

"Just doing my job." She let her head fall backward when he lifted her up his body so that her breasts were in his face. "God, crap!" she howled, digging her fingernails into his shoulders when he bit down on one of her nipples.

The sweet pain shot through her body like an electrical current, sizzling straight to her clit, which pulsed violently in reaction. She hissed in a breath, wrapping her leg over his thigh and feeling moisture pool between her legs.

Noah chuckled, lapping at the nipple he had just tortured and then sucking it into his mouth. The moist humidity soothed her but at the same time made her crave more from him. No one in a million years would have made her believe she liked being treated so roughly.

She dug her nails into roped muscle and dragged them

down his arms, feeling him twitch under her touch. What she wouldn't do to return the aggressive play.

When he moved to the other breast, Rain pushed against his arm, rolling him onto his back, and then mounted him. The thick length of his shaft throbbed between her legs. She rubbed her moisture against him, easing her hips back and forth as she lubricated him. The growl that emerged from deep in his lungs vibrated through his body as his grip on her tightened.

"Woman," he rumbled, his voice thick with need.

She smiled, not answering, and arched her back, leaning into him, smothering him with her swollen, aching breasts. She locked her arms on either side of him and pressed her hands flat into her blankets, keeping her body against him but riding him slowly, torturing him and herself, and fighting not to let him slide inside her.

"Don't even think you're going to get away with that," Noah roared, coming up off the bed and flipping her off of him and onto her back.

Just as quickly he spread her legs; positioning himself between them, he grabbed her ankles and locked them in a tight grip as he thrust deep inside her.

"Oh my God!" She covered her face with her hands as the pressure built quickly when he impaled her with his engorged cock.

"Rain." His baritone rumbled before her closed eyes.

She moved her hands, reaching for him. His shoulders were slick, a sheen of perspiration making it easy to glide her fingers over corded muscle.

"More." She didn't sound too authoritative, but she ached to control his actions. "Give me more, Noah."

"You've got all of me, darling." He kissed her nose and then rose over her, straightening and giving her a view to die for.

He ran his hands down the backs of her legs and she rested the weight of them against his grip, allowing him to keep her spread open. She wanted to feel him, enjoy him inside while running her hands over his chest, his arms, and losing herself in his sensual gaze.

Then gripping his waist, the heat of his body flowing through her fingers and deep inside her to her womb, she pulled him closer. "Deeper. Faster. Noah, God, please."

Noah chuckled, but his expression remained serious. He gazed down at her with so much warmth that she recognized it instantly. If he'd looked at her like that before, she hadn't noticed. But acknowledging the emotions inside her, knowing she was experiencing love, Rain understood the heat that warmed his dark eyes. He loved her, too.

They hadn't known each other long. And Rain wasn't foolish enough to demand a commitment when there was still so much to learn about him. Not to mention, even if he claimed this wasn't good-bye, he was leaving. Such thoughts made the pressure inside her turn to pain. To a sensation that filled her and demanded relief.

Rain dug into his waist, lifting her ass off the bed and adjusting the angle he entered. And with every stroke she wanted more, ached for everything he could give her, again and again.

"You're perfect, sweetheart," he whispered, forcing her gaze back up to his eyes. "Feel that? Feel how perfect we are?"

"Yes. Oh yes," she wailed, again shifting her rear end and feeling herself grow more wet with each thrust.

His body was tight, every inch of him hard as steel. But his gaze was so warm and sensual she drowned in it. If she could make it so this never ended, she would.

"A perfect fit. You were meant to be mine."

She stared up at him, positive her heart quit beating while she let his words sink in. "You keep saying things like that . . ." She couldn't finish, couldn't offer an ultimatum. There wasn't anything either of them could do about their careers taking them in different directions.

Noah lowered himself, slowing the pace and thrusting

deeper than before. "You better get used to hearing them," he whispered, his nose practically touching hers.

"Oh?" She rested her hands on his shoulders, unable to move.

"I'm not letting go of you, Rain. Whatever it takes, we're staying together." He thrust one last time as he spoke.

Whether it was his actions or the words, Rain couldn't say. But the dam broke. The pressure filling her and pulsing out of control as wave after wave released inside her like molten lava. Her orgasm damn near ripped her in two. Noah growled, suddenly picking up pace, like it was a race and he was the grand-prize winner, ready and willing to show off his skills and claim his victory.

She continued coming when he pressed his mouth to hers and impaled her with his tongue. When the low growl started deep inside him and he filled her, throbbing and pulsing, Rain knew she'd taken him over the edge with her.

"Come for me, Noah," she whispered, her lips moving against his. "Show me we can make this work together."

"Oh, baby, we can!"

He exploded inside her, his eyes so close to hers when he came that her vision was blurred as she stared at him.

"I love you, Rain."

"Oh, Noah." She wouldn't cry. No way in hell would she cry. "I love you, too."

Maybe she drifted off to sleep. Rain opened her eyes and stared into her dark bedroom. She listened as her shower quit running and cuddled farther under her covers, knowing she should get up and wash as well. She would in a minute. Noah's cell phone went off in the other room and his slow, confident footsteps sounded in the hallway. He must have left his phone in the living room. How long had he been in her home before she got here? Coming home to him after a long day's work would be paradise. But again, she wouldn't let her heart attach to ideas that just weren't going to happen.

"Special Agent Kayne," he said seriously. "Ethan! How the hell are you doing, my man?"

Noah's excitement piqued Rain's attention and she sat up in bed, turning her head to hear more.

"No shit. Man, that sucks," Noah continued, his voice soft and suddenly sounding full of concern. "Damn it," he hissed. "God, there is nothing worse than a child being murdered. You're right; it's the worst of all crimes. I know you'll nail the bastard."

Rain didn't have a clue who Ethan was, but obviously he was one of Noah's buddies and it sounded like he was dealing with a bad situation. She would agree with Noah; learning a child had been killed tore her up worse than anything she'd ever seen. She stood, not bothering with clothes but instead leaving her room and walking down the hallway.

"Man, I'd make arrangements to drive down there in a second if I could get it approved. But you're a few hours too late. I put in a request this afternoon to work at the field office here in Lincoln, Nebraska."

Rain froze. Noah wasn't leaving? She didn't mean to squeal when she heard him speak, but when she did, Noah turned around. His dark, brooding gaze warmed as he stared at her in the darkness. As soon as her heart quit pounding so hard that the sound stormed in her ears, she would rush to him. Excitement hit her so hard, though, that her legs started trembling and she fell into Noah instead of jumping into his arms like she wanted.

His powerful arm wrapped around her while he continued with his conversation. "Maybe I can swing it to come down there for an afternoon sometime soon. It's been a while." Noah listened to the man on the other end of the line, but all Rain focused on was the steady beat of his heart.

Maybe she was frozen in place, too stunned at his news to be able to function, but Noah wasn't going anywhere. His strong hold on her felt better than anything she'd ever known.

"I don't know, my man. You were always the wild one. I don't want you getting me in trouble." Noah chuckled, kissing Rain's forehead. "I've found me a lady and I'm not going to do anything to lose her."

Rain couldn't hear the man through the phone other than his tone turned very excited. If it weren't for the ringing in her head she might have been able to follow the conversation better, but between her heart about to explode in her chest and the happiness filling her so quickly she got dizzy, it was all she could do to hear Noah speak.

"No way, man. It's not lust. It's love! And I'm never going to let her go." Noah continued holding her.

Rain relaxed against his chest, feeling more at home and loved than she had in years. Somewhere in her fogged brain she swore she heard her father's voice. *Good job, princess. This one is a keeper.*

Read on for an excerpt from
Lorie O'Clare's next book

STRONG, SLEEK AND SINFUL

Coming soon from St. Martin's Paperbacks

Her heart thumped in her chest as she turned off the light, locked the door to the middle room, and headed down the hall to the front door.

"Yes?" she said, placing her hand on the door handle and leaning against the front door.

"Open the door, Kylie." Perry's deep voice sounded all business—or pissed.

She slid the chain into place on the door and unlocked the deadbolt. Opening it as far as the chain would allow, she flipped on her porch light and watched him squint as she blinded him.

"What did you want?"

"Open the damn door and let me in," he growled.

It was tempting to spar with him, but she closed the door, slipped the chain free, and then stepped out of the way when he pushed the door hard enough that it swung open. She grabbed it before it hit the wall, staying clear while he stalked into her home.

"What were you doing?"

"When?" She watched him as he stopped in the middle of her living room and turned to face her.

"Just now. When I knocked on the door."

She was toying with him just a bit. It was so easy to do, and she kind of liked how she could make his eyes darken with her comments.

"What do you think I was doing?" she asked, turning from him and closing the door. "I was studying."

"Where are your books?" he asked, his demanding tone pushing as he continued watching her, slowly crossing his arms. Apparently he had the night off as he was still dressed in his T-shirt and jeans. God, he made simple clothing look deadly.

Kylie took her time answering, unwilling to spar with him full force. Already she felt the charge in the air, the sexual energy radiating off him. It was best to keep her head clear, stay focused on the fact that she had quite possibly just communicated with their killer. Although that would mean Perry was innocent, it also meant that if her man was online right now, she needed to take this opportunity to get to know him.

"Why are you so interested in my studies?" she challenged, crossing her arms over her chest and watching his expression harden.

Perry walked toward her. If she didn't move, he would have her cornered.

"I think you're avoiding the answer to a simple question." He grabbed her arm when she tried walking past him. "Where are your books?"

"I do most of my work on my computer," she said honestly and looked down at her arm. "Is there a reason you're restraining me?"

His hand was large and his fingers long. His skin was tanner than hers. She watched his fingers wrap around her forearm and then his grip loosened and slid down to her wrist.

"This isn't restraint, darling," he drawled. "When I restrain you, you won't be able to move."

"That is what restraining means," Kylie laughed, walking away from him and pulling her arm free as she headed toward her kitchen. Perry let go of her but followed when she walked around the open living room that turned into her small kitchen. "You never told me why you're here," she said, keeping her back to him.

She grabbed a plastic cup from her cabinet and then filled it with ice from the icemaker in her refrigerator. She hadn't tried to grocery-shop yet so other than the leftover pizza, which fit in one box and took up a shelf in her refrigerator, there wasn't any food in her kitchen.

"Because I know what you're doing."

Kylie put her cup under the faucet and let it fill with tap water.

Then taking her time turning around, she brought the cup to her lips and watched him while sipping.

"Then why did you ask?" An ice cube brushed against her lip and she savored how cold it was. Anything to help keep her grounded.

"Ask what?"

"You asked me what I was doing when you walked in the door, yet now you say you know what I'm doing." She smiled, sipped again, focused on the cold water soothing the fire burning inside her. "Did you learn this by my actions after entering my home?"

"No." The hungry look in his eyes made them brighter. But it was the way he pressed his lips together, not frowning or smiling, that made him look dangerous, like a deadly predator who ruled all around him, and contemplated making her his next conquest. "Who is your professor?"

Kylie rolled her eyes, although she needed to play out her next card very carefully. If and when she nailed her guy, it would come out that she was FBI. She wouldn't insult Perry too much for questioning her.

"You don't believe I'm a student." She put her cup down on the counter and sighed, sounding frustrated as she started around him.

Once again he grabbed her arm, this time turning her to face him with enough force that she slapped her palm against his chest to balance herself. Tingles shot through her hand when she touched muscle that was solid like steel.

"Where are you going?" he growled, searching her face.

"I don't have my professor's information memorized." She gestured with her free hand. "I was going to get you his phone number so you can call him and prove to yourself who I am."

"And will this professor also confirm what it is you're writing your thesis about?" he asked.

"You can ask him, or believe me," she said, softening her tone and looking up at him through her lashes.

"Here's what I think. You might be the student you claim you are, and you might be working on a paper or thesis." He let go of her arm but then gripped her neck, his long finger pressing under her jaw until she tilted her head back further. "I also think you've stumbled onto something, crimes that intrigue you, and now you think you're Agatha Christie."

"You see me as an old woman with a British accent?" she retorted, pulling free from him and hurrying out of her kitchen. She needed him to leave and the longer he kept his hands on her, the harder it would be to get him out of her house.

He was behind her faster than she imagined he would be. "Hardly," he growled, flipping her around to face him once again and this time pulling her into his arms. When he kissed her, the savage hunger he displayed had her insides boiling feverishly within seconds.

Kylie tried moving her hands to his chest. Maybe he thought she meant to push away from him, and in some part of her brain, she knew that she should. Get him to leave. Return to work. Her thoughts grew more muddled the longer he devoured her mouth. Not to mention the way he tightened his hold on her, pinning her with his arms against his rock-hard body, turned her on a hell of a lot more than she should let it.

There was something about a man who got a bit rough, though. Something about how a demanding nature, taking and controlling and leaving no room for any reaction other than submission, got her so hot she swore she'd be a puddle at his feet in moments.

"Perry," she gasped, managing to turn her head and break the kiss. Her lips tingled and a pang of regret hit her when she sucked in a deep breath. If she moved her face, looked into his intense eyes, she would initiate the next kiss. And she couldn't do that. "Why are you doing this?" Her voice was no more than a raspy whisper.

"To get it out of the way." His voice was rough.

"And that was necessary?"

He moved his fingers through her hair and then brushed them across her face. She needed distance, for him to quit touching her, and then her thoughts would return to normal.

Kylie stared at her hand, resting against his chest, and moved her fingers. Roped muscle quivered under her touch. A sense of control rushed over her. Maybe he could turn her brain to mush and create desire inside her stronger than anything she'd felt in years, but she was doing the same thing to him. He wasn't the rock of solid determination he wanted her to believe he was.

"You tell me." He gripped her chin, forcing her to look into his eyes.

"I think it was necessary for you. Maybe you worried your rock of resolve might crumble if you didn't taste me."

"Are you always this stubborn?" he asked, chuckling and then letting his fingers stroke her neck, move lower and brush the swell of her breast before he quit touching her.

"I'm being stubborn?" Kylie felt control once again and sucked in a fresh breath, strengthening her resolve. "You should go, Perry. I've got work to do."

"Show me this work."

That was the last thing she wanted to do. "I'll show you when it's done, if you really want to see it." She headed to her front door and rested her palm against the doorknob. It was cool and made her realize how hot and damp her hand was. "And I'm not going to get it done if you don't leave." She offered him a smile that she hoped reassured him she wasn't getting rid of him, although that was exactly what she needed to do.

"I think you promised me a name and number to call." He didn't budge.

"Oh yeah." Kylie turned, padding barefoot down the hallway to her bedroom. Paul had made business cards for her in case she needed to back up her story, but they were in her briefcase. That wouldn't be a problem if she could keep Perry at bay long enough to fish them out.

She squatted in her dark bedroom and unzipped the side pocket to her briefcase as her bedroom light turned on. "Tell me you're not trying to play detective and I'll be satisfied," Perry said, leaning in the doorway and crossing his arms.

"I'm not," she said, taking in how his jeans molded over long muscular legs. He made T-shirts look like body armor, the way they sculpted over his broad chest and the sleeves hugged well-defined biceps. Eye candy barely described how tempting he looked. "What has you so worried, though?" she asked, deciding that turning the tables and putting him on the defensive would keep her head clear, in control, and probably make him leave sooner. "Are you on some investigation right now?"

She knew the look people gave her when they asked about what crimes she might be fighting to solve. That look of excitement, eagerness to hear the inside scoop. It caused people's faces to light up, their eyes to spark with curiosity. Kylie looked up at Perry from her squatting position and knew she gave him that exact look when his expression turned wary.

"No," he said simply, surprising her, but there was something that clouded over his gaze that grabbed her attention.

"Oh," she said, not needing to pretend to sound disappointed. "Then what are you worried about?"

She looked away from him before he answered and fished through the pocket of her bag, which leaned against the side of her dresser, until she found the card she needed.

"My nieces think the world of you."

The admission startled her.

"And they're my responsibility to protect. If you're using them in any way to gather information because you're trying to find a criminal, no matter how good you feel your intentions are, you're going to stop right now. I'm not going to let you put yourself, or them, in harm's way."

Kylie stood and ran her hand down her dress, straightening it while she watched Perry's attention shift down her body. She moved toward him slowly, holding out her hand with the card in it.

"I'm going to let that comment slide," she began and his gaze snapped to her face, "because you don't know me that well. But you better believe that I would never do anything to harm your nieces, or any other child, ever."

He took the card, and slid it into the pocket on his chest without looking at it. She worried he'd trap her in her bedroom, but he turned and started down the hallway. Kylie was right behind him, but he stopped, causing her to almost run into his backside. He grabbed the doorknob to her middle bedroom and turned, then frowned when it was locked.

"Why do you keep this room locked?"

"It's where I work."

He looked down at her. He was easily over six feet tall, with his broad shoulders and thick chest aiding in him looking fierce. His dark eyes and short, almost black hair, not to mention that tiny scar on the side of his jawbone, made him appear dangerous. Kylie could hold her own with the self-defense classes she was required to take, a black belt in karate, and years of experience handling criminals who were twice her weight and body size. Nonetheless, she felt the danger radiating from his pores. His body was a weapon, and if she weren't careful, she'd be his target practice.

"Unlock the door," he ordered.

She smiled easily. "No way. It's locked for a reason. My work is private until I'm done. If I allow anyone to give their opinion on what I'm writing, it distracts me," she added for good measure. Then keeping her expression light she said, "You really should go now, Perry."

He turned on her and she barely had time to raise her hand in protest before he pushed into her, proving how solid and invincible that body of his was.

"No, don't," she managed to get out before he knocked the wind out of her when he shoved her against the wall and pounced on her mouth.

God. She loved it rough. And obviously Perry did, too. He impaled her mouth, devouring her before she could catch her breath. His fingers scraped over her shoulder, pushing the strap of her dress down so that she couldn't raise her arm. He squeezed her breast and growled into her mouth.

Kylie swore her world turned sideways. She had one free arm and she grabbed his shoulder, fighting to stay grounded as she opened to him, taking what he insisted on giving her and drinking him up as fast as she could.

She kept her fingernails short, yet filed and painted, her personal vanity. And with what nails she had, she dug into his shoulder, feeling how solid he was and rubbing her fingers over the swell of roped muscle. Then wrapping her fingers around the side of his neck, she lost herself in the solid repetitive beat of his heart as it pulsed through the vein in his neck.

"Don't tell me 'no' again," he hissed into her mouth, moving his lips over hers.

Her eyes were still closed and she relaxed between the wall and his virile body. "Don't do anything that I wouldn't want," she challenged, and then blinked several times, her vision blurring when she gazed into his face.

His eyes pierced her soul. "I haven't so far," he growled.